Dr Dan's Casebook

Laurie Graham

First published in 2019 by

Laurie Graham

Copyright © 2019 Laurie Graham

ISBN 9781080342259

All rights reserved.

ISBN:

Dedicated to my readers, who kept the faith even when my publishers didn't

CHAPTER 1

I'd decided against wearing my lucky, white cotton, nervous-sweat absorbing shirt because I hadn't told Chloe I was going to meet my new Educational Supervisor and see what was likely to be my new workplace for the next twelve months. It was probably a bad idea - the shirt and the not telling her - but my career plans were still a delicate subject. Her father had offered me the golden pathway to easy hours and big money with his ENT practice in Harley Street and I'd turned him down. It was touch and go between me and Chloe for a while after that and although love had conquered, the topic still wasn't a happy one.

I'd wanted to be a GP almost as long as I'd wanted to be a doctor, and that dated roughly from the time I realised that getting capped for Wales was a daft schoolboy's dream. Now I was embarking on the last lap. I was just finishing a six month placement with a practice in Dudley and I'd been due to start my final year as a trainee with John Sillitoe. John had been my training supervisor all the way through my specialty training. I'd liked him. He was a quiet, rather shy man, but very pleasant. I'd looked forward to working alongside him. Then he died.

It was a suicide that no-one had seen coming. He'd left behind him a mess of devastation for his family and partners and my career was just a minor casualty. Black Wednesday was approaching: one of the two days of the year when the merry-go-round music stops and junior doctors move on to their next gig.

I needed a new supervisor for my final pre-registration placement and I needed one fast. The Deanery had reassigned me to a practice in Sedgley. The Lindens.
It was one of those muggy, late July days. My drip-dry, everyday work shirt was clinging not dripping. There was a holdup on the Wolverhampton Road because a traffic light was out and then, when I got to Tipton Road West, I couldn't find The Lindens. I drove by it twice before I spotted it, set back from the road. The sign had been vandalized. It said THE   DENS.

Five past two. I was late, my face looked like a boiled radish and the door to the surgery was locked. I hammered and eventually a woman appeared, grey-haired, cross-looking. She shouted through the glass that they were closed.
I shouted back. 'Dan Talbot to see Dr Buxton or Dr Vincent.'

She unlocked the door, reluctantly, and opened it an inch. I told her I had a two o'clock appointment.
'Are you sure?' she said. 'Surgery's not till 3 o'clock and it's Dr Buxton's afternoon off.'
Another woman appeared behind her, younger, in a health care tunic. She was eating a yogurt.
'Everything all right, Mary?' she said.
The Mary woman said, 'I don't know. This young man seems to think he's got an appointment. I suppose I shall have to

let him in while I sort it out.'

I was allowed in. They both went behind the reception desk and peered at a computer screen. There was a lot of head-shaking.

Mary said, 'Trevor's gone and done it again. Booked in an extra and not put it on the system. I could strangle him.'

I said, 'The Deanery office said Dr Vincent would be my new supervisor. I'm Dan Talbot.'

But Mary wasn't listening. She said she could squeeze me in with Dr Antony at 11.30 on Friday.

I said, 'I'm not a patient.'

And the one in the nurse's tunic said, 'He's a new trainee, Mary. Are you here about the ST3 job?'

'I am. So are neither of them here?'

At that very moment a figure slipped past the open door behind them and I discovered that this Mary, the receptionist, had eyes in the back of her head. Many women do.

'Dr Buxton!' she roared. 'Where do you think you're going?'

'To the bog,' said a disembodied voice. 'Then home via a possible pit stop at the Black Bear.'

'And what about this young man for a 2 o'clock interview?'

'Dr Talbot,' added the nurse, trying to be helpful. 'The trainee.'

There was a pause.

'Bugger,' said the voice, eventually. Then he appeared.

Trevor Buxton, silver hair, pink face, crumpled linen jacket.

'Wednesday,' he said. 'Damn it, it's Wednesday.'

He looked at me, puffed, beckoned me to walk round behind Mary's little kingdom and follow him.

'If Mrs Buxton phones,' he called back over his shoulder, and Mary finished the sentence for him. 'You're tied up. No

idea how long you'll be.'
'Good girl,' he said. He calls her that even though she must
be 60 if she's a day.

He showed me into his room, told me to cop a squat while
he went to the toilet.
'Paperwork. Phone calls. Morning surgery,' he said.
'Madness. You'd think the Black Death had returned. Not
even time for a bowel movement. Talbot, right?'
'Yes. Dan Talbot.'

When he came back he turned on a noisy old electric fan,
knocked a pile of papers onto the floor and invited me to
take my jacket off. It was very warm in his office.

'Now,' he said, 'Dan, we do have a slight complication. As
the senior partner I'm very happy to have a chat, but Dr
Vincent would be your training supervisor and I'm afraid I
may have neglected to remind her you were coming in today.
I'm easing into retirement and she'll be taking over at the
end of the year anyway. So she's the woman you need to
meet. Are you in a particular hurry?'

I wasn't. I'd taken the afternoon off and I definitely didn't
want to have to come back another day.
'Good,' he said. 'Then bear with me while I see if I can track
her down.'
He leaned back in his chair, scratched his head, picked up an
ancient-looking mobile phone and held it at arm's length
while he jabbed at the keypad.
'A word from the wise,' he said. 'Never let your wife know
you have one of these mobile jobbies.'
Dr Vincent answered.
'Helen, my love,' he said. 'Are you anywhere nearby?

Because I have an excellent young chap here to be interviewed with a view to joining us. He's a pre-reg, ST3, left orphaned by the Sillitoe tragedy and he already has six months in grimmest Dudley under his belt.'

There was a raised voice on the other end. Dr Vincent wasn't happy.

'So sorry,' he said. 'I thought we'd discussed it. I mean, I could take him on myself, but he needs a 12 month placement, which might be more than I can manage. To lose one supervisor could be regarded as a misfortune. To lose two might scar him for life.'

Could I hang on for half an hour? I said I could. I was rather hoping to go home with things settled. For one thing I needed to keep my training on track and for another, I thought it might help Chloe to unwind a little. She had big exams coming up, plus tough competition for a job on Barrington's firm. Getting myself settled for the next year would remove one uncertainty from our lives.

'I'll see if I can rustle up some tea,' he said. 'Helen shouldn't be too long. Pedicure. Final stages of.'

He came huffing back, popped a piece of nicotine gum.

'The char-wallah has things in hand. So Dan…Dan…?'

'Talbot.

'Dan Talbot,' he said. 'Of course. We can have a general chat while we wait. Terrible about the Sillitoe chap. I didn't know him, personally, but tragic. His wife had left him, I gather.'

'They say he was depressed.'

'There's a lot of it about. If his practice was anything like ours, he was treating dozens of patients for it. But nobody was looking after him. Very sad. Now, Dan Talbot, tell me your story.'

So much for my carefully crafted CV. I don't think he'd even looked at it. I offered him a copy, but he waved it away.

My story. I was in the final stages of my GP training. Thirty and still a trainee. My Nan thought I'd be a consultant by now. I graduated from Birmingham Medical School in 2005, did two stints as houseman at the Good Hope and then went to the Queen Elizabeth to do my core training. That's where Chloe and I got together.

I said, 'I've always wanted to be a family doctor.'

'Really?' he said. 'Didn't you ever want to be Spider Man? My son did.'

'What did he end up doing?'

'Medicine. Urology. Because he's smarter than his old man. Urology's where the money is, Dan. Private practice. Rich old men with the dribbles.'

'It wouldn't appeal to me.'

'No? Dermatology's another good one. No emergencies. You don't get dragged off the golf course for a case of eczema. You don't get hauled out of bed because somebody's got acne. Wives hate the night calls. Are you married?'

Chloe and I are engaged. We live together but she's doing her MRCP Part II so she doesn't want the distraction of a wedding just yet.

'Well here's the thing,' he said. 'Helen and I have had a number of trainees over the years and they've all gone on to greater things, apart from our sainted Dr Vaz who registered earlier this year and has chosen to stay on with us. I've generally supervised most of the training but as I mentioned, I'm winding down. For health reasons.'

'COPD?'

'Correct. Two-packs a day emphysema. Well observed.'

It wasn't a wild guess. Quite apart from the flushed face and the puffing trout lips, the nicotine-stained fingers were a giveaway.

Mary brought in two mugs of very strong tea.

'Mrs Buxton phoned,' she said.

'Not here. Whereabouts unknown.'

'Yes, I told her that. But can you please pick up some tonic water on your way home? If you happen to get this message.'

'Excellent woman, that,' he said when she'd left.

'Mary?'

'Yes. We have two of them, sisters. One's Mary and the other one's Moira but I can't always tell them apart. They're like peas in a pod and they seem to own identical cardigans to add to my confusion, so I tend to call them both Mary. They've been here since the year dot. Elephant memories and lion hearts. They protect us from the demanding hordes. If it wasn't for the Marys we'd never get out of here. We wouldn't even have time for a pee. You'd like to know a bit about the practice, I dare say. Three partners, me, Helen Vincent and Bruce Macdonald. Then we have a part-timer, Dr Parker, who deals with ladybits, two afternoons a week, and Dr Vaz, our junior.'

'Mary mentioned a Dr Antony?'

'That's Vaz. A very nice Indian fellow. I can never remember if his name's Antony Vaz or Vaz Antony but he answers to either.'

'And nurses?'

'Two. Both very competent.'

He told me he'd been 37 years in the practice. It had been his father's originally.

'I've got patients I've known since before they were born.'

'That's exactly my idea of a satisfying career.'

'We weren't always in this building, of course. My father used to see patients in one of our drawing rooms. Mother answered the phone, typed the letters, topped up the autoclave. No appointments, just open surgery hours. You could work like that in those days. People weren't such malingering, entitled nuisances. They'd have a bath and change their underwear before they came to see you. The old boy wouldn't recognise this place. We have a Patient Participation Group now. Have you come across Participation Groups yet? And Quality and Outcomes Framework points?'

I had.

'Such things are sent to try us. We moved here in the Eighties, after the old fellow retired. Brand new building, cracks and all. Tiles drifting down off the ceiling. Don't let the name mislead you, by the way. The Lindens. Linden Lea and all that. Within the woodland, flowr'y gladed. Most of our clients are from Brook Glen and Cherry Tree, both ironically-named estates full of lorazepam addicts. We do have a few loyal souls who've moved out to Wombourne or Himley and stayed on our books, but we don't see so much of them because they hate to be any trouble. They only come in when they're really, really worried about something.'

'It's a pleasant name though, The Lindens.'

'Yes. Buggered if I can remember how it got it. I suppose there used to be some trees. The Marys will know. Now what's your thing, Dan?'

'My thing?'

'What really interests you? Mac, for instance, is our geriatrics man. Myself, I'm interested in the mysteries of human nature. It's not a recognised clinical field but we have daily contact with it. Dr Vincent's very good on Parkinson's, referred pain and backs. We see a lot of chronic backs here and they're time-wasters mainly, so you need to be on the qui vive for a genuine cause for concern. Such as?'

It was the first clinical ball he'd bowled me.

'Heart disease, pancreas, gall bladder, epidural abscess, pressure from an abdominal or thoracic mass.'

'Good, good. But I interrupted you. You were going to tell me what interests you.'

Now I know him I realise that was classic Trevor Buxton. If he senses you're nervous he rabbits on a bit, to give you time to relax.

I'd done six months of General Medicine, six of elderly care, six of old age psychiatry. I mentioned I was interested in diabetes. He nodded.

'Big growth area, that. We have a diabetes support group, by the way. Chris runs it. She's our Nurse Practitioner. You met her out at the front of the shop. Support groups, nurse practitioners. My father wouldn't know what the hell we were talking about. How about paediatrics? Round here they breed like E fucking coli.'

I'm actually a bit nervous around children, particularly very small ones but I thought it best not to say so. I suppose you get over that when you have your own.

I said I was interested in preventative medicine, generally. Improving outcomes for children and adults, supporting good lifestyle choices. Diet, exercise, smoking. As soon as I'd said 'smoking' I wished I hadn't, but he smiled.

'All very commendable,' he said. 'But I should probably break the news to you that most of our patients don't have a lifestyle. Chaotic existences would be more accurate. Many of our patients, Dan, are shit conduits, pure and simple. They eat shit, watch shit, talk shit. Shit in, shit out. Booze, drugs, impulsive and regrettable actions, dinners from the chipper, volatile relationships. The only regularity in their lives is getting their Job Seeker's money.'

'Is there a big drug problem?'

'Hard to judge the size of it. It's slippery thing. A year ago I'd have said it was mainly prescription drugs. Now there's all kinds of stuff out there. Just when you think you know what you're dealing with they find something new to stick up their nose or down their throat. I imagine it's the same in Dudley.'

In fact, at the Panwar surgery I hadn't felt we were in the middle a drug war. Domestic violence, yes. Unemployment and poverty, yes. And some cultural issues.

Trevor Buxton smiled when I said that.

'Ah yes' he said. 'Cultural issues. And what would they be?'

The Muslim population was quite small but a challenge. The older women and the very young girls were kept closeted. We only saw them when their menfolk deemed it really necessary, and they weren't particularly healthy. When I told Mam I'd seen two cases of rickets in as many weeks, she didn't believe me. She thought rickets had gone out with horse trams and collar studs. Yasmin Panwar wore hijab herself but she had a sun lamp at home so she and her daughters could top up with Vitamin D.

And then there were the birth defects. In my six months there I'd logged two stillbirths, a baby born without any eyes, and another born with fused fingers. All most likely the result of cousins marrying cousins. It was common practice, and as Dr Panwar said, how do you even begin to tackle that?

I heard women's voices outside the door. Mary, the receptionist's and a younger, clearer one.

'Aha,' says Trevor Buxton, 'I believe Dr Vincent is about to join us.'

CHAPTER 2

I was expecting…. What was I expecting? A woman who was about to become senior partner. Short, sensible hair, sensible shoes? Somebody who looked like Mam, basically.

I put Helen Vincent's age at around 50. She could have passed for younger but she had a pair of reading glasses hooked over the neck of her T shirt and that's a pretty accurate guide. She was tall, sporty-looking, bare legs and strappy, non-sensible sandals. I could imagine her in a tennis skirt, but I tried not to.

'For fuck's sake, Trevor,' were her first words. So not like Mam at all. 'When was this arranged?'

He said he was sure he'd mentioned it to her. He couldn't find my CV but I handed her a copy. That was when she acknowledged my presence and gave me a once-over.

She said, 'Trevor, can we please open a window? Your office smells like an ashtray and Dr Talbot looks very warm.'

She was scanning my CV and talking to Trevor Buxton at the same time.

She said, 'What about the Korean girl? I thought we were going to take her? She was very keen on paediatrics. She'd have been useful to have around.'

'Helen,' he said, 'You've had children, I've had children, Pam Parker's had children. We're not exactly wanting in the paediatric department.'

He tried to open the window and failed.

'Also, you said I must under no circumstances call that girl 'sweetheart.' Or even 'dear'.'

'Damned right. Jesus, Trevor, it's 2012. You'd be accused of sexual micro-aggression.'

'Well bugger that for a game of soldiers, Helen. I'm still the senior partner here and I'll call people whatever I like. Besides, she probably wouldn't last five minutes. She was a delicate little thing. Send her on a house call to Bonny Brook Glen and she might never be seen again. All they'd find would be a pile of bones.'

Dr Vincent turned to me.
'John Sillitoe was your supervisor?'
'Yes. I still can't believe what happened.'
'So damned selfish. He's caused so much inconvenience.'
Trevor Buxton said, 'And grief, Helen. Let's not forget the bereaved.'
She ignored that.
'And you've been on placement with Yasmin Panwar? I know her. We were undergrads together. Dudley. So you're used to a mixed practice. The Lindens is very mixed. I see you've done a lot of ENT. Why is that?'

The bit of my CV that I regret, the bit that shows indecision on my part. Best to be honest about it, I thought, so I told them about the offer I'd felt under some pressure to accept. How Chloe's father had taken me for drinks at his golf club and made me a serious offer. It was a fantastic opportunity. Everybody said so. A four and a half day week including one minor surgery session. Elegant consulting rooms. A licence to print money. I'd have been mad to turn it down, but I did. Halfway through my second ENT rotation I couldn't take any more of tonsils and ear grommets and I knew I absolutely didn't want to work with my father-in-law looking over my shoulder. I jumped ship and went back to my original plan to be a GP.

Trevor Buxton said, 'Bloody hell, lad. I bet that didn't go down too well.'

It didn't. Chloe's still a bit mad about it. Her father just thinks there must be something wrong with me. I'm sure he wonders if his super bright daughter is marrying an idiot.

Helen Vincent was studying me. I got the feeling she quite liked my story. But Trevor Buxton just shook his head and said, 'ENT. Early Nights and Tennis.'
It was true. Laurence Swift's idea of unsocial hours is a 6pm consultation at two hundred quid a pop.
Dr Vincent went back to my CV.
'You're from Abergavenny?' she said. 'You haven't got much of an accent.'
I've been gone from Wales nearly twelve years. The accent wears off, I suppose.

They didn't seem to have an interview routine. No good cop, bad cop, and I'd been expecting more of a clinical test from them. Referred pain in an acute abdomen? Signs of fulminant bacterial meningitis in infants? That kind of thing. But no. If it was up to Trevor Buxton, I was probably in. For Helen Vincent, the Korean girl was still a possible candidate.
'What's your personal situation? Married? Single and carefree? You'd be expected to do some out-of-hours shifts. We use Sterling.'
'My girlfriend's at the Queen Elizabeth. SHO in Acute Medicine. She's taking her Part II. We're used to shift work.'
Then her questioning swerved in a different direction. Was I religious?
I do go to church occasionally, especially if Chloe's working on a Sunday. She's very anti but I prefer to keep the God question on the table. And I enjoy singing hymns. Mam and Dad are Methodist, but I like to go to the cathedral, to the choral Eucharist.
I sensed 'not particularly' was a safe answer. I guessed what

was coming next.

'No problem with requests for terminations, for instance?'

I said I believed in judging each case on its merits, which seemed to satisfy her. Her final question: did I have any funny-bunny baggage? I had no idea what she was talking about.

'Crystals, auras, high colonics, homeopathy? I had a trainee a few years ago who kept trying to detect patients' auric eggs. Drove me crazy.'

I was able to say, with all honesty, that I wouldn't know an auric egg if I saw one.

She said, 'You know what I'm thinking, Trevor? He's a good-looking young guy. It could be a problem. Sorry to talk about you like this, Dan, but we may as well cut to the chase. No sense in wasting your time or ours.'

I think I turned an even deeper shade of red. Nobody had ever called me good-looking before, at least, not in an interview. I mean, Chloe finds me attractive, obviously, but that's different. Mam always says there's somebody for everyone.

Trevor said, 'We can fit him with a patent chastity belt. Make sure he always keeps the consulting room door open. Wide open.'

He turned to me.

'Helen's worried you'd be catnip to some of our female patients. She may have a point.'

I said, 'I haven't had a problem in Dudley.'

'No? Maybe it's the air out here. We're practically rural. We've got a country park, you know? Opened by Princess Anne, no less. What else have we got, Helen? Subsidence. Quite a bit of that, from the old mines. Pound shops. Women who go shopping in their jarmies. Our flaxen-haired maidens don't get up to much but they're always on the lookout for fresh meat. You should just be aware. Anyway Helen, he's got a fiancée so it's not like he's a complete innocent.'

'Well then,' she said. She sat looking at her toes. The nails were painted the colour of an orange iced lolly. She had great legs, for her age.

Trevor Buxton folded a prescription blank into an airplane and aimed it at her. I wondered if it was my cue to leave them to talk but he gestured to me to stay put. There were more voices outside the door. Mary and another woman.

Helen Vincent muttered, 'Stephanie.'

Trevor Buxton said, 'Our esteemed Practice Manager, Dan. Whose opinion weighs heavily even when it hasn't been sought.'

'We agreed she could sit in on any future interviews.'

'Did we? I don't remember that. And not for a trainee, surely? What about the girl who cleans for us? Do we need to consult her as well?'

Helen Vincent tossed my CV onto the desk. Was that it? Were we done? It was the rummest interview I'd ever experienced. She asked if I'd ever taken a workplace safety course, for doctors working in the community. Risk assessment, de-escalation techniques, that kind of thing. I hadn't. I'd worked Saturday nights in A&E though.

Trevor Buxton said, 'I don't know, Helen. That course sounds a bit war-zone to me.'

She said, 'It is a bloody war-zone. Getting to be. What about the incident in Friar's Green?'

I'd read about Friar's Green. A GP making a home visit had been threatened with a rounder's bat and forced to open the boot of her car. The thief was believed to have stolen two

GTN angina sprays and an EpiPen.

He said, 'We ought to piss in a few old pethidine vials. Let them rob those. That'll teach the blighters.'

'Well I'm just thinking, if we organise a course for Vaz we should see if we can get a discount for Dan at the same time.'

For Dan? Did that mean they were offering me the job?

'Any questions, Dan?'

'How do you arrange training here? Do your trainees move around the practice or just shadow one partner?'

'The former, although I don't have as much time as I'd like. Let's say I'll be your supervisor, but you'll probably sit in with Trevor mainly, at least for a start. We should use his vast experience while we still have him. If you can bear the smell of his cigarettes, that is.'

It was the first glimmer of a smile from her. He gave me a little nod.

She said, 'Trevor, how much longer do you think you'll be working full-time?'

'I don't know. There's been talk of going on a cruise.'

He said it like it was a death sentence. He looked so sad.

'But having a trainee will cheer me up no end. We do see life here, Dan. I'll need to make sure your Chav-speak is up to snuff. Do you speak Chav? Try this one. Iffee dow gerriz tablits iz sindrome comes on everso badly.'

We all laughed.

He said, 'I'll go when I have to, Helen, but don't worry, come January it'll all be yours and you can bring in the Thought Police. Purge anyone who calls a female 'darling'.'

'Have you talked to Mac yet?'

'Yes. No. I will. Bit of a power struggle, Dan,' he said. 'Between Helen and Mac. It's been like the Tudors and that other lot. The Plantagenets. But Helen's going to be senior partner. She'll be your boss.'

I looked at her. She looked at him.

I said, 'So you want me?'

'Oh yes,' he said. 'Definitely. When were you supposed to start with Sillitoe?'

'August 8th.'

Helen looked at a calendar on his desk. She said, 'The thing is, I'll be away for two weeks. Let's say, the beginning of September. Can you keep yourself usefully occupied till then?'

I was sure I could.

'And when do you think you'll take your Applied Knowledge?'

In the interests of domestic harmony, I didn't want to be studying at the same time as Chloe. She had her Part II coming up in November and she'd get her results in January. I was thinking I'd do the Applied Knowledge paper in the spring and then my clinical assessments later in the summer. We might even fit in a wedding.

It was nearly time for afternoon surgery to begin. More voices, phones ringing. You could feel the place revving up. When we opened Trevor Buxton's door a woman was hovering outside. She had a face on her that'd stop a clock.

'Stephanie,' he said. 'Only whisper her name and she appears. Dan, this is our practice manager. Stephanie, this is Dan Talbot. He'll be joining us as a trainee.'

I offered her my hand. She ignored it.

She said, 'Why wasn't I told?'

'You just were, dear.'

'We have recruitment procedures in place.'

Trevor Buxton said, 'Indeed we do. But we're the clinical trainers. No need to take up your valuable time. Dr Talbot should have been going to the Sillitoe practice but that's all

17

gone tits up. Our gain though, Stephanie. We're lucky to nab him. So now over to you, at your convenience, of course.'

I said I could stay, if she needed to talk to me. I was trying to be helpful.

'No,' she said. 'It'll have to be next week. I'm far too busy now. You'll have to phone and make an appointment.' And she walked away.

I said, 'That wasn't a good start.'

'Pay no heed,' says Helen Vincent. 'She's more bark than bite, and anyway it's not her business. You're my trainee.'

'Our trainee,' said Trevor. 'I'm rather looking forward to it. Now Dan Talbot, are you quite sure you wouldn't rather be Spider Man? Or a Harley Street glamour boy with a brand new Beamer?'

'Quite sure.'

'Good man,' he said. 'Welcome to The Lindens.'

CHAPTER 3

I felt on top of the world. Trevor Buxton seemed like he might be fun and Helen Vincent seemed like she might be a good trainer, an efficient, no-nonsense type. It wasn't a huge practice, so I might actually get to know some of my patients, and its catchment area was mixed, everything from tower block poor to comfortable suburbs. Twelve months at The Lindens and I'd be ready to apply for my MRCGP. Sorted.

I bought steaks on the way home and flowers and a bottle of champagne. Well, not actual champagne but something with a cork to pop. Chloe was working an early shift, so she was due home by seven. She got in just after nine.

'Oh,' she said when she saw the table set ready for dinner. 'I really need to shower first. Do you mind if I eat in my bathrobe?'

Chloe had had a good day. She'd done an unsupervised ascitic drain which is a pretty nerve-wracking procedure. If you push the needle in a tad too far you can puncture the intestine and then you're in trouble. She was feeling very pleased with herself. I didn't want to spoil her moment with my news. Timing is everything with Chloe so I showed an interest.

'Was it a cancer patient?'
'Cirrhosis of the liver. Portal hypertension. A hopeless case really. A chronic boozer.'
'That's sad. What was his story?'
'Who?'
'The patient.'

'No idea. It was a she. Completely away with the fairies. Hepatic encephalopathy, liver flap, the works. The son had to sign the consent.'

'I wonder what drives people to drink like that?'

'Who cares? People make choices. We're just there to pick up the pieces. This is nice. Is it champagne?'

'It's a New Zealand sparkler. How did you judge where to go in with the needle?'

'Percussion. Well, okay, the ultrasound tech had put a marker for me. X marks the spot. But I confirmed it by percussion.'

Tell her, Dan. Stop feigning interest in ascitic drains and tell her about the Lindens job.

'I'll put the steaks on.'

'Actually, would they keep? I fancy something lighter tonight. Like a salad. Once you're into the abdominal cavity the main thing is to make sure the catheter doesn't kink. We drained nearly three litres out of her in six hours. It was like a balloon going down.'

I turned the flame up under the pan.

She said, 'I thought we just agreed we wouldn't have the steak tonight?'

'No, we agreed you wouldn't have a steak. I'm having mine. I've been looking forward to it.'

Now. Tell her now.

'We're supposed to be cutting down on red meat.'

'Says who?'

'You know it makes sense. We had lamb at the Greek place and that was only four days ago.'

'Well I thought we'd celebrate.'

'My putting the drain in?'

'No. Me getting my ST3 placement.'

'What? How?'

'I had an interview this afternoon.'

'Why didn't you tell me?'

'Because I didn't want you giving me your begrudging face.'

'I wouldn't have. I'm resigned to it. It just feels like you're giving up too easily.'

'There you go. Giving up what? I want to be a GP. It's not a booby prize.'

'So you've got a new supervisor?'

'I've kind of got two. Trevor Buxton and Helen Vincent.'

'Mopping up the Sillitoe mess. Why two?'

'Because he may have to retire before my year with them is up. He's got COPD.'

'Eww! Smoker?'

'Yes.'

'Has he quit?'

'He's trying.'

'You don't have much luck with supervisors, do you? Where's the practice?'

'Sedgley. Well, more Tipton really.'

She groaned.

'What?'

'You know what. Why must you gravitate to these places? Are you trying to be some kind of Welsh Mother Teresa?'

Chloe has led a relatively sheltered life. Between leafy Warwickshire where she grew up and a documentary she saw about the streets of Calcutta, there's a big gap in her knowledge of the world, even of the Black Country, which is practically on our doorstep.

I said, 'It's a busy practice, very mixed. It'll be terrific experience and I liked Trevor Buxton very much.'

'What if I get a job in London?'

'What if you do? We'll cross that bridge when we get to it. You haven't even passed your Part II yet.'

'Oh cheers. Thanks for that vote of confidence.'

'I'm just saying. This is where you need to be right now, therefore it's where I want to be, and I've been offered a good placement. You could be pleased for me.'

'Okay,' she said. 'I'll put my pleased face on. I'm sorry. Well done.'

Chloe isn't very good at faking a pleased face.

'Go on then. Give me the gruesome details. It's in Tipton and your supervisor is a chain smoker. Who's the woman?'

'Helen Vincent. She's taking over as senior partner. She actually knows Yasmin Panwar. They trained together. So that went in my favour. There's also a Dr Mac-something. I didn't meet him. He does most of the geriatrics. Then there's an Indian called either Antony or Vaz, and a woman who does the obs and gynae twice a week. Dr Parker. Two nurses. I met one of them. And a practice manager.'

'How many patients?'

'About 8000.'

'Eight thousand specimens of pond life. Isn't it all council estates out there?'

'Don't be so judgmental.'

'Do you actually know anyone who lives in a council flat?'

'Yes.'

'Who?'

'My Nan Talbot. And Aunty June.'

'Family doesn't count.'

'Aunty June isn't family. She's Mam's friend. Anyway, Sedgley and Tipton are quite mixed. I drove around a bit, had a look. High-rises, retirement bungalows, private houses. And the practice covers parts of Wombourne and Himley too. They're nice enough areas.'

'You'll have to get a better car.'

'Why?'

'Because yours doesn't always start first time. You'll be

making house calls on those horrid estates. You need to be able to make a fast getaway.'

'Don't be so melodramatic.'

'I'm not. Call Watkins's tomorrow, see what they'll give you on a trade-in.'

I said I would although I was pretty sure I knew what Watkins's would say. A ten year old Vectra isn't worth a light.

'You should get a stab vest too. But the practice should pay for it.'

She was serious.

'Dan,' she kept saying, 'you have to realise. Those people. They're lawless. They'll do anything for a few pills.'

I love Chloe very much but one rather annoying thing about her is she'll say she's not hungry for dinner and then spend the evening snacking. She watched me eat my steak and then went looking for biscuits. That was when she noticed the flowers.

'Aw,' she said. 'Are those for me?'

'Obviously. Flowers for you, fizz for both of us, steak for me.'

'Aren't you sweet. By the way, I hope there aren't any sexy young females at this practice you're joining.'

'Nobody under the age of 50,' I assured her.

'Good,' she said. 'Because sometimes I think you don't realise how oddly adorable you are.'

I was having a proper day of it. Helen Vincent had said I was good-looking young guy and now Chloe had confirmed that she still found me oddly adorable in spite of my career choice. I left the dishes in the sink and we went to bed for conciliatory sex which was great for me and Chloe said it was really terrific for her, so I probably shouldn't feel too guilty that I'd kept thinking of Helen Vincent in a tennis skirt.

CHAPTER 4.

The Panwar practice presented me with a T shirt after my last surgery, as a souvenir. Survived Leopold Street, it said. Will go far.

Dr Yasmin said, 'I told Helen Vincent, you're going to make a very good doctor.'

'You spoke to her?'

'She called me.'

'What's she really like? She asked me some weird things, personal things. And she agreed to be my supervisor but then she kept emphasising how busy she was. I hope it's going to work out.'

'I don't know. We were classmates but we weren't friends. She's very bright though. I was quite surprised to hear she'd gone into general practice. I'd have thought she was consultant material. I suppose it's the old story. If you're going to have kids it's very tough to keep your place in the scramble to the top.'

Everyone says that. It makes me wonder about Chloe. She's very ambitious. She says she wants to have children but will she really want to take time out? Will we be one of those families dropping the kids off at creche at seven in the morning? Of course, it all depends on her getting her Part II. It's her second go at it. Maybe if she doesn't pass this time, she'll rethink.

It was a great morning for the immersion heater to pack in. Chloe was off down to London on a course: percutaneous cardiovascular interventions. And I was starting at The Lindens. I had to boil a kettle for my shave.

Chloe thinks I should get an electric razor but when you have a dark beard like mine you get a closer cut with a wet shave.

She said she'd shower at the gym before she went to the station. She was meeting Hua and Jamil there at 9.30. Hua's a Chinese girl, another cardio wannabe. She and Chloe have been pals since med school. Jamil was a name I seemed to be hearing more and more often.

'Where has this Jamil sprung from?'

'He's with Kirkpatrick's firm,' she said. 'Studied at Manchester. He's Lebanese.'

'Is he tall, dark and handsome?'

'No. He's short, dark and handsome. And rolling in money.'

'Should I be jealous?'

'It wouldn't hurt. Keep you on your toes. And please call someone and get the hot water fixed.'

I got to The Lindens by 8 o'clock. I wasn't sure if the woman on Reception was the one I'd already met. It wasn't. This was Moira, and she was too busy answering the phone and pulling files off the shelves to talk to me. There was a man in the kitchen, slim, greying temples, a three-piece suit and a very nice silk tie. Not a look you'd see around Tipton very often, I imagined. I introduced myself.

'Bruce Macdonald,' he said. 'Want a coffee?'

He tapped his chin. Chloe hadn't bothered to remind me I'd stuck a piece of tissue on a shaving cut.

I felt a bit spare. I didn't know who I was supposed to be sitting with for my first morning.

'It won't be me,' he said. 'I'm out all morning. Nursing home rounds. But you're welcome to join me once you've settled in.'

The practice manager appeared. Stephanie. She said Helen Vincent had a Clinical Commissioning Group meeting, likely to last all morning. Mac said it was high time they got a decent coffee machine. Stephanie said she had bigger fish to fry, like getting everyone in the practice to make better use of their computers. Moira had overheard.

'We do use the ruddy computers,' she said. 'It's not our fault if they go wrong. Give me a biro and a piece of paper any day. And I'll tell you another thing. The older patients don't like knowing their private particulars are on some machine. They don't trust it.'

'Yes,' says Stephanie, 'but they'll soon be dead and gone.'

I asked if Trevor Buxton was expected.

'He's already in,' says Moira, like I was supposed to know. 'He'll be waiting for you. And he's run out of nicotine patches so he's in a right old monkey mood. Just to warn you.'

'Should I go and see if I can find a pharmacy that's open?'

She said Linda, one of the nurses, was picking up some patches on her way in.

Trevor Buxton was doing paperwork and looking grim. Letters, test results. It's the same routine in any practice. He grunted, told me to leave the door open and beckoned me to pull up a chair beside him.

'It was a quiet weekend by the look of things. Nothing much from out-of-hours. A kiddie with earache. A senior with urinary retention, sent to A&E. A death at the Sorrento nursing home. That's Mac's territory.'

There was a hospital letter he sat and looked at for a lot longer than it took him to read it. He passed it to me. James Riley. Stage 4 gastric adenocarcinoma, liver and bone metastases, palliative care only.

'Mary!' he yelled.

No reply.

'Mary! This is your master's voice.'

I said, 'I think it's actually Moira out there this morning.'

Moira appeared in the doorway.

'Darling girl,' he said, 'would you please give Jimmy Riley a call and ask him to come in. Maybe first appointment tomorrow afternoon?'

'You've got twelve booked already and your 3 o'clock's taken.'

'Well then ask him to come at 2.30, God damn it.'

She left but he kept talking to her anyway.

'And don't call him yet. Please. Let him have his breakfast, poor bugger. So, Dan Talbot, here we are again. It's Monday, it's piddling rain and we've got sixteen booked for morning surgery, but are we downhearted? No. Are you a betting man at all? Fancy a wager on the number of no-shows?'

'Are we betting for money?'

'No, no. Who needs money? We'll do a spread bet over the week. Loser buys the first round on Friday. The Black Bear, after close of play.'

I guessed there would be three no-shows.

'Very conservative,' he said. 'I'm betting five and I hope I'm right and you're wrong. Those little interludes are precious. They give you time to think, time to pick your nose.'

Moira brought in a stack of files. She asked if I wanted to order a sandwich for my lunch, but I'd brought my own. I'd learned the hard way my first week at the Panwar practice. There was rarely enough time to go out and buy something.

He gave me the files and told me to have a quick look. I asked him how he felt about computerised records. He curled his lip.

'This bloody thing,' he said, banging the top of the

monitor. 'It's all Stephanie's doing, and Helen's. They gang up on me, these women. What happens if it breaks? There go all your records.'

'But I expect everything's backed up to a cloud.'

'So they say. A cloud. Whatever that means. And what if the cloud disappears? But I'll tell you what I really object to. I get these messages popping up. Refer to weight-loss clinic? Refer to QUIT smokers' group? A machine telling me my job! I've tried typing in BUGGER OFF but it won't accept it. And in my opinion patients like to see you jotting things down not rattling away on a keyboard like a shorthand typist.'

I started to look through the files. The first name was Coco Tomlinson. A three-year old.

'Tomlinson,' he said. 'That's Kelly and her exotically named tribe. She's also got a Levi and a Sienna, if I remember rightly. Clear the desk of anything they can nick or stick in their ear.'

It would have been a job and a half to clear Trevor's desk. Nurse Linda arrived with nicotine patches.

'Ministering angel,' he said. 'How can I thank you?'

'Give me a pay rise,' she said, then she turned to me. 'So you're the tasty new doctor we've heard about. I'm Linda. Second door on the left, if ever you need anything. And I'm single.'

He said, 'The man's spoken for,' but she'd gone. 'Sex mad,' he said. 'A good nurse, though. Strong stomach. And an excellent wound dresser.'

Kelly Tomlinson looked very young to have three children. Coco had pink, gummy eyes.

'Hmmm,' says Trevor. 'What do we think, Dr Dan? Viral or bacterial? And what, if anything, are we going to do about it?'

I hadn't expected to be consulted. I thought I'd just be observing for a while. The main thing with gummy eyes is to stop it spreading to other children. The baby, Levi, was asleep but his eyes looked all right. Sienna was cranky and I thought one of her eyes looked a bit inflamed.

Kelly said, 'That's because she don't sleep. Are you going to be here permanent then?'

I explained I was a trainee.

'Oh,' she said. 'So you're not a proper doctor yet?'

I'd heard that a few times. Still studying then? That was another one.

Trevor told her how to bathe the eyes, boiled water, cooled to tepid, one wipe in an outward direction then throw the cotton wool away. She wasn't really listening.

'Don't I get a prescription then?'

'No need. We don't want to be giving her antibiotics for no good reason. Did your man go for the snip yet, Kelly?'

'No,' she said. 'He's fucked off with some minger.'

'Pity,' he said, after she'd left. 'That was one of the more successful relationships on our books. Three children all by the same father. Remarkable around here.'

By 10.15 we'd had a tickly cough, a chronic depressive for a prescription repeat and two no-shows.

'It's the rain' he said. 'The miraculous healing power of a downpour. I sense a question on your lips.'

'Do you always see patients if all they want is a prescription refill?'

'No, they can just ask at the desk for refills and generally I only have them come to see me after six repeats. But as you'll have gathered, Mrs Wilyman likes to have a chat. She's decided she's never going to feel any better and she wants to make sure I won't stop her pills. Of course, we don't know how she feels. Her idea of depressed might be your idea of doing okay.'

'She's not a suicide risk?'

'No, no. If you listen to her, she's quite interested in life. She just sees it all in shades of grey.'

'Has she tried counselling?'

'Counselling, aquarobics, going to Tenerife in the winter, Prozac 20mg, we've tried it all. The bottom line is she's happiest taking the pills and telling everybody they don't really help.'

Elsie Turney was next in, to get her blood pressure checked. Another job for the nurse, I'd have thought. 'Same principle as the Wilyman woman,' he said. 'In my opinion, it's time well spent. Elsie's 85, so she's earned a bit of attention and I'd rather see a dozen Elsies than one of the Cherry Tree time-wasters.'

Actually, so far we hadn't seen any time-wasters. He said that was because they wouldn't be up yet.

'Wait till the afternoon,' he said. 'Oh and I'll give you evens on Elsie telling you the story of the boiled egg.'

Mrs Turney was a smiley old lady, and pretty nifty for 85. Trevor said, 'I've got a treat for you today, Elsie. I've got a handsome young doctor to check you over.'

She laughed.

He said, 'Elsie's been with us since I was in short trousers. Isn't that right, Elsie?'

'Oh yes,' she said. 'Old Dr Buxton delivered both of my boys. He was a lovely man. He'd give you all the time in the world.'

Her blood pressure was 155/85. Excellent for her age. The computer screen flagged 'Candidate for statins?'

Trevor looked at me.

'See what I mean? Big Brother.'

'What's your general policy on statins? For the over 60s,

say?'

'My policy is not to have a policy. Know your patients, that's the thing. And I happen to know that in this particular case statins would get flushed round the U-bend.' I said, 'You're very healthy for your age, Mrs Turney. What's your secret?'

'Well' she said, 'I allus has a cooked breakfast and I allus has a nip of rum in my cocoa, so I sleep well.'

'And what she's not told you, Dan, is she never sits still. She's always running errands and for people who are a sight younger than herself. No sign of you easing up, eh?'

'If I ease up you might as well measure me for my box. And you know something I shall never forget about old Dr Buxton. When my Leonard was born, I needed a bit of repair work, you know? Down below. So Dr Buxton says, "I'll tell you what Elsie, it's not even seven o'clock and we've both done a day's work already. How about I boil us each a nice egg and I'll sterilise my darning needle at the same time. Kill two birds with one stone." He was a proper gentleman.'

She squeezed my elbow as she was leaving.

'Thank you very much, young man,' she said. 'I reckon you'll make a bostin' doctor.'

She left. I pressed him about statins. Yasmin Panwar prescribed them for most of her patients over 50.

He said, 'Well for one thing, the jury's still out. They're not without their side effects. And with a patient like Elsie you have to ask yourself, what would be the purpose? She's buried her husband and both brothers, she's seen her grandkiddies into the world and I don't imagine she wants to live for ever. But that's my opinion. You'll make up your own mind, as you go along. I was right about the egg story though. I realise I had inside information but a bet's a bet. I win. You fetch the coffee. Mine's white, two sugars.'

I glanced into the waiting room as I passed. Every seat was taken. The window was steamed up. Nurse Linda was in the kitchen, microwaving porridge, Moira was arranging biscuits on a plate.

'One per person,' she said.

I said, 'I was taking the other one for Dr Buxton.'

'Yes, well,' she said. 'I'm just saying. Butter shortbread doesn't grow on trees. And don't leave a wet spoon in the sugar.'

It seemed I had uphill work ahead of me with Moira. Antony Vaz came in to make himself a mug of tea. Short, slim, smiley. He pumped my hand, asked me where I'd trained, where I was living, was I married?

Linda said, 'Vaz is looking for a wife. He's too young and innocent for me, though. I'm looking for a man who knows his way around.'

She winked at me.

Stephanie appeared. She said, 'You're running very late again, Dr Vaz. Your 10 o'clock is still in the waiting room.'

'Because ten minutes is not enough for consultation,' he said. 'A doctor must be thorough. Even 20 minutes is not enough.'

He picked up his tea and went back to his office.

Our next patient was Freda Jarrold. She had quite a thick file and on the manila cover in black marker it said BOG.

'Ah yes,' says Trevor, 'that's my shorthand. You'll find quite a number of those. It's an aide-memoire for me and a handy hint for those who come after me. BOG stands for Been on Google. Freda just used to drop by with unexplained twinges and niggles but since she got a computer she's detecting all kinds of conditions that have

escaped my notice. A few weeks ago she had erysipelas.'
'Really?'
'No. A touch of lichen planus, possibly. But she likes to keep us on our toes, does Freda. I rather enjoy her. There's no telling what she'll come up with next.'
Mrs Jarrold was a woman in her fifties, nicely dressed, clearly intelligent. She was concerned that she might be magnesium-deficient.
Trevor wrote down her symptoms. Night cramps, unexplained fatigue, palpitations.
He said, 'Shall we have a listen to your ticker?'

Her heart sounded fine to me though of course palpitations can be fleeting. In a quick examination you can easily not catch them. Freda said she felt what she needed was a serum magnesium test. She seemed very well-informed.

'Dr Dan,' says Trevor, looking at me over the top of his glasses, 'what's the latest thinking on the serum magnesium test? It used to be considered rather unreliable.'
'Still is,' I said. It seemed to be the answer he wanted.
'Freda,' he said, 'how's the catarrh? Did you try that decongestant spray I recommended?'
She said she had.
'Because that has an ingredient that can cause palpitations. Nothing to worry about.'
She looked dubious. 'But what about the night cramps and everything? I definitely think I need my magnesium checked.'
He said, 'Dr Dan? Any thoughts?'
I said, 'Brazil nuts are very good.'
He looked at me. 'Brazil nuts?'
'They're very rich in magnesium. My girlfriend eats them a lot.'

'Hmm,' she said. 'I don't know if nuts are a good idea for me. I've got a very delicate stomach. And you know, Ron says I've undergone a complete personality change. Which is another symptom of magnesium deficiency. He says he's never known me to be so irritable.'

Trevor said, 'Well here's a plan. Let's try a month not using the catarrh spray and eating a few brazil nuts a day. If that doesn't help, we'll look at other options.'

'Like the serum test?'

'Yes.'

'Because I was reading that magnesium deficiency can lead to heart failure.'

'Don't worry, Freda,' he said. 'We're not going to let that happen.'

As the door closed he said, 'Heart failure? See what I mean? Change that BOG to BOBG. Been on bloody Google.

'What about the personality change? Did you think she seemed any different?'

'Not at all. It's probably the menopause. Wife goes through the change, a lot of husbands wonder what's hit them.'

Morning surgery was supposed to run till 12.30 and thanks to the no-shows we were actually finished by just after 1 o'clock.

'Right,' says Trevor. 'House calls. One quick phone call, one not so quick pee and then we'll hit the road. We'll go in my car. I've seen the rust bucket you're driving.'

He called Ladbroke's, placed a bet on the 3.30 at Plumpton then sloped off to the toilet. Helen Vincent was in the kitchen eating a salad with a plastic fork.

'Quiet morning or baptism of fire?'

'Fairly quiet.'

'Wait till Friday afternoon when they all want their pills for the weekend. Are you starting with Sterling this week as well?'

Sterling is the out-of-hours service. Yasmin Panwar used a different company, so Sterling were treating me like a rookie, putting me through my paces before I was let loose on any patients.

'I'm sitting in with a triage nurse on Wednesday evening.'

'Good,' she said. 'And tomorrow you can sit in with me.'

She had a drip of vinaigrette on her chin but I didn't like to say. Trevor Buxton appeared, unwrapping a Mars Bar.

'First surgery and our apprentice has blotted his copybook already, I'm afraid, Helen. Inappropriate contact with a patient.'

'Oh yes?' she said. 'Anyone who's likely to sue?'

Stephanie materialised. One minute she wasn't there, next minute she was.

She said, 'Who's likely to sue?'

'Nobody,' says Trevor. 'Young Dan here allowed Elsie Turney to squeeze his elbow. Not only that, but I have a strong suspicion that if I hadn't been there to keep things under control, she'd have pressed him to a Werther's toffee.'

'Take care, Dan,' says Helen. 'Some older women are friskier than you might think.'

I smiled. I think she was joking but it was hard to tell.

And Stephanie said, 'Dr Talbot, you have read the Guide to Professional Conduct and Behaviour?'

I assured her I had. It was one of the items she'd given me when I met her to put all my paperwork in order. That and a Best Practice Toolkit. I'd tried a couple of times to read them but somehow I always fell asleep. I kept seeing the words 'provider units' and it was only when I read on a bit that I realised it was referring to hospitals.

'Helen dearest,' said Trevor, 'what green horror is that

you're eating?'

'Spinach, celery, pine nuts.'

'Yum' he said. 'Come on then, Dr Dan. Let's go and see what Rene Spooner's been up to.'

Trevor Buxton drove an old Volvo.

'I keep the convertible for weekends,' he said. 'Strictly speaking this is Mrs Buxton's car but she got a three-year ban and this is a handy vehicle for trips into the war-zone. It's not sexy enough for anyone to nick.'

'Stephanie seems very earnest.'

'Oh yes. Totally humourless. Efficient though, I'll give her that. Everybody gets paid on time. We never run out of printer cartridges. If it's humour I want, I look to my patients.'

'A three-year ban must be tough.'

'Not really. Mrs Buxton never did a lot of driving. Shopping, hairdressers, that's about all. And there's always taxis.'

'She doesn't work?'

'Not since the kiddies came along. Drink-driving, you see? Second time. If it happens again, she'll get banned for life, but I don't think she will. Drive again, I mean.'

I didn't know what to say.

'We all have our flaws, Dan. We all have our weaknesses. She's a wife in a million, though. Still got her looks too, still got her figure.'

They'd met in A&E, same as me and Chloe.

'North Staffs Infirmary. I was clerking and she was a runner-up to Miss Cannock Chase 1967. Or was it 1968? I can never remember. She'd broken her ankle. It was love at first sight.'

'And you've got a son?'

'And a daughter. Alice. James is a urologist, did I tell you?'

'Yes. Making bags of money.'

'Bags of money and he needs it. He's got a serious skirt-chasing habit and that can get costly. Don't know where he got that from. Not me. Alice runs a little shop. Candles, scarves, birthday cards, that kind of thing. Up in your neck of the woods as a matter of fact. Betsy something.'

'Betws yn Rhos? Betws-y-coed?'

'That's the one.'

'Snowdonia. North Wales. I'm from the south.'

'Ah yes, Abergavenny. Alice is a lesbian. She lives with a friend. Special friend.'

'No grandchildren?'

'No, I think the Buxton line is doomed to peter out. Now, let me tell you about Rene Spooner. She's in her eighties and she's got a touch of dementia. Well, more than a touch. She should probably be in residential care by now, but she lives with her daughter, Margaret. It's Margaret we're really checking on, but discreetly. With cat-like tread.'

'Is she ill?'

'She will be if she doesn't watch out. Round-the-clock carer. She's running herself into the ground.'

'Doesn't she get any help? Is there any other family?'

'Yes, there's a horde of them but nobody else can be arsed to help with the old lady.'

'Can't we get her some outside help?'

'We could, but here's the problem, Dan. Margaret won't agree to it. She says her mother wouldn't like having a stranger come to the flat, but you don't know till you try. Get the right person, Rene might enjoy it.'

Rene and Margaret Spooner lived in a council flat on the Cherry Tree estate. Margaret was a tired-looking woman, late fifties, early sixties. Rene was a pacer and a fiddler. Some people with dementia just sit in a chair and doze but Rene was one of the restless variety. She was very deaf too, which made her voice harsh.

Margaret offered to make us a cup of tea.

'Sit down, woman,' says Trevor. 'We're awash with tea.'

She perched on the edge of the sofa. Rene picked up my coat and started going through the pockets. Margaret jumped up to try and stop her. I assured her I didn't mind but she still got into a tussle with Rene, a tug-of-war with my coat. Lesson learned. When visiting Rene Spooner, keep coat on.

Margaret said the evenings were the worst, from around five o'clock till her mother fell asleep. That was when Rene got aggressive.

'You're giving her the Ativan?'

'When she needs it. I don't want her getting addicted.'

'Margaret,' says Trevor, 'the dose I've prescribed, a mouse wouldn't get addicted. Give it to her every night. Then as soon as she settles, get your own head down. Sleep when you can. You don't manage to go to choir practice, I suppose?'

'How can I? She can't be left.'

'Your Maurice still not taking a turn? Or Steve?'

'It's no job for a man, Doctor.'

'Why not? She's their mother too.'

'What if she messes herself? I couldn't expect a man to deal with that.'

'I don't know, Margaret. It's an equal opportunities world now. They must miss you at St Peter's. Margaret has a great voice, Dan. You should hear her sing The Lost Chord. It'd make the hair stand on the back of your neck. Now Rene, what's your story today?'

Mrs Spooner said she'd been robbed of £1000.

'Have you?' says Trevor. 'Well that's a very serious matter. Have you reported it to the police?'

'Ten thousand pounds,' she barked.

'I'll tell you what I'll do,' he said. 'I'll drop by the police station and mention it to them. Are you all right for a few bob, in the meanwhile? Was it pension day today?'

'Pension day today,' she said.

'You're okay then. You've probably got more than I have. Now listen, would you like to go to the Day Centre some time?'

She looked at him.

He said, 'They have music one of the afternoons. Cup of tea and a singalong. What do you think?'

She said she'd get her hat.

'No hurry,' he said. 'Wednesday's the day. Your Margaret'll organise it.'

Margaret showed us out.

She said, 'She won't go. You know that. She tells you she will but it's a different story when I try to get her there.'

'Keep nudging though. One of these days she might.'

We walked back to the car.

He said, 'Did you get the picture, Dan?'

'The daughter looked exhausted.'

'She's knackered. But did you get the true picture? Margaret's a big part of the problem. If she bundled Rene into a taxi, took her to the Day Centre, left her there for two or three hours the old girl would enjoy it, guaranteed.'

'So why doesn't she?'

'Because her mother's become her life's work and she won't let go. What's she going to do with herself when Rene doesn't need her every minute, night and day?'

'What can we do?'

'Not much, Dan. Keep an eye. That's the best I can suggest. Margaret's a very stubborn woman. I mean, a sense of duty is all well and good, but there's no need for heroics. Now while we're here I'll take you to see another of our home visit regulars. She's just around the corner.'

Marion Flitwell was a morbidly obese shut-in with diabetes and mobility issues. The district nurse visited her once a week to treat recurring skin infections in her skin folds. I had no idea what 450lbs would look like.
The husband came to the door. A normal-looking middle-aged bloke.
'In the neighbourhood,' says Trevor, 'so we thought we'd drop in.'
'Smashing,' says Mr Flitwell. 'She always enjoys a visit.'
There was a sour smell in the flat. Marion was in a reclining chair in the living room. She was enormous, like a human bouncy castle and yet she had a pretty face.
'Hello Dr Buxton,' she said, 'I hope you've not come to nag me.'
'I never nag you,' he said. 'I've brought Dr Talbot to meet you. He's just finishing his training and he's interested in diabetes. So how's the diet going?'
'Pretty good,' she said. 'Doing our best aren't we, Terry?'
There was a litre bottle of Fanta on the table beside her, half empty, and the corpse of a box of Fondant Fancies.
I asked what kind of weight loss regime they were following.
'Salad dinners,' says the husband. 'Every day.'
Trevor looked at me, one eyebrow raised. I know that eyebrow signal very well now.
Mr Flitwell said, 'The thing about Marion is, she can't lose weight like you and me can. It's her glands.'
Marion said, 'That's why I need the operation.'
Trevor said, 'And I've told you before. You have to lose some weight first. You have to show you can stick to a diet.'
'Well it's very depressing,' she said. 'Because I hardly eat a

thing. It'd just be easier if I had the operation.'

'It's not that simple, Marion. I'm not nagging. I'm just giving you the facts. No surgeon is going to operate at your current weight. Dr Dan will tell you and he's much more up to speed on hospitals than I am.'

I said, 'Dr Buxton's right. An operation could be high risk at this point. Having an anaesthetic and being immobile. A surgeon needs to consider the big picture.'

I found myself wondering if I should have used the word 'big.' I don't know why. People like Marion annoy me. I mean, I like Fondant Fancies myself but heaven's above, a whole box?

'Have you had your lunch yet, Marion?' asks Trevor.

'Just a drop of soup,' says Mr Flitwell. 'And a couple of Ryvitas.'

'Drop of soup my arse,' says Trevor when we got back into the car. 'Well, Dan? Still want to be a GP? Have we achieved anything at all in the past hour?'

'We checked Mrs Flitwell's haemoglobin glucose. And her feet.'

'The visiting nurse could do that.'

'And we were probably the only non-demented people Margaret Spooner will see today.'

'True. So we've brought some company and cheer to one poor sod's existence. But the Flitwells? What can you do?'

'It's the husband, isn't it?'

'Of course it is. Marion can't get down to Asda to stock up. She's not been out of the house for at least three years.'

'Doesn't he understand that he's killing her? He seemed bright enough.'

'He understands. He likes her the way she is. When Marion carks it, which she will before long, he'll find somebody else to stuff like a fucking Strasbourg goose.'

When we got back to the surgery the sign had been tampered with again. Instead of saying THE   DENS it said H   ENS.

Trevor said, 'You know, credit where it's due. That's quite creative.'

CHAPTER 5

I ate my sandwich at Trevor's desk and checked a pile of prescriptions while he made phone calls. Afternoon surgery started at 3 o'clock. Fifteen appointments, three no-shows, one fungal toenail, one pulled back muscle, a sore throat, two patients feeling listless, a bunch of people needing sick notes and then Kyle Bibby.

'Aha,' says Trevor. 'You've hit the jackpot on your first day. I wondered how long it'd be before you met Kyle. Did I write anything useful on the front of his file?'

I couldn't see anything.

'Pass it over,' he said, and he wrote TFDOS.

'Take a guess?'

'Does the F stand for the F word?'

'It does. And the T stands for 'total'. Total. Fucking. Drain. On. Society. Our Kyle is 23. Never worked a day. Hobbies, getting off his head and distributing his DNA as widely as possible.'

How many children does he have?'

'I shudder to think. He wouldn't be able to tell you but to be fair to Kyle probably neither would some of the girls. These are not carefully considered acts of procreation, Dan. These are random shags. Let's get him in. I imagine he'll be looking for something to get him through the week. Valium. Temazepam.'

'Will you give him something?'

'Possibly. If I don't, he'll buy some on the street, or steal some. If I do, he might sell them. There's an entrepreneurial side to Kyle.'

'How do you decide whether to prescribe?'

'Depends on my mood, if I'm tired of his bullshit or if I'm just plain tired. You'll notice Kyle always takes a late appointment. He thinks I'll do anything to get rid of him so I can go home. He's quite a psychologist, Kyle. Sometimes he's right, but sometimes he's dead wrong.'

Kyle Bibby was a lanky specimen. Loping gait, cheeky smile. He did a very theatrical double take when he saw me.

'Hello, hello, hello,' he said. 'What's this? You being inspected, Dr Buxton?'

Trevor said, 'This is Dr Talbot. He's going to be around for a while so why don't you tell him a bit about yourself? Tell him why you're here?'

Kyle settled himself. He was quite the performer.

'It's me anxiety disorder,' he said. 'It's really doing my head in.'

I asked him what he thought was causing it.

'Relationship issues,' he said. 'Fucking Jade Shotton says that kid's mine and it never is. So I've got her giving me brain-ache. Then my brother died, Dr Buxton'll tell you.'

'Scott was in Winson Green,' says Trevor. 'He suffered a coronary thrombosis.'

'Only on remand, mind,' says Kyle. 'Innocent until proven guilty. They say it was his heart, but I say there should be an inquiry. Else how can I get closure?'

'So you sometimes feel anxious?'

'Not sometimes, doctor. All the time.'

'You do realise the pills can make things worse?'

'How's that then?'

'I see you've been taking temazepam for a long time now. Your body's become accustomed to it. So when the dose is wearing off you're bound to feel worse. For a while.'

'That's what I'm saying. If I don't get me tammies I'm liable to go off on one.'

Trevor said, 'What do we think, Dr Talbot? 10mg?'

Kyle said, 'You're kidding me. Tens don't even touch me.'

I said, 'They would. You might not think so, but they'd help you to cut down. Gradually reduce your dependency.'

'But not while I've got issues, doctor. I'm not in a good place at the moment.'

We gave him a prescription for Temazepam 20mg. He seemed happy enough with that.

Trevor said, 'Of course he's bloody happy. He'll go straight from the chemist's to the estate and sell them. He'll make enough profit to buy himself 30mg, which is what he was angling for. But don't be downhearted, Dan.'

I did feel Kyle Bibby had defeated us.

'Look' says Trevor. 'Whatever we do he's going to take something. If he doesn't get what he wants from us he'll go robbing to pay for something down the souk.'

'Where's the souk?'

'Outside Karim's Kabin or the Brook Glen offie. Or in any underpass between the aforementioned. You see what we're up against? The Kyles on our books aren't interested in having a pill-free life.'

'So we just give them what they demand?'

'The way I look at it is, it might spare some poor old dear getting knocked down for her purse. And then, to take the longer view, it's unlikely Kyle'll be around ten years from now. One of these days he'll neck something dodgy and it'll be night-night Kyle. Think of the money that'll save the system.'

I'd heard the same argument from Yasmin Panwar. Still, it wasn't a great end to the day.

There was a lone figure hunched over in the waiting room. Down jacket and a woolly hat even though it was a mild evening. I asked him if he was waiting to see Dr Buxton. He looked up at me. Late teens, early twenties, bad skin.

'No,' he said.

'Who are you here for?'

'What's it to you?' he said. 'You the trainee?'

I said, 'I'm Dr Talbot. Who are you waiting to see?'

He sniggered. 'Not you, Mr Learner Doctor.'

I went to Reception to ask about the charmer.

'That's Miles,' says Moira through lemon lips. 'Dr Vincent's boy. He's waiting for a lift.'

I was in no hurry to go home. Chloe was staying at her brother's place in London overnight, so she could go to the final cardio wet lab the next morning. I phoned Matt, to see if he was up for a beer.

Matt, Rob and I were mates all the way though med school. Rob's in Australia now and Matt's doing orthopaedics at the Queen Elizabeth. I hadn't seen him for months. Somehow the timings never worked out. He said his fracture clinic should be finished by 5.30 so we arranged to meet in The Green Man.

I had a surprise when he walked in. It was the first time since our pre-clinical years that I'd seen him clean-shaven. He said the beard had had to go: when you're doing ops there are infection considerations. He's in theatre three or four sessions a week, plus he has to do trauma assessments in A&E, and then there are the out-patient clinics. He looked very well though. When we were junior housemen he always looked wrecked. Long days, late nights and too much booze.

'So,' he said, 'how are things in the ranks?'

Now he's an apprentice surgeon he thinks he's a bit superior to the rest of us but from what I understand, a lot of the time all he'll be doing is closing the patient up after the Great Panjandrum has done the tricky stuff and gone home. I always hated surgical rotations myself. I like to be able to see the whole patient, not just a bit of them through a hole in a sterile drape. I like patients I can talk to.

I told him about The Lindens.

'Sooner you than me, mate,' he said.

I might have said the same about his life. Knees are his major interest. Knees, knees and more knees. And he has his FRCS exams coming up. Without that, his career will stall. Matt always seemed to breeze through exams but it's one thing when you're a full-time student and quite another when you're holding down a job as well.

'You still with Chloe?'

'Getting married next year.'

'Wow. A married GP. You'll be joining a golf club next.'

'You seeing anyone?'

'Nobody special. I'm spoiled for choice. Pick of the chocolate box. When you're a surgeon you don't get left with the nougat nobody else fancied. Nurses, physios. They really go for a guy in scrubs. So when's the wedding?'

'To be decided. Chloe's doing her Part II in November. We have to get through that first.'

'Want me to organise your stag?'

'No thanks.'

'Prague's great, or Riga. I've been to both. The drink's cheap and the girls are gorgeous.'

'I don't think so.'

'You mean you don't fancy some wild, no-strings sex before the cell door slams shut on you? Dan, you are middle-aged before your time.'

I'd intended suggesting we go for a curry, but I thought better of it. I didn't have much to say to Matt anymore. Funny how things change. When we were first year students, starting our anatomy course, Rob, Matt and I had been allocated the same cadaver. First day in the dissection room we were all a bit queasy, what with the smell of the formaldehyde and the realisation that this was an actual deceased human being we were cutting open. But we blagged our way through the first session and we just clicked. After that we always sat together in the refectory, always revised together, even lived together eventually. But now, all Matt talks about is knee surgery and one-night stands with physios.

Mam phoned me later that evening. I should call her more often, but she works shifts so it's hard to know when's best to catch her and Da doesn't always bother answering if Mam's not there.

She said, 'What it is, I'm a bit worried about your Nan.'

Nan Talbot is Da's mother. She's in her eighties and still living on her own. Mam said she was getting forgetful.

'Just forgetful?'

'A bit pixilated too. She thinks the woman next door stole her floor cloth.'

'Apart from that, how is she?'

'Right as rain. A touch of arthritis but nothing else.'

'Has her GP seen her?'

'She won't go. You know what she's like. Stubborn as a cat. I mean, it's not that I'd mind having her to live with us, but then I'd have to give up work. I've got a year and a half to go yet.'

Mam's a midwife at Nevill Hall in Aber. She loves her work. I can't imagine her retired.

'Do you want me to come down and see Nan? Give you my expert medical opinion?'

'Very funny. No, you're busy. It'd be a long trek for you.'

'It wouldn't. I'm waiting to get my new out-of-hours rota. As soon as I know which weekends I'm off, I'll come down.'

'It'd be lovely to see you. How's your girlfriend?'

'Say her name, Mam. She's not my girlfriend. I'm going to marry her.'

48

'So you say. What year will that be?'

'Next year. When she's finished her exams. Say her name.'

'Chloe. What it is, Dan, we hardly know her.'

When we got engaged Mam and Da drove up to Birmingham and we all went to Pizza Express. It went off okay, except Da's not that keen on pizza and Chloe made a fuss about too much rocket in her salad. They might not have got the best impression of her.

'How about we come to you for Christmas?'

'That'd be fabluss. I'm just saying Ed, it'd be fabluss if Dan and his girlfriend, if Dan and Chloe came for Christmas.'

Mam's phone conversations are always relayed to Da. Sometimes you can hear him making interested noises in the background but usually not.

I said, 'I'll run it by Chloe when she gets back from London.'

It might have been better if I'd done that before making rash suggestions.

'But I'll come down sooner than that, one of the weekends, if you want me to take a look at Nan.'

'Well,' says Mam, 'let's see how we go. I'm probably worrying too much. I'm just saying, Ed, no need for Dan to come trekking down here in a hurry when he's so busy with his doctoring.'

I hope I'll never be too busy to give my folks a hand. It wouldn't hurt my brother to step up occasionally. Adam lives in Cardiff. He's a maths teacher, single, no dependents. He could drive there in under an hour, but I don't think they see him any more often than they see me.

CHAPTER 6

Helen Vincent was in with Trevor when I arrived the next morning.

'Dan,' she said, 'sit with me for morning surgery today. It's important for you to spend time with each of us. You'll find we have very different styles.'

Trevor said, 'That's a gentle dig at the Buxton Method. Which is, watch, listen, follow your instincts.'

She said, 'But also ignore current recommendations and refuse to make friends with technology.'

'I don't need a machine telling me my job. You can take him, Helen, but I want him back by 2.30. I've got an SPO coming in and I want Dan there. It'll be useful Bad News training.'

SPO. Spare Parts Only. He was referring to Mr Riley with his Stage 4 cancer.

I followed Helen into her office. Trevor had had me sit beside him where I could see whatever popped up on his hated computer screen. Helen parked me in a chair by the wall, like a rookie student. She looked through her letters in silence. I felt like she'd forgotten I was there.

'Right,' she said. 'Who do we have?'

Her first patient was Michael Ward. A 42 year old with a history of digestive problems. He was suffering from cramps, flatulence and a burning sensation in his anal sphincter.

'So, your old problem. When did this latest bout start?'

'Last week.'

'Monday? Friday?'

'Can't remember. It comes and goes.'

'Are you still drinking?'

'The usual.'

She said, 'Mr Ward, how many times have we had this conversation? Six cans of Frosty Jack's a day is too much.'

He said, 'It can't be the Frosty's causing it, Doctor. My guts is used to that.'

She sighed.

'Dr Talbot? Any thoughts?'

I said, 'Query IBS?'

She gave me a little smile.

'Mr Ward,' she said. 'I don't want to send you to hospital for tests but if you keep presenting with these symptoms, I shall feel obliged. Do you really want a colonoscopy?'

'I don't know. What is it?'

'Having a camera shoved up your back passage.'

'A camera?'

'Yes.'

'What, a real camera?'

Poor Mr Ward was probably picturing a Canon Powershot pushed up his fundament.

'Yes, a real camera.'

'No way. I could try the Imodium again.'

'You could, although it's not really the answer. You need to cut down your drinking and eat some proper food.'

'I do. I get a doner most days.'

'Where from?'

'Kebab King.'

'No wonder you've got the runs.'

'So do I get a prescription? For the Imodium.'

'No. You can buy it over the counter. Off you go.'

That was Helen Vincent's style. Crisp, impatient. Sandra Kerridge, feeling low? 'Think of those less fortunate. Try some volunteer work.' Cheryl Yeomans hoping for a brow-lift on the NHS. 'Not a chance. Don't waste my time.' She wasn't the kind of GP you'd go to for a reassuring chat.

Keith Sideaway was her last patient of the morning. He had a drooping eyelid. He said it had come on suddenly. Helen read his notes on her screen while I leafed through his file, such as it was. He hadn't been to see a doctor in more than three years.

'Dr Talbot,' she said. 'Perhaps you'd like to examine Mr Sideaway?'

A healthy-looking 52 year old male with sudden onset unilateral ptosis and mydriasis. His left eyelid was half closed. His left pupil was very small. Or was it that his right pupil was dilated? Helen was watching me. And I felt myself beginning to suffer a brain-fade. Think, think, sympathetic nervous system, parasympathetic nervous system, cranial nerves. Suddenly I couldn't remember a thing.

I'll put my hand up and admit, I'm not great under pressure. Rob, my best mate from med school, he actually thrives on it. He's in Australia now, working in Major Trauma. It would be my worst nightmare.

She said, 'Don't keep your thoughts to yourself, Dr Talbot. Talk me through your thinking.'

'There's no sign of trauma. No facial palsy.'

'Any strabismus?'

'No.'

'Anything else you'd like to check?'

I couldn't think.

'Would eye drops be of any use?' she hinted.

I was sweating. 'Hydroxyamphetamine?'

'Yes. They'll have some in the nurses' room.'

Nurse Chris found some Paredine drops.

She said, 'Are you okay? You look a bit flustered.'

'I think I'm flunking some basic neurology in there.'

'Oh dear,' she said. 'Well, being put on the spot can be a

good way to learn. Do you want a glass of water before you go back into the lioness's den?'

Helen applied the eye drops to Mr Sideaway.

'Now,' she said, 'what are we looking for here?'

'To see if the contracted pupil dilates?'

'Yes. Which might indicate?'

I knew she was checking for damage to one of the nerve trunks. I just couldn't think which. I decided a guess would be better than a dithering silence.

'A problem in the sympathetic nerve trunk?'

'Yes.'

Relief. But I wasn't out of the woods yet. She perched on the edge of her desk while we waited for the eyedrops to take effect, asked about Mr Sideaway about his general health. He said he was fine.

'No aches and pains?'

Just a touch of arthritis in his shoulder, he said.

'Both shoulders?'

'No, only the left side. I had a torn rotator cuff a while back.'

She commiserated, said she'd had that herself, years ago, and it had prevented her doing weights at the gym for a long time. She asked me to check his grip. His left hand was significantly weaker than his right.

'Have you noticed any change in your voice?'

'Don't think so.'

'It's not a little hoarse?'

'It might be.'

'Any cough?'

'No.'

'Hoarse voice? Cough? With a drooping eyelid. Where was she going with this? We checked his eyes again. Helen wears a very nice perfume. Chloe wears Wild Bluebell. I like that too.

53

The left pupil had dilated.

Helen looked at me.

'So?'

'Possible lesion.'

'Yes, but where?' She sounded exasperated. I knew what she was getting at. Was the problem pre or post ganglionic? I honestly couldn't remember how that worked. The only thing for it was another guess.

'Preganglionic.'

She nodded. My luck had held. It was like being back in first year clinical, praying the consultant wouldn't pick you, wouldn't put you on the spot in front of a patient and all the other students. She went back to her desk.

'Are you a smoker, Mr Sideaway.'

'Used to be. I gave up years ago. Haven't had a cigarette since January 1st 2002.'

'Good for you. I'm going to refer you for a chest X-ray.'

'Why's that?'

'The human body is a mysterious thing. Sometimes a problem in one part makes itself known as a symptom in a different area. For instance, your eyelid problem. It could be caused by pressure on a nerve somewhere else. In your chest, say, where you've got a lot of wires in a confined space.'

'Sounds like my job', he said. He was a cable-puller. They'd just finished a big contract for North Staffs hospital, installing the electrics for a new scanning unit.

She said, 'We'll see you again after your X-ray. But you never know, that eyelid thing might resolve itself before then.'

Keith Sideaway left. I started gathering up the patient files.

'Leave those,' she said. 'That's Mary's job.'

She left the room. I followed her to the kitchen. Dr Mac was in there and Vaz and Stephanie and both nurses. I don't know if it was the coffee, but my head suddenly cleared.

Eyelid droop and possible referred shoulder pain. It had been in one of Chloe's revision quizzes.

I said, 'That last patient? Are you thinking it might be Horner's Syndrome?'

'Yes,' she said. 'I wouldn't necessarily have expected you to pick up on that. It's fairly rare. It was your neurology that was found wanting, Dan. You need to get your textbooks out. Back to basics.'

Everything went very quiet. Nurse Chris grimaced. Vaz looked at his feet. Mac said, 'Helen, did you never need to sneak a wee look at a cribsheet? Are ye so damned perfect?'

Helen grabbed her salad box from the fridge.

She said, 'Dan's here to learn and there are some things that should be second nature to him by now. No sense sugar-coating it. Right, I'm gone. Another bloody CCG meeting.'

As she left, Trevor appeared.

He said, 'What's going on? You should see your faces. Has Helen been reading the riot act? Or were you talking about me?'

Mac said, 'Our trainee just got a slight public bollocking. He took it like a man, though.'

Nurse Linda said, 'She was well out of order. Narky cow. Not Dan's fault if she's not getting any.'

Mac said, 'Pay no heed, laddie. You should come out with me, maybe Thursday. No textbooks required around the nursing homes.'

I was grateful to him for his show of solidarity, but I could have done without being called 'laddie'.

Trevor and I took our lunches to his office.

'And what was all that about?'

I told him about Keith Sideaway.

'Horner's Syndrome?' he said. 'What the hell is that?'

'Disruption of a nerve supply to one side of the face.'

'And?'

'Possibly due to pressure from a thoracic mass. We sent him for a chest X-ray. But it was my shaky neurology Helen was criticising. I deserved it. I couldn't think straight.'

Mary brought in the files for afternoon surgery. Jimmy Riley's was on the top of the pile. Stage 4 adenocarcinoma of the stomach, metastases in the liver, spine and ribs.

Trevor said, 'Have you had much experience of delivering bad news, Dan?'

I hadn't. That's to say, I'd done it, but I suspect not very well. They didn't really teach us stuff like that in medical school. They're starting to now, apparently. Role play. They take turns to be the anxious patient or the messenger of doom.

'A few times, in A&E mainly. In the relatives' room.'

'Cup of tea. Box of Kleenex. Sympathetic face.'

'Yes. I could never work out how long I should sit with them. How to end the conversation.'

'It may surprise you to know that it doesn't get any easier. Harder for us GPs, in a way. You get to know your patients. Take Jimmy. I've known him since I first started in the practice. And his wife, and his kids.'

'And you want me to sit in?'

'Definitely. You'll be a bit of a distraction. And I want you to hear what I'm prescribing.'

'Pamidronate for bone pain?'

'Yes.'

'What about steroids?'

'Possibly. Maybe some Ativan, if he's feeling anxious.'

'Will you talk about hospice care?'

'Play it by ear. We don't have to say everything today. No sense in overloading. Sometimes you've winded people with the bad news so they aren't really listening anyway. Sometimes they're way ahead of you and they've already worked things out.'

'Anything else?'

'Yes. I'm going to the Black Bear for a fortifying double.'

He was back from the pub, on the phone placing a bet on the 2.30 at Uttoxeter, when Mary put her head round the door to say the Rileys had arrived.

'Bring them in, dear girl,' he said. 'And no interruptions. Please.'

He signalled me to sit in his seat.

'Try it on for size,' he said.

Jimmy and Connie Riley came in and Trevor pulled a chair round to sit with them.

He said, 'This is Dr Talbot, our very bright assistant. He's driving the desk this afternoon.'

Mr Riley looked like a sick man.

'Now Jimmy,' says Trevor, 'you've been through the mill lately. How are you feeling?'

'Terrible,' says Jimmy. 'I suppose you've got me in to show me the red card?'

'Well yes. It looks like an early shower, for you and me both.'

'I heard you were retiring. Is it cancer?'

'Emphysema.'

You'll be missed.'

'Missed but replaceable, that's what I hope. I'm about ready for the knacker's yard.'

'You're too young for that.'

'I'm 65, Jimmy. Time to let the youngsters run the show. Dr Vincent's taking over the practice when I go.'

'Well I won't be around. I'm 73. I've had a good innings.'

'Not bad. How do you think he seems, Connie?'

'He's not eating. How can he get his strength up if he's not eating?'

'It'll be because of the growth in his stomach. Did they

explain it to you at the hospital? The appetite goes. Just give him whatever he fancies.'

'All he wants is ice cream. There's no nourishment in that.'

'Ah go on,' says Trevor. 'Indulge the man. I like a bit of ice cream myself. Caramel swirl. Are you sleeping all right, Jimmy?'

'Not so great. I lie awake thinking.'

'We can give you something for that, if you'd like. And I want you to see the nurse while you're here today. She'll get you in every week or two for a special treatment, in case your bones start giving you pain. It can happen.'

'Special treatment?'

'You'll be on a drip and it'll take an hour or two, so bring a paper to read. Or one of those saucy magazines.'

Jimmy laughed. His wife said, 'And that'll fix him will it, Dr Buxton? The drip thing? Because the hospital hasn't done a thing for him.'

Trevor paused.

Then he said, 'Not a lot they can do, Connie. The main thing now is to keep him comfortable. Maybe a little pill to help with the sleeping? We'll take it a week at a time. See how things go. How are your boys?'

She said their sons were both doing well, both very busy. Roger was working overseas, Derek was in West Bromwich.

'And does Derek get over to see you? Give you a hand?'

'I don't need a hand. I need His Nibs to buck up.'

Jimmy said, 'What do you reckon, doctor? Christmas?'

'Touch and go, Jimmy. It's hard to say.'

Mrs Riley said, 'Well I hope he is right by Christmas. It won't be worth getting a turkey if all he wants is ice cream.'

Trevor took them through to Chris, to set up an appointment for the first pamidronate infusion. He came back.

I said, 'His wife doesn't get it, does she?'

'Oh, I think she does, Dan. She's not a stupid woman. It's her way of coping. He certainly does. Couples are funny, the ways they find to muddle along. As you will discover.'

We did letters and prescriptions till our 3 o'clock arrived. Tara Beamish, with a livid rash. Trevor said he'd known Tara since she was a positive pregnancy test.

It was a strange rash, on the back of her neck, her scalp and her hands, but nowhere else. Trevor guessed what it was immediately.

He said, 'You've gone auburn since I last saw you. Have you been dyeing your hair?'

She said it was just a wash-in colour you could do at home.

'Did you test it on a patch of skin first?'

'No.'

'Well there you are then. Mrs Buxton gets hers done at the hairdresser's, costs a bloody fortune, but if she wants to change her colour, they do a skin test first. Calamine lotion, my dear. That'll soothe it. And learn your lesson. Always do a skin test. How's your Mum?'

Tara said her mother just got engaged.

'Did she, by jingo? Good for her. Is he a nice chap?'

'Don't know,' she said. 'He's in Africa.'

'Is he? Where did she meet him?'

'Internet.'

'So is he moving here? How does that work?'

'He has to get a visa first. Mum's going over there to get married.'

'To Africa?'

'Yes.'

'Taking a chance, isn't she?'

Tara shrugged.

She said, 'He's nice-looking. I've seen his photo. He's only 29.'

'Well tell your Mum, Dr Buxton says to take care. And to get her vaccinations. That's important. Where exactly is she going?'

She thought for a minute.

'Niagara?'

'Nigeria, maybe?'

'Could be.'

'Then she'll need a lot of vaccinations. Dr Dan'll tell you.'

I was winging it. These things change all the time, but I was pretty sure she'd need shots for typhoid, cholera, yellow fever and Hep A and B. Tara promised to pass on the advice to her mother.

'Fucking Niagara,' says Trevor. 'They're a nice family, just not much going on between the ears. Trolling off to Nigeria to marry a 29 year old she's never met? Can you believe these people?'

'She should probably get the rabies vaccine too. I forgot to mention that. And take anti-malarials.'

'She should get her bloody head looked at, Dan. Never mind about vaccinations. She needs a shot of common sense. One thing about this job, there's always something to entertain you. It's better than the telly any day.'

CHAPTER 7.

Chloe texted me to say she was back from London. It was nearly 7 o'clock by the time I'd finished writing up notes. The cleaner was in, pushing a squeegee mop over the waiting room floor. Antony Vaz was in the kitchen eating peanut butter on crackers.

'Lining for my stomach,' he said. He was going on a date. 'Do you think I look all right?'

He hadn't met the girl before and I had a feeling the sleeveless pullover wasn't the coolest fashion choice. But she might be an old-fashioned kind of girl and anyway, I'm no great expert on clothes. I told him he looked fine. He was using an Internet site called Match. They were going to meet at a wine bar in Wolverhampton and he was fretting about what to order.

I said, 'She'll tell you what she wants.'

'But what about me? I don't like alcohol.'

'You could have a zero alcohol wine. Tell her you're a doctor on call. Women love that.'

'Do they?'

'Never fails. The only thing sexier than a doctor on call is a vet on call. Do you want me to phone you later, with a fake medical emergency?'

'I think this will not be honest.'

'What do you know about her?'

'She is a hairdresser.'

'Anything else?'

'She liked my picture.'

Trevor came in, cigarette case in his hand, battered old Panama jammed on his head. He looked tired.

'Clear off, the pair of you,' he said. 'Then I can do likewise.'

I asked him if his horse won at Uttoxeter.

'Pulled up,' he said. 'Bloody donkey.'

Chloe was asleep on the sofa with the British Journal of Cardiology. She surfaced when she heard me.

'Good course?'

'Yeah.'

'Get any hands-on?'

'A bit. But we watched a load of procedures on a video feed.'

'Stents?'

'Balloon first, then the stent. But the balloon was coated with slow-release paclitaxel. It delays re-stenosis. Which overall gives you a better outcome.'

'You go in through the groin, right? Femoral artery?'

'Or the wrist. You were supposed to buy milk. Barrington's a groin man.'

Barrington's her consultant.

'I had a drink with Matt.'

'What's his story? Let me guess. He's diddling some nurse.'

Chloe doesn't really like Matt.

'Several, from what he says. A different one each night of the week. There's plenty of milk in the fridge.'

'It's out of date.'

'By one day, max. I sniffed it and it seemed fine to me.'

'Well a best-before date is on it for a reason and I'm not risking it. You dropped the ball, Dan.'

'Okay, I'll go and buy some if it's really that important. When I was a kid my Nan Talbot used to use what she called 'paralysed' milk.'

'What's that?'

'It was sterilised milk, like long-life. Because she didn't have a fridge.'

'Why didn't she have a fridge?'

'She wouldn't have one. She was afraid it'd catch fire. Actually, she didn't need one. She was in the old house in those days. She had a nice cool pantry and a meat safe with a wire mesh door.'

'Gosh, how primitive.'

'She's got one now. A fridge. Da insisted, when she moved into her flat.'

'Quite right. Why did she say her milk was paralysed?'

'She took 'sterilised' and 'pasteurised' and kind of invented a new word.'

'Why?'

'It was a joke.'

'Don't get it.'

Chloe's family don't go in much for silliness. Her brother Charlie might tell an off-colour joke, after the ladies have left the room, but they generally play everything very straight. I'd rather hoped she'd cook, as she'd had an easy day, but she said she was too tired to eat.

'In that case I'll get a takeaway. I really fancy a Chinese.'

'Ooh,' she said, 'get Pekin duck and pancakes.'

'So you're not too tired to eat?'

'Actually, get an Indian. They deliver faster. And don't forget the naan.'

I ordered from the Star of Madras and ironed a couple of shirts while we waited for the delivery.

'What's the rest of your week looking like?'

'Echograms. Valvular regurge. Septal defects. Yada yada.'

'You don't sound very interested. Are you sure cardiology is your future?'

'I'm just tired, Dan. I'm working, I'm studying.'

'It'll soon be over. The studying.'

'Yeah.'

'And now you're supposed to ask me about my first two days at The Lindens.'

'As long as you don't tell me about any no-hopers and druggies on benefit because it'll just annoy me.'

'Okay, well let me think.'

I told her about poor Margaret Spooner, struggling to cope with her old Mum. I told her about Freda Jarrold thinking she had magnesium deficiency.

'Brazil nuts.'

'Exactly what I told her. We call people like Mrs Jarrold, the Worried Well. They go on the Internet and find diseases they might have. I suppose it's always happened. People used to read Pears' Medical Encyclopaedia.'

'Time-wasters. And you've been with that smoker. I can smell it.'

'I only saw him have two cigarettes all day.'

'It's still disgusting. I hope he doesn't smoke in the surgery.'

'I think he used to. His office does smell. They're getting it deep-cleaned when he leaves. Vaz was going on a date tonight.'

'Who's Vaz?'

'The junior. Antony Vaz. He's a really nice bloke.'

'You think everyone is a nice bloke.'

'No, I don't. I think your brother is a tosspot. Anyway, Vaz is desperate for a girlfriend and he'd been on a site called Match and got himself a date. I wasn't sure he was dressed right but I didn't like to say anything.'

'Not a blazer? Please tell me he wasn't wearing a blazer.'

'Your father wears a blazer.'

'Because he's old. What was this Vaz wearing?'

'A pullover.'

'You mean a sweater?'

'No. A pullover. Sleeveless.'

'Eww. Not Fair Isle?'

'What's that?'

'The patterned kind that grannies used to knit.'

'His was plain maroon.'

'Still, a pullover. He sounds like a bit of a clueless knob. Your Worried Well woman, is she taking a calcium supplement?'

'No. I don't know. Why?'

'Think, Dan. Magnesium, calcium. How does that relationship work?'

'Go on.'

'Where do you find the highest concentrations of magnesium?'

'South Africa?'

'In the body, you twit.'

'Well as I'm talking to a cardiologist, I'm going to guess the heart.'

'Yes. Left ventricle. And what role does magnesium play in the metabolism of the heart, Dr Talbot?'

'Something highly beneficial, I'm sure.'

'It controls calcium levels. So, if magnesium levels are low, calcium can flood in.'

'And that's bad?'

'Very. It can cause strong arrhythmias.'

'Wow. I'd forgotten that.'

'If your woman is taking extra calcium, which a lot do when they get to a certain age, worried about osteoporosis, she could be right to ask about her magnesium levels. She could be a heart attack waiting to happen.'

I made a mental note to discuss it with Trevor.

Chloe cleared away while I made myself a packed lunch for the next day. I'd stuck my Sterling schedule on the fridge door.

She said, 'What's this?'

'My out-of-hours shifts for the next month.'

'Daniel!' she said.

This always signals trouble. It was the same when I was a kid. I was Dan or Danny until I'd done something wrong. Then I was Daniel.

She said, 'You can't work on that weekend. It's Daddy's birthday lunch.'

I hadn't really looked at the dates.

'I'll try to change it.'

'Not try. Succeed. Do it. Tell them it's absolutely non-negotiable.'

'I'll see what I can do, but I don't want to give a bad impression. Messing up the rota when I've only just started with them.'

I don't actually think Chloe's father would have been heartbroken if I'd missed his birthday lunch, but I was on thin ice with Chloe. Mahatma Ghandi, Nelson Mandela. Her father's right up there. It's a daughter thing.

'I could always put in a brief appearance at lunch and then drive back in time for the evening shift.'

'That would be incredibly rude.'

'Would it? Your Dad's a doctor. He'd understand.'

Of course, Chloe's father isn't any old doctor. In recent years the most he's worked is three full days and two half days a week. As he explained it to me, there's no point in working Friday afternoons or Monday mornings in Harley Street because his patients are either on their way to a weekend in the country or on their way back from a weekend in the country. Also, being a top-drawer throat man, he has a lot of patients who are singers and actors and they don't get up till late.

Chloe said, 'You'd have a different attitude if it was your father's party.'

'Da wouldn't have a birthday party. He hates that kind of thing. I will move heaven and earth to attend your father's birthday. Okay?'

'Okay.'

'But while we're talking about families, perhaps this is a good moment to talk about Christmas?'

'Christmas? It's September. Anyway, I can't think about things like that. You do realise it's only eight weeks till my exams?'

'Yes, darling, I had heard. But Christmas will still happen. I thought it'd be nice if we went to my folks. Give them a chance to get to know you.'

'I'd kind of assumed we'd go to the Chummery. I'd quite like a bit of pampering, after my exams.'

The Chummery is Chloe's family home and it's not a place I'd associate with pampering. The bathrooms are arctic and the food is pretty basic. Vinnie, my future mother-in-law, lives on cream crackers and Laurence generally eats dinner in town before he goes home.

I said, 'It was just a thought. We don't have to decide yet.'

That was a fib. Now I'd opened my big mouth Mam was very likely planning major refurbishments.

Chloe said, 'You haven't promised them?'

'Not promised. But hinted we might. If you want to go to the Chummery, fine. But I'll definitely go to Wales. For one thing, I want to see my Nan. And Mam and Da. I see more of your family than I do of my own.'

'Will your parents think I'm horrid if I don't go with you?'

'Probably.'

'Seriously, Dan.'

'Yes. They'll say, "What kind of toffee-nosed little madam are you walking out with? Our hovel not good enough for her, is it? Is she worried about the slag heap in the back yard?"'

'I love it when you talk Welsh.'

'That's not Welsh. That's my Max Boyce impersonation.'

'Who? Anyway, I know you don't have any slag heaps.'

'Nowhere near. We have the Black Mountains. It's lovely. Come with me.'

'I'll think about it. I don't want your family thinking I'm standoffish.'

'They won't. They don't.'

This wasn't strictly true. Mam does a bit, if I'm honest, but that's because she hardly knows Chloe yet.

'What do they say about me?'

'They don't say anything about you.'

'Because they don't like me.'

'Okay, do you really want to know what my Da said about you?'

'Yes.'

She made a wincing face.

'He said, "I reckon you're punching above your weight there, Dan boy".'

'Is that good?'

I love it when she says something dim. Not very street-wise, Chloe. Although she has picked up 'clueless knob' as a derogatory term for unsophisticated men who wear sleeveless pullovers.

She spent the rest of the evening doing a revision quiz. She tried out a few questions on me.

'A 7 year old child, of short stature, presents with excessive thirst, lassitude and increased urination…'

'Type 1 diabetes.'

'Hold on, I haven't finished. A 24 hour urine collection reveals hypercalciuria. Is the most likely diagnosis a) Gitelman's Syndrome, b) Liddle's Syndrome, c) Renal tubular acidosis or d) Bartter's Syndrome?'

'Isn't Liddle's a supermarket?'

'You're not taking this seriously.'

'No, because I'm not taking my MRCP. And I'm watching Pointless.'

'Well the answer is renal tubular acidosis.'

'Right. Was the short stature a false clue?'

'No. RTA can cause rickets. Try this one. A patient with Crohn's disease is unresponsive to steroids and anti-inflammatories. What is your next step?'

'Liquid diet?'

'No.'

'Colon resection?'

'I'm glad you're not my doctor.'

'Me too. How about immuno-suppressants?'

'Correct. I'd prescribe azathioprine. London's great. There's so much going on.'

'Such as?'

'Pubs, restaurants, theatres, museums.'

'There are theatres and museums in Birmingham. We just don't go to them. And I thought you were on an exhausting intensive course?'

'So? I'm still allowed to unwind and go out for a drink.'

'I thought Hua doesn't drink?'

'Hua didn't come.'

'You went pubbing on your own?'

'No. But what if I did?'

'You went pubbing with what's his name? Jamil?'

'He's a colleague.'

'Isn't he a Muslim? Do they go to pubs?'

'For goodness sake, Dan. He's not that kind of Muslim.'

'What kind is he? The kind who takes another man's fiancée out for the evening?'

'You're jealous. That is such a turn on. Let's have sex.'

To be honest my Balti was sitting a bit heavy, but the offer was irresistible. It seemed I was forgiven for not buying milk and for even dreaming of missing her father's birthday lunch. Most important of all, I still compared favourably to some Lebanese playboy doctor. It wasn't until afterwards that I realised the Balti wasn't the only cause of my discomfort. There was also a very crumpled edition of the British Journal of Cardiology under my lumbar region.

CHAPTER 8.

I looked in on Vaz. He was already at his desk, doing letters.

I said, 'How did it go last night?'

He shook his head, said there must have been some confusion.

'She didn't turn up?'

'I waited one hour. Should I have waited longer?'

'First date? No way. She didn't phone?'

'No.'

'And you didn't phone her?'

'I didn't have her number. We spoke only on Internet.'

'And you were sitting where she could see you? You weren't hiding in a corner?'

'I sat by the window. Perhaps she was ill.'

Or perhaps she saw a guy in a sleeveless pullover and decided to activate the ejector button.

I asked him if there was any chance of him swapping his Sunday out-of-hours shift with me. His face lit up. He dislikes working on Sundays.

'Happy to,' he said. 'Now I can go to later Mass.'

So that was Chloe's Dad's birthday lunch sorted.

Helen's door was open. I asked her who she wanted me to work with. She barely looked up from the letter she was reading.

'Trevor,' she said. 'Sit with Trevor this morning and Pam Parker this afternoon.'

Trevor came in breathless, ten minutes before surgery was due to start.

'Apologies, apologies. Blocked drain. Not the end of the world but Mrs Buxton gets in a tizz. So, what have we this morning? Sniffles, twinges, general feelings of what's-the-fucking-point. The usual mix, I expect.'

I'd sorted the day's paperwork into things that needed action and things that didn't. We had twelve appointments booked but there are only two of them I remember clearly.

Stuart Curtain's file cover bore a Buxtonism. GOK.

Trevor smiled. 'Think about it,' he said. 'If you don't get it now, I think you will after you've spent ten minutes with him.'

Stuart was a man in his late fifties, average build, very quietly spoken, a bit tense. He sat on the edge of the chair. He said he just didn't feel right. I went through the list. Any unexplained weight loss, pain, insomnia, bowel changes, cough? Nothing. He just didn't feel right.

I tried coming at it from a different angle. Compared to when he did feel right, what had changed? He said he couldn't put his finger on it. Had there been any major life changes recently? Not really. Did he think he might be depressed?

'I might be,' he said. 'I don't know. You're the doctor. Do you think I'm depressed?'

Trevor didn't make an actual sound, but I was already getting that I could tell when he was stifling a laugh. He'd get out of his chair and go to the window or across to his old bureau, as though he'd suddenly thought of something urgent.

Stuart's blood pressure was good, he didn't look anaemic, his reflexes were all normal.

I said, 'Well let's take some blood and see if that tells us anything.'

He seemed to perk up when I said that and started to roll up his sleeve.

I said, 'No, Nurse Chris will do your blood tests.'

I conferred with Trevor. 'Full blood count? ESR? Thyroid

function?'

He concurred. Stuart shook my hand. 'Thank you, doctor,' he said. 'For being so thorough. Because I have to tell you, I just don't feel right.'

'Well?' said Trevor when he'd gone.

'Hypochondria?'

'I'll say. You can see how many times we've looked at his bloods.'

'Perhaps he is depressed. He lives alone. He's not working. I should have asked him more about that.'

'He used to look after his mother, but she's been gone years. He'd find it hard to get back into work now. You could try him on Prozac, next time he comes in, but I'm not convinced he needs it. He might just be bored with life and we haven't got a pill for that.'

I hate consultations that appear to go nowhere. Had I missed something? Had I wasted ten minutes?

I said, 'God only knows what that was all about.'

'See,' says Trevor. 'I knew you'd get it after you met him. GOK. God Only Knows.'

Glenys Allsop was a 56 year old woman with no significant medical history. She had itchy ankles. There were no signs of a rash or insect bites or chilblains, just a couple of patches of broken skin where she'd scratched. She said when it started it had only troubled her at night but now it was all the time and sometimes not just her ankles. Had she changed her washing powder? No. Her bath soap? No.

Trevor clicked his biro.

He said, 'What do we think, Dr Dan? Anything we'd like to investigate?'

Itching can sometimes be a sign of liver problems, but Mrs Allsop showed no sign of jaundice, so that seemed to rule out biliary obstruction. It can be a symptom of diabetes too. I wondered if we should check her urine for sugar.

'Not a lot of use', he said. When he suspected diabetes, he preferred to do a blood test and one that was properly set up, so we knew how long it was since the patient had eaten. Click, click, click went his biro. He was thinking.

'Okay Glenys,' he said. 'Here's a plan. Try keeping your ankles a bit cooler at night. Stick them out from under the covers. I'll share a little bedroom confidence with you. Mrs Buxton's feet are like hot potatoes. They never used to be. It's since the menopause. Give it a week or two. If that doesn't help, make an appointment to see one of the nurses and we'll check your blood sugar. How does that sound?'

She seemed satisfied. She got up to leave. Her hand was on the door.

She said, 'When you go to the toilet, it should be proper brown, right?'

Trevor beckoned her to come back and sit down.

'What colour are your stools, Glenys?'

'Not the usual.'

'Compared to Dr Dan's sweater? Darker? Lighter?'

'More like your tie.'

His tie was pale beige, knitted.

'Now we're cooking,' he said, 'Now we've got something to work with. We'll get one of the nurses to take some bloods. Complete blood count, ALT, AST, Alk Phos. What else, Dan?'

'Albumin, bilirubin?'

'Yes.'

Glenys said, 'Is it serious?'

'Probably nothing at all, my love,' he said. 'But we'll check you over anyway. A full liver MOT test.'

She went off to the nurses' room. He leaned back in his chair.

'That,' he said, 'was a good consultation. A textbook example of the exit reveal. It happens a lot if it's something they're embarrassed to mention. Halfway out the door. "Oh, by the way, doc, I've got a suppurating dick." So always watch them as they're leaving. You can usually tell if there's something on their mind, something else they need to say.'

'She doesn't look jaundiced.'

'True, but she's naturally rosy-cheeked. If it's a mild case, you don't always pick it up with that colouring. The other thing, Dan, is that I addressed her as 'my love' which is of course strictly forbidden. Helen Vincent and our stern practice manager would string me up for less but as I'm on my way out I really couldn't give a damn.'

'I don't think Mrs Allsop even noticed.'

'No. She's got more important things on her mind. Such as faeces the colour of my tie.'

He took it off and tossed it in a drawer. He said he'd never really liked it anyway.

It was his afternoon off. We did hospital letters and test results together before he went home. I mentioned Chloe's idea about the cause of Freda Jarrold's palpitations. He sighed.

'Talking shop at home, Dan? Not sure that's a recipe for a happy marriage.'

'There's not much else to talk about at the moment. Chloe's revising.'

'Yes, you said. Well that'll change. Down the line you'll find other topics of conversation. Curtains. School fees. I'll tell you what I predict with Freda. Next time she comes in she'll have forgotten about the bloody magnesium and found something else to fret about. But mark her file if you like. Query calcium imbalance. Are you sitting in with Helen this afternoon?'

'Pam Parker. I haven't met her yet.'

'Oh, you'll like her. And her surgery could be fun. We get

the Kyle Bibby faction of the community, but Pam sees the distaff side and believe me, they can be just as entertaining.'

'What will you do on your afternoon off?'

'Get home in time for the first race from Newton Abbot. Pull up a chair, sip a Gaelic coffee, rest my eyes between races. Heaven. Enjoy your afternoon with Pam. You might have to take a shufti at a few manky undercarriages but it's what we do, Dan. It's what we do.'

CHAPTER 9.

I was leafing through Clinical Neuro-physiology when Helen looked in.

'Has Trevor gone already?'

'Home. To watch the racing.'

'It was you I wanted to see anyway. How's it going?'

'Early days, but it seems fine.'

Was I about to get an apology for yesterday's public drubbing? She sat down. White shirt. Denim skirt, bare legs. It was a warm day.

'You'll find my style is very different to Trevor's.'

'Yes.'

'He's not great at time management.'

'We seem to get through surgery pretty much on time.'

'But he sees a lot of patients who could just as easily be dealt with by Chris or Linda. Doing routine blood pressures because it's some sweet old lady or somebody you've known since they were in junior school, it's very inefficient. Once you start flying solo I'll expect you to offload all that stuff to the nurses.'

'Okay.'

'You don't sound convinced.'

'It's not a bad thing though, is it, the rapport he has with his patients? It must have some value. And I'm learning a lot from him.'

'Such as?'

'He acts very casual, but he really notices things.'

'Yes, he's good, in his own way. Just don't model yourself on him, that's all I'm saying. His style of doctoring is a thing of the past. You can sit in with me again any time you like. Tomorrow. No, not tomorrow. Friday.'

So, no apology. Perhaps I wasn't owed one. Or perhaps a

chummy chat was her idea of an apology. After she left the room, I found myself feeling oddly unsettled. Was it because of her little snipe at Trevor? Or was it because of her perfume and the fact that her shirt was unbuttoned quite a lot lower than I'd have expected?

Dr Parker was late for her 3 o'clock. Mary had predicted she would be.

She said, 'It's the same every week. She'll blame the traffic, you'll see.'

And right on cue she came bustling through the door laden with Tesco bags.

'Call off the Mounties,' she said. 'I'm here. Ruddy traffic. Mary love, could you pop my lamb chops in the fridge?'

Dr Parker was a motherly little body, almost as wide as she was tall. I introduced myself, told her I'd been instructed to sit in on her surgery.

'Yes, pet,' she said. 'I've been told to take care of you. Follow me.'

Pam Parker shared an office with Bruce Macdonald. As she said, they were like those little figures on a weather house. When one was in the other was out.

She changed her shoes, washed her hands, asked me about my Obs and Gynae experience, which didn't amount to much. I assumed most women would rather see a female Ob/Gyn if they possibly could. She laughed.

She said, 'Round here they're generally quite happy for anybody to have a decko. Roll up, roll up. And anyway, once you've given birth most of us couldn't care less. Once you've been in stirrups with your kit off it's all over, modesty-wise. Right, what have we here? Sheila Mount. She's having the slowest moving menopause on record. I wish she'd just get it over with.'

'Do you prescribe hormone replacement therapy?'

'Happy to, but she's refused it. Worried about cancer.'

'What else can you offer?'

'Nothing much. A natter. Let's get her in.'

Mrs Mount wanted to know what Dr Pam thought of green tea for hot flushes and night sweats.

'Some women say it helps,' says Pam. 'I can't speak from personal experience. I'm using the patches myself. Have you thought any more about that?'

'I don't want to catch cancer.'

'Look, we've talked about this before. You don't smoke. There's not been a lot of cancer in your family, certainly not the lady cancers. You're not high-risk, Sheila. But it's up to you.'

'And you haven't tried the green tea?'

'No. Well I did, once, but I didn't like it. Builder's, with milk and two sugars, that's me. Do you like green tea?'

'I don't think so.'

'Well then, why make yourself miserable? What do you think, Dr Dan? Try the patches? Try the tea? Open the box or take the money?'

I said, 'Just one thought. My Mum's been taking citalopram for the night sweats.'

'Right. It can help. So that's another possibility, Sheila. It's like an anti-depressant. Do you want to try that?'

'And I won't catch cancer from it?'

'Look love, I can't promise you that you're never going to get cancer. But taking something to get you through the menopause, I don't think that's going to tip the scales. How old's your Mum, Dan?'

'Fifty five, fifty six.'

'Same as me. Same as you, Sheila.'

Mrs Mount said she'd think things over.

'See?' says Dr Pam, 'She just wanted a natter.'

'Does she come in a lot?'

'Quite a lot. Do you think she wasted my time?'

'No. I don't think it's a bad thing if people want to manage without drugs.'

'Sheila's a worrier. Friendly Chats PRN, that's my prescription. Who's next? Amina Lohani. I don't think I've seen her before.'

Mrs Lohani was dressed in shalwar kameez. It was hard to put an age to her. Her hair was grey but she had no lines on her face. She was accompanied by her husband. He stalled in the doorway when he saw me.

Pam said, 'Dr Talbot is our trainee. It's very important that our young doctors see as many patients as possible. Is it all right with you and your wife if he sits in?'

'No,' says the husband. 'It's not all right. Lady doctor only.'

I left the room, went and hung out with Nurse Linda. She's the younger of the two nurses. Late thirties, wears blue mascara.

'You in trouble again?'

'No. What do you mean, again?'

'I'm just teasing you. Has Dr Parker chucked you out because of the Paki couple?'

'The husband didn't want a male doctor in there.'

'You know why he's come with her, don't you? I'll bet you she doesn't speak English. They keep them under lock and key, some of those Muslim husbands. I saw you had Kyle Bibby in the other day. How did that go?'

'He seems to be quite a character.'

'Cunning, that's what I'd call him. You need to watch him. When he's on his way out of the surgery he always wanders in here, pretends he's taken a wrong turn. He must think I was born yesterday. Give him half a chance he'd be in here nicking stuff. Hi Mac. You off visiting?'

Over my shoulder she'd noticed Bruce Macdonald sliding past. He back-tracked.

'Dovecroft,' he said. 'Edie Miller's on her way out.'

'Bless,' says Linda. 'How long's she been in Dovecroft?'

'Too bloody long.'

He left.

Linda said, 'They love Mac at the nursing homes. He's brilliant with the old ladies. Well, the men like him too. But the old ladies love him.'

And not only the old ones, it seemed.

Pam Parker appeared. She needed an aspiration needle, 21 gauge, and some iodine solution.

'Breast lump,' she said. 'It feels like a cyst, so I'll have a little poke, see what's in there.'

I stayed out of sight until the Lohanis had left the building. I could hear Mr Lohani haranguing his wife. Pam was washing her hands.

'Were you right about the cyst?'

'Yes. Nice clear fluid and the lump resolved. Needless to say, she's never had a mammogram.'

'She must have been offered one.'

'Oh yes. They get the appointment card, she can't read it and her lord and master bins it. He probably thinks breast clinics are full of pervs who want to look at his wife's boobies.'

'Will you see her again?'

'I told him she needs to come back in six weeks, just for me to check her, and I want her to have a mammogram. He'll ignore me though. I can feel it in my water.'

It's funny what things stick in your mind about a surgery. Nicola Willetts was a no-show, but I remember her because of Pam Parker's thumbnail sketch of her.

'Nose stud, one side of her head shaved, refuses to have her kids vaccinated.'

'And yet she made an appointment to see you?'

'Only because the health visitor threatened her. Her latest baby isn't thriving. He was low birth weight and he's still not gaining like he should.'

'What was the threat?'

'Social services. I don't like interfering in people's lives, Dan, but girls like Nicola get on my pippin. Baby not gaining. Kiddies not vaccinated. She thinks measles is nothing. She thinks whooping cough is nothing. Her oldest has started school now. We could have an epidemic on our hands and all because of the Nicola Willettses of this world. Have you got kids?'

'Not even married yet. Next year, we hope. Chloe wants to get her MRCP first.'

'Good for her. Mind you don't leave it too long though. I was 40 by the time we had our two and childbirth is for the young, let me tell you.'

Pam has two teenage daughters. Her husband's a dentist. Bob Parker. They have his father living with them. Bob Senior. She refers to him as 'Senior'.

She said, 'Senior's gone a bit doolally since Bob's Mum died so we moved him in with us. He's not bad. Just a bit forgetful. Killed a few kettles, left a few taps running, you know the kind of thing. Right, who's next? Amber Evans. Fasten your seat belt. Amber definitely won't ask you to leave the room.'

Amber is the other patient I remember clearly from that afternoon. Her file had KDO scrawled on the front.

'Is that one of Trevor's labels?'

'Yes, that's a Buxtonism. It means Keep Door Open. Sound advice, actually. Quite a nympho, our Amber. When she comes in it's usually about something below the waist so if ever you have to deal with her make sure you have one of the nurses with you. Better still, send her to me or Helen.'

Amber said she didn't at all mind me sitting in on her consultation.

'You know me, Dr Parker,' she said. 'Anything to help.'

Pam said, 'Yes, Amber, I do know you. So what's ailing you today?'

She said she had a bit of a discharge. This turned out to be the understatement of the year. Pam examined her.

'That,' she said, 'is one very inflamed cervix.'

Amber said she thought she'd had that before.

'Yes, you did. And now it's back. What have you been up to, my girl?'

Amber grinned. 'Just the usual.'

I didn't go in too close. Things seemed pretty purulent down there.

Pam took two swabs. One for gonorrhoea, one for chlamydia. Amber was very chatty. Being naked from the waist down didn't seem to affect her conversational skills. She asked me where I was from. Like the Queen, working a reception line.

I said, 'I'm from Abergavenny.'

'Where's that?'

'South Wales.'

'You look like that actor, don't he Dr Parker? Off The IT Crowd.'

Pam said, 'I don't know. I'm not sure I've ever seen it.'

'You know who I mean, Doctor. What's your name again?'

'His name's Dr Talbot and junior doctors don't have time to watch TV.'

'Well it was on Channel 4. He's like, dopey looking, but quite tasty.'

'KDO,' says Pam under her breath. 'As previously recommended. Now, in cases like this we do bloods as well as swabs. Might as well cover all the possibilities. It must be like a theme park for STDs down there.'

She took samples to test for syphilis and HIV.

'Will you prescribe anything before you get the swab results back?'

'Oh yes. Oral Zithromax. And a shot of ceftriaxone.'

Amber had started to put her jeans on.

'Leave them off a minute. I'm going to give you an injection.'

'Not in my bum.'

'Where do you want it then?'

'Just not in my bum. It hurts.'

'I'll put it in your thigh. It's going to hurt wherever I do it. Actually, Dr Talbot will do it while I label your samples.'

How often had I given intramuscular injections? More times than I could count. But Amber made me nervous.

1. Prepare site with alcohol wipe. 2. Remove needle cover. 3. Pull skin tight and insert needle at 90 degree angle. 4. Retract plunger a little to check for blood.

She said, 'Are you a proper doctor then?'

I said, 'No. I'm a trainee butcher at Morrison's.'

'I can't watch.'

'Neither can I. I just close my eyes and take a stab at it.'

5. If no blood appears, proceed to inject slowly. 6. Withdraw needle. 7. Dress site with sterile gauze. 8. Dispose of syringe in sharps' bin.

'Hurry up. You're giving me the willies.'

'It's done. You can get dressed.

'Really? I never felt nothing.'

250mg ceftriaxone injected into the rectus femoris and the patient never felt nothing. Dr Pam gave me an approving nod.

She said, 'The question is, Amber, where could you have picked this up? Who are you going with these days?'

'Nobody.'

'You haven't had sex with anyone?'

'A bit.'

'Anyone in particular?'

'Not really. I'd have to think.'

'Well you should do that. Because whatever you've got, they've likely got it as well. See, there's no point me treating you for this if you're going to keep shagging the bloke you caught it from or gave it to, excuse my French, Dr Talbot. Why don't you use johnnies?'

Amber shrugged. 'They don't like it.'

'They won't like it if their dick turns green either.'

'They're a price though, aren't they?'

'If I give you some will you use them?'

'Okay.'

Pam opened a drawer in her desk, brought a cellophane-wrapped 12-pack of condoms, wrote a prescription for Zithromax.

'Amber,' she said, 'you are dicing with your health. How many times do we have to go through this? One of these days you're going to get an infection that drifts north and you'll end up losing your girlie plumbing. Ovaries, tubes, the lot.'

Another shrug and a sly smile.

'You won't be smiling if you have to have a hysterectomy, my girl. Take it from one who knows. These capsules, you're to take them all today. Two as soon as you get home, two before bedtime. Got that? And use the damned johnnies or better yet, stop having sex for a while. Give your body a little holiday.'

Amber's parting words were, 'Chris O'Dowd, that's who you look like. I bet he's from round your way.'

Dr Pam sat with her head in her hands for a while.

'Give me strength.'

I said, 'So is she an actual sex worker?'

'Sex worker? You mean professionally on the game? Not really. She's more like the Wavy Line store for sex in her tower block. Open all hours. But I don't think she charges. It's more of a barter system. A couple of cigs for a hand job. A few pills for the á la carte. She's a very happy person, as you could see. Always cheerful.'

'Does she ever get pregnant?'

'Not lately. Her tubes are probably clagged up. And you know, these blokes she goes with, they may not like using condoms but some of them might have the wit to get off at Rowley Regis.'

'Rowley Regis?'

'Coitus slightly interruptus, dear. She had two boys, but they were taken into care.'

'That's sad.'

'I don't know, Dan. Amber doesn't seem bothered and it was better for the kids, poor little sods. They're probably in some nice foster home. Getting three meals a day and a bedtime story.'

'Do you think she'll use the condoms?'

'Very unlikely. She'll trade them for something. But it's up freed a bit of space in my drawer.'

'What about the Zithromax?'

'I doubt that has any street value. I might be wrong. Some people'll try anything, to see if they get a buzz. Whether Amber actually takes them as instructed, that's another matter.'

'Do you ever get disheartened?'

'About the Ambers of this world? No. I refuse to. I come here twice a week, do my best by them, then I go home and forget about them. We can't perform miracles, Dan, and we have to look after our own lives. Keep our own house in good order. I'm sure I don't need to tell you the statistics?

Divorce, drug abuse, alcoholism, suicide. You name it, we're right up there in the league tables.'

'John Sillitoe was my supervisor.'

'Shit. I'd forgotten that. I'm sorry.'

'I didn't know him that well. It was still a shock though.'

'Of course it was. We're supposed to be pillars of society. You're just starting out, Dan. Start as you mean to go on. Don't take your work home. Keep your balance. Have a laugh, take a break, have a Kit-Kat. Did Amber say Chris O'Dowd? Stupid girl. He's not Welsh. He's Irish. You do look a bit like him though. A younger version.'

CHAPTER 10.

Chloe's parents have a very nice house near Bishop's Wapshott, not far from Leamington Spa. It's called The Chummery, which is something to do with colonial life in India because great-grandpa Orde-Sykes was in the Punjab, and the house has been in the family for three generations. The Chummery is detached with a huge garden and no neighbours in sight. Mam'd love it. She's been watching a series called Downton Abbey on the telly so she's into big houses. Whether she'll ever get to see The Chummery, I don't know. I think we might have the wedding there. Marquee on the lawn, that kind of thing.

Chloe's mother was born at The Chummery. Vinnie, which is short for Lavinia. I'm supposed to call them Vinnie and Laurence since Chloe and I got engaged. Apart from a few ruffled feathers about my not wanting to go into ENT, I think they like me. It's hard to tell though because they never really look at you when they're talking to you. Vinnie's always straightening the cushions or jumping up and rearranging things on the mantelpiece. 'Do carry on,' she says, but I'm sure she's not really listening. Laurence looks over your shoulder while you're chatting. It's a habit some people have, always to be on the lookout for someone more important to talk to. I imagine he's more attentive with his patients.

Vinnie is Ladies' Captain at the golf club and Laurence plays a bit too. He's very fit and dapper. Vinnie's parents are still alive too. Granny and Grandpa Orde-Sykes. They live in very expensive sheltered accommodation in Leamington Spa. She still has her legs but her mind's gone and he still has his mind but bad legs and they take their meals in a kind of communal dining room with tablecloths and flower arrangements and a glass of sherry before dinner.

We drove down to Bishop's Wapshott on Saturday morning after a slight delay caused by a disagreement over dress standards. Chloe, who was, admittedly, looking gorgeous in a dark turquoise dress with a sticky-out skirt, said I should wear a suit, but I stuck to my guns and went in cords and my nice pink sweater. It was a family lunch, after all, not some grand, formal occasion.

Chloe said, 'Well don't come crying to me that you feel inappropriately dressed.'

I said, 'I won't. I'll feel comfortable and warm.'

Vinnie and Laurence don't believe in heating. They think of it as burning money, which I suppose it is, but to good purpose as far as I'm concerned. I'm all for fresh air, but not indoors in November. The Chummery has very high ceilings and old windows that rattle in their frames.

I said, 'Also, if your nieces decide to use me as a climbing frame again, I won't have to worry about my suit getting ruined.'

Chloe has a sister, Flora, known as Flo, and a brother, Charlie, generally known as Slow. He got the nickname at school possibly because of his surname being Swift, but Chloe reckons it was also an accurate assessment of his intellect. He should care. He may come across as a twit, but he makes a very good living selling prestige cars, Jags and Bentleys mainly. Anyway, within the family the siblings are known as Flo, Chlo and Slow.

Flo is married to Henry, a pleasant man of private means who breeds British Saddlebacks, so come the wedding my father will have someone he can talk to. Although Da's a sheep man principally, he's perfectly willing to talk pigs if the occasion calls for it. Flo and Henry have three daughters. I'd never realised little girls could be so boisterous until I met

Daisy, Poppy and Lily. Poppy is eight, Daisy is six, Lily is four. I'm sure they'll make very pretty flower girls. Feral, but very photogenic.

I said, 'Do we have a present for your Dad?'

'Of course. Why do men always think about presents at the 59th minute of the 11th hour? It's in the envelope in my bag. Flying lessons.'

I couldn't recall any discussion about such a lavish present.

Chloe said, 'It's not lavish. It's just a taster lesson and then he gets a discount if he decides to sign up for the full course. It is his 65th, Dan. You have to give something special for significant birthdays.'

'What's special about 65?'

'I don't know. It just is.'

'My Da got a liquorice allsorts selection box for his 60th.'

'That will have been a joke present. I'll bet your Mum got him something special.'

'Such as?'

'Cuff links?'

'Nobody wears cuff links nowadays.'

'Daddy does.'

'Well mine doesn't.'

'What if he has to go to a black tie do?'

'He doesn't. He wouldn't. Da's not a black tie type. He's a Dickies safety boots and Raintite jacket man.'

'Gosh. Still, there's surely a time and a place for everything.'

Charlie roared up the lane behind us in a Jag coupe and overtook us on a blind bend, reckless git that he is, so we were the last to arrive. Vinnie and Flo both air-kissed me, Laurence shook my hand and young Lily hurled herself at my family jewels. Henry gave me a wan and weary smile.

Drinks were being served in what they call the drawing room. The senior Orde-Sykeses were already installed and an actual fire had been lit. Elm isn't the most giving firewood in the world, but the Swifts have quite a pile of it and waste not, want not. The nibbles and lunch were being catered by an old schoolfriend of Flo's, Annabel, who had recently gone into the party catering business. Little chicory boats filled with cream cheese, cocktail sausages wrapped in cold bacon and rounds of baguette spread with a paté made from aubergines which Granny Orde-Sykes took one look at and leapt to her feet.

She said, 'Lavinia, the cat's been sick on this plate,' and she tossed the whole lot into the fire. It made quite a blaze. Better than the elm, any day.

Flo threatened withdrawal of TV time for any child who blabbed to Annabel about the paté, but in my experience Flo's warnings to her children never bear fruit. Counting to ten is one of her disciplinary techniques but she never seems to get beyond eight.

I was the designated driver for our journey home, so I only had half a glass of fizz. Charlie said it was a nice drop of shampoo.

'It's from Aldi,' Vinnie whispered to me. 'Simply marvellous. Do you have one in your part of the world?'

Our part of the world. Somehow, she can never bring herself to say 'Birmingham.'

Laurence opened his presents. He was delighted with his flying lesson. Grandpa Orde-Sykes said, 'What type of crate do they give you?'

The voucher didn't say.

'I once had a close call in a Tiger Moth,' he said. 'Hopping over to Alderney with Tommy Ironside for a spot of lunch. Ran into thick fog. Bit of a sphincter-clencher, I can tell you.'

Charlie's gift was a case of Dow's 1983 port. It was ready

for drinking, he said, but good enough to keep for a while too.

Chloe said, 'Slow, you are so flash.'

Henry and Flo had commissioned a painting of The Chummery. The perspective was a bit off. I wouldn't have dreamed of saying so, but Chloe tends to speak her mind.

Flo said, 'It's modern. No-one does perspective anymore.'

Vinnie said she thought it was quite lovely and Laurence agreed.

The Orde-Sykeses gave him a giant crossword toilet roll.

Flo said, 'What did you give him, Mummy?'

'Guess.'

'Fountain pen?'

'No, they only get stolen.'

'Cuff links?'

'No, he loses them. I'm getting him automatic garage doors.'

'And about bloody time too,' said Charlie. 'Get back from London at God knows what hour, the last thing you feel like doing is jumping out of the motor to open the garage. Torture.'

Lunch was smoked salmon on sliced Hovis, duck breasts for the grownups, very pink, almost still quacking, and turkey goujons for the kids, followed by a chocolate gateau which hadn't quite defrosted.

Chloe said, 'Somebody's clearly been to Iceland. Flo, are you sure Annabel's cut out for this catering business?'

And Flo said, 'Don't be so bally critical.'

Daisy said, 'Mummy, what does 'bally' mean?'

Poppy said, 'It's the same as saying 'don't be so fucking critical' but it's more polite because we're at Grandpoppa's birthday party.'

Henry mouthed, 'Sorry.'

Flo said, 'Look, Annabel's been through a beastly time. She lost an absolute packet at Lloyds. The very least we can do is put a little business her way.'

'The least we can do?' says Chloe. 'Really? Are we a rescue service for Lloyds names? Just don't imagine I'll be hiring her for my wedding. Don't even think of it.'

And Flo muttered, 'Wedding? Ha! If it ever comes off.'

There's this thing they do at the Chummery at the end of a meal. Vinnie and any other females go to the drawing room for coffee and peppermint creams. Laurence and the men stay at the table for something a little stronger. Personally, I'd rather go with the ladies but when I told Mam about it she said, 'Sounds lovely. Upper crust. Just like in Downton.'

It being Laurence's birthday, a bottle of the vintage port had been decanted and Annabel brought in a modest cheeseboard and said she hoped we'd enjoyed everything. We assured her we had. Henry gave me a quizzical smile and lit a small cigar. I asked after his pigs. It's the only way into a conversation with Henry.

His Lord Topnotch had been runner-up Best Boar at the Leominster show and he had two gilts due to farrow any day. Lady Lobelia and Lady Marigold. Henry names all his females, pig and human, after flowers.

I said, 'I'm surprised you dared to leave them for the day. First pregnancies and all that. Aren't you worried about complications?'

'Laurence's birthday. Three-line whip, old boy,' he said. 'But my pig man's on duty. He'll let me know if anything starts.'

Laurence said, 'So I gather you're sticking with General Practice, Dan? Rum choice. A bit like working in a department store, one imagines. One minute you're required in Gents' Footwear, the next you're needed in Ladies'

Lingerie.'

I said, 'That's part of its appeal. In your business, you know that everyone who consults you has a problem with either their ears, nose or throat. We never know what's coming through the door.'

Charlie said, 'You get to see a fair amount of pussy, I imagine?'

And a vision of Amber Evans's vaginal swab rose before me just as I'd helped myself to some Brie.

I said, 'We have a lady doctor who deals with most of that, Charlie. And anyway, you don't think of patients that way. If you did, you'd soon be in trouble.'

Laurence said, 'Damned right. You've got plenty of insurance, I hope? Too many bloody patients on the make these days. Looking to catch you out in some minor indiscretion and cash in. It was the Americans who started it.'

Grandpa Orde-Sykes said this was typical of Americans.

'Always barging in, late to the party and throwing their weight around,' he said, which seemed to contradict Laurence's point about them setting trends. 'Look at the last show. It was the beginning of 1942 before there was any sign of them.'

I said, 'The practice I'm working in, the senior partner's a Bart's man, about your age, Laurence. I wonder if you knew him? Trevor Buxton. You might have been in the same year.'

Laurence couldn't place a Trevor Buxton. He said he'd kept up with a few classmates, but their numbers were dwindling.

'Cruikshank's just dropped off the twig. Melanoma. Heighton's in prison for fiddling with children. Been at it for years apparently. I suppose that's why he went into paediatrics. Terrible business. The wife had no idea.'

Grandpa Orde-Sykes said that kind of thing had never

gone on before the war and he wondered whether the cause was perhaps over-heated houses, or the free orange juice the Health Service had doled out at great expense to the Exchequer. I hadn't heard of any free orange juice. Laurence said it was a post-war thing. Cod liver oil too. It was discontinued in 1951 and he doubted Heighton's history of molesting children had anything to do with it.

We rejoined the ladies, Downton-style. Chloe was looking peeved.

Vinnie said, 'Chlo's cross with us for talking about wedding dates. I think you should at least name the day. Weddings take a huge amount of organising. Why delay?'

I said, 'I'm ready when she is. But her mind's on her exams at the moment so I think we should take the pressure off.'

Chloe slipped her hand in mine.

Flo said, 'As long as you don't do something mean like sneaking off to a horrid registry office.'

And Chloe said, 'What a very good idea.'

Everyone looked at me.

I said, 'Look, whatever Chloe wants. I think my parents would enjoy a nice wedding though. I'm sure Mam would. It might be her only chance. My brother doesn't show any signs of settling down.'

Adam is three years older than me and if he has a girlfriend, she's a well-kept secret.

Vinnie said, 'I didn't know you had a brother. How old is he?'

'Thirty-three. He's a maths teacher, in Cardiff.'

'Thirty-three! He has acres of time. Will he be your Best Man?'

'I haven't really thought that far. Getting him into a suit might be a struggle though.'

Poppy said, 'Why, is he fat?'

'No. Just more of a sweatshirt and jeans type.'

'Good,' she said. 'In that case I'll be able to wear dungarees instead of a sick-making dress.'

There was some discussion about Annabel and whether she should get a tip as well as her agreed fee. Chloe thought definitely not. I stayed out of it.

She said, 'What on earth is the point of rewarding incompetence? She needs to go to cooking school if she's determined to pursue this career.'

Flo said, 'She had cooking lessons at Vieux Glion. We all did.'

Vieux Glion was a finishing school near Geneva.

Vinnie said, 'Flo darling, that's almost 20 years ago. Perhaps a little refresher course is in order for Annabel? One hates to criticise but my duck was fearfully stringy.'

Granny and Grandpa Orde-Sykes had both fallen asleep, Flo's girls were unfurling the crossword toilet roll to create an obstacle course and Henry took a call on his mobile to say that Lady Lobelia had begun nesting. The party broke up.

I love it when Chloe rests her head on my shoulder but not when I'm driving.

She said, 'Flo makes me so cross. Why must she encourage these no-hopers? Bloody Annabel. A bought gateau! And it was rock solid in the middle. I don't believe she's ever cooked anything in her life.'

I said, 'How come they didn't send you to Vieux Glion?'

'Because I have a brain. Charlie got seed money for his business and Flo went to Switzerland to get finished. It was where they sent you if your only hope was to nab the right kind of husband.'

'And was Henry the right kind of husband?'

'I suppose.'

'I like Henry. He's laconic.'

'What does that mean?'

'Unhurried. Economical with his words. Poppy's a riot.'

'She's a little shit. They all are. We may have to give them Ritalin if they're going to be bridesmaids.'

'Or we could just elope.'

'Would your parents mind?'

'Yes. They'd say they didn't, but Mam would. She's probably got her eye on a hat already.'

'I should revise when we get home. I haven't even looked at dermatology yet.'

'You have all day tomorrow. I'm doing a double shift at Sterling. Your doctor recommends you take this evening off.'

'Okay. Actually, I'm ravenous. Let's stop for burgers.'

Which we did. I was waiting to lock the car and she was searching for something.

'Fuck!'

'What?'

'My scarf. I must have left it at the Chummery. We'll have to go back.'

'Are you crazy? We're not going all that way. You have dozens of scarves.'

'But that one's special.'

'Then call your mother and ask her to post it to you.'

'She'll say she will and then she won't. She'll hang on to it and then swear it belongs to her. It's vicuna.'

'I don't care. I'm not driving back, and you can't. You're way over the limit. If Vinnie nabs it, you'll just have to buy a replacement.'

'I can't. It cost, like, at least a thousand.'

'You bought a £1000 scarf?'

'It's not mine.'

'Whose is it?'

'Jamil's.'

I might have known.

'Jamil gave you a valuable scarf?'

'He lent it to me, when we were in London. It was cold when we came out of the restaurant.'

'I thought you just went to a pub?'

'I knew you'd be like this. You have completely the wrong idea about him.'

'I don't want to have any ideas about him. I don't even want to hear his name. Are we getting burgers or what?'

'Forget it. You've ruined my evening.'

I'd ruined her evening. I mean, who did this Arab jerk think he was, swaddling my girlfriend in a scarf worth more than my entire wardrobe? We drove in silence.

By the time we got to King's Heath I was feeling a bit of a chump. Lending a girl your scarf on a chilly evening isn't exactly a capital offence. I suppose I'd do it myself and not think anything of it. I apologised for being a jealous idiot.

'Jealous idiot is right,' she said, but by the time we were driving through Harborne her head was back on my shoulder and I was seeing things more clearly. I might be an unambitious, Welsh hick but I was the one Chloe wanted to marry. This Jamil sounded like a bit of a joke. A vicuna scarf? He probably wore Cuban heels, to boost his height. Very likely he had a hairy back too.

CHAPTER 11

I settled into a sort of routine at The Lindens. Most of the time I shadowed Trevor, on Wednesday afternoons I'd sit in with Pam Parker and occasionally Helen would commandeer me but there was never any predicting when that would happen. Sometimes I felt she'd forgotten I was there, sometimes she'd clearly thought I'd benefit from seeing a particular patient. David Millichamp, for instance, who had Parkinson's.

Mr Millichamp was a 70 year old retired car mechanic. He'd been diagnosed five years ago. Helen asked me for the cardinal symptoms. No problem. Resting tremor, muscular rigidity, bradykinesia and postural instability.

'Good,' she said. 'David presented with tremor and cog-wheel rigidity. He's been on Sinemet since 2005. Recommended dose?'

'Start on 25mg, increasing to 100mg three times a day, as required?'

'Yes. He's been on the 100 mgs since the beginning of the year. So what might you be looking for today?'

'Signs of reduced effectiveness?'

'And?'

'Dyskinesia?'

'Yes. Good. Let's get him in.'

David was recognisably Parkinson-y. He stooped forward as he walked, no arm swing, face inexpressive. He also had a head-bobbing tic.

Helen said, 'That's new. When did it start?'

He said he'd had it for a week or two. His voice was very quiet.

She said, 'You may remember I told you this can happen when you've been on the levodopa for a while. But we can do something about it. Dr Talbot? What would you suggest?'

I was ready. I'd been warned that Parkinson's was one of Helen's things.

'Reduce the Sinemet dose? Or add in a dopamine agonist?'

'Okay. How would you reduce the Sinemet exactly?'

'A lower dose four times a day instead of three?'

'Yes. And that's what we'll try, David. We might try you on some Neupro skin patches too. See if we can smooth out the tics for you.'

It was the first time I'd seen her give a patient more than his allotted ten minutes. After he'd left she quizzed me a little more.

'Possible side effects of a dopa agonist?'

'Nausea, constipation, orthostatic hypotension, compulsive behaviour.'

'Yes.'

'Does he have any history of falls?'

She checked his file.

'Not that he's admitted to. He's a very proud man. Divorced, lives alone and very fierce about his independence.'

'I see he's still riding a bike. That's something.'

'Is he? Did he say?'

'No. But he was wearing bike clips.'

She laughed. Not a thing you see her do very often.

'That,' she said, 'is a very Trevor Buxton thing to notice. Well, well. Your neurology might be a bit shaky, but you have keen powers of observation. Good work.'

Praise from Helen Vincent. I felt rather pleased with myself. And when we took a break for coffee and she was reaching round me for the milk she found occasion to put her hand on my back, around L2 or L3, which is a few vertebrae lower than you might expect from your boss. Or so it seemed to me.

Trevor had a slight cold. It was making him quite breathless. He'd turn away occasionally, brace himself on the arms of his chair and take a few breaths with his lips pursed. I wasn't supposed to notice.

He was still smoking. Not during working hours because it wasn't allowed, but as soon as he got in his car and all the time when he was at home, I imagined. He said he'd cut down.

'Look,' he says, 'the damage is done, entirely self-inflicted. So now I have a choice. Slowly suffocate in a state of relative contentment or slowly suffocate while craving a cig.'

It was a fair point.

'Tell you what,' he said, 'you can run the show today. You don't need me spoon-feeding you. I'll sit to one side and wheeze words of wisdom. If required. I was thinking, about your future father-in-law?'

I'd asked him if he remembered Laurence from his student days.

'As I recall there were two Swifts, one in my year, one in the year below. Glenys Allsop's blood results are in, by the way. Albumin's down, bilirubin's elevated and so is her alk phos.'

'So it looks like she does have a biliary obstruction? She's the right age for gallstones, but you'd think she'd be getting pain.'

'You would. I don't like the look of it, Dan. I don't like the look of it at all. We'd better get her in for a chat, pronto. Your Swift fellow, has he got a very narrow head? Like it's been in a vice? Like one of those Easter Island statues?'

'That's him.'

'Then I do remember him. Most of us didn't start acting like pompous pricks till we were let loose on the wards, but

Swift was way ahead of us. Dressed like a consultant, wore a bow tie, even as a first year.'

'He still wears a bow tie.'

'I shouldn't call him a prick. I didn't really know him. He's obviously done very well for himself.'

'There's a story in the family that he's treated royalty, but he doesn't talk about it.'

'Well he wouldn't. I imagine they make you sign the Official Secrets Act before you're allowed to peer into a royal cakehole or up a royal nostril. Is he still trying to tempt you with Harley Street?'

'He's given up on me. He thinks General Practice is for losers but lately he's been decent enough not to say it in so many words. Anyway, it doesn't matter. This is what I want to do.'

'Good. Right, what have we this morning? Bad backs, warts, hacking coughs? Oh, Paul Styles. You'll enjoy him.'

Mr Styles's file had TMS scrawled on the cover.

'TMS?'

Trevor said, 'Think about it while I make a quick call to the bookies. See if you can guess.'

He placed a bet on the 2 o'clock race at Wincanton.

'And?' he said. 'TMS?'

'Thinks Medics Stupid?'

'Try again.'

'Totally Mentally Something or other.'

'No, no, no. Too Many Symptoms. Paul hasn't worked for a while. It's not really his fault. He's in his fifties and there's bugger all jobs around here. He was at Tipton Castings till they closed down. I think he goes into town and hangs around the medical section in Hudson's bookshop. Looks things up. Makes a few notes. It's like a hobby really.'

'So how do you handle him?'

'I listen sympathetically. Suggest remedies he can buy over

the counter. That usually satisfies him. He's not a difficult character, just a bit tedious. But we have to listen, Dan. One of these days he might have a real symptom and we don't want to miss it just because he's a lonely hypochondriac.'

Paul Styles reported a headache over one eye, bleeding gums, itching palms and a painful left knee. I recommended paracetamol and a check-up with the dentist. I didn't think the palms were significant. My Nan always says itchy palms mean money. Right palm if you've got money coming to you, left palm if you'll be paying out.

He said, 'You don't think it's something more serious? I was reading about this syndrome. Shenk-Moller, I think it's called. Or it might be Moller-Shenk.'

I said, 'That's a very, very rare condition, Paul.'

'Yes,' he said. 'I realise that. But I mean, somebody suffers from it, don't they? Else it wouldn't exist.'

I asked him which of his symptoms was troubling him most. The knee, he said. And the palms. And the headaches.

I said, 'We'll certainly keep an eye on things, Paul. Knees can play up as we get older. But let's see if the painkillers help, and maybe a support bandage. You know a lot of these things resolve themselves without us doctors interfering, and we don't want you hanging around in hospital waiting rooms unnecessarily. Knee clinics are very over-subscribed.'

'So you don't think it's the Shenk-Moller thing?'

'I'd be very surprised.'

'Thank you, Doctor,' he says. 'I've been really worried.'

'And worrying won't help with the headaches. You might think of coming to some of our relaxation sessions. Have a word with Nurse on your way out. And don't forget to see your dentist about your gums.'

As soon as the door closed Trevor said, 'What the fuck is Shenk-Moller syndrome?'

'Moller-Shenk? It's a recessive autosomal condition. Rarely seen outside of Polynesia.'

'Is that so?'

'You haven't heard of it?'

'No.'

'Neither have I. Like I said, it's extremely rare.'

Trevor laughed so hard his face turned purple. I offered to fetch him oxygen, but he shook his head. He leaned back in his chair, exhausted.

He said, 'You had me there. I told you you'd enjoy Paul.'

'Did I handle him okay? I meant to reassure him, not mock him.'

'And you did. Moller-Shenk Syndrome. You're coming out of your shell, Dan Talbot. I like it.'

I said, 'Why don't you go home? I'll finish your surgery. Anything I'm not sure about I can ask Helen.'

He shook his head.

'It's not an auspicious day to be at home,' he said. 'Mrs Buxton's sister is visiting. But ask Mary if she's booked me for any house calls.'

He had two. Rene Spooner and Harry Darkin. I said I'd do them. I'd already met Mrs Spooner and Mr Darkin's was only a friendly check-up. He'd just been discharged from Sandwell after a fall.

He hesitated. Then he said, 'All right, but go with Vaz. He usually has a couple of home visits to do.'

'You don't trust me to go on my own?'

'No, it's that old banger of yours I don't trust. We don't want you stranded on Cherry Tree with dead electrics. Now when you go to Rene Spooner, make sure you do the talking. In fact, leave Vaz in the car. She doesn't like foreigners. You know what I mean?'

'Should we pander to her?'

'She's old, Dan. Old and demented. When she was young

you never saw a brown face around here. We don't try re-educating people like that. This isn't the bloody Soviet Union.'

We ploughed through the morning's list. A lot of coughs, a lot of catarrh, two cases of anxiety and one bad back.

'And not forgetting,' says Trevor, 'a possible case of the extremely rare Moller-Shenk syndrome. Pass me the phone.'

He called Glenys Allsop's number and got her answering machine. He didn't leave a message.

'I never do,' he said. 'If you leave a message you don't know who'll listen to it. What if she's not told her husband she's been to see me? What if she calls me back and I'm not available? Then she'll be left worrying. I'll try her again later. Wait till I can speak to her in person.'

Trevor's full of surprises. He comes across as such a shambles. Piles of paper everywhere, phone calls to the bookies, refusing to use the computer. But underneath the chaos he thinks about his patients a lot.

Vaz said he was going to have a slice of Nurse Chris's birthday cake, then he'd be ready to go out on calls. There was quite a crush in the kitchen.

I said, 'So is this the tradition? If it's your birthday you bring cake?'

'Yes,' says Chris. 'When's yours?'

I said, 'I'm not telling. I'll let it be a surprise.'

Practice Manager Stephanie said, 'I can easily find out from your contract.'

Helen Vincent said, 'But nicer not to, eh Stephanie? Nicer just to mind your own business and enjoy your cake.'

It was coffee and walnut. I asked if it had to be homemade.

'No,' says Helen. 'It just has to be edible, which in my case means purchased from M&S.'

Trevor appeared, leaned against the door frame. He

105

looked grey.

Helen said, 'You look like a corpse. Go home. We can divvy out your afternoon list. Mac can take a few, I can take a few. Dan can sit in with me.'

Trevor said, 'I don't want to go home. I'll be fine. I'll take tomorrow morning off. Dan can do my list. He's perfectly capable.'

Stephanie said, 'Is that wise. He's barely been with us a month.'

'But he was studying medicine while you were still a trainee tea-maker at Nettlefold's, so allow me to know what's wise and what isn't.'

Stephanie scowled at me.

'And Dan,' he said, 'As you're seeing Harry Darkin, you might look in on the Rileys as well. See how Jimmy's doing. They're neighbours, practically.'

Vaz's calls were both on the Cherry Tree estate too. It's mainly high-rises, with a few blocks of maisonettes and retirement bungalows. I went to check on Mrs Spooner while Vaz braved the dreaded Tower C, home to a particularly high number of delinquents. Birds of a feather, as Trevor said. 'Clans like the Bibbys and the Dearloves like to roost together. It's handier for interbreeding and threatening each other with GBH.'

Margaret Spooner didn't look very happy to see me.

'Oh,' she said. 'We usually have Dr Buxton.'

I said, 'He's a bit under the weather today. You do know he'll be retiring soon?'

'Yes,' she said. 'And then I don't know what we'll do. Mum doesn't like strangers.'

I said, 'Well I'm not exactly a stranger. I have seen your mother before.'

'She won't remember that. When will Dr Buxton be back?'

'I don't know. Do you want to see if Dr Vincent will do a home visit? Would that help?'

'No,' she said. 'Mum doesn't trust women doctors. You'd better come in.'

So for Rene Spooner it had to be a white male doctor already well known to her. Not too demanding then.

She was a bit chesty. Her lungs were rattling and her pulse was raised. She was drooling too. I asked her if she ever had trouble swallowing. She just looked at me.

Margaret said, 'She gobbles her food. She wolfs it down, then she starts choking and coughing.'

Aspiration pneumonia. It's common in the elderly, especially when you have dementia in the equation.

I said, 'We'll need to keep an eye on that, Margaret.'

Should I have called her 'Margaret' or 'Miss Spooner? Trevor was on first name terms with both of them. What if she wasn't 'Miss Spooner'? What if she'd been married and went by some other name?

I said, 'It's the Alzheimer's. The body gradually forgets how to swallow and then there's a danger of food getting into the lungs.'

'And what am I supposed to do about it?'

I didn't really know what to say. That's how people like your Mum end up being tube-fed? Or they get pneumonia and die? Surely she knew that anyway.

I wasn't sure whether to prescribe antibiotics. The chestiness might not be an infection. It could just have been the stomach acid irritating the lungs. I wondered whether I should prescribe steroids instead. Or both. I felt at a loss without Trevor at my side.

I wrote a prescription for Augmentin.

Margaret said, 'It's no use giving her pills. She'll spit them out.'

'This is a liquid. You'll need to keep it in the fridge and

give it a good shake before you pour it. Give it to her before a meal. And use it all. Don't stop just because her chest sounds clearer.'

'What about a chest X-ray?'

'I don't think she needs one, but I'll ask Dr Buxton what he thinks.'

'Yes, you do that,' she said. 'Dr Buxton knows what's what.'

That annoyed me. I wasn't so unsure of myself anymore.

I said, 'The thing is, Margaret, getting an X-ray means a trip to hospital. Then they might decide to keep her in and patients like your Mum don't do well in hospital. Strange surroundings, infection risks. She's better off at home with you, if you can cope with her. But I realise that's a big 'if.' Maybe you'd like some respite? Would you like Rene to go to a nursing home for a week?'

She looked at me.

'We could arrange that, if you need a rest.'

'I don't,' she said. 'I just want a proper doctor when I ask for one.'

A proper doctor. How much longer was I going to have to put up with that? I knew I looked young for my age. I tried a moustache for a while when I was working for Yasmin Panwar. Chloe loved it but Mam said it made me look like a spiv.

Vaz was frustrated. The lift was out of order in Tower C so he'd had to climb the stairs. One of his calls was to two children with mild coughs. No need to see a doctor at all. The other was to a woman called Swinton. She had a history of drug use and paranoid episodes. Somebody had phoned the surgery to say she was behaving erratically, talking to herself and refusing to leave her flat, but when Vaz got there, there was nobody at home.

I said, 'Are you sure? Could she be lying unconscious on the floor? Or hiding, too disturbed to open the door?'

'No,' he said. 'Neighbour saw her go out. Now I'll have to come back.'

'Why bother? If she's gone out, it sounds like she's feeling better.'

'But her file says she has mental health issues. What if she comes to harm and I didn't make extra effort? No, I will come back this evening. It is my duty.'

Harry Darkin was having beans on toast for his lunch. He still had a bit of bruising down the side of his face.

I said, 'You're not black and blue. More yellow and purple.'

He said he was fine, never better.

'I'm 92,' he said. 'Watch this.'

He got up, lifted one leg until it rested on the chair back and then leaned over till his face almost touched his knee, like a ballet dancer at the barre.

I said, 'You're more limber than I am.'

'Royal Navy fitness exercises,' he said. 'I've done them all my life.'

'How did you happen to fall?'

'Granddaughter's dog legged me over,' he said. 'It wasn't his fault. He's only a pup. I reckon he was more shook up than I was, but they said I had to go to the hospital, on account of my age. What a waste of time and money. I'll make you a cup of tea.'

I said, 'Next time, Harry. This is a flying visit. We heard you'd been in the Sandwell, so we just wanted to check up on you. I need to get off now and see Mr Riley.'

'Jimmy?' he said. 'He's not long for this world. Last week he really went down. They have one of those special cancer nurses now, comes twice a day. I do a bit of shopping for

Connie but if you ask me it'd be better if she did her own shopping while I sit with Jimmy for an hour. She never leaves the house.'

'I'll suggest it to her.'

'Yes, you do that. She might listen to you. Dr Buxton retired, has he?'

'Not yet, but he wasn't feeling so good today.'

'He's another one, ruined his health with the smokes. We used to get them duty free in the Navy, you know? During the war. I was in Combined Ops. Trained up in Scotland, at Inverary. Smokes were sixpence for twenty. That was in the old money, of course. But I never smoked. I was already engaged when I joined up, you see, to my Winnie, and she was asthmatical so I thought well smoking'll never do. Because once you've started it's very hard to stop.'

'As Dr Buxton is finding. Is that your wife?'

There was a 1950s wedding photo on the sideboard.

'That's her. Still keeping her beady eye on me. 1992 she passed away. How long's that? 20 years. I manage all right. My daughter and my granddaughter do my washing. I could do it myself only they like to feel useful. I still talk to Winnie, tell her what's going on.'

He chuckled.

He said, 'I talk to her, but one good thing, she can't talk back. You married?'

'Next year, I hope.'

'My granddaughter's not married. They just live over the brush. I can't understand it. What's wrong with putting a ring on a girl's finger? Well good luck to you, Doctor. If you're half as happy as me and Winnie were, you'll be champion.'

The Rileys' bungalow smelled of Dettol. Jimmy was in a hospital bed in the living room. He'd only managed to come to the surgery for one pamidronate infusion and then he'd become too weak to leave his bed.

Connie said, 'Look at it. Ugly great thing. There's hardly room to swing a cat in here.'

Jimmy was gaunt, propped up against pillows, but smiling, toothless. His dentures were soaking in a pot on the windowsill.

I said, 'How's the visiting nurse arrangement working out?'

'Lovely girls,' says Jimmy. 'Both of them. Always cheerful.'

Connie said the cheerfulness grated on her.

Jimmy said, 'Go and make the doctor a cuppa, woman. He looks parched.'

I nearly said not to bother. I'm glad I didn't. Jimmy wanted her out of the room. The minute she'd gone he grabbed my hand.

He said, 'I'm afraid Connie don't appreciate how things are. She thinks I'll shake this off. She's been talking about booking for our usual two weeks at Llandudno next June. We go to a caravan there. Done it for years. I don't want her wasting money on a deposit. I'll be six foot under by then. But if I try to say it, she won't listen.'

I promised I'd have a word.

I said, 'Are you comfortable, Jimmy?'

'Not bad,' he said.

'Does your son come over at all?'

'I think he does. I sometimes forget who's been. Or what day it is. I think it's the medicine they're giving me.'

He closed his eyes and drifted off to sleep. I went to find Connie in the kitchen. She'd made me a very milky tea. She signalled to me to shut the door.

I said, 'He seems very peaceful.'

She said, 'That's because he don't understand how bad he is. I don't let on. I've told him I'm going to book for Llandudno next year, just to buck him up. Give him something to look forward to. I won't do it of course. He'll be gone by then, won't he?'

'I think we're talking weeks, Connie, not months.'

'That's what I think. The way he's looking, I can't see him lasting much longer.'

'So we'll just keep him as comfortable as we can. Is he constipated?'

'He was. One of the nurses gave him something. Laxido.'

'And how are the nights?'

'Not so good. He imagines things. He said there was a dog on the bed last night, but we've not had a dog for years. It didn't bother him. He kept reaching out, like he was patting it.'

'It's the Oramorph. People see things that aren't there. But the pain's under control?'

'Most of the time. He's got a spray, for when he has a really bad turn.'

'Fentanyl. And that helps?'

'It seems to. Like when we move him, to wash him, that pains him, but he squibs the Fentywhatever up his nose and then he's alright. His mouth gets dry after he's used it, but I'll tell you what he likes. Pineapple chunks. He can't chew, to get them down, but he sucks on them and it moistens his mouth. He's always loved pineapple chunks.'

'You look very tired, Connie. Would you think of having a night nurse?'

'No.'

'Not even for a couple of nights a week? It'd give you a break?'

'I don't need a break. It's my job to sit with him. It won't be for much longer.'

'What about your boys? Could they take a turn?'

'Roger's not here. He's working in the Gulf. He'd come if I asked him, and so would Derek. But they're busy people,

Doctor. They've got their own lives. And our Derek needs his sleep. He always did.'

'When was the last time you left the house?'

'Can't remember. I don't need to. Derek does me a Tesco order on his computer and they bring it in a van. And if I run out of milk or bread, I watch for Harry Darkin going to the shop and he fetches it for me.'

'I was just visiting Mr Darkin. Did you know he'd had a fall?'

'I saw him go off in an ambulance, walking though. He wasn't on a stretcher. Is he all right?'

'He is. And he told me he'd be happy to sit with Jimmy any time, so you can go out and get some fresh air.'

'Yes, well,' she said. 'You know why he's offering?'

'No, why?'

'He's setting his cap at me.'

Vaz was in the car swiping through pictures of women on Match and looking depressed.

He said, 'Many ladies are not honest.'

He'd been on five dates and he said none of the women looked anything like their photos.

I said, 'Are their looks important to you?'

'Not so much. But I don't like this piggery-jokery, putting up pictures of ten years ago. I'd like to meet a nice honest Christian lady.'

Vaz is a Catholic.

I said, 'There must be dating sites for Catholics.'

'Oh yes,' he said. 'But those ladies, mostly they are not in West Midlands. Mostly they are in South America.'

I said, 'When Chloe's finished her exams I think we'll have a party and invite all of her single girlfriends. There's somebody out there for you.'

'Thank you, Dan,' he said. 'You are a very kind fellow.'

When we got back to the surgery I found Trevor half
asleep on the examination table.

'Everyone's telling me I look like death warmed over so I
thought I'd have a little kip. Recharge the batteries. How
were the shut-ins?'

'Harry Darkin was doing thigh stretches over the back of
a chair. Jimmy Riley's on his last legs but he's got good pain
control. I'd say his main problem is communication.'

'Has he had a stroke?'

'No. Just wires crossed. He thinks his wife doesn't
understand that he's dying and she thinks the same of him.
Barmy really.'

'Yes, but none of our business. The main thing is, they
each in their own way get the picture. And what about Rene
Spooner?'

'Aspiration pneumonia. Her daughter says she gulps her
food down.'

'Basal crackles?'

'Yes. And she was a bit tachycardic. I prescribed oral
Augmentin but I wondered about giving her a steroid as
well?'

He shook his head, said he was never convinced it made
any difference in such a case.

'If you're in Casualty and you're dealing with some young
idiot who's got bladdered and aspirated vomit, yes. But an
old lady who's had a slight acid regurge, no.'

'The daughter wasn't very happy about me turning up
instead of you. I think she felt she was getting second class
service, so I promised her I'd check with you, whether Rene
should get a chest X-ray.'

'Absolutely not,' he said. 'For one thing, Margaret doesn't
drive. They'd be sitting around for hours waiting for
transport, then waiting for the X-ray, then waiting for

transport home. No, Rene's better off at home watching the telly and taking her chances.'

'That's roughly what I said.'

'Good,' he said. 'Now Glenys Allsop's coming in at 2.30. As soon as I've seen her, I'm going home, sister-in-law or no sister-in-law. Helen'll be around if you need a second opinion on anything.'

CHAPTER 12.

Glenys Allsop arrived early. She looked anxious.

She said, 'Is it bad news?'

Trevor said, 'First things first. How are you feeling?'

'I'm all right,' she said, 'apart from the itching. It's not just the ankles. I itch everywhere now but I still haven't got a rash.'

Was it my imagination or was there a slightly yellow cast to the whites of her eyes? You see things differently when you know what you're looking for.

Trevor said, 'Well we got your results back and some of your bloods are a bit out of kilter so we might be closer to explaining it.'

'Out of kilter' was putting it mildly but he was being gentle with her.

He said, 'Dr Dan and I think the next step is to send you for a scan.'

She said, 'But what will they be looking for?'

'We're wondering if you might have a little blockage in your bile duct. It could be a gallstone. Have you had any pain at all since we saw you?'

She'd had no pain. Normally I'd be pleased to hear that, but gallstones would have been a happier explanation than something else causing a blockage.

She said, 'I suppose there's a long waiting list for scans.'

He didn't mention urgent referrals. He just said, 'There can be, but I think we can pull a few strings. Lord knows they get plenty of time-wasters, plenty of people not turning up for appointments, and I don't see why somebody like you should be kept waiting.'

'And it'll just be for a scan? I won't have to stay in or anything?'

'Just a scan.'

'But what if they find something? Because if I had to go into hospital, I don't know how my Pete'd manage.'

'One step at a time,' he said. 'A scan only takes half an hour. And you know, Glenys, helpless husbands are usually only acting helpless.'

He looked across to me. I could see he was flagging. Talking was taking a lot out of him. He needed me to wind up the consultation.

I said, 'So Dr Buxton will make that call today. If you don't hear about the scan appointment within a week, let us know. Sometimes things fall between the cracks and we don't want you sitting around worrying.'

She couldn't thank us enough. She said it was a great weight off her mind knowing somebody was taking her itching seriously. She stood up to leave and promptly burst into tears. Trevor was out of his chair in a flash.

'Sit down, my dear,' he said.

She said she didn't want to hold us up when we had so many patients to see.

'You're not holding us up,' he said. 'We've got all the time in the world.'

He pulled his chair over and put his arm around her shoulder.

He said, 'Don't cross your bridges, Glenys. Life's complicated enough. Go for the scan and then we'll know what's what. And get somebody to go with you. Waiting around in hospitals, it's nice to have company.'

She said she didn't think her husband would be able to get time off from work. I was about to say something about employers generally being sympathetic regarding hospital appointments, but Trevor was way ahead of me. He'd already formed a picture of the Allsop marriage.

He said, 'Does your Pete know you've been to see us?'

'He knows I came about the itching.'

'But you didn't talk to him about your liver tests?'

'Pete's not good with illness,' she said. 'He'll only think the worst and get himself in a state.'

'Men do. It's a well-known fact. Even doctors. Especially doctors. When Mrs Buxton gave birth, she didn't even want me in the same building, never mind the same room.'

Glenys smiled and blew her nose. She said she might ask her sister to go with her to the hospital.

'Top idea,' says Trevor. 'Women are much better company. But make sure you tell that man of yours what's going on. That's what husbands are for. In sickness and in health and for when you can't get the top off a new jar of jam.'

As soon as she'd left Trevor called someone he knew at the Queen Elizabeth. He was promised a liver and gallbladder scan for Glenys within two weeks. Then he called Ladbroke's. He was on that call when Moira brought the files in for afternoon surgery and gave him the thumbs up. He blew her a kiss.

'That,' he said, when he got off the phone, 'is what I call a good outcome. We've got Glenys on track. HappyasLarry just came in at 12-1, won by a length. And Mrs Buxton's sister is on her way to the station.'

'How do you know?'

'Mary gave me the signal. She made some discreet enquiries.'

'That was Moira by the way, not Mary.'

'Of course it was. How come you're so good at telling them apart? You've only been here five minutes.'

'Moira wears her reading glasses on a gold chain, Mary's is silver. And Moira's got a chipped front tooth.'

'Good grief, you've made a close study of them. Anyway,

whichever. I love that woman. I love them both.'

He pulled his coat on, checked his pockets for his keys and his smokes and shuffled off.

'Don't tidy my desk. Don't examine unchaperoned women. Don't run with scissors in your hand.'

The afternoon list was pretty straightforward. An insurance check-up, one case of ringworm, one of cystitis, a couple of bad backs. Pat Bovey had seen a gadget advertised, a kind of gum shield, supposed to prevent snoring, and wondered if I thought it'd work on her husband.

I said, 'Will he wear it?'

'He swears he doesn't snore.'

'Then you might be wasting your money. Does it disturb your sleep?'

'It's terrible.'

'Do you have another room you could sleep in?'

'Not really. We keep the budgies in the other bedroom.'

The Boveys breed budgerigars.

'When he snores, are there times when he goes quiet, as though he's holding his breath?'

'Oh yes. Then just when you think you can get to sleep, he lets out this great big snort and it starts up again.'

'That type of snoring can be bad for the heart. He should come in for a check-up.'

'He won't. He doesn't like doctors.'

'It's called sleep apnoea. Tell him you read about it in a magazine.'

'He won't fall for that. We only get Budgerigar World. What about a chin strap? I've heard that can help.'

You get patients like Mrs Bovey. They ask for your advice but somehow it's never quite what they wanted you to say.

Jill Bloxhall, who was waiting for a new knee, wanted to know what I thought about a glucosamine supplement and Taryn Gilbert had self-diagnosed ADD. Attention Deficit

Disorder.

She said, 'I need assessing.'

She was having difficulty holding down a job. Shelf-stacking, office-cleaning, sandwich prep. Nothing suited her. She got bored, couldn't concentrate on the task in hand, messed up.

'What happened with your last job?'

'Got the sack.'

'Why?'

'Gobbed in the mayonnaise.'

'That's not an attention problem, Taryn. That's just bad behaviour.'

'But I need assessing.'

'I'm assessing you. You need to grow up and exercise some self-control.'

'Still, you're not a proper doctor, are you? Dr Buxton'd get me assessed.'

'Do you think so? Okay, come back and see him then. He should be in next week.'

Her parting shot was, 'I'll go private.'

'Good idea.'

I'm afraid I carried my irritation over into the diabetes clinic. People who forget to come to their appointment, or pretend they're trying to lose weight and still keep piling it on. I told Brian Longmoss he was digging an early grave with his knife and fork and Nurse Chris gave me a reproving look.

I didn't care. Was I sharpening my teeth with patients like Taryn and Mr Longmoss? Was I tired of being Nice Dr Talbot, or just plain tired?

Wednesday came and Trevor was still out of action. Stephanie was pushing to get a locum in. Helen said there was no need because I could cover for him. Another vote of confidence.

Mac said, 'A pound to a penny Trevor'll be back tomorrow.'

Helen said, 'I don't know why he doesn't just jack it in.'

I said, 'His sisters-in-law seems to feature in his retirement fears. He doesn't like to be at home when they visit.'

Helen said that was a load of nonsense.

'They've got an enormous house. He can make himself a nice little downstairs snug and shut the door. He doesn't even need to see them.'

Mac said, 'Cut the man some slack, Helen. This place has been his life. Let him go in his own good time. Are you coming out with me this afternoon, laddie?'

I was to have my promised tour of the nursing homes.

Bruce Macdonald drives a Merc. Leather seats, surround-sound audio. Of course, Mac didn't generally make house calls on Brook Glen or Cherry Tree so he didn't need to worry about driving a thief-magnet.

He had four calls on his list.

'Dovecroft first', he said.

We'd just set off when he got a call to say there had been a death at Twycross Lodge.

'Does that mean a change of running order?'

'Not at all,' he said. 'He'll still be dead when we get there. Always attend to the living first.'

We got a very warm welcome at Dovecroft. It was like arriving with some big celebrity. Mac worked the Day Room like it was a cocktail party, old ladies beaming at him and clutching at his hand. The charge nurse said she didn't have much for us to do. Mrs Wells had a sore patch on her foot but the chiropodist was keeping an eye on it. Mrs Geary was refusing to eat. And Herbert Cousins' breathlessness had worsened.

Mac said he'd see Mrs Geary first. He offered Mr Cousins to me.

He said, 'Go and introduce yourself. Herbert's a Wolves supporter.'

I said, 'I don't follow the soccer much.'

'Rugby union, I suppose, where you come from? Doesn't matter. Herbert's got vascular dementia as well as congestive heart failure so you might not get a lot of sense out of him anyway. He can be a bit of a flickering light bulb.'

Mr Cousins was in his room. It was quite pleasant. He had an en-suite shower and toilet and some of his own furniture and odds and ends. He was in a reclining chair, still in his pyjamas. His ankles were very swollen even though he was wearing pressure socks.

I listened to his chest. His lungs sounded clear but his jugulars were distended and he had heart gallops, Lubbity-dubbity instead of lub-dub.

I said, 'I hear you're a Wolves man?'

He smiled.

I said, 'What do you think of their new manager?'

'Not much,' he said. 'Billy Wright, now he was a great player.'

I'd never heard of Billy Wright.

I said, 'They'd better bring him out of retirement then.'

Herbert said, 'He's married to one of the Beverley Sisters.'

I'd heard of the Beverleys. My Nan liked them. They did a song called The Little Drummer Boy and she used to sing it to me and Adam when we were kids.

I said, 'Mr Cousins, I'm going to have a word with Dr Macdonald, see about changing your water pills. It might ease your breathing.'

He was already taking Lasix and he was on a low-salt regime.

'Don't bother,' he said. 'Just shoot me.'

There were photographs on the chest of drawers, three boys in school uniform.

'Are those your grandchildren?'

He snorted. 'Little fuckers.'

There was a box too. Cremation ashes. The metal plaque said NELL.

I asked if it was his wife.

'Dog,' he said. 'Wife's buried. She left instructions. Marble headstone with an angel. Waste of bloody money.'

'What kind of dog was Nell?'

'Bitser.'

'Bitser this and bitser that?'

'Best dog I ever had.'

There was a new diuretic I'd read about but Mac said it was too expensive to prescribe.

I said, 'It seems a pity. Herbert's on his way out. It'd be nice to make him more comfortable for however long he's got left.'

'Aye,' says Mac, 'but the bean counters won't wear it. I'll up his Lasix dose, see if that helps.'

'What was Mrs Geary's problem?'

'She's had enough. Wants to die.'

'What can you do?'

'Not much. Keep her hydrated. She'll drink but she won't eat.'

'No tube-feeding?'

'Nothing. She stipulated that when she arrived, all in writing. And no resuscitation.'

'Can the family over-rule her?'

'Not if I'm around. Right, next stop, the Sorrento.'

Dovecote, Woodleigh Grange, Waterdene, Sorrento. What lovely names they give those places people go to to die. Like hotels, a lot of them, that's what people say. Choice of menu, on-site hairdresser, sing-alongs and Bingo. It's not home though. I can't imagine putting my Mam or Da in a place like that, but I suppose that's what everyone says, until it comes to it.

I said, 'Doesn't geriatrics get you down sometimes?'

'No,' he said. 'Paediatric oncology would get me down.'

'Yes, I can see that. Do you have children?'

'No.'

The best thing about the Sorrento nursing home was its name. It was Sixties-built unit, badly in need of updating. The only private rooms were for the dying. If they moved you there, you knew they were talking days or hours, not weeks. They'd just finished serving lunch and everyone was in the day-room. The TV was on but the only people watching were the staff. The place smelled of school dinners and urine.

Mac had been asked to see a resident with late-stage dementia. Stanley had only been awake for a few minutes on and off in the previous 24 hours. The nursing manager wondered if he should be transferred to hospital for fluids by IV. Stanley himself hadn't ever stated his wishes.

Mac said, 'No need for that. He's in the home straight now, so just warn his daughters and keep his mouth swabbed with iced water.'

Stanley was pushed along the corridor to the end-of-life accommodation.

'When the patient hasn't put their wishes in writing, do you use your discretion?'

'Yes, I suppose I do. Hospital's not the place for him and the Sorrento can't manage IV fluids. Chances are he'd end up with an infection or a thrombus. The staff are okay but they've no great clinical skills. Mopping, lifting and spoon-feeding, that's about their limit. And you know, dehydration when the end is nigh, it's not so bad. People imagine it'd be like crawling across the Sahara without water, but you saw Stan. He's not distressed. Quite the opposite. He's slipping peacefully away. And don't forget, if he's not peeing at least he won't get a sore backside to add to his final joys.'

'I try to imagine what it feels like, going into residential care, knowing it's the end of the line. Do you ever picture yourself somewhere like that?'

'No. I have an exit plan. Bottle of vodka, a handful of Seconal and a whacking big insulin shot, for insurance. On which cheery note, let's go and certify Albert Gosling. Have you had much experience of death certificates yet?'

I hadn't. Very few of Yasmin Panwar's patients died at home.

'Okay. This will be an instructive one.'

'How so?'

'You'll see.'

Mac said the Harold Shipman scandal had provoked a big shake-up over certifying deaths. I was still at school, doing A Levels, when that case was in the news. I remembered the pictures of him in the papers. Glasses and a beard. I don't know how many patients' deaths he was charged with, but I know he was sentenced to life without parole and I know he hanged himself in prison. I was in med school by then.

He said, 'Pre-Shipman there only used to be cross-checks if the relatives wanted a cremation but now any certificate that won't be going to the coroner's office has to be countersigned by another doctor. It's a nuisance but you can understand the reasons. You won't be countersigning for a while, of course. You have to be registered for a few years before you get that job.'

The nursing manager at Twycross Lodge looked about seventeen. She had a nose ring.

She said, 'Albert's son is here. He's got his solicitor with him.'

I looked at Mac.

'Pleural mesothelioma,' he said. 'Listen. Do ye hear the chink-chink of a compensation payout? We'll see the deceased first, lassie.'

Mr Gosling had received last offices. He looked to have been a tall man, but was very emaciated. Skin grey, features flat, pupils dilated and fixed. Definitely dead. The manager said he'd had a sudden attack of breathlessness and died within minutes. An auxiliary had been with him.

Mac said, 'When you fill in the form, on the first line you need to write the immediate cause of death. To the best of your knowledge. So in this case we'd say?'

'Pulmonary embolism?'

'Yes, very likely. Then on the next line, you write the underlying condition, if there is one.'

'Mesothelioma.'

'Yes. And that's as far as we go because this now gets referred to the coroner's office. Because?'

'There's likely to be a court case?'

'Yes. Notification of any death that might be due to an industrial disease goes to the coroner. Albert worked at C&W, building train carriages. Forty years inhaling asbestos.'

Mr Gosling's son and the solicitor were waiting in the manager's office. Dr Mac shook the son's hand but just nodded to the lawyer.

'Clifford,' he said.

'Mac,' says the lawyer. 'Form going straight to the coroner I presume?'

'As soon as the ink's dried.'

Mr Gosling's son wanted to know when they could go ahead with a cremation.

'It's up to the coroner's office,' says Mac. 'But they'll

usually release the body as soon as they've done a post-mortem. You shouldn't have too long a wait.'

We walked back to the car.

I said, 'The nose-ring was a surprise. I'd have thought that might be a safety hazard for a nurse.'

'Well,' he said, 'she's the manager. I don't think she does a lot of hands-on. But I take your point. A sharp tug from a stroppy resident and she could end up with one very big nostril.'

I said, 'Is it common for a lawyer to turn up when someone dies?'

'Not at all. But if young Gosling asked him, Clifford wouldn't refuse. He'll always be happy to oblige, at his usual hourly rate.'

'You obviously know him well.'

'Do ye not know who that was? Clifford Vincent. That was our Helen's dear husband.'

Helen Vincent's husband. Would I recognise him if I saw him again? Fifties, brindled hair, dark suit. I wished I'd paid more attention to him. Then I wished I wasn't so interested.

'Things seemed a bit frosty between you. Don't you get on?'

'We don't need to. Our paths don't cross very often. Lawyers, lad. Henry VI Part 2.'

He'd lost me there.

I asked him if he thought things at The Lindens would change much once Trevor had retired.

'Bound to,' he said. 'Mind, Helen's been wearing the troosers for a good while. Trevor's not interested in the business side and these days ye have to be. Try talking to Trevor about budgets and he switches off. So you might say we're already easing into the new regime.'

'You didn't want to take over?'

'I gave Helen a wee fight over it, but nothing serious. She really wanted it and I wasn't hungry for it. I'm happy enough with what I've got. I wouldn't be clinging on like Trevor. Early retirement is what I fancy. No, Helen's welcome to it. She likes to keep busy. It takes her mind off her own problems.'

'What are they?'

'Life with Clifford, for one. And then there's the son. Miles.'

'I saw him at the surgery one evening. He was quite surly with me.'

'Doesn't surprise me. He's quite the Prince Charming.'

What's his story?'

'He's a deadbeat. Doesn't work. Doesn't do anything as far as I know except take pills. Helen's gye too soft with him. If he was mine his bags'd be on the doorstep and the locks changed. Come to think of it, if she changed the locks that'd fettle Lightning as well.'

'Lightning?'

'That's what they call Clifford at the Rotary. Lightning, as in zipper. Clifford has trouble keeping his fly closed.'

'Poor Helen.'

'Anything young, anything in a skirt.'

'And she's such an attractive woman. For her age.'

Did I say that? I shouldn't have said that.

'I'll drop ye back at the surgery.'

'Are you finished for the day?'

He wasn't, quite. He had a monthly private geriatric clinic in Bromsgrove from 4.00 till 6.00. Then he was off for the rest of the week, going up to Galashiels to see family and play golf. Bruce Macdonald seemed to have his life very well sorted.

I asked him what had ever brought him to the West

Midlands.

'A woman,' he said. But he didn't elaborate.

CHAPTER 13

I was slightly alarmed to see Amber Evans on my afternoon list. KDO.

I said, 'Dr Parker's in today. You should see her.'

'Can't,' says Amber. 'She's full up. I need a doctor though. I've got summink stuck up me fanny.'

'That's definitely a job for Dr Parker.'

'Well her on the desk said Dr Parker's not got no appointments and I need to get it seen to.'

'Then you should go to A&E.'

'I can't hardly walk.'

'Are you in pain?'

'Terrible. And I need me phone.'

'Your phone?'

'It's stuck up me fanny.'

I'd have suspected someone was pulling my leg, but this was Amber Evans. I told her to stay put while I checked on something. I caught Pam between patients.

I said, 'I've got Amber Evans.'

'Have you, indeed? Yes, I thought she might latch on to you.'

'I'm not sure if I've understood her correctly but I think she's saying she has a mobile phone stuck in her vagina. I know you've got a full list but I wondered…?'

Pam laughed till she cried. She wiped her tears.

'Give me a minute compose myself and then wheel her in. But do sit in on the consultation, Dan. This'll be one for your memoirs.'

Amber seemed to be walking normally, considering what she claimed to have in the cargo hold. Could she possibly be having us on?

'Now,' says Pam. 'Are you telling me your phone is actually, really and truly up and under? Don't waste my time, Amber.'

'I'm not. It is.'

'Right. Drawers off, if you're wearing any, and get yourself up on the table. Why did you go to Dr Dan with this? I do the ladybits.'

'They said you was busy.'

'I am.'

Amber did indeed have a phone in her vagina. It wasn't a smartphone. Just an old-fashioned flip-top.

Pam bit her lip.

'Who put it up there?'

'I did.'

'Why?'

'There's an app.'

'An app?'

'Vibrator.'

'And do you have that app, Amber? Can you get such a thing on an old phone like yours?'

'Dunno.'

Pam did a cursory examination.

'It's well and truly stuck.'

'Can you get it out?'

'I'm not even going to try. This is a job for A&E.'

'Fuck no. I'll have to wait ages.'

'Not if you go now. This time of day is usually pretty quiet.'

'Can you give me a letter?'

'No. I've got patients to see. Make yourself decent and get down to Sandwell pronto, tonto. Did you take the Zithromax I gave you?'

'I think so.'

'The last time you were in? You had a discharge? Dr Dan

gave you an injection and I gave you a prescription. Did you take the pills?'

'Yeah.'

'You certainly look a lot cleaner down there. But if I were you, I'd give your phone a good wipe when you get it back.'

Amber zipped up her jeans. I got a big smile but all Pam got was a sigh.

'Thank you, Dan,' says Pam. 'You've made my day. Just when you think you've seen it all, along comes Amber.'

'So she'd put her phone up there hoping it'd vibrate?'

'Yes. There is an app. She was right about that, but it's meant for the clitoris, stupid girl. I mean, who'd want their cervix tickled? And anyway, why would you mess up your phone? Why not send off for a vibrator? You did the right thing coming to me though. I see her little game. She was hoping to get you up to your elbow in her lady parts.'

'Was the phone really stuck or did you just want to get rid of her?'

'No, it was jammed in the fundus. People don't realise, what goes up doesn't necessarily come down.'

'Maybe having to wait to be seen in A&E will make her think twice about pushing anything else up there.'

'Don't bank on it, pet. Some of them actually enjoy A&E. Playing on the wheelchairs. Getting dinner from the vending machines. It's like Alton Towers with the possible bonus of drugs.'

'Dan,' she said, as I was halfway out the door. 'I'm just wondering. Do you think she'd get a signal with it up there?'

My last patient of the afternoon was Barbara Humphries. Her face fell when she saw me. Where was Dr Buxton?

'Off sick. How can I help you?'

She wanted to talk about getting her bunions done. She

said it wasn't that they pained her, but her daughter was getting married next July and she'd like to able to wear some nice shoes. I was frank with her. The chances of her getting her bunions done on the NHS just so she could wear heels were not great. Plus, the operation wasn't the half of it. Two or three weeks off your feet, another five or six weeks when you can't drive. My Aunty June had it done and she nearly went out of her mind, stuck indoors, depending on friends to do her shopping.

Mrs Humphries said, 'I know what's involved. I've read up on it. I'd still like to get it done.'

I said I'd take a look at her feet.

'Don't bother,' she said. 'I'll come back when Dr Buxton's here. He's looked after all of us Humphries for years. He'll be able to help me.'

It was interesting, occupying another doctor's seat. The newbie sitting in for the venerable senior partner. Some patients, the Kyle Bibbys of the world, saw opportunity. They'd push, to see what they could get out of you. Patients like Mrs Humphries saw you as an obstacle, a disruption to their well-ordered lives. Trevor Buxton was their GP, had been for years, and they weren't going to let go of him that easily.

I had to attend the Patient Participation Panel that evening, as Stephanie reminded me every time she saw me. I'd already missed the September meeting, with the cast-iron excuse of doing an out-of-hours shift at the Sterling call centre. Stephanie was supposed to run things but she had competition from a man called Ron Jarrold - I assumed he was somehow related to Been on Google Freda. Ron loved meetings and was a stickler for procedure. 'Through the chair, through the chair, if you please,' was one of his favourite challenges.

The other patient participants were Sandra Kerridge, Betty Cheever, Maureen Haycock and Chandeep Rajput, a local businessman. Pam Parker and I were there to represent the practice.

Ron Jarrold wanted it put on record that he'd been caused considerable inconvenience because the meeting had been rescheduled at short notice.

'We give of our time,' he said. 'And we're all busy people.'

Betty Cheever said she wasn't. Mr Jarrold persisted.

'Most of us are very busy people. I think we're owed a little more consideration.'

'Noted,' said Stephanie. 'Mr Rajput. You wanted to say something about the on-site pharmacy.'

Pam said, 'What on-site pharmacy?'

He said, 'The one that would be a great asset to this practice.'

Stephanie said she was very much in favour but a decision would have to wait until Dr Vincent took over as senior partner.

Pam said, 'I don't see the need for a pharmacy. What's wrong with people walking down to the one on the Parade?'

'Pharmacies can be big earners,' says Stephanie. Mr Rajput nodded.

'And it'd be more convenient for us patients,' says Mrs Cheever. 'You can wait for ages for your tablets down at the Parade, and they've only got two chairs. You get mothers in there hogging the seats and letting their kiddies sit down when there's pensioners standing.'

I asked where they thought they'd find room for a pharmacy. The Lindens isn't a big building.

'Yes,' says Pam. 'We're tight for space as it is. You'd have even more people clogging the waiting room.'

Someone said, while we were on the topic of the waiting room, it'd be nice if we had a coffee machine in there.

Stephanie made a note.

'Or tea,' someone else chipped in. 'Not everybody likes coffee.'

Ron Jarrold raised his hand.

'At the risk of sounding like a broken record,' he said, 'what's happening about introducing on-line appointment booking? It's the way to go.'

Stephanie said, 'You don't need to convince me, Ron. Believe me, I'm pushing for it.'

Mrs Haycock said she was against it. She didn't have a computer, so how was she supposed to manage?

Ron said, 'There'd still be the telephonic option, for those who choose not to go online. Then you'd be able to phase that out as the older people died off.'

Mrs Haycock said she was only 67.

'Through the chair, Maureen,' says Ron.

Pam Parker said, 'We have two receptionists who do a perfectly good job with the system we've got, but neither of them will see 60 again so I say, if we must do this on-line thing, we wait till they retire. What do you think, Dr Dan?'

I agreed. I also thought the whole meeting was a waste of time but with Ron Jarrold around it was hard to get a word in.

He said, 'If you computerised everything you could manage with one receptionist and afford another doctor. Then people wouldn't have to wait so long to get an appointment. Take my wife. The last time Freda needed to see Dr Buxton she had to wait a week.'

I said, 'You won't get another doctor for the price of a receptionist and anyway, I don't think we need more doctors. I think we need more patients taking responsibility for their own health. And that includes not missing appointments.'

He bristled.

He said, 'My wife never misses appointments.'

I said, 'I'm not talking about your wife.'

'I am,' he said.

That's the problem with these panels. They turn into personal wittering sessions.

I said, 'At a typical surgery we're getting 20% no-shows. On-line booking isn't going to change that, and neither is employing more doctors.'

Mr Rajput suggested fining people. Sandra Kerridge said she didn't see how that would work. 'Those kind of people never pay fines,' she said. 'They get let off because they're on the social.'

He said, 'But next time they come, the receptionist can say, "sorry Mr No-Show, you can only see a doctor after you have paid this fine" This will teach them a lesson.'

Not a bad idea.

Pam kept looking at her watch. Mrs Cheever and Mrs Haycock both picked up their handbags. I thought we were done. But Ron Jarrold had his finger in the air again.

'It also seems to me,' he said, 'that a lot of time could be saved by email consultations. Take your typical patient. He has to take time off work, drive through traffic to get here on time, then he sits in the waiting room for an hour just to get ten minutes with the doctor. It's highly inefficient. Now, if he could email the doctor, outlining the problem, suggesting a possible diagnosis if he has a shrewd idea what's wrong with him, he might well avoid having to come in at all. The doctor could attach a prescription to his reply, and Bob's your uncle.'

I said, 'Mr Jarrold, an important part of a doctor's job is sitting with the patient and noticing little things that might be significant. What the patient thinks is wrong with him, what his ostensible reason is for coming in, they might be red herrings.'

'Spot on,' says Pam. 'Well said, Dr Talbot. Anyway, Bob's not my uncle but I've got two of them at home and one of them is my father-in-law who needs his dinner at a regular time so can we please finish?'

After much to-ing and fro-ing a date was fixed for the November meeting.

'Another hour of our lives we'll never get back,' Pam muttered as she was leaving. 'And I can't wait to hear Trevor's views on email consultations.'

Chloe was home well before me. She'd finished work early to have one last blast of revision. Textbooks everywhere. She was not in a good mood.

'Take a break. Have a glass of wine and ask me about my day.'

'I'm not drinking. I have exams next week.'

'Cook you a stir-fry?'

'I couldn't eat a thing.'

I went to the chipper, got the Fish of the Week meal deal and ate it in the car.

When I got back Chloe was making coffee. She said she couldn't remember a single clinical fact.

'Stop trying. Relax. I'll tell you a story. A day in the life of a GP. Guess what one of my patients had shoved up her vagina?'

'A drug baggie.'

'No.'

'A courgette.'

'No.'

'Give up.'

'A mobile phone.'

'That's not possible.'

'Of course it is. If it can accommodate a full-term baby it can accommodate an old fliptop.'

'I don't know how you can bear dealing with such stupid people.'

'I went out on rounds with Mac too. We had a mesothelioma death to certify. Oh and I met Helen's husband.'

'Who?'

'Helen Vincent's husband. He's a solicitor. He's handling the mesothelioma compensation claim. Asbestos related death.'

'I'm too stressed to chat.'

'I'm trying to distract you.'

'I'm going to fail, miserably, and my career will be in ruins.'

I put my arms around her.

I said, 'Well first of all, you're very unlikely to fail, but even if you did, it wouldn't be the end of the world.'

'Yes it would,'

You can take the exam again. Or rethink your career. It isn't carved in stone. CHLOE SWIFT MUST BECOME A CONSULTANT CARDIOLOGIST.'

'Daddy would be disappointed.'

'No he wouldn't. You're already his star child. Sister, farmer's wife. Brother, car salesman.'

'Charlie's a bit more than a car salesman. You smell of chips.'

'It's possible.'

'You had chips and didn't bring me any?'

'You said you couldn't eat a thing. Do you want me to fetch you some?'

'No. They'll make me sleepy and I still have stacks and stacks to revise.'

'Don't overload.'

'I'm not.'

'Sex might be a good idea. It'd help you relax?'

'I'm wearing my onesie.'

'I know how to deal with a onesie. Trust me, I'm a doctor.'

Afterwards, lying in bed, she said, 'You do talk about this Helen Vincent a lot. Do you have a crush on her?'

I said, 'Darling, Helen Vincent is my training supervisor. She's also old enough to be my mother.'

Which was completely beside the point, but I felt very much better for saying it.

CHAPTER 14.

Chloe's exams took place over two days. After the first day she was all gloom. She came home and went straight to bed with her stuffed Eeyore. As a rule I won't have him in bed with us so he sits on the chair where she dumps her clothes, but her need for him is a pretty accurate indicator of her stress levels so I let it pass.

Day 2 was a different story. She felt it had gone very well and she went out for the evening with her friends, to celebrate the end of revising. She mentioned Hua and Mun-Hee. I didn't ask if Jamil was going. I'd decided to be a grownup about him.

I phoned Mam to see how my Nan was doing. She'd managed to persuade her to see their GP and his verdict was that she was suffering from mild cognitive impairment.

Mam said, 'Well I could have told him that. Forgetting things, imagining things. Otherwise, she's tip top. Her blood pressure's better than mine. So all we can do is keep an eye. You'll see for yourself how she is. You still coming for Christmas?'

The unresolved C question.

I said, 'I think so.'

'Smashing. I'll borrow Aunty June's air bed.'

'Why?'

'Chloe can have your old bed and you can have the box-room.'

'There are two beds in my old room. We do live together, you know?'

'I know. I just feel a bit funny about it, Dan. You two sharing when you're not married yet. What will your Nan think?'

'She doesn't need to know. Is Adam coming? If he's staying over, put him in the box-room.'

She started the relay-to-Da routine. I've shown her how to use speaker-phone but she never remembers.

'Dan's saying why not put him and Chloe in together and give Adam the airbed.'

I heard Da say 'Right you are.'

I don't think my father could care less about the sleeping arrangements.

'Come Christmas Eve, can you? Or earlier?'

'It'll depend on Chloe's shifts.'

'And go to the match with your Da, on Boxing Day?'

'I think I've got an out-of-hours shift on Boxing night.'

'He might not get to the match with you, Ed. He might be working.'

'Right you are.'

Going to the match is one of our Boxing Day family traditions. The menfolk freeze their backsides off at Bailey Park while the women stay home, watch the telly and eat chocolate.

I said, 'And has Adam actually said he's coming?'

'You know what he's like. He never organises anything till the last minute. I reckon we shall have to bring him handcuffed and shackled to your wedding.'

'If he doesn't want to come, I won't want him there.'

'But he'll be your Best Man.'

He won't. You need somebody you can rely on. I didn't say that to Mam though.

'And you still haven't fixed the date?'

'No, but we're hoping it'll be in the summer.'

'You keep saying that, but what blooming century? I don't know why you don't just get on with it. How hard is it to arrange a wedding? Book the chapel, book the hall, buy a dress. You could get it all done in one day.'

'I think it'll be a bit more elaborate than chapel and the village hall. I think Vinnie has big plans.'

'Who's Vinnie?'

'Chloe's Mum. Lavinia.'

'Well then I hope she'll be paying for it. I don't want you bankrupting yourself. The money people spend on weddings these days. Remember Ceri Hargest?'

'Vaguely.'

'Ginger hair. She used to be a scrawny little thing. Turn her sideways she'd disappear, although she's put up a lot of weight lately. She married a boy from Blaenavon only they went to Jamaica for the wedding. Jamaica! What must that have cost? And then her dress went missing. Lost in transit. It only arrived the morning of the wedding. I'm just saying, Ed, how Ceri Hargest nearly had to get married in the clothes she stood up in. And her father got mugged. He only stepped outside the hotel for five minutes and boom, he was robbed.'

'Don't worry, we won't be going to Jamaica to get married. What shall we bring, for Christmas? A couple of bottles?'

'That'd be nice. I like that Pink Blush. You can bring your washing as well.'

'We have a washing machine here, Mam.'

'All right. Well bring your shirts for ironing. It's a pity you can't stay longer.'

'Everybody wants time off over Christmas, Mam. I don't mind working. A few years down the line it'll be different, once we've got a family.'

'Let's get you married first. The girls I get on the unit, Dan, there's hardly any of them married. They come in with their boyfriend. Next time you see them, next baby, it's a different boyfriend. I delivered one last week. Second baby and the chap who came in with her wasn't even the father. Whoever the father was, he hadn't lasted the nine months.

Nice girl, but I ask you! Posterior presentation so she was very slow to dilate. She said she intended getting married when her kiddies were old enough to be ring bearers. The world's gone mad. In our day you got married and you kept a tier of the wedding cake for the first christening. I'm just saying, Ed, in our day....'

Mam rang me back three times that evening. The first time, to tell me not to bring presents.

'Save your money, boy,' she said. 'Me and your Da have everything we need.'

Then to say she'd just spoken to Adam and he most probably would come for Christmas, but he'd let her know nearer the time.

'So the usual non-commitment.'

'He doesn't like to be pressured. You know that.'

'Mam, do you think it possible Adam has a life we don't know about?'

'How do you mean?'

'Maybe he's in a secret relationship. Something he doesn't want to tell us?'

'Such as?'

'Like having an affair? Married woman, maybe?'

'Don't be daft. Adam doesn't like complications, you know that.'

'Could he be gay?'

'Never!'

'Think about it. Has he ever mentioned a girlfriend?'

'Not that I'd mind if he was.'

'Da might not be too thrilled.'

'Anyway, he's not. I'm his mother. I'd know if he was. Elton John... now he's, you know...'

'Yes, but Elton John's possibly not the best litmus test, vis-à-vis Adam.'

Third call.

'What it is, I've been thinking about what you said, about your brother, and I don't see there's any way… you know? I won't say the word because your Da's in the room. Adam played rugby for heaven's sake.'

'Er, how about Gareth Thomas?'

Silence.

Then, 'No, Gareth Thomas played full-back. Your brother played prop forward.'

I said, 'You're right, Mam. I should have thought of that. Adam can't possibly be gay.'

Chloe came in very late and very drunk.

'Nice evening?'

'I think so.'

'Relieved it's all over?'

'Yeah. No more exams. Ever. Ever.'

'I was thinking, now you don't have to study, we could have some people over for dinner.'

'Why?'

'I'd like to invite Vaz. I don't think he has much of a social life. Maybe try to fix him up with one of your friends. Who's single?'

'Everybody.'

'Who's single and would like not to be?'

No reply. She'd fallen asleep. I put Eeyore back on his chair, picked up her coat from the floor. And her gloves and scarf. The vicuna scarf, worth a king's ransom, left at the Chummery, posted back to us by Vinnie after some serious, daily nagging and returned, or so I thought, to its owner, the Lebanese moneybags. My girlfriend was wearing Jamil's damned scarf again.

It was almost the first thing I thought of when I woke. To say something, or not? I decided not. Could I honestly, cross my heart and hope to die in a cellar full of rats, say that I had never looked at another woman since Chloe came into my life? There had been a very pretty nurse at the Panwar practice. Not that I'd have dreamed of doing anything about it, but I had enjoyed the view.

Trevor was back at work by Friday. He looked much better.

'A Combivent nebuliser and three days at home with Mrs Buxton. It does wonders.'

'Is that because she's a good nurse?'

'She can plump a pillow with the best of them, yes, but she has the additional restorative feature of sisters who like to visit. If it isn't one of them it's the other. A threat like that can make a man rally.'

'How will you cope when you retire?'

'I've been thinking about that. I might buy a garden shed. Or I might just carry on working till I drop. But don't tell Helen. She'll be planning to go through the place like a dose of Epsom salts, as soon as she's shot of me. She won't want me hanging around, making the place look untidy.'

I couldn't say what I was thinking: that work would become impossible for him eventually. COPD can be a slow-moving animal but there comes a time when you're breathless even sitting in an armchair. Getting dressed knocks you out. Then the strain on your heart starts to show. But Trevor knew all that.

He said, 'I need a retirement plan. I might work on developing a few vile habits, something to repel the sisters-in law. Gratuitous farting. Walking around with my tackle hanging out. So what have I missed?'

'Ron Jarrold is lobbying for consultations by email.'

'Ron? As in Ron and Freda, Been on Google?'

'You know he's on the Patient Panel?'

'I try not to know anything about the Patient Panel. I pretend it doesn't exist."

'Well it does and Ron Jarrold's on it, and he thinks patients should be able to email their GP with a list of their symptoms, so they don't have to wait for an appointment or sit in the waiting room getting coughed and sneezed on. Have you got email, Trevor?'

'Probably. It sounds like the kind of thing Stephanie would have insisted on.'

'You'd better make sure Ron and Freda don't get hold of your address.'

'People like the Jarrolds soon won't need us, Dan. All those years, all those exams, it's all going down the crapper. Everyone'll go on Google and we'll be redundant.'

'What is your email address, out of interest?'

'Haven't the faintest. Got a pin? Here, pick a horse, any horse. You can't do any worse than me.'

My biro landed on Man Overboard in the last race at Sedgefield.

'Not a chance,' he said, but he phoned the bet in anyway.

He said, 'I hear you've managed very well without me so you might as well carry on. You take surgery and I'll just sit behind the Racing Post and eavesdrop.'

I went out to fetch the mail. Helen was in Reception.

'Dan' she said, 'two things. Could you fit in a visit to Woodleigh Grange at lunchtime? Mac's not back till Tuesday.'

'Sure. Who's the patient?'

'I don't know. Mary'll tell you.'

She started to walk away.

'You said there were two things?'

'Did I? Oh yes. Do you remember Keith Sideaway? Drooping eyelid and reduced pupil?'

'How could I forget!'

'Come in after morning surgery. I'll show you his

radiology report.'

Glenys Allsop's scan results had arrived as well. Trevor read the hospital letter and then passed it to me.

'Not good,' he said. 'Not good at all. Should we get her in today? No, leave it till next week. The hospital will have given her enough to think about.

'Primary biliary cholangitis.'

'We used to call it cirrhosis but they changed it. I don't usually approve of changing the names of things but in this case I think it was justified. People heard the word 'cirrhosis' and they assumed you must be an incurable drunk. So, what would be your care plan, Dr Dan?'

'Reduced fat diet? Oral cholestyramine?'

He nodded.

'Will you talk to her about a transplant, or do we leave that to the hospital? Will they have discussed it with her?'

'Possibly, but we shouldn't take it for granted. No use us assuming she's on the waiting list for a liver when she might not be. We could make enquiries. No, let's see if she brings it up. Play it by ear. Now, what delights have we got this morning?'

The first patients were Wolf and Bronte Shotton. The surname seemed familiar, but I definitely hadn't seen them before. Wolf was five, Bronte was two. The mother was a very big girl in leggings and saggy sheepskin boots. Jade. She was pushing one of those double-decker pushchairs, with a baby in the top layer and Bronte grizzling on the lower deck. Wolf hung back by the door.

Trevor said, 'Hello, Jade. Dr Talbot's going to look after you this morning.'

Jade said both the boys were cranky and kept rubbing their eyes.

They looked hot. Bronte's temperature was 101 degrees.

He had a runny nose and red eyes. Wolf wasn't keen on having his temperature taken. Trevor made an airplane out of an eating disorders pamphlet and flew it at him. That coaxed him a little further into the room. Another paper plane and he allowed me to use the tympanic thermometer on him. He was burning up. 102 degrees.

I said, 'Do your boys usually look this pink?'

Jade said she didn't know. I took a peep at the baby. She was sleeping and not at all pink. She was coffee-coloured.

Trevor looked over the top of his newspaper.

'Any Koplik spots?' He pointed into his mouth.

I checked Bronte. He had tiny white spots on the insides of his cheeks. Wolf wouldn't open his mouth.

Trevor said, 'Jade, have your boys had their MMR jabs?'

Then I understood what he was getting at. They weren't pink just because they were hot. They both had big flat red spots, so many they were practically joined up. Measles.

'I think so,' says Jade.

'Well young Wolf would have had his second shot a few months ago, before he started school. You'd remember that.'

'No. I don't think so. There's too much to remember.'

'The clinic would have written it on a card for you.'

He went back behind his paper.

I said, 'Has anyone else in his class been off sick?'

'Don't know.'

I said, 'Okay. Take them home. Give them plenty to drink. Calpol if they can't sleep. And keep the curtains closed while their eyes are bothering them.'

She said she hadn't got curtains.

'Then find something to hang over the windows,' says Trevor. 'Or buy them some Mickey Mouse sunglasses from the chemist. And if the baby doesn't get a rash, make sure you get her vaccinated. How old is she?'

'Nearly one.'

'Right. When you get the appointment card, take her to the clinic. Don't ignore it. What's her name?'

'Nivea.'

'Very nice.'

Wolf went and stood right by Trevor. He was hoping for another plane.

'You're in luck, young man,' says Trevor. 'I'm allowed one more piece of paper today.'

He made a fighter jet. He's very good with children. It's a pity he doesn't have any grandchildren.

'Fucking Nivea,' he said, when Jade had left. 'What kind of a name is that to give a child? And measles. I thought those days were gone forever.'

'I'd never seen it before.'

'You wouldn't have. And you shouldn't have. It ought to be a thing of the past.'

'Pam Parker was predicting there'd be an outbreak. She's got several mothers who don't vaccinate. It's a notifiable disease, right?'

'It is. There's a form. And make sure it goes off today. One of the Marys can fax it to the Health Department.'

'Jade Shotton. Is she the one Kyle Bibby was talking about? Said she was claiming he was the father of her baby?'

'Very likely. Kyle gets around and God knows, so does Jade.'

'Well I don't think that baby can be Kyle's. She looked mixed race to me.'

'There you are then. Kyle Bibby isn't a complete idiot after all.'

A verruca, a painful mouse-click wrist, various coughs, chesty, tickly and dry, a 77 year old who was getting forgetful, a couple of lonelies who needed to chat and a woman called Raquel who wanted breast augmentation on the NHS.

I was about to say her breasts looked all right to me but

then thought that wouldn't sound quite right. I asked her why she felt she needed bigger breasts.

'For me self-esteem,' she said.

I said, 'I have to tell you, that kind of procedure is very low priority.'

'Practically non-existent,' says Trevor, over the top of his racing paper.

I said, 'To give you some idea, we have patients waiting months even for urgent hip replacements.'

'Important though, isn't it? Self-esteem. What if I topped myself?'

'Do you ever think about doing that?'

'No. But I might do, if I don't get implants, I could get depressed. Then there's no telling.'

'You don't strike me as lacking self-esteem, Raquel. You strike me as quite a confident person.'

'No. I did a quiz about self-esteem, in Take Five, and I've definitely not got it. I need you to write a letter.'

Trevor put his paper down.

He said, 'Leave it with us, Raquel. Like Dr Dan said, you'll have a long wait. Come back in twelve months, if you haven't heard anything.'

'But I bet they get cancellations,' she said. 'Great. Thanks Doctor. I'm going to get DD cup.'

She went off smiling. A happy end-user, as Stephanie would style it.

I said, 'We're not actually going to write that letter, are we?'

'Letter?' says Trevor. 'What letter?'

'And what do we say when she comes back complaining that she hasn't heard from the hospital?'

'Things get lost in the system, Dan. Fact of life. Non-urgent referrals. It's like the Bermuda Fucking Triangle.'

I looked in on Helen.

'About Keith Sideaway?'

'Yes. Come in. It's very interesting. He has a Pancoast tumour in the apex of his left lung, Stage III. His chest X-ray looked clear but they did an MRI as well, given his symptoms. And there it was, tucked behind his collar bone, an adenoma. It could easily have been missed. He has spots on two vertebrae as well, and two ribs.'

'Will they operate?'

'Tricky, given where the tumour is. They've offered him neoadjuvant chemo and/or radiation. They'll try to shrink the mass, then they'll assess him for surgery.'

'Not a good prognosis is it?'

'Not great. So, there you have it. Horner's Syndrome and a Pancoast tumour. You'll probably go the rest of your working life and never see either of them again.'

CHAPTER 15.

Mac was away and I was asked to visit one of his nursing home patients. Hilda Ruck was an 89 year old resident of Woodleigh Grange. She'd been having episodes of breathlessness. The nursing manager, Carmel, thought they were just a bid for attention.

Hilda's chest sounded clear. She looked anxious though.

'Where's Dr Mac?' she said.

'On holiday. He'll be back next week.'

'Will he come on Monday?'

I said, 'Miss Ruck, are you worried about something?'

She beckoned me to go closer, so she could whisper.

She said, 'I don't want that woman listening to my affairs.'

She meant the manager.

I said, 'Carmel, Miss Ruck and I are going to go for a little walk, so I can see whether she gets breathless when she's active.'

'She won't do,' says Carmel. 'She only gets breathless when it suits her.'

But she left us alone.

Miss Ruck held my hand.

She said, 'It's a secret.'

'Well you can tell me if you'd like to. It's up to you.'

'I don't want to make Dr Mac cross.'

'Does he get cross?'

'Not at all. He's very kind. He's a wonderful doctor. But he might get cross if things don't get done.'

'And what needs to be done?'

'Two things. I'm supposed to change to the coloured doctor.'

'Dr Vaz?'

'I think that's his name.'

'And why are you supposed to change?'

'Dr Mac said it would be for the best, but I don't really want to. It's not because the other doctor's coloured. I just don't like change.'

'Neither do I. And I can't think of any reason why you should need to change doctors. Dr Mac visits all the nursing homes. I think there might have been a misunderstanding. You can talk to him about it when he gets back. And what was the other thing that was supposed to happen?'

She hesitated.

'It's the solicitor, you see. Holding things up. He says I should talk to Michelle about it, but it's none of her business.'

'Who's Michelle?'

'My niece. But what's it to do with her? I never see her. Dr Mac's the one who visits me.'

'Is it to do with your Will or something?'

'Yes. Well no, not exactly. It's private. It's between me and Dr Mac.'

'I'm sure he wouldn't want you worrying on his account.'

'No, but a promise is a promise. And that solicitor has no right. I was never going to leave anything to Michelle anyway. I don't like her.'

I said, 'Today's Thursday. Nothing gets done over weekends. But I'll ask Dr Mac to come and see you as soon as he gets back. Try not to get worked up about it. Like you said, Dr Mac is a kind man.'

She seemed calmer. She smiled. Her dentures were a bit loose.

'Thank you, Doctor,' she said. 'You're very young.'

'I'm 30.'

'Dr Mac's 52. Some of them in here call him my boyfriend but there's nothing untoward between us. He's my friend and they're just jealous.'

Carmel gave me a long, hard look as we were leaving.

I said, 'I think Miss Ruck could use some denture fixative.'

I sat in the Lindens car park for a while and tried to get my thoughts in some sort of order. What to do? Should I do anything? Hilda Ruck had spoken to me in confidence. Mac was a respected partner in the practice. If a grateful patient chose to leave her doctor something in her Will, was there anything wrong in it? She might be leaving him a fortune. Or just a pair of china dogs. What if she was dotty? What if she wasn't?

Trevor rapped on the glass. I lowered my window.

'Fathomed it out yet?'

'What?'

'Whatever it is you're puzzling over.'

That was when I decided I wouldn't say anything. I'd make a few discreet enquiries. I'd maybe discuss it with Chloe.

Three times during the afternoon list the computer flagged CANDIDATE FOR STATINS? One of the patients actually requested them. They'd been offering cholesterol tests at one of the shopping centres and he'd been told his LDL was high. I prescribed Lipitor 10mg.

At the end of surgery Trevor said, 'Let's talk about statins.'

I said, 'I know you don't approve.'

'Not strictly true,' he said. 'It's more complicated than that. They have their uses. We're overdue this conversation. Here or the Black Bear?'

'Here. I've got a shift at Sterling.'

'Okay, once upon a time I had a patient, let's call her Mrs Smith, early sixties, fit as a fiddle, but her brother had just had a triple bypass so she was worried about her arteries and she wanted me to start her on statins. We looked at her

154

cholesterol, LDL 120, HDL 60. I told her, enviable numbers. So I thought I'd put her mind at rest but apparently I hadn't because a week or two later she went to see another doctor, who shall remain nameless. The next time I saw her, getting on for a year later, she had chronic diarrhoea and brain fog. She was like a different woman, Dan.'

'Because she was taking statins?'

'Because she'd gone from taking nothing to taking five medications. The statins had made a slight difference to her cholesterol, but she'd developed muscle pain. It's quite a common side effect. She took ibuprofen every day for the myalgia, which led to a stomach ulcer and hypertension. So then she was put on a proton pump inhibitor for her stomach and a beta-blocker for her blood pressure, and as if all that wasn't enough she was popping loperamide like Smarties because she was afraid of being caught short when she was out shopping.'

'But if the statins had been better monitored…'

'Yes. Or not prescribed at all. How about that? I mean, what kind of margin of improvement are we looking for?'

'What would our position be if, say, Mrs Smith had taken your advice, stayed off the statins and then had a stroke?'

'Our position would be the same as it always is. We prescribe based on our considerable experience and we aim to do no harm. We don't always get it right, but equally, patients are mere humans too. They ask for advice and then ignore it. They fuck up with their meds. Their bodies get sick and wear out. We're not in the immortality business, Dan.'

'I understand.'

'It's my perspective, that's all. You can work out your own policy on statins and a dozen other thorny questions. Things used to be easier.'

'In your father's time?'

'Even in mine. When I was your age patients didn't come

in and tell you what they wanted. God Almighty, they practically bowed when they saw you.'

Miss Ruck's generation.

I could have sounded out Vaz, to see if he knew anything about Mac transferring a patient to him. Bad idea. Vaz was both a worrier and an open, honest man. Not the type to keep possibly dodgy secrets. I could have asked the Marys whether any of Mac's patients had asked to change doctors, but I was still a bit afraid of them. They both tended to sigh a lot if I asked them for anything.

I was the last to leave the building that evening, apart from Stephanie. I was hurrying to my car when I heard someone say, 'Hello Doctor. Cold innit?'

Two of the lights were out in the surgery car park so it was hard to see. She came closer. It was Amber Evans.

I said, 'Surgery's closed.'

'Yeah,' she said. 'I was just passing. Give us a lift, can you?'

The letters KDO flashed before my eyes. KEEP DOOR OPEN.

I said, 'I'm sorry, Amber. I'm on an urgent call.'

'I don't mind,' she said. 'I'll come with you. Then you can take us home.'

'No, I really have to hurry.'

'I can be quick,' she said, and she opened her puffa. I can't swear to any details, but she was wearing very little.

I said, 'Go home before you catch your death. I do not give lifts to patients. Ever. It's strictly against the rules.'

'Give you nice blowjob,' was the last thing I heard her say before I slammed the car door.

I don't know how I got to Sterling. I'd have missed a green light if the driver behind me hadn't parped his horn. Thank God I didn't miss a red light. What if Amber accused me of doing something? I had no witnesses. It'd be her word against mine. As soon as I got to the call centre I phoned Trevor. He just chuckled.

He said, 'She's a trier, that one. But don't worry. We've got security cameras. Had them installed after somebody tried to break in last year.'

'Do they cover the whole car park?'

'Buggered if I know. But nothing happened. Please tell me nothing happened.'

'I drove away, fast.'

'Then you don't have anything to worry about. Nobody'd take Amber's word anyway. She's well-documented as the community bike.'

'Has she ever tried anything with you?'

'No, I don't think even Amber's that desperate. But as I recall she did once offer Mac a quickie. One thing, Dan. I think we'd better adjust her file cover. In surgery KDO. In car park KDL.'

'L?'

'Locked, lad. Locked. Relax, don't fret.'

It was after midnight when I got in, but Chloe was still up. To tell her about the Amber incident? To tell her about Hilda Ruck? Neither. Chloe was eager to tell me about her day. She'd been called down to A&E.

She said, 'Okay, see what you make of this, Dr Talbot. A 73 year old male, no significant history, admitted with gradual onset sub-sternal chest pain and diffuse elevated ST waves.'

'Myocardial infarction.'

'Wait, wait. They'd given him nitroglycerin in the ambulance but the pain worsened.'

'A very severe myocardial infarction?'

'His temperature was 101.'

'I'm obviously missing something here. Was it an acute

abdomen leading you astray?'

'That was what Mun-Hee thought. I went to have a listen to his heart and I noticed that when I got him sitting upright the pain wasn't as bad.'

'Positional pain.'

'Correct. And then what do you think I heard?'

'Classic FM? Go on.'

'Pericardial rub.'

'You are so clever. What does it sound like?'

'Squeaky leather. He had pericarditis.'

'Brilliant. So what, drain the fluid and start him on antibiotics? Or is it usually viral?'

'I haven't finished my story. While the senior reg was listening, confirming my diagnosis, the old boy's blood pressure suddenly went through the floor and he lost consciousness. PEA.'

Remind me.'

'Pulseless Electrical Activity. He'd suffered a cardiac tamponade.'

'Caused by pressure from the inflamed pericardium?'

'Right.'

'But you got him back?'

'No. We shocked him three times, then we called it.'

'Fuck. I'm sorry.'

'Why? I made the diagnosis, Dan. I was the one who noticed the pain was positional, plus he had a fever. I was the one who put two and two together.'

'But he then died.'

'Well he was 73.'

I suppose everyone has a different idea of what constitutes a good day.

'Can I run a hypothetical case by you?'

'Why? I've finished my exams.'

'It comes to your notice that a frail old lady, with no close family, is apparently making some kind of deal, possibly financial, with her attending physician. What do you do?'

'Are you talking about Trevor Buxton?'

'No.'

'The Vincent woman?'

'No. It's a hypothetical scenario.'

'Bet it's not. It must be the other one. Macwhatsit. Does he seem like a criminal?'

'He doesn't wear a mask and carry a bag marked Swag. And I'm not saying it is him. I'm just wondering about the ethics.'

She said, 'I'm sure Daddy's been remembered in a few Wills. By grateful patients.'

'But without exercising undue influence? Your father's patients aren't confused. They're not vulnerable.'

'Daddy and Mummy had a lovely holiday in the Virgin Islands one time. Gorgeous beach house. It belonged to some old pop singer Daddy treated for vocal cord nodules. I mean, would you consider that unethical?'

'No. A bit icky, but not unethical. If, say, you thought Barrington had benefited financially from a patient who didn't know what they were doing, would you say anything?'

'Barrington? He doesn't need to rob old ladies. He's loaded.'

Chloe can be extremely dense sometimes.

She was in the mood for sex. I wasn't much. The Amber thing was on my mind. But I was open to persuasion.

'I've run out of pills so you'll have to wear a noddy.'

'I don't think I have any. We haven't used those for ages.'

'Well that's no fucking use.'

'The SPAR is probably open. I could go and buy some.'

'Forget it. It doesn't matter. By the time you get back I'll have gone off the idea. I thought boy scouts were always prepared.'

'I wasn't in the scouts. St John's Ambulance, me.'

I would have gone. It's never a bad idea to be prepared with a pack of noddies. But then her phone rang.

'Who the hell phones at 1 a.m?'

'It's Hua. She's on nights.'

Hua was having a slow shift and if she couldn't sleep, she didn't see why anyone else should. She'd heard about Chloe and the pericarditis case.

'No Hua girl,' I heard her say. 'Mun-Hee so did not diagnose it. I did.'

Flaky behaviour from Mun-Hee, apparently. Those cardiology wannabees could be so ruthless.

I went in to work early. I was feeling ropey, not enough sleep, but I wanted to check the security cameras. Trevor might not be concerned about Amber Evans's little games, but I wanted solid evidence, just in case she made any allegations.

I got to The Lindens just before eight. There was a police car parked in Pam Parker's space. My stomach did that oh-shit, freefall thing.

CHAPTER 16

Like all innocent people, I get nervous around the police. When you're working in A&E and there are police in attendance, it's different. You're comrades in arms, almost. They're trying to hold the thin blue line, you're trying to manage the blood red one, and you know that you, personally, are peripheral to their inquiries. But when you think you might be questioned about an encounter with a half-dressed patient in a dark car park, boy can that put the wind up you.

Stephanie was in, and so was Helen. She had bed hair and her coat buttons were out of sync.

'We've had a break in,' says Stephanie. 'They were after the drugs' cabinet.'

Someone had broken in through a window at the rear of the building, into Helen's office. There was a boot print on the door to the nurses' room where it had been kicked in. Trevor arrived just after me, then Mary, then Nurse Chris. She went with the policeman to check what had been taken.

Trevor said, 'I suppose we have to go through the motions but it's a waste of time. They never caught the varmints who did us last year.'

I said, 'But you've got security cameras now.'

'Oh yes,' he said. 'The security cameras. They'll make interesting viewing. Have you all heard about Dan's encounter with Amber Evans?'

No-one seemed interested.

'Last night, in the car park. She flashed him and offered him a blowjob. I tell you, there's never a dull moment around here.'

Stephanie said, 'Was there any physical contact?'

I said, 'Of course not. I jumped in my car and drove off.

The cameras will show that.'

But Helen said there wasn't anything on the tape.

'Don't tell me the camera didn't cover where I was standing?'

'No. The machine wasn't working. I already checked.'

And Stephanie said, 'Actually, it was working until you messed with it. I told you not to touch it till the police had looked at it.'

'Oh for goodness sake,' says Helen. 'What does the tape matter anyway? A blurry image of some dipstick from Cherry Tree and no doubt wearing the same hoodie as all the other dipsticks. Whoever it was, he'll have nicked a few high value items like tube bandages and sold them for a can of cider. It's not exactly the crime of the century.'

I said, 'Are you saying there's nothing on the tape?'

'Wiped, apparently,' says Stephanie. 'Brilliant, eh?'

I said, 'But that tape might have saved my skin if Amber Evans starts making allegations.'

'Amber Evans?' says Helen. 'She's just simple-minded. Everybody knows that. She won't be any trouble.'

Stephanie said, 'Still, how about covering Dr Talbot's back instead of worrying about your own?'

Everything went very quiet. Then Helen said, 'What do you mean by that?' and Stephanie said, 'You known damned well what I mean.'

Chris and the policeman emerged from the nurses' room. She said some Co-Codamol had been taken and a box of xylocaine sprays. The locked cabinet where we keep the morphine sulphate vials had been wrenched off the wall, but they hadn't managed to open it.

Trevor said it was nothing to lose sleep over, but Chris was upset. She said, 'I'm sure I locked the door.'

'You did,' said Stephanie. 'I always check before I leave.

But that door is nothing but hardboard panels and egg boxes. I've been saying we should get something stronger. No-one listens to me. What about the boot print?'

The copper said there was a partial one on Helen's windowsill as well so someone would come and photograph it before we got the glass replaced, but he didn't hold out much hope. He said half the usual suspects would be wearing the same knock-off trainers.

Vaz arrived. The police left. Helen went home for a quick shower before surgery started. As she was leaving she said, 'Cheer up, Dan. You look like you lost a pound and found a penny.'

I said, 'I'd be a lot happier if the tape had recorded what happened to me last night.'

'Oh that,' she said. 'Forget it. Amber Evans is just a silly cow, the break-in was just vandalism and now we all need to get on with the day's work.'

Stephanie followed me into Trevor's office.

'Dr Buxton,' she said. 'I'd like a word. Regarding the security cameras.'

He said, 'You don't need to say it.'

Stephanie was red-faced with fury.

'But I will say it. I won't be silenced. Dr Vincent wiped that tape.'

'Are you sure about that?'

'Absolutely. Because I got here first. I saw the broken glass, called the police, called Dr Vincent because that's the agreed procedure now you're retiring. Then I checked the security tape. There was definitely stuff on it. She turns up and the first thing she does is go into Reception and start messing with the machine. And we all know why.'

Trevor took off his specs, rubbed his eyes.

He said, 'That's a big leap, Stephanie.'

But there was no stopping her.

'We all know about Miles Vincent. Every time he comes here to get money from her, he's snooping around. I've caught him in the nurses' room more than once.'

'Miles has his problems.'

'Yes, and she thinks it could have been him. And now she's destroyed the evidence. That's called obstructing the course of justice.'

Trevor said, 'Still, just a few pills taken. And the police have enough to do, catching real villains. Let Helen deal with Miles.'

I said, 'And what about me?'

But no-one was listening. Stephanie had turned on her heel and left the room. Trevor was rattled. Moving things around on his desk, taking his cigarette case out, looking at it, putting it back in his inside pocket.

Eventually he said, 'Don't fret about Amber. Everyone knows what she's like. She's probably offered it to half the constabulary. She won't be making any allegations.'

Don't fret Dan, they all said. Everyone knows what Amber's like, they all said. Let Helen deal with Miles. Were Stephanie and I the only people in the practice who took things seriously?

I said, 'If it was Helen's son it might be doing both of them a favour if he got his collar felt. It might be what he needs.'

'Do you think so?' says Trevor. 'His old man's a solicitor, don't forget. You can be sure Clifford'd find a way to get him off. No, best to clean up the mess and carry on as per. Keep it in the family.'

Family. That's what they were at The Lindens, and I was just a lodger, passing through.

'By the way,' says Trevor, 'Man Overboard won by a nose. Incredible. I think I'll let you pick my bets again.'

By lunchtime the police had finished gathering evidence, Helen's window had been repaired, the carpenter was on his way to hang a new door and I had become a figure of fun. Nurse Linda came in, even though it was her day off. She'd heard about my encounter with Amber. She said she'd come to help Chris clear up, but she kept bumping into me and giving me a knowing smile. Even Pam Parker had heard the news and dropped in to add her twopennyworth.

'Amber Evans strikes again. Was she starkers?'

'Bra and pants, I think. It was pretty dark out there.'

'Be thankful for small mercies. She has plenty of previous, of course.'

'So everyone tells me.'

'And she's just the latest in a long line of fuckbunny nutcases. Trevor'll tell you. There was one patient, I can't remember her name, not in the first flush, her charms had moved south, but she was still on the prowl. I'm talking about years ago, pre-kids, when I was still working full-time. I went out to her on a house call. She was expecting to see Trevor. She came to the door, the dressing gown fell open and I got the full frontal. I don't know who was more surprised, me or her.'

'What do you think about the break-in?'

'It's not the first time and I'm sure it won't be the last.'

'It's a pity the tape got wiped.'

'Did it?'

'Helen wiped it.'

'Right.'

Pam gave me a what-can-you-do shrug.

'Well,' she said, eventually, 'you have to feel sorry for her. What an embarrassment.'

'So you think it could have been Miles who broke in?'

'Does a wooden horse have a hickory dick?'

'You don't think it's wrong to cover it up?'

165

She said, 'Listen, we're the Six Musketeers here. All for one and one for all. The main thing is, he didn't get into the morphine cabinet. And I'm not one to judge another parent. Someday you'll have kids. You'll find out. Are we chucking Amber off our list?'

'I don't think so. But I won't see her. From now on if she wants to see a doctor it has to be you or Helen.'

'Definitely. I mean, in a way I'd be sorry to lose her. Who else offers free bareback rides to an entire community? Who else would shove an old Nokia up her joy trail? We've had three more measles cases, did you hear? And who's the common denominator? Nicola Won't Bloody Vaccinate Willetts. They're all in the same class as her boy, Conan.'

Trevor went to the pub, Helen took her salad into her office. I decided I'd walk down to the Wavy Line, get some fresh air and a meat pie. Vaz asked if he could come with me.

As soon as we were outside he said, 'This is very serious matter, Dan. I have thought of this all morning.'

'About Helen's son?'

'No. What about Helen's son?'

'Nothing. What's on your mind?'

'About the lady in the car park. Is Helen's son sick?'

'No. He does drugs. Stephanie thinks it might have been him who broke in last night. She accused Helen of wiping the security camera pictures.'

'This is also a serious matter. But about the lady in the car park. How did you know what to do?'

'I didn't. It all happened so fast. Jumping in the car seemed the only option. Thank God it started first time. When it's cold it can take a couple of tries.'

'What would you have done if she had been lying on the ground?'

'I don't know. Driven round her?'

'But what if she seemed to be in distress? What if she made cries of pain? This could happen.'

I hadn't thought of that.

I asked Vaz what he was doing for the weekend. Nothing much apart from church and a Sunday evening shift at Sterling. I invited him to dinner. It was spur of the moment thing but the more I thought about it the more I liked the idea. Chloe's exams were over and Vaz was a nice guy. He said he'd like to come, very much.

There was more trouble when we got back to the surgery. The carpenters had arrived so Helen had told Nurse Chris to take her afternoon dressings appointments in Stephanie's office. Stephanie said she was far too busy to give up her office and Chris would have to make alternative arrangements. Chris burst into tears.

I offered to clear a bit of space in the little room where they kept an overspill of patient files. 'Dr Talbot,' says Helen, 'you're here to practice medicine, not move furniture. Please attend to your patients.'

Another telling off, carpeted by the headmistress, or was I being over-sensitive. Trevor appeared.

'Now what?'

Helen said, 'We can't use the nurses' office while the carpenters are here.'

'Why not?'

'Patient privacy.'

'And why is Chris crying?'

'Nothing to do with me,' says Helen. 'Stephanie's upset her.'

Trevor said, 'I'll do dressings. Chris, go home.'

Helen opened her mouth to object but he waved her away.

'Give the girl a break, Helen,' he said. 'She's had a shit

morning. And I'll bet she's got a pile of ironing needs doing at home. Three growing lads. Off you go, sweetheart. Send me your corned beef can cuts and weeping ulcers. Clear the decks. I'll do them in the kitchen.'

I started afternoon surgery solo. I wasn't sorry. I was feeling stung by Helen and a bit awkward around Trevor. I wanted to talk to him about Mac and Hilda Ruck but how to broach it? He didn't agree with me about Amber Evans or Helen and the security tapes. He didn't agree with me about statins. I was an outsider. The boy scout. Not one of the musketeers. But of course, he didn't know how I was feeling.

When he'd finished dressings, he joined me for the rest of surgery. He was waving a piece of paper.

'Remember Stuart Curtain? His bloods are back. I thought they'd disappeared down the lab plug hole. And guess what?'

'All normal?'

'All perfect. He must be the healthiest man in Tipton. But…, kindly fill in the dots, Dr Talbot.'

'He just doesn't feel right?'

We had a good laugh. My cloud lifted a little. Our 4 o'clock was a no-show. I made two mugs of tea.

'Female patients,' says Trevor, out of the blue. 'On the whole it's not so much the barmpots like Amber you need to watch out for. It's the seemingly normal women who fall in love with you.'

'Pam Parker was telling me about one of your patients she went to. Came to greet you at the door in the altogether?'

'Oh yes. That was, can't remember name. Sad soul. Lonely. Yes, I've had offers. Not recently, I might add. Quite surprising, though, a couple of them. Sometimes passion seethes beneath a Marks and Sparks blouse.'

'What did you do?'

'I expressed gratitude for the compliment and passed their

files straight to Helen. I also used to keep a photo of Mrs Buxton and the kiddies on my desk, to discourage any triers. You might think of it. A nice big picture of the girlfriend. Some women have a thing about doctors. Maybe it's the Mills & Boons they read. No, actually, I think it was Dr Kildare who started it.'

'Was he in the practice?'

'No lad, he was a telly doctor, before you were born. In the Sixties. Richard Chamberlain. It broke Mrs Buxton's heart when someone told her he was a woofter.'

'Vaz raised a good point. What if Amber Evans had feigned being ill? If she'd been on the ground, pretending to cry out in pain, say, my first instinct would have been to go over to her. Next thing you know, I'm caught on camera bending over a half-naked female patient. Then what?'

'Hmm,' says Trevor. 'I'll have to get back to you on that.'

Mary looked in before the next patient.

'Dr Buxton,' she said, 'I thought I'd put the Christmas decorations up on Monday. Do you have any objections?'

Trevor said, 'No. Proceed. But nothing musical, please. And nothing with flashing lights.'

'I don't need telling that. How many years have I worked here?'

'I dread to think. Have you ever thought of a change? You'd make a very good warder at Drake Hall.'

'You've got Kevin Hodge next and serve you blummin' well right.'

'Moira,' he called as she was closing the door behind her. She came back in.

'While we're on the dreaded topic of Christmas, has anybody thought about the staff party?'

'Dr Helen's choosing a date,' she said. 'And I'm Mary.'

'I know you are,' he said. 'Just making sure you know who you are. Just keeping you on your toes.'

I said, 'What's Drake Hall?'

'Women's prison,' he said. 'It's between Stafford and Stoke-on-Trent. Quite progressive, I believe. They can train to be hairdressers or beauticians before they're tipped back into society. Mary'd soon lick them into shape. So would Moira. Either of them.'

I'd already encountered Kevin Hodge. He wasn't a troublesome patient as long as a) you gave him a sicknote and b) he got his temazepam prescription. The problem with Kevin was body odour. Trevor lit one of his forbidden cigarillos and left it burning on an ashtray.

'All set,' he said. 'Bring in the dead.'

Kevin's always very cheery. 'I've just come for me jellies,' he says, as if he's in a sweet shop picking up a regular order. But unlike many of our locals, he doesn't go out and sell them on the street. The first time I met him he said, 'Don't worry, Doctor. I'm not one of them scrotes as lets kiddies get hold of them. If I seen anybody dealing on my walkway, I'd dob them right in.'

Like Trevor says, Cherry Tree folk can be as civic-minded as the best of us. As long as they get their jellies.

As I was leaving, Mary beckoned to me.

'Dr Talbot,' she said, 'Don't you worry about Amber Evans. She won't get past me nor Moira. Next time she shows her face in here she'll be told. She can either see Dr Parker or sling her hook.'

Those were the kindest words I'd ever had from her. Moira had become slightly more friendly, once I'd passed some secret initiation test known only to her. She now accepted me as a member of the Lindens team, but it was taking longer with Mary.

I thanked her. She offered me a toffee. Was this perhaps the moment to ask her about any patient transfers from Mac to Vaz? No. It was Friday, the week had been long and challenging and I needed to get home and break the news to Chloe that we were having a dinner party in just over 24 hours.

CHAPTER 17

Chloe said, 'You are kidding? A dinner party, tomorrow?'

'Just friends round for something to eat. I'm not working, you're not working. Let's do it.'

'It's a huge amount of work.'

'No it's not. I'll cook. I want you to invite your nicest single friends. Vaz needs a girlfriend.'

'Vaz needs a change of name. And do you really think my friends don't already have plans for Saturday night?'

'Only one way to find out.'

By the time I got back from the supermarket she was on the sofa, channel-surfing.

'And? Guests for tomorrow?'

'Hua and Mun-Hee.'

'See? How hard was that?'

Her phone rang. I heard her say, 'Between seven and eight. Great. See you then.'

Another taker. Things were looking good.

'Who was that?'

'Jamil.'

'Jamil?'

'Don't start.'

'We're supposed to be finding Vaz a girl.'

'No, this Vaz thing is your project, not mine. I'm not hosting a meat market, Dan. Anyway, we need another man to even up the numbers.'

Chloe can be ever so slightly anal about even numbers. She gets it from her mother. Vinnie has this friend, Verity, who was widowed last year and the golf club ladies don't invite her to dinner any more. Vinnie said, 'Verity understands perfectly. Female odds are such a pain. There are never enough spare men.'

With Jamil on board, Chloe seemed suddenly more interested in our plans, or was it my imagination? She said she'd make her tuna dippy thing to have with drinks. And she'd be i/c vegetables because I always overcook them.

'What about pud?'

'We don't eat pud.'

'I do, given the opportunity. Tiramisu is nice, although you really need to start that the day before. And we don't have any Marsala.'

'No, too faffy and too fattening. Get mango sorbet. And put pistachios on the shopping list, and hummus. Jamil loves hummus.'

'Does he? Anything else I should know about him? Like why he keeps giving you his ludicrously expensive scarf to wear?'

'You're in a mood but I'm not rising to it. I think I'm being jolly decent about you foisting your sad, undateable friend on us. Do we have six wine glasses?'

We did. But we only had four chairs. Chloe made another call and Mun-Hee said she'd bring a canvas garden chair. I'd have to sit on the kitchen step-ladder, with a couple of cushions.

Saturday morning everything was going smoothly until I returned to the topic of Christmas. I was thinking that if Chloe could get time off, we could drive to Abergavenny on the 23rd.

She said, 'What do you mean, drive to Abergavenny? I'm going to The Chummery for Christmas.'

'You said you'd think about coming to Wales.'

'I have thought about it. I'm going home.'

'Mam will be disappointed.'

'Then you shouldn't have promised her. What is it with you, Dan? Making all these arrangements without considering me? It's very high-handed of you.'

Her phone rang. All I could hear were sympathetic noises. Someone was crying off. I was praying it was Jamil. It wasn't.

Mun-Hee thought she was going down with a bug. I said we had to find someone else, otherwise Vaz's only prospect was Hua. Not that there was anything wrong with Hua. She's actually very pretty, but she's also very quiet and from what I'd heard, the only thing she thinks about is work, so perhaps not looking for a relationship. Even Chloe agreed we had to find another female. It took a few calls but she managed to get Dee, an Obs/Gyn registrar,. Australian. I'd never met her but I'd heard a few reports.

I said, 'You don't think she'll be a bit too wild for Vaz?'

'Why?'

'Isn't she the one who turned up at somebody's birthday with a gang of bikers?'

'Three bikers, Dan. Hardly a gang. Anyway, what am I supposed to do? Dee's single, she's fun and she's available this evening. My friends aren't exactly lining up to meet a GP who wears sleeveless pullovers. And do we have to call him 'Vaz'? Every time you say it I think of scrotums.'

'Antony. His name's Antony. If Mun-Hee's not coming what about the extra chair?'

'Shit. I'll have the stepladder. You'll have to perch on the arm of the sofa.'

Vaz was the first to arrive. I knew he would be. He brought a very nice box of chocolates, a bottle of red and a bottle of sparkling water. He was driving.

Chloe whispered, 'I thought you said he dresses like a nerd? His jeans are a bit 'grandad' but he looks okay to me. Quite cute actually.'

It was a very promising start to the evening which then went downhill fast. Hua and Jamil arrived together. Hua doesn't drink. She'd brought her own bottled water and a copy of The American Journal of Echocardiography for Chloe. Jamil brought flowers, a very nice Burgundy and a lavish box of little Lebanese cakes. He's short, slightly podgy, very pleasant. He asked me about General Practice. We even had a laugh about Wales winning the Six Nations. He's a France supporter himself. I found I quite liked him.

Eight o'clock came and went, then half past. Dee arrived nearly an hour late by which time I'd had more to drink than advisable when in charge of cooking dinner, Chloe was at the pink and giggly stage and Dee herself had clearly had a few before she rolled up. She kissed me on the lips and I was so flustered and worried she'd do the same to Vaz I introduced him as 'Vaz' instead of 'Antony' and she roared, 'you're kidding? Vaz? What's the surname? Deferens?' But at least she didn't kiss him.

I dished up my slightly over-crisped cottage pie and Chloe's defeated broccoli and snow peas. I tried perching on the arm of the sofa but it was uncomfortable. Jamil offered to share the stepladder with Chloe to free up a chair for me but I wasn't having him sitting thigh to thigh with my girlfriend. I just leaned against the kitchen counter and after a while nobody seemed to notice that I wasn't actually sitting at the table.

Vaz, Antony, was doing well. I could see he was interested in Hua. She has beautiful black hair, almost blue, and a very quiet voice. He asked her lots of questions about cardio-version, which is her current area of interest. What phase of the sinus wave works best? What drugs do they use before applying the current? They use the procedure for atrial fibrillation mainly, or atrial flutter, but Hua said they're now trying it in some cases of ventricular tachycardia where there's a pulse.

I said, 'And if there's no pulse?'

Chloe said, 'If there's no pulse we're talking flatline, you dimwit. If there's no pulse we're talking defibrillation or sending for a porter.'

Of course. Still, there was no need to call me a dimwit. I was only trying to join in the conversation. I think Jamil felt she'd overstepped the mark too.

He said, 'Dan and Antony have a different skill set, don't forget. They usually see patients who've definitely got a pulse.'

Chloe said, 'A pulse but not much brain activity. Tell them about that girl, Dan. With the mobile phone.'

I told them about Amber.

Dee said, 'Terrifying. And what's worse, these people are breeding.'

'Not in this case,' I said. 'Not any more. Her tubes are too battle-scarred.'

Dee said if she had her way every girl would get a contraceptive implant as soon as she reached puberty. No arguments, no questions asked.

I said, 'But surely we should be discouraging girls from having sex at such a young age, not making it easier?'

'Bullshit,' says Dee. I saw Vaz flinch. 'Fourteen year olds are going to have sex whatever you think about it. It's the norm now. And an implant's a lot more efficient than a termination.'

I said, 'Excuse me, but isn't there a law about age of consent?'

Chloe said, 'Okay Dan, so what will you do if a 14 year old comes to you, Monday afternoon, and says, "I'm having sex with my boyfriend. Give me the Pill"?'

I said, 'I'll send her to Pam Parker, who knows a lot more about this than I do, and I'd hope Pam would talk to the parents. In my opinion fourteen is too young. That's why there's a law.'

There was howl of dissent from Dee and Chloe.

Dee said, 'Chlo, where did you find this throwback?'

And Chloe said, 'You'll have to excuse Dan. He's from darkest Wales.'

I was trying to think of a devastating retort. It usually takes me a few hours. But suddenly Vaz, who'd been very quiet, jumped in.

He said, 'I agree with Dan. A girl should treasure her virginity. Fourteen is too young for childbearing and sex is intended for procreation.'

Dee said, 'Procreation? Not round mine it's bloody not. Sex is for pleasure. Simples.'

Chloe said, 'And the kind of people you're dealing with, Dan, do we really want them crapping in the gene pool? Those estates, if you ask me, they should put contraception in the tap water.'

'Yeah, right,' says Dee. 'The world's overpopulated anyway.'

Jamil said, 'Do you want us all to stop reproducing, Dee?'

'Wouldn't be a bad idea.'

I said, 'Then who will look after us in our old age? If we stop having children who's going to be paying taxes 50 years from now, and working in our hospitals?'

'Who cares?' she said. She was drunk. 'If you ask me, there are too many squawking brats in the world.'

I said, 'That's an interesting attitude. Isn't a big part of your job helping women to have children?'

'Or not to have them. I'm pro-choice one hundred percent, down the line. Not for budging.'

'Me too,' says Chloe. Her wine glass nearly went flying.

I said, 'But hang on, you were just advocating compulsory implants and spiking the Brook Glen water with contraceptives. That's not choice. You're contradicting yourselves.'

Chloe glared at me. She knew I was right. Vaz had been folding and refolding the little paper case from his chocolate.

'Excuse me,' he said. 'I hear a lot of ladies saying this 'I am pro-choice' but nobody can tell me, is this choice just for ladies? Do they ask this baby, 'would you like to live?''

Dee said, 'Sorry, are you some kind of religious nut?'

Everything went quiet.

Eventually Chloe said, 'Coffee everyone?'

Hua said, 'Not for me. I get taxi. Anyone coming?'

Vaz said, 'I can drive you.'

'No thank you,' she said. She had her phone in her hand. 'There is taxi five minutes away.'

Dee and Jamil said they'd share her cab. They couldn't leave fast enough. The evening was a washout and it certainly wasn't my fault.

Jamil shook my hand, thanked me for dinner. Chloe got two kisses. She's taller than him. Dee ignored me but she made a big thing of hugging Chloe. What was that about? A you-poor-thing-living-with-a-dimwit-throwback hug?

She said, 'Cheers, girl. It's been an evening to remember. I'll bet Mun-Hee didn't have as much fun.'

Chloe said, 'Yeah, she was feeling fluey.'

Dee said, 'Fluey? Is that what she told you? The lying bitch. Feeling crook? Feeling up old Barrington, more like. I wonder where he took her?'

When Chloe's upset but she doesn't want to show it she presses her lips together and does a tight little smile.

Vaz insisted on helping to clear the dishes. I thought he'd never leave. Chloe had gone straight to bed, hadn't even said goodnight to him.

I said, 'I'm really sorry about Dee. She stepped in at the last minute and she wasn't at all what I had in mind for you.'

He said it had been a great honour to come to my home and the evening had been very interesting. When I went into the bedroom Chloe was wide awake with a fighting face on. She'd used her stuffed Eeyore to effect a cordon sanitaire between herself and my side of the bed.

I said, 'That was fun.'

'Are you serious?'

'Of course. I cooked, I stood up to eat, I cleared away. I exposed Vaz to your gobby Australian friend. Got called a dimwit by my fiancée. All in all, I had a really great evening.'

'Not my fault if your friend's a God-botherer.'

'Since when do you call people God-botherers? I go to church. Is that what you call me behind my back?'

'You only go because you like singing.'

'Not entirely. And anyway, I thought we were going to get married in a church?'

'That's nothing to do with anything. It's just a venue.'

'I notice you didn't give Jamil his scarf back. It's a cold night. He might have been glad of it. Unless, of course, he's given it to you to keep?'

'So that's what's bugging you. You can be such a bore, Dan.'

'If you say so. I'll tell you who is a bore. Hua. Does she ever talk about anything but work?'

'Hua is super smart. Anyway, she's not interested in your Antony Vaz Deferens. She told me when I was letting her out. Definitely not her type.'

'Yeah, I think he got that message. And what about Mun-Hee? Chucked you so she could have dinner with the big chief. You need to keep an eye on her.'

'It won't be anything like that. Barrington's old enough to be her father. As a matter of fact, he knows her father. They trained together.'

'She lied to you, Chloe. She said she was too sick to come.'

'Dee might have got it wrong.'

'Ah yes. Dee. What an adornment to the evening she was. The words bull and china shop spring to mind.'

'Why? Because she's lively and so not boring? She's actually bi.'

'Bipolar?'

'Not bipolar. Bisexual.'

'Is that why she had her tongue in your ear?'

'You are too ridiculous.'

I lay awake for a long time. I felt terrible for Vaz. He'd had a horrid evening, but he'd been so polite about it. My cottage pie had dried out, I had a red wine headache, and a niggling voice was asking me whether Chloe and I really had a future together.

Sunday was tense. Usually, when neither of us is working, we sleep in, have a Full English and then go out for breakfast. I didn't try for sex, but I did make coffee and bring it to her in bed. She was monosyllabic. I was going to have to be the grownup. She schlumped around for a while and then suddenly appeared, showered, dressed and with her coat on.

'Christmas shopping.'

'Want me to come with you?'

'No. You hate shopping. I have no idea what to get the she-brats.'

I suggested books but she didn't think Flo's daughters were big readers.

'Fairy outfits, then. Don't all little girls like to dress up as fairies?'

'Demons, more like. Yoblets with hair ribbons. I wish I could just give them vouchers.'

'Why can't you?'

'Because aunts are supposed to bring magic into children's

lives. Slow gives them money. Idle git.'

'But I'll bet they love getting money. They can spend it on voodoo dolls and whoopee cushions.'

I don't want it to look like I don't care.'

'What, by selfishly lobbing them a voucher to go and spend on their heart's desire? I think vouchers are definitely the way to go.'

'You're only saying that because you want to stay at home and watch the rugby.'

'I cannot tell a lie. But I'll come if you want me to.'

She shook her head. I told her not to spend too much on me, but she was in no mood for a joke. I mean, I'd made her a proper cappuccino and I'd offered to forgo watching Wales hammer New Zealand and go shopping with her. I felt I could do no more.

CHAPTER 18.

We were halfway through the morning list when Mary came to the door.

'John Adkins,' she said.

Trevor pointed to me.

'Dr Talbot,' she started again. 'John Adkins is outside. He's booked for a dressing change at eleven o'clock but he's effing and blinding and refusing to get out of his daughter's car. Linda's been out to him, but he won't move. Any suggestions?'

Trevor said, 'That doesn't sound like John. Well, let's try taking the water-trough to the horse.'

We went out to the car park. I'd never met Mr Adkins before. He was a sharp-featured man in his eighties. He had a surgical dressing over his ear and he hadn't shaved. He glowered at me through the car window. His daughter was pacing back and forth, very apologetic.

Trevor knew her.

'Susan,' he said. 'What's the old so-and-so up to?'

'I don't know,' she said. 'He's woken up with the very devil in him.'

'Did he eat his breakfast?'

'No. He wouldn't touch it.'

'What's with the dressing?'

'Rodent ulcer on the rim of his ear. Dr Vincent sent him to have it removed.'

'And he was alright yesterday?'

'Yes. He was playing dominoes at the British Legion all afternoon.'

Trevor looked at me.

'Thoughts?'

Sudden onset aggression in the elderly? Possible delirium due to a urinary tract infection.

Trevor opened the car door. Mr Adkins told him to fuck off.

Trevor said, 'I wish I could, John, but I'm stuck here till closing time. I haven't seen you for a while. How are you keeping? Are your waterworks okay?'

No reply.

'It's brass monkeys out here. Will you come in and have a cup of coffee with me?'

No reply.

'I was just telling Dr Dan here about time you got bitten by a snake. Was it in Aden?'

'Cyprus. Akrotiri.'

'National Service, Dan. Before your time. Before mine, too. I just missed that. They should bring it back. Some of the layabouts around here. Two years in the army'd sort them out. What do you say, John?'

'Airforce,' says Mr Adkins. 'I was in the Air Force. RAF Akrotiri. Fucking snake bit me and my foot swole up so big I couldn't get my boot on.'

He reached for his stick, got out of the car and walked with Trevor into the surgery.

'Mary,' shouts Trevor, 'we'll have two white coffees and a plate of biscuits, if you please.'

'Dr Buxton,' shouts Mary, 'that'll be Starbucks you're looking for. There's one in Wednesbury.' She did make the coffee though.

Trevor ushered Mr Adkins into Pam Parker's empty room. The daughter went to follow them but Trevor shook his head.

'This is man talk,' he said, 'My money's on a bladder infection. Getting a urine sample could be interesting but I'll give it a try. Dr Dan'll write him up for Amoxycillin anyway.

Give us half an hour, sweetheart. Have you got a bit of shopping to do? Or there's last month's Vogue in the waiting room, donated by Mrs Buxton.'

Trevor rejoined me towards the end of morning surgery. We had Glenys Allsop coming in for a review of her hospital results.

'Sorry to take over like that with John,' he said, 'but sometimes, with the older patients, you've got to go the long way around for the shortest.'

'Did you get a urine sample?'

'I did. It wasn't exactly mid-stream, but he's definitely got an infection. Nitrites, leucocytes. Enlarged prostate, more than likely. His bladder's not emptying properly. He sits for hours playing dominoes and puts off going to the bog because he knows it'll be such a slow dribble he'll be in there for ages and he'll miss valuable playing time. Such are the things old men talk about.'

'I couldn't have spent that amount of time with him.'

'No, you couldn't. Terrible, isn't it? My Dad could have. But in his day he didn't have sixteen patients to see and half of them not really sick anyway. Helen ought to keep me on, just for patients who need a cuppa and a chat.'

I said I thought that was a very good idea.

'I'll suggest it.'

'Save your breath, lad. Our esteemed practice manager will shoot you down in flames. There's not a QOFs Reassuring Chat box for her to tick. Anyway, I'm supposed to retire and go on holiday. Mrs Buxton says so.'

'Where will you go?'

'Wherever I'm told.'

'What do you fancy?'

'Bit of sunshine, cheap booze, racing on the telly. No real need to go away for that. Come July I can have it all in Wombourne and without any bloody suitcases to lug. The

Allsops just got here, by the way, so shall we get on with it?'

Trevor said he wanted me to lead the conversation.

'That's what you're here for, Dan,' he said. 'All the stuff they don't teach you in medical school.'

Glenys looked very well, considering her diagnosis. Her husband was with her. Pete. Glenys unbuttoned her coat, Pete didn't even take his gloves off. He didn't want to be there.

I said, 'So we finally have some answers.'

'Yes,' said Glenys. 'After all those ruddy tests. And to think, I only came to see you because of the itching.'

'Thank goodness you did. Now we can start dealing with it. So I expect the hospital will have explained things to you. What's your understanding of your condition?'

'It's my bile duct.'

'Yes. Biliary cholangitis. Did they talk to you about adjusting your diet?'

'Low fat, they said. But we've been low fat for years haven't we, Pete?'

Pete nodded.

'And they've given me a powder to take. To help my digestion.'

'Good. You seem to have everything sorted, for the time being. Down the line we might need to review things.'

I was about to mention transplants, but Glenys had something else on her mind.

'I'm all right,' she said. 'It's my Pete I'm worried about. He's been really down lately.'

Pete looked at the floor. I asked him if he was feeling depressed. He shrugged.

I said, 'I imagine you've both been under a lot of stress, worrying about Glenys's health.'

'We have,' says Glenys. 'But I'm all right now they've

185

sorted me out. I just need Pete's spirits to pick up.'

I saw Trevor's eyebrow twitch.

I said, 'Pete, how do you feel about Glenys's diagnosis?'

'She's been off work a lot.'

'Has that affected you, financially?'

'Of course it has.'

Glenys patted his hand. She said, 'We'll be okay.'

I said, 'Have you talked about making some adjustments? You know Glenys really needs to look after herself now, not get over-tired.'

He looked up at me.

He said, 'She needs to get back to work. She's had her tests, she's got her medicine. It's time to get back to normal.'

That was when I knew I had to venture into deeper water. Either the hospital hadn't explained the gravity of Glenys's condition, or she and Pete were both in denial. Or, as Trevor said later, Glenys was putting on a brave front and Pete was a clueless prick.

I said, 'I understand you want to get back to normal, as long as you both realise it'll be a new kind of normal. Glenys needs to keep herself in the best possible health so that if a transplant becomes available she can give it her absolute best shot.'

The word 'transplant' landed with a thud. They both looked at me. The transplant question had evidently not been addressed by the hospital.

Trevor shifted in his seat but said nothing. He was leaving it to me.

'Your condition,' I said, 'is a progressive one. It will gradually get worse. The diet and the cholestyramine powder, those things will help, but ultimately we'd be looking at a liver transplant.'

I had their attention.

I said, 'The hospital didn't talk to you about an assessment?'

'I don't think so. I have to back though, the week after next. It's for a check-up.'

'That's good. They'll probably be assessing your suitability for a transplant and I'd say you'd be a very promising candidate. You don't drink, don't do drugs, you're not overweight.'

'When you say 'a transplant' do you mean from a dead person?'

'From an organ donor, yes.'

'I don't think I fancy that. What about from somebody who's alive?'

I had heard of attempts at partial transplants from living donors, but I wasn't going to go into that with the Allsops.

'Not really. People only have one liver. It's not like donating a kidney.'

'What if I don't get one?'

'You will,' I lied. I actually had no idea what her chances were, but I pressed on anyway. 'And as Dr Buxton will tell you, they have a very high success rate with livers these days.'

Trevor gave her an encouraging smile.

She said, 'I'm all right to go back to work though?'

She worked in a fabric shop, but behind the scenes, doing alterations.

'I don't see why not. Would you be able to cut down your hours if you start to feel tired? Perhaps you should discuss it with them.'

Pete said, 'No, no. She's only part-time as it is. They won't want her messing them around. They'll sack her, more than likely. No, the less they know the better.'

I said, 'It's up to you, Glenys. But good dressmakers don't grow on trees. I'm sure they won't want to lose you. And the better you take care of yourself the longer you'll be able to work. Do you see what I'm saying?'

She nodded, only half listening. Pete glared at the floor, annoyed, with me, annoyed with progressive biliary cholangitis and life in general. They were both miles away. Parachuted into unknown territory. A life-threatening condition. Best hope a transplant from some healthy, unsuspecting, soon-to-be-dead donor. A new kind of normal.

Trevor thought I'd handled it well.

He said, 'They weren't really paying attention. He's worried about money. She's worried about him worrying.'

'What's the transplant waiting list like?'

'Six months, at least. She might make it. Her serum bilirubin's very high, but you never know. It might settle down. You should give the hospital a call. No, I'll do it. I'm not pulling rank on you, but I do know a few people. I'll make sure they're following through. If she gets on the waiting list sharpish, this is the best time of year.'

'Is it?'

'Winter,' he said. 'Black ice. Fatalities on the roads. You can get quite a crop of motorcyclists with good, healthy livers. Nice woman, Glenys. Pity about the husband.

There was paperwork to catch up on. It was going to be a desk lunch day. I'd just been to the kitchen to toast my cheese sandwich when Mary appeared again.

'I've got Connie Riley on the phone,' she said. 'Will you have a word?'

Trevor picked up.

'Connie, my dear,' he said. He listened. 'And when did that start?'

He told her we'd be there within a quarter of an hour.

'Jimmy,' he said. 'Sounds as though he's going. You'd better come with me. You've been his most recent 'attending.'

We drove in silence. Connie had left the door off the latch so we could let ourselves in.

She said, 'I didn't mean for you to come dashing over. It's just that his breathing's gone a bit haywire this morning.'

Jimmy was Cheyne-Stoking. His breathing was noisy and laboured, then it would stop and there'd be absolute silence. Was it over? Just when you thought it might be, he'd start snoring again. His feet were cold and mottled. His pulse was fast but very weak.

Trevor said, 'Did you call your boys?'

She said Derek had promised to come over after he finished work. Roger was still away, working in Abu Dhabi.

'Is it the end?' she said.

Trevor nodded. He took Jimmy's hand.

He said, 'Can you hear me, Jimmy? Are you comfortable? Can you give my hand a squeeze if you're comfortable?'

Did his hand twitch? I couldn't be sure. Trevor seemed to think so.

'Good man,' he said. 'Your Connie's here. She's going to hop up beside you like the spring chicken she is.'

She said, 'That's too high for me. I can't get up there.'

'You can if I lift you,' says Trevor and with that he deposited her on the bed next to Jimmy. Connie Riley's built like a little sparrow but the effort fairly winded him.

He said, 'Now you snuggle up with him, while Dr Dan makes you a cup of tea. Have you had anything to eat today?'

She said she wasn't hungry.

Trevor said, 'Well I'm not leaving till you eat something, woman, so what's it to be?'

In the time it took for the kettle to boil and me to butter a teacake, Jimmy's breathing had become quieter and the gaps between breaths were longer. He died at 2.10 with Connie's head resting on his chest.

'Is that it?' she said. 'He went very easy.'

I called the son, Derek. I found myself shaking as I dialled his number. I'd seen plenty of dead patients on my hospital rotations, but I'd never been present at the very moment of a death at home.

Derek said, 'What, gone? Well that's a bit sudden. Was I told it was likely to be so soon?'

I said, 'Your Dad's cancer was too far advanced for treatment. He's been getting palliative care for the past two months. Dr Buxton's your father's GP and as far as I'm aware you haven't been in touch with him, to discuss the likely outcome.'

'It's his job to get in touch with me,' he said. 'I'm a busy man.'

I said, 'Well your father died peacefully a few minutes ago and your mother now urgently needs her family around her.'

I ended the call before I added, 'And I'm sorry for your loss, arsehole.'

Connie was very calm.

She said, 'I'd better call the funeral people.'

Trevor said, 'There's no hurry. Leave all that to Derek. You sit with Jimmy for a while.'

He and I went into the kitchen. He got out his pen. In the surgery he uses whatever biro comes to hand but when he's certifying a death, he likes to use a proper ink pen.

'Pulse absent, pupils fixed. Life extinct. Right Dan, what are we going to give as cause of death?'

I thought cachexia or broncho-pneumonia.

'Let's put both. Underlying condition?'

'Gastric adenocarcinoma. Do we mention the metastases?'

'No harm. Better to give too much information than too little. The main thing is to be precise. You can't put 'bored with life' or 'chronic stupidity' as a cause of death. Even if it happens to be true.'

'I should be getting back for surgery. Are we okay to leave Connie on her own till her son gets here? There's Harry Darkin two doors away. I'm sure he'd come and sit with her.'

'She'll be fine. Women like Connie are made of steel. But don't worry about being late for surgery. Give me five minutes, just to tidy him up, and then we'll be on our way. Let the surgery crowd wait. Half of them haven't got anything ailing them anyway.'

Funny, it was the exact opposite of Mac's motto. Always attend to the living first.

When we went back in, Connie had already made a start. She'd put a rolled towel under Jimmy's chin, to stop his mouth gaping, and she'd straightened his arms. She was wiping his face with a wet flannel.

Trevor said, 'Dear God, Connie, where did you learn to do that?'

She said she'd done a bit of nursing before she was married.

'Only State Enrolled,' she said. 'I didn't have the brains for anything higher.'

'I doubt that,' says Trevor. 'They have to have a degree these days, but it doesn't mean they're any better at the job. When my father was in practice a lot of patients died at home. It was common back then. He had a couple of local ladies who did last offices for him.'

Connie said, 'I know he did. My Aunt Peg was one of them. She'd nursed in the First World War so dead bodies didn't bother her. She'd seen it all. And if it was too far away for her to walk, old Dr Buxton used to fetch her in his car. We didn't see many cars on our street in those days, so if Dr Buxton pulled up outside, we knew somebody had died. It was a nice bit of extra money for her. She didn't have a lot, being a spinster. Should I open a window, do you think? Aunt Peg used to do it. She said it was to let the departing spirit out.'

'Up to you,' says Trevor. 'I wouldn't, personally. It's a bit parky today. And Jimmy'll find a way out when he's ready to go.'

A car passed us going at speed the other way on Churchfield Road.

Trevor said, 'That was Derek Riley, giving it some welly. Was he upset when you called him?'

'More annoyed than upset. He seemed to think he should have been informed his Dad was going to die today.'

'It happens. I got punched once.'

'For what?'

'Failing to keep somebody's mother alive. She was 97 but feelings can still run very high. Are you alright, lad? You look a bit dazed.'

'It all happened so fast.'

'It did. I thought he might be waiting till Connie left the room. They do sometimes, you know? Like it's easier to go if you don't have your loved ones hovering and dabbing their eyes. But anyway, she was with him. Powerful, isn't it? Being there at the end?'

'Very. Like an honour.'

'I suppose it is. It's the same being at a birth.'

'You've delivered babies?'

'We used to. Home births. Not any more, of course. I wouldn't mind. Pam Parker could do them but Helen won't hear of it. She thinks it's too risky.'

'You know what really got to me with Jimmy just now? Seeing Connie combing his hair so gently.'

'Yes, that's devotion for you. Taking care not to scratch your scalp even when you're dead and gone.'

As we came back into the building Mac was on his way out. Trevor asked him if he'd had a good break in Scotland.

'Pissed rain every day,' he said. 'My clubs never saw daylight.'

I told him I'd been to the Woodleigh to see Hilda Ruck.

'Panic attack by the sounds of it,' he said. 'She has them from time to time. She's a lonely old soul. Craves a bit of attention.'

My heart was pounding but I thought, 'Press on, Dan.'

I said, 'She seemed anxious about transferring her file to Vaz? She said you'd advised her to do it.'

'News to me,' he said.

'And she was talking about her lawyer delaying something. She was quite upset.'

'Oh aye, that's a frequent bee in her bonnet. She's forever changing her Will.'

'Is she wealthy?'

'I doubt it. And if she ever was, she won't be for long. Living in a place like Woodleigh, you'll soon run through your money.'

So Hilda Ruck was just a lonely old lady, obsessed with her Will, a bit confused, and Mac was one of the few people who gave her any attention. I felt relieved.

Barbara Humphries, the bunion woman, was on the afternoon list. I told Trevor about my previous encounter with her.

'In that case I'll sit in the driving seat,' he said. 'No disrespect, Dan, but I know Barbara. We have to use a bit of psychology here.'

'Oh,' she said, when she saw me. 'You're still here.'

'Dr Talbot is my assistant,' says Trevor. 'And a very good one, too. Now Barbara, what can I help you with?'

She told him her bunion story. Daughter getting married, wanting to wear high heels.

He said, 'Well let's have a look. And if you don't mind, I'll ask Dr Talbot to examine you first because he's here to learn.'

As soon as she peeled off her knee-highs I could smell something wasn't right. At The Lindens it wasn't uncommon to get patients with ripe feet, but Barbara was an immaculate, well-dressed woman. I checked her notes. Type 2 diabetes, insulin-dependent but well-controlled. This was basic stuff.

She had an open sore on the sole of her right foot. It stank. I prodded it and she didn't react.

I said, 'Do you get your regular foot check at the diabetes clinic?'

'Of course I do,' she said.

'And the most recent one was when?'

'September.'

Trevor strolled over.

'Mind if I have a gander?' he said. He took his glasses off and examined her feet at close quarters. He has a stronger stomach than I do. He beckoned me to go in closer and used a tongue depressor to point to two tiny patch black patches on the underside of her toes. Gangrene.

He said, 'So which of your girls is getting married?'

'Joanne,' she said. 'We're having it at Peyton Bridge Country Club.'

'That'll give you a pain in your cheque book.'

'Well you want to give them a nice send-off, don't you? I love a good wedding. Yours must both be married by now.'

'No. Neither of them. Barbara, my dear, you've got a couple of patches on your feet I'd like somebody to look at. You know how it is with diabetes. You have to watch every little thing.'

'Oh I do. And my eyes. I'm ever so careful.'

'Good girl. Now Dr Dan here'll send off a referral. And we'll ask Nurse Chris to put a dressing on that ulcer. No we

194

won't. I'll see to it, to save you hanging about.'

He sent me across to the nurses' room for an alginate dressing and a roll of gauze bandage, took off his jacket and rolled up his sleeves.

She said, 'I suppose there's a long waiting list for the foot people?'

'No. We'll get somebody to see you within a few days.'

'Wonderful,' she said. 'And while I'm there I can ask them about getting my bunions done.'

I had to go outside for a breather after Barbara had left. When I came back Trevor had the window open a crack and a cigarette in his hand.

'I'm only having a couple of puffs,' he said. 'Replacing the pong of putrescence with the sweet smell of the dreaded weed.'

'I was ready to gag.'

'My sense of smell's not what it was,' he said. 'It's a dividend of getting older. When you send the referral form, make sure you write URGENT DIABETIC FOOT on the top. And underline it. Now who's next? Usman Okeke. That's a new one. Why are they giving me new patients when I'm ready for the push?'

'Helen's out a lot. She seems to have a lot of CCG meetings.'

'Sooner her than me. They sit around a big table, dream up a few new labels for things, have a cup of tea and a Hobnob, then spend half an hour deciding on a date for the next meeting. She likes that kind of thing though.'

'It leaves us a bit short-handed sometimes.'

'It does. Are you angling for a permanent job, young Talbot?'

'Might be. It's too soon to know.'

'And it'll be in Helen's gift, when the time comes. But you'd get my backing, for what it's worth. Okay, let's get Mr

Okey Cokey in. After we've seen him, I think I'll call it a day. Let you finish the list.'

Mr Okeke turned out to be a Mrs with a six week old baby, Usman. She unwrapped him and lay him on the desk. He was wide awake.

Trevor said, 'He's a bonny little lad. What's the problem?'

'Time for you to cut him,' she said, and she opened his disposable. She'd brought Usman to be circumcised.

'No, my dear,' says Trevor. 'We don't do anything like that here.'

'But it's time,' she said. 'This is important.'

'Listen,' he said, and he closed up the nappy. 'First of all, I'm afraid I don't believe in it. Not unless there's a problem. Foreskin won't retract, something like that, but it's far too early to know. He looks fine to me. Time will tell. Then, if it does need to be done it should be in a hospital, by somebody who knows what they're doing.'

'But it must be done now,' she said. She reopened the Pampers. 'This is our custom.'

'Then phone the hospital and ask them. They might be willing, but I think you'll find they won't do it till he's older. In any case, I don't circumcise healthy little boys in my surgery. And that's that.'

Usman peed on Barbara Humphries' file. His nappy was opened and closed several times before Mrs Okeke admitted defeat. She was very angry.

'I will report this,' she said.

'Go ahead,' said Trevor. 'I'd sooner have a complaint against me than a mutilated child.'

She left, but we could hear her out in Reception, haranguing Mary. Trevor peered round the door.

He said, 'Where's the practice rottweiler when you need her?'

196

But Stephanie had taken the afternoon off.

'Perhaps she's gone for a job interview. We can but hope.'

'Do you get asked to do circumcisions very often?'

'I honestly can't remember the last time.'

'No Jewish patients?'

'No. You'd get that more around Edgbaston and Moseley. And Solihull, of course. Anyway, Jewish parents wouldn't ask me. They'd go to a mohel, and a medically trained one most likely. This is a West African thing. They might oblige her at Sandwell. Customer demand, cultural sensitivity and all that. On the other hand, they might not.'

I wiped the pee off Barbara Humphries' folder. Trevor put his overcoat on and shuffled through the rest of the afternoon's files.

'Nothing you can't handle,' he said. 'If in doubt you can draw on the combined wisdom of Helen and Vaz.'

Lisa Packer came in. She wanted a different inhaler for her asthma.

'How often do you use the Ventolin?'

'All the time.'

'It's not meant to be used all the time, Lisa. It's just for when you feel an attack starting. How often does that happen?'

She shrugged.

I said, 'Did you drive here today?'

She'd walked.

'Where's your coat, where's your scarf?'

'Haven't got none.'

I said, 'Lisa, it's a very cold day. If you're asthmatic you need to wrap up, put a scarf over your nose and mouth when you first go out, warm the air before it gets to your lungs.'

She gave me a dead-eyed look.

'Do you understand what I'm saying?'

'Yeah. Put a scarf on. So can I get the other inhaler?'

She had a friend who'd been given a Serotide dispenser. Medication envy, pure and simple.

I said, 'Serotide isn't the same as Ventolin. It's a preventative, for really severe cases. Your asthma isn't life-threatening so Serotide isn't the right thing for you.'

She wasn't happy.

She said, 'Can I get a different puffer then? I'm bored of this colour.'

I prescribed Salamol. Lisa had a very distracting cleavage on display and I wanted to be rid of her.

She said, 'What colour is it?'

'Blue and white, I think. The kind of inhaler you need, they're mainly blue.'

'I wish I could get a red one,' she said. 'Or purple, like Tia's.'

Reece Hopkins was a regular. He needed me to sign him off unfit for work. He had a history of tonic-clonic seizures since suffering a concussion when he was nine. He also suffered from anxiety attacks. He took Keppra for the epilepsy and Paxil for the anxiety.

I said, 'When did you last have a seizure?'

'Can't remember, offhand.'

I looked back through his notes. 2007. Five years without a seizure.

I said, 'You're doing very well on the medication. Wouldn't you like to get back to work?'

'Not really,' he said.

'Don't you get fed up, sitting at home?'

'I go out.'

'Be nice to be earning though, wouldn't it?'

'Thing is,' he said, 'I get more on Incapacity than I'd get on Jobseekers. Plus, I can take my kiddie to the park. I can get down the shops when they reduce stuff. I've got quality of life.'

'What about the anxiety?'

'It comes and goes.'

'But it sounds like you're functioning pretty well. We might think of tailing off the Paxil.'

'I don't know as I'd feel easy about that, Doctor. I mean, what if I was out with the bab and I had an attack?'

'How old's the baby?'

'Three. She's a caution. The things she comes out with.'

He showed me a picture on his phone. A cute little girl in a Burger King crown.

I signed him off sick. Gave him a repeat prescription for Paxil. Whatever happened to improving patients' lifestyles, Dan Talbot? Whatever happened to weaning people off drugs they don't need?

The cleaner was in, mopping the waiting room floor. Vaz's door was open and the light was off. He'd left already. There was a man in Reception, leaning over the counter, his face right in Mary's. It was Miles Vincent.

He said, 'I'm in a fucking hurry, right?'

Mary said, 'Dr Vincent said you're to wait till she's finished surgery. And kindly watch your language.'

I heard him mutter, 'fuck you.'

I said, 'Good Evening, Miles. Everything okay, Mary? Can I help?'

'Thank you, Dr Talbot,' she said, 'but we're quite alright. Miles is just waiting to have a word with his mother. Who has a patient in with her just now and isn't to be disturbed.'

Miles gave me the finger.

He's tall, like Helen, but dark, like his father. Camouflage parka and a beanie. Sulky-looking. Given to tantrums and swearing at nice old ladies. He moved away from the desk and studied a poster on the notice board. Pre-natal yoga.

'By the way,' says Mary, 'I don't know if anyone told you, but we do Secret Santa for the Christmas party.'

She produced a paper bag.

'Draw a name. And don't tell me who you get.'

'What if I get my own name?'

'Then you put it back and try again. I sometimes wonder what they teach you people at university.'

I drew Helen's name.

'How much am I supposed to spend?'

'Ten pounds. Not more than fifteen. And it's a secret, right? They won't know who bought their present and you won't know who bought yours.'

The phone rang. Miles Vincent wandered off.

'Keep your eye on him,' she said.

I found him in the doorway to the nurses' office. He said he was just looking for the toilet.

I said, 'We haven't moved it. It's still next to the waiting room. Why don't you wait in there?'

'And why don't you mind your own fucking business?' he said. 'Mr Learner Doctor.'

He called after me, 'Mr Learner Doctor who bricked himself over some old slag flashing him in the car park.'

It appeared I'd been made a figure of fun in the Vincent household too. Miles had a jackass laugh. He could have been a good-looking boy but he had that pallor people get when they stay in bed half the day. Father a solicitor, mother a respected GP. Been to a good school, no doubt. They must have had high hopes for him. What went wrong?

It had been quite a day. John Adkins, the Allsops, Jimmy Riley, the Okeke baby. And to top it off, Helen's bristly, grubby, insolent son. I was glad to be out of there. I wanted to get home, bump the thermostat up, open a bottle and mend a few fences with Chloe.

I'd had a glass and bunged the lasagne in the oven before I went into the bedroom. The first thing I noticed was that Chloe's big wheelie suitcase was gone. The second thing I noticed was that Eeyore was gone. The third thing I noticed was the note.

CHAPTER 19

Need some space, the note said. Nothing else. Not even one of her sad or smiley faces. Her phone was turned off. I tried The Chummery. Vinnie said she hadn't heard from her.

I said, 'Is it possible she's gone to stay with Charlie?'

'I don't think so. He doesn't really encourage visitors.'

'Could you please check with him anyway?'

'I suppose I could. He can be terribly difficult to track down, you know, and I have a tournament tee-off at ten tomorrow. What have you quarrelled about?'

'Just silly little things.'

'So it's just a lovers' tiff. Nothing too anxious-making. Do calm down, Dan.'

All very well for her to say.

Where could she have gone? Not to Mun-Hee. Whatever loyal protestations Chloe had made on Saturday night, my guess was Mun-Hee was now on her shit list. Hua was a possibility, or Dee, but I didn't have either of their numbers. And then there was Jamil. Was that who she'd run to? If it was him, game over.

I ate one forkful of lasagne. It tasted of nothing. I went back into the bedroom. Suitcase still gone, bloody Eeyore still gone. There was still some of her stuff hanging in the wardrobe but then, Chloe did have an awful lot of clothes. Her electric toothbrush was gone and her very expensive skin repair cream. Her coloured contacts were still there. What did it all mean? It meant she'd lost interest in wearing her coloured contacts, that's all. I phoned Mam. Da answered.

He said, 'She's working nights.'

'Okay. Just called for a natter. I'll try her some other time.'

'Right you are.'

One more forkful of lukewarm lasagne. I needed to talk to someone, anyone. It was 8 am in Sydney. I Skyped Rob.

He said it was great to see my ugly face. We talked shop. I told him about Keith Sideaway's drooping eyelid and my brain fade.

I said, 'And it wasn't even an emergency. How the heck do you cope, when every second counts?'

'Mate,' he said, 'It's just the way I tick. As soon as we get a trauma call, I'm in the zone. And anyway, Trauma's teamwork. Everybody knows what they have to do, plus a lot of it's rote. Airway clear? Respiration impaired? Vital signs stable? Mental status? The only thing is you really need to be on your game with kiddies or seniors. Things can go pear-shaped quicker with them. You still with Chloe?'

I said, 'Yeah.' Because I had no idea how even to begin to explain.

'You named the day yet?'

'Next summer, I hope.'

Really, Dan? She's taken her iPod and her Bodum travel mug. Do you really think she's intending to come back and marry you?

He said, 'You should come to Sydney for your honeymoon. You'd love it.'

I miss Rob. He, Matt and I shared a grotty flat in Selly Oak our final two years as students. He's got an Australian girlfriend now, so I don't think he'll be coming back to England in a hurry.

''I saw Matt last week.'

'I never hear from him. Is he doing his Fellowship?'

'Doing his Fellowship and getting a lot of sex.'

'So he says.'

'Do you think he exaggerates?'

'Didn't he always? The more they talk about it, the less

203

they're getting. That's my beeper. Got to go, mate. Great to have a yarn, though.'

I did nod off, eventually, but it was more a cheap wine coma than true sleep. My phone woke me.

Mam said, 'Your Da said you called last night and you sounded upset.'

There's more to my Da than meets the eye. He might be a man of few words, but he takes a lot in. Those powers of observation he brings to bear on livestock, sometimes he uses them on human beings too.

I said, 'Me and Chloe have had a bit of a bust-up.'

Mam said she was sorry to hear that. I said I might take a couple of days off and go down to Abergavenny.

Mam said, 'Well I'm on nights again tonight and then your Da's taking me away for a few days. He booked it all without telling me, hotel and everything.'

Even more to my Da than met the eye.

'Paris?'

'Don't be daft. You know your father doesn't hold with 'abroad.' We're going to the Cotswolds. It looks lovely, Dan. Log fires and everything. You even get a complimentary glass of bubbly on arrival. We'll be back home on the Monday night. You can come if you want. There's always a bed for you, you know that, but it hardly seems worth it when you'll be coming for Christmas. It's nearly on us, Dan, and I haven't even put the marzipan on the cake yet.'

'Right.'

'Driving all the way down here. You'd be better off kissing and making up.'

'Yes.'

'Or not. I mean, sometimes these things don't work out. But that's for you and Chloe to decide.'

'I think she might have met someone else.'

'Well I'm sorry for your troubles, Dan, I really am, but I'm not going to take sides. I'm not going to say a bad word about the girl because the next thing you know, you'll be back together and I'll be left with egg on my face.'

'You're right. As usual.'

I went through the motions. Showered, shaved, made a sandwich, drove to The Lindens. I was hungover.

'Dr Dan,' says Linda, 'you'll have come across Marion Flitwell.'

'I have. Morbidly obese, Type 2 diabetes.'

'That's her. Guess what? She's lost weight. Five kg. And guess how she did it? Her husband's in hospital. All she's getting is Meals on Wheels.'

'So as soon as he goes home, she'll pile the weight back on.'

'But that won't be for a while. Two broken femurs and an unstable pelvic fracture. He got knocked down by a van. By the time he gets home she could be down to a size 10.'

I'd heard about a pedestrian being run over. It had happened in Tipton, late one evening. Driver over the limit.

Linda said, 'And here's the amazing thing. He tried to stand up, What's-his-face Flitwell. A busted pelvis and he tried to pick himself up off the floor. Everybody was saying 'don't move, don't move', but he'd bought fish and chips and he wanted to get them home while they were still hot. He's lucky to be alive. And he's had phlebitis.'

'How do you know all this?'

'The district nurse who goes in, to clean Marion's skin folds. She's in my Pilates class.'

Stephanie materialised in the doorway. Not a sound. Suddenly she was there. It's like she floats through walls.

She said, 'I hope you're not breaching patient confidentiality, Linda.'

'No,' says Linda. 'The whole of Sedgley knows Marion

Flitwell's a tubster and her hubby keeps her that way.'

Stephanie narrowed her eyes. 'Be very, very careful,' she said, and dematerialised.

Trevor had decided to start sorting through his personal effects, preparing to vacate his office.

'Bookshelf,' he said. 'That's where I'll start. Anything you'd like, just speak up.'

There were some old editions of MIMs that were only fit to be tossed. You can look up all the drugs online these days and the information is kept up to date. There was a Gray's Anatomy. That's a good old standard. The body doesn't change. I already had a copy though.

I said, 'Why don't you take the books home with you, when you retire?'

'Less of the R word, if you don't mind. I don't know, Dan, it's not like I'll ever open them again. Mrs Buxton's a great reader but Essentials of Clinical Medicine isn't really up her street and Dick Francis is about my limit.'

'Is Helen going to have this office? When you…if you ever… you know?'

'I doubt it. According to her the smell of my cigs has penetrated the brickwork. Anyway, I've not gone yet. I might prove harder to get rid of than a verruca.'

It was an unremarkable surgery. Coughs and sneezes, an ingrowing toenail, a small lipoma that would be a five minute excision job for Nurse Chris, a perforated ear drum. I referred Mrs Wade for a bone density scan and flagged Walter Topham to have his blood pressure checked again in the New Year.

Trevor said, 'Are you coming down with an attack of QOF-itis, Dan Talbot? Has dear Stephanie nobbled you?'

I said, 'It just seems to me to make sense, to catch health problems before they become serious. If the practice gets rewarded for doing it, that's a bonus. I'd much rather manage Mr Topham's hypertension than deal with him having a stroke.'

'Quite right,' says Trevor. 'I was pulling your leg. And yes, if we can catch things early, we should. The only thing I'd say is, if you look hard enough for problems, you'll find them. All this scanning and monitoring. Like this memory test they want us to give the oldsters, early detection of dementia. Where's the gain? Why ruin somebody's day? It's not like there's a cure. What do we say? Here's some pills that might slow it down a bit but in the long run you're fucked?'

'People might prefer to know, so they can put their affairs in order while they're still capable.'

'Some people, yes. Not everyone wants to know their fate.'

'But in the case of a 70 year old man with slightly raised blood pressure?'

'Yes, yes. You're probably right about Walter Topham. You know, I might be better disposed towards these QOFs if they hadn't given them such a stupid name.'

'So you don't disagree with what I've done?'

'I'd tell you if I did. Though a 24-hour BP monitor would give you a more useful picture than a random reading. But be your own man, Dan. You're not a student anymore.'

'Although Helen's son did call me 'Mr Learner Doctor'.'

'Did he, the little prick? What was he doing here? Tapping his mother for a few quid, I'll be bound.'

'He's not what you'd expect, is he? Quite rough-looking.'

'Last time I saw him he looked like he needed a bath and a shave.'

'Poor Helen. I wonder what went wrong?'

'I'm not supposed to say this but, you know, a working mother, feeling guilty because she's not at home, knitting bread, a kid can get spoiled rotten. I don't think Miles ever heard the word no.'

'You don't think mothers should work?'

'I just think they can pay a high price. It depends how they manage things. Pam Parker seems to have it figured out, but Helen would never have settled for being a part-timer. And even with a stay-at-home mother, things don't always turn out brilliantly. Look at my Alice.'

Trevor hardly ever mentioned his daughter. He said her teenage years had been very troubled.

'You name it, Alice did it. Shaved her head, bunked off school, cut herself.'

'Self-harming?'

'That's what they call it now. Of course, we realised later she'd been struggling with the lesbian thing. It wasn't all over the papers like it is today. You knew it existed, well I did, but not in Wombourne. Daft really. And you see, Mrs Buxton's a very feminine person. She was trying to get Alice to wear pretty dresses and Alice wasn't having it. She's not manly, not at all. Quite nice looking actually, considering she's never looked after herself, but I don't think she owns a dress. They were at loggerheads for years. It's better now, not warm, but civil.'

'Do you ever go to visit?'

'To Betsy-whatsit? No. We went once, when they first settled there, when they bought the house and the shop, her and Micky. Once they'd got a mortgage together, we knew it was serious so we made an effort, you know? Tried to play Happy Families.'

'Do you like Micky?'

'No, I don't. I have my reasons. Now, Dan Talbot, if you don't mind my saying, you're looking a bit seedy today.'

'I didn't sleep well.'

'Neither did I. But I've got a home visit in Himley. Come with me and get some country air.'

CHAPTER 20.

Trevor's house call was to Eileen Prior. She had multiple sclerosis.

'Is she housebound?'

'Not at all. She usually comes into the surgery, but she's got the relapsing-remitting type and apparently she's not doing so well at the moment, so I said we'd go and see her.'

'What medication is she on?'

'Injects herself with Avonex once a week. She's very low maintenance and if she's going to relapse it's usually when we have a spell of hot weather. This time of year she's generally pretty stable. Anyway, Eileen's a trouper. I'd never begrudge her a visit.'

'What about Copaxone?'

'We tried her on it, but she had some side effects.'

'Nettle rash?'

'Nettle rash, puffy face, palpitations.'

The Prior house was a big detached property on Churn Hill. Double garage and a Toyota 4x4 parked out front.

Trevor said, 'See, this is the more genteel side to the practice? The husband's a pilot. Flies out of Birmingham. Eileen manages a dress shop. Posh frocks. Mrs Buxton goes there if we're invited to anything fancy.'

It turned out that Captain Prior didn't just fly out of Birmingham. He had also flown from the marital home and Eileen wasn't a poster girl for her posh frock shop. She was in her dressing gown, her hair needed washing, and she was in a foul mood.

She said, 'I told you not to come. Waste of fucking time.'

Trevor said, 'And I told you you're never a waste of time. Are your legs playing up?'

'Legs, hands. Rick's fucked off with a trolley-dolly. And I'm sick of people pitying me. I'm sick of people giving me those bloodhound eyes.'

'How long since Rick left?'

'A few weeks.'

'He'll come to his senses.'

'I don't think so. You can't blame him. I'm not much cop in the sack anymore.'

'How are the kids?'

'Horrible. All they do is roll their eyes and demand money.'

Trevor said, 'Normal teenagers, then. We could try the Copaxone again. It can reduce the relapse frequency.'

'No thank you. I felt like shit the last time I took it.'

'But you feel like shit now.'

'True. That was a different kind of shit.'

'Well think about it.'

'I will.'

'And get dressed. Sitting around all day in your jarmies, it's no wonder people give you pitying looks.'

'I can always rely on you to cheer me up, Dr Buxton. So, I hear we'll be getting Dr Mac as a neighbour.'

'What, our Mac? First I've heard. Are you sure?'

'The big white house, set back from the road, near the turn for Wombourne? It's three old cottages knocked into one.'

'And Mac's bought it?'

'That's what I heard. It needs a lot of work. There used to be an old lady living in it. I suppose she died. Funny, I never saw it advertised. If I'd seen a For Sale board I'd have gone to have a look at it.'

'You're not thinking of moving?'

'I might have to, if Rick stops paying the mortgage. But no, I'd just have viewed it to be nosy.'

'Talking of being nosy, why don't you give Dr Dan the tour? Show him your swimming pool. It'll make a change from the puddles of piddle he has to step round in the Brook Glen towers.'

There was a garden room at the back of the Priors' house, with potted palms and cane chairs and a heated pool. Eileen said she hadn't been in it for a while. I was about to say if I had a pool like that, I'd swim every day, but she read my mind.

'Not if you had MS and you were feeling crap, you wouldn't.'

'Get your roots done,' were Trevor's final words to her. 'Doctor's orders.'

At least he got a smile from her.

I said, 'She's depressed.'

'Oh yes.'

'Will you flag her for a review in a few weeks?'

'Could do.'

'I think the QOFs recommendation is 'within a month'.'

'I'll take your word for it.'

'That way we're covered.'

'Whatever you think, Dan. But Eileen's not a likely suicide, not at the moment anyway. She's got a lot of fight in her. She'll want to stick around to see her husband rue the error of his ways. What a plonker. Now, let's take a little detour and have a butcher's at this house Mac's supposed to have bought. It's news to me.'

But perhaps not to me. As soon as Eileen Prior mentioned Mac and an old lady, the thought of Hilda Ruck had slithered back into my mind.

'I don't want to make Dr Mac cross, she'd said.

'Does he get cross?'

'Not at all,' she'd said. 'He's very kind. But he might do if things don't get done.'

Halfpenny House was a run-down property. The garden was very overgrown and the wooden window frames were in bad condition, but you could see it had a lot of potential.

Trevor lowered his window.

He said, 'I've been in that house. I'm pretty sure my father had patient who lived there. I reckon I did a house call. A long time ago, mind. I'd have been like you, just starting out. A chap living there with his daughter. An old maid type, you know?'

I said, 'It's a lot of space for one person. Mac's not married, right?'

'No, the carefree bachelor. He has little romances, but he never gets in too deep. A bit like my son. Fearful of losing the thrill, fearful of getting too comfortable. See Dan, losing the thrill never bothered me. I like knowing exactly what Mrs Buxton'll say if I get butter in the marmalade. Or marmalade in the butter. I don't know, I can't see Mac buying a house like this. It's a fixer-upper. It's not like he's a handyman. Unless it was going for a song. And why would it, the prices places fetch around there? No, I reckon Eileen must have got the wrong end of the stick. Do you fancy a quick half in the Dudley?'

'Not really.'

'You all right, lad? You seem out of sorts.'

So I told him. Chloe left me. He said nothing. Pulled into the Dudley Arms car park.

'Have a tonic water, at least,' he said. 'You can either tell me all about it or sup in silence.'

He listened. About Jamil, mainly, and about Saturday's nightmare dinner.

'It was nice of you to have Vaz over,' he said. 'I don't think he gets out much. This Jamil, do you think he's made a play for her?'

The truth was, I thought it more likely Chloe had made a

play for Jamil, but it was too humiliating to say.

'You might get home tonight and find she's come back.'

'I don't think so.'

'And if she has come back, my advice is to keep your powder dry. No inquisition, right? If there's something she wants to tell you, she will. The ladies love discussing things. Relationships. Feelings. If you ever flick through one of their magazines, you'll see.'

'You don't think I should go to the Queen Elizabeth, wait for her to finish her shift and have it out with her?'

'Under no circumstances.'

He looked at his watch.

'Let's go and see Marion Flitwell while we're out and about. I hear she's lost a lot of weight.'

Marion was using a walking frame. It took her a while to come to the door. She was still enormous, but the change in her was astonishing. Her features were in sharper focus.

Trevor said, 'If you keep this up Terry won't know you when he comes home.'

Her lip trembled.

'He'll be gone for weeks,' she said. 'He's got to go to rehab and I do miss him. I can't even visit him. I tried going in a taxi but the driver got that impatient. It's the getting in and out of the car. And then there's the steps, when I get back here. If the lift's bosted, the stairs'd kill me.'

'There are volunteers, you know? People who'd drive you. Have you asked your district nurse? She'd know where to ask.'

Marion said she did feel better for losing some weight, but she was still hungry all the time.

'The nights are the worst,' she said. 'When Terry's here he gets up and brings me a snack. But I haven't got anybody to fetch stuff in for me. Terry always makes sure we've got plenty of cake in. These meals they bring you, you don't get much. I could eat the whole van load.'

Trevor said, 'Ask the nurse about getting a lift with a volunteer. Tell her Dr Buxton said so. Go and visit your man. That'll cheer you up. And treat yourself to a new blouse. I see you've got the Littlewoods catalogue.'

We sat outside the Flitwells' building while he smoked half a cigarette.

He said, 'Sometimes I'm not so much a doctor as an agony uncle. Keep your powder dry. Get your hair done. Buy yourself a new top. Still, it's all part of the service.'

'Marion won't keep the weight off.'

'No. As soon as Terry gets home from rehab he'll resume the midnight cake delivery.'

Back at The Lindens Moira was draping tinsel along the top of a door frame and Vaz was holding the step-ladder steady.

Trevor said, 'Halfpenny House, between Himley and Wombourne? Did we have a patient there once upon a time?'

'Yes,' she said. 'Old gentleman with softening of the brain. The first Dr Buxton used to go out to see him. He used to play dominoes with him.'

'Name?'

'I'll have a think.'

'See?' says Trevor. 'We don't need computerised records. Moira's got it all up here.' He tapped his head. 'And she puts up Christmas decorations. At no extra charge.'

Stephanie appeared. I think she must have the place bugged.

'We do need computerised records,' she said, 'because Moira won't always be here. December 21st, staff party, after evening surgery. Other halves are invited, Dr Talbot.'

214

Other halves. Another reminder. It was an expression Chloe hated.

'Do we have to bring stuff?'

'No, the partners all chip in and then Linda goes to Costco.'

I was sitting in with Helen for afternoon surgery. I always felt like a spare part. She never allowed me to conduct a consultation and sometimes she didn't even introduce me to the patient. Moira brought in the files.

I said, 'You didn't happen to remember the name of the gentleman who had softening of the brain?'

'I did,' she said. 'I just told Dr Buxton. It was Jesse Ruck. And he had two daughters. Hilda and Delia.'

When Moira had gone, Helen said, 'Softening of the brain? Dan, we do not use that expression. Encephalomalacia, please.'

I said, 'But I don't think our receptionists would necessarily know that. I said "softening of the brain" because that was the term she'd used.'

'Okay,' she said, 'keep your hair on. Someone's obviously had a bad morning?'

So, Halfpenny House, formerly the home of the Ruck family, had possibly been sold to Mac. Who happened to have been Miss Ruck's doctor but had recently suggested she transfer to Vaz. The same Miss Ruck who'd been fretting about lawyers and her dear Dr Macdonald?

Helen often doesn't stop for a break. She likes to power through. By 5 o'clock we'd seen her last patient.

She said, 'Trevor's still got a few to see, unless you want to get off early?'

Getting off early was the last thing I wanted. To go home to an empty flat? Besides, I had an out-of-hours shift to get through.

She said, 'You all right, Dan? You're not your usual self.'

I told her I was fine. Just tired. She put her hand between my shoulder blades. It felt warm. I rather wished she hadn't. I kept remembering it all evening. That and her perfume.

I waited until Trevor's final patient left. How to broach it? Was it any of my business? Why was I feeling like a snitch?

I said, 'Moira has an amazing memory.'

'Terrifying,' he said. 'And not just for patients, past and present. She remembers birthdays, wedding anniversaries, where you've been on your holidays. I'll bet she could tell you what year Mrs Buxton and I went to Lake Garda.'

'She told me she'd remembered who used to live in that house.'

'Yes. The Rucks.'

'Funny, the name rang a bell with me. I couldn't place it straight off but then I remembered. One of Mac's old ladies in Woodleigh Grange is a Miss Ruck. I wondered if that property could be hers.'

'Could well be,' he said. 'Ruck. It's not that common a name.'

'Only, if it is her, she's the patient I visited while Mac was away. She was having anxiety attacks, worried about something to do with Mac and a lawyer.'

'Oh yes? And what did Mac say about it?'

'That she often got confused.'

'You're giving me your boy scout look.'

'I just wondered…'

'Spit it out.'

'Miss Ruck is elderly and arguably demented. Mac's her attending doctor. Although according to Miss Ruck, Mac told her to transfer to Vaz's list.'

'According to Miss Ruck who's arguably demented?'

'Yes, but now Mac appears to have bought her house. Which wasn't on the open market.'

'According to Eileen Prior. Could just be Himley gossip.'

'Right. Gossip's not good though, is it? For the practice?'

'What do you want me to say? You want me to grill Mac?'

'Not grill. I'd just have thought you'd want to be sure that everything is above board.'

He said, 'I imagine Miss Ruck's solicitor will have made sure it is, don't you? And haven't you got worries enough of your own to deal with?'

There was a steeliness in his voice I hadn't heard before. Mac was a respected partner and I was a trainee, just passing through, sticking my nose in, stirring up trouble, too assiduous with the QOFs, the boy scout. As far as he was concerned the matter of Halfpenny House was closed.

Time and again he fools me. I think he's switched off but behind those rheumy eyes he's cogitating.

There was still no message from Chloe. One minute I felt furious with her, the next I'd have given anything to hear her voice. I drove to the Sterling call centre. I was glad of the prospect of distraction for a few hours.

Out of Hours could have its lighter moments. One evening there was a woman who called us because she'd been waiting two hours for a pizza delivery. When we told her that we couldn't help her she said it was absolutely disgraceful and in that case she was going to call the police. And then there was a man who phoned because he didn't like the way his brother was looking at him. We had a laugh about it, but afterwards I started thinking, should we have treated it as a possible mental health issue? What if things kicked off and somebody got hurt? I had Neil, a very experienced nurse practitioner, sitting in with me that evening.

He said, 'Dan, you could drive yourself round the bend with what-ifs. We can't be dispatching police and ambulances to what-ifs. We're just doing triage here, till the surgeries open in the morning. And after you've done this job for a while, you get a feeling about calls. You get an instinct for serious stuff.'

The panicky call about a sick baby was what I really dreaded. Are they teething? Is it just a cold? Or could it be bacterial meningitis and I'm going to end up facing bereaved parents at an inquiry?

Things were fairly slow. It was a typical Tuesday. Fridays, Saturdays, Bank Holidays, that's when things can get hectic. Then Pauline, one of the nurses on duty, took a call that bothered her. She was having difficulty understanding what the woman was saying. I heard her tell the caller to calm down and speak clearly. Then the call dropped. She tried to call her back a few times but the line was busy.

She said, 'I think it was about a baby, but she was yelling so loud I couldn't tell what she was saying. Foreigner. Polish probably. I reckon she might have been in labour.'

Neil said, 'Don't worry, flower. She probably popped it out or realised she'd be better off calling 999. Who's for a cup of cocoa?'

I hoped there'd be a light on when I got home. There wasn't. I fell asleep in front of the telly, woke around midnight with a crick in my neck, ate a whole bag of M&Ms and sent a pathetic text to Chloe. Hyperglycaemic stupidity. I tried sleeping on her side of the bed to see if that felt less lonely. It didn't. I checked my phone every five minutes. Sod's law prevailed. The minute I was asleep she woke me with a message. Stop pressuring me. Need time out. If Net-a-Porter parcel arrives, pls advise.

Trevor had abandoned his bookcase sorting project.

'I'll leave it,' he said. 'It's quite decorative. But I will clear out the Bureau of Doom. God knows what's in there.

Woodworm I shouldn't wonder, apart from anything else.'

I took surgery, with him in the background, coughing and grunting and going through the contents of his battered old bureau. It was stuffed with papers and the overflow was piled on the top. Nothing was said about Mac or Miss Ruck. Nothing was said about Chloe.

It was a pretty average morning. Sciatica, catarrh, tinnitus, itchy haemorrhoids, feelings of listlessness (mine as well as the patient's), a self-diagnosed case of IBS and Mandy Povey, whom I'd never seen before.

'Mandy Povey, says Trevor, 'is Stinky Hodge's girlfriend.'

Mandy was a well-upholstered woman of about forty. She wanted a weight loss pill.

I said, 'There's only one way to lose weight and that's slowly and sustainably.'

'How do you mean?'

'You need to change what you eat and how much you eat, and permanently. There's no quick fix.'

'But there's definitely pills. It was on the telly.'

'We won't prescribe them.'

'So how am I supposed to fit in my new jeans?'

I suggested she take them back and get a bigger size.

She said, 'Well you're not much help. I shall have to get a second opinion.'

As I told her, a second opinion is often a good idea.

Trevor said, 'And so the new, tougher Dr Talbot emerges from his trainee cocoon.'

Lunchtime I did letters and prescriptions and ate my sushi at his desk.

Trevor said, 'Like that Japanese stuff, do you?'

'It's okay. Low in fat, high in protein. Actually, I don't like it that much. I only eat it, only ate it, to please Chloe. I think I'll walk down to the Parade and get some chocolate.'

'Ah,' he said, 'rebelling against the guiding hand of the future lady wife. Any news on that front?'

'Nothing.'

'I'm sorry to hear that. Dietary guidance isn't something I've ever suffered from because Mrs Buxton isn't very interested in food. I've been left in peace to poison myself. You know, whenever people talk about sushi I immediately think of two things. Number one, tapeworms. Have you ever seen a tapeworm?'

'Only in the museum at Med School.'

'Horrible things. We had a case once. A chap who'd been working out in Uganda. He'd lost a bit of weight and he had gut pain. First thought of course was the Big C. Then one morning he brought in a lump of faeces and there were tapeworm segments in it, still moving. Sorry. Didn't mean to spoil your lunch.'

'What did they look like?'

'Like a little necklace of rice grains. I can picture it now. It was in a pickle jar, still had the label on. It put me off pickled onions for years.'

'How did you treat him?'

'Oral Distoside. As I recall he needed a couple of doses. You have to kill the head, otherwise they just grow a new body. What was God thinking? I mean, I don't like rats but at least you can say a rat brings pleasure to other rats. You can't say that about a tapeworm.'

'No?'

'They're hermaphrodite, lad.'

'What's the other thing sushi makes you think of?'

'What those Japs did to our boys. Mrs Buxton had an uncle who was a POW in Changi. Are you going to the Parade, then?'

'For a Twix. Do you want coffee when I come back?'

'Yes please. And if you're going to the shop, get me a

packet of salt and vinegar crisps and 20 Benson & Hedges.'

I was almost out the door.

'Oh, by the way' he said. 'I had a word with Mac. He did indeed look at Halfpenny House but not for himself. His sister's thinking of moving down here.'

'Thinking of moving?'

'Actually, she is moving. They made an offer, she made an offer, and it's been accepted.'

'By Hilda Ruck?'

'If that's who owns it. So there we are. Mystery solved.'

There were some new mugs printed with 'The Lindens'. A gift from one of the drug reps. When I went back into the office Trevor was using a wire coat hanger to fish papers out from behind the bureau. Each piece he retrieved, he read. I could see it was going to be a very drawn out job.

He looked at the coffee mug.

'What's this? Something to treasure from Big Pharma?'

'From TheraMed.'

'TheraMed. I can remember when they used to ply us with real treats. Tickets for Twickenham. Hospitality tent at the Cheltenham Gold Cup. Not that it was necessarily a good thing. I'm not saying that. I was never for sale, but there were plenty who were. Now all we get are pens and diaries. And mugs.'

He went back to sifting. Some of the papers were yellow with age.

'Look at that,' he'd say. 'Lionel Cherry's hospital discharge letter. August 2002. Well he's definitely been discharged now. Discharged to Fallings Heath Cemetery.'

I said, 'A paper-free office would suit you.'

'You sound like dear Stephanie. Doctor-free surgeries, that'll be the next thing. Everybody'll sit at home, stooped over their phone, asking Google what's up with them.'

He was looking at a homemade card.

'I'll keep this,' he said. He passed it to me. It was a child's drawing, sun in the sky, ambulance with a big red cross and a stick man doctor with a stethoscope dragging on the ground. Inside it said Thank you you Dokter Bukton. From Bobby.

'A happy customer?'

'That was Bobby Tyrell. Acute lymphoblastic leukaemia.'

'How did he do?'

'Didn't make it. He had a bone marrow transplant, but it failed after a year. He was a smashing little lad.'

'I haven't had anything like that yet. Dealing with a really sick child, dealing with the parents. It's something I dread.'

'Bound to, Dan. It puts you in your place. All those years of training, brass plate with your name on and you think you're the mutt's nuts. Then a Bobby Tyrell comes along and reminds you just how bloody powerless you are. But there's no ducking out of it.'

He threw me his racing paper.

'Pick a horse, any horse.'

I jabbed with a pen. Bowl of Cherries in the 3.20 at Fontwell. I reached for my bookbag.

'Are you leaving me? Are you sitting in with Helen this afternoon?'

'Pam Parker.'

'That'll cheer you up. I have a suspicion Pam gets more entertainment per minute than we do.'

Pam laughed when I told her.

She said, 'If Buxton's idea of entertainment is vaginal thrush and breast lumps, he's welcome to join me any day.'

But sure enough, we did get one moment of light relief. Tegan Strange wanted to know how to get a black baby.

Pam put on her serious face. She said, 'Tegan, are you having sexual intercourse with anyone?'

'Yeah.'

'And what colour is the man you're having sex with?'

'Morocco.'

'Is that a colour?'

'It's where he's from.'

'Okay. So he's, what, darkish-skinned?'

'Yeah.'

'Therefore, any baby you have with him is going inherit some of his colouring. Could be anything from Tipton beige to toffee brown, but probably not black. That's how inheritance works.'

Tegan didn't look convinced.

She said, 'My sister's got a black baby.'

'That'll be because her Baby Daddy's black.'

'No. He's from Wednesbury.'

'But black.'

'No, he's white. And any road, he's away. He's in Brinsford.'

Tegan left, probably not much wiser than when she'd arrived.

Pam said, 'Eleven years of being educated at tax-payers' expense. Literacy and numeracy, bog basic, I'd say. Biology? Nothing. Although she's very likely learned how to put a condom on a carrot.'

'What's Brinsford?'

'A Young Offenders' place. He's going to be thrilled when he comes home and finds a black baby in the cradle. It could be enough to drive him back to a life of crime.'

There was a crowd in the kitchen. It was Linda's birthday and she'd brought in cake. The phone rang in Reception. Stephanie went to answer it. Trevor had his coat on and an unlit cigarette in his hand, ready for the drive home.

Helen said, 'Have you thought of trying those e-cigs?'

'No,' he said. 'Have you thought of leaving a man in peace with his modest pleasures?'

'By the way, what happened to Mrs Buxton's Vogue you brought in? It's not in the waiting room.'

'Then I suppose somebody nicked it. One glossy mag, hardly read. It has to be worth something down the souk. Funny, nobody ever takes the National Geographic.'

'Damn,' says Helen. 'I was looking forward to a bubble bath, a G&T and a nice long browse.'

Stephanie rematerialized. She normally has a florid complexion but her face was quite pale.

'Dr Buxton, Dr Vincent,' she said, 'We have a situation. My office, please. I need a word, in private.'

Pam said, 'I hope you don't need me. I've got dinner to cook and a parents' evening to go to.'

'No,' says Stephanie, 'I don't need you, but no-one is to leave until I say.'

Trevor gave me a mystified look. The three of them trooped into Stephanie's office and she closed the door.

Pam Parker said, 'A situation? Uh-oh.'

Vaz came into the kitchen.

He said, 'You are all standing like statues.'

Linda said, 'Something's up. Stephanie's put us on lock-down. Well fuck that. It's my birthday and I'm meeting my mates at Fusion. There's a Screaming Orgasm out there with my name on it.'

And she left.

Pam said, 'Wait for me. There's cauliflower cheese and the Screaming Ab-dabs out there with my name on them.

Vaz said, 'What is a lock-down?'

'It means no-one's supposed to leave till Stephanie says so. I have no idea what's going on.'

'But Nurse Linda has gone. Dr Pam has gone. I have 7

o'clock shift at Sterling. I think I must go.'

Vaz left. And as I couldn't think of any earthly reason why I should need the practice manager's permission to leave the building, I was about to follow him when Stephanie's door opened.

'Dr Talbot,' she said. 'Would you step in here, please.'

Everyone was standing. Trevor looked grim. Helen looked grimmer.

Stephanie said, 'Usman Okeke.'

Trevor said, 'The black baby.'

'Please don't interrupt,' says Stephanie. 'Time is of the essence. And by the way, the colour of the child is irrelevant.'

'Not entirely irrelevant,' says Trevor. 'The very reason the mother wanted him circumcised was because they're from West Africa. Where people are black, mainly.'

Helen hissed at him to shut up.

I said, 'I was with Trevor when he saw Mrs Okeke. I heard the advice he gave her. He told her the only place to get the baby circumcised was a hospital. Has she lodged a complaint?'

Helen said, 'The child's dead, Dan. Bled out. And there are seven shades of shit about to hit the fan.'

Mrs Okeke hadn't listened to Trevor's advice. She'd gone to some Nigerian woman in Handsworth who styled herself a wise-woman, healer and midwife.

Trevor said, 'Wise-woman! Witchdoctor, more like. What else does she do, on the side? Mend shoes?'

Helen said, 'Trevor, your attitude isn't helpful.'

'I haven't got an attitude. I've done nothing wrong and yet I've been hauled in here like a schoolboy caught smoking behind the bike shed.'

Stephanie said, 'Trevor can't remember whether he took notes when he saw Mrs Okeke.'

Trevor said, 'I see 30 patients a day. I can't remember everything I do, but I remember her clearly. And I probably took notes. Possibly.'

Helen said, 'On the computer, Trevor? Not on the back of a betting slip.'

I said, 'I took notes.'

And Trevor murmured, 'Thank you, Dan.'

I said, 'I don't see the problem anyway. Trevor gave Mrs Okeke very clear reasons why he wouldn't do the procedure. It's hardly his fault if she ignored him and went off and made her own arrangements.'

Stephanie said that would be for a court to decide if the Okekes made a claim for clinical negligence.

'Which they are threatening to do.'

'Really?' says Trevor. He was leaning on Stephanie's desk, bracing himself, trying to get his breath. 'Threatening legal action? With a six week old child lying cold in his little box? You'd think they'd be prostrate with grief, not talking to lawyers.'

Helen said, 'Do you want me to call Cliff?'

'No way,' says Stephanie. 'He's your husband. He can't get involved.'

'But he can give us some informal advice.'

'We don't need informal advice. We need someone who knows what they're talking about.'

Helen didn't like that.

Trevor said, 'No offence, Helen, but it's hardly Clifford's area of expertise. That's what the GMC is for. We'll talk to them in the morning.'

'And in the meanwhile,' says Stephanie, 'No-one's to discuss this with anyone. Not even at home, Helen.'

Helen glowered.

I said, 'When did this happen? Was it last night, by any chance?'

'Yes. Why?'

'I was doing a shift Sterling and one of the triage nurses took a call she couldn't understand. It was someone who didn't speak very good English. She thought it was about a baby, but then the caller rang off.'

'That was probably it. The kid was DOA at Sandwell.'

'Has anyone been arrested? That'd be manslaughter, right? Involuntary.'

'Not our concern,' says Helen. Our business is the good name of this practice. And not getting sued. That could wipe us out, and even if we won, God knows what it'd do to our insurance premiums.'

Trevor's breathing had worsened.

He said, 'I'll talk to the GMC first thing in the morning. Now I'm going to light my cancer stick and leave the building.'

'No Trevor,' says Helen. 'You're going to leave the building, then light the cigarette.'

He stumbled on the way out of Stephanie's office. I caught him by the arm, but he was a dead weight. He sank to the floor. His face was purple.

Stephanie said, 'Does he need oxygen?'

'Yes,' says Helen, 'and an ambulance.'

Everyone had left. Even Vaz had disobeyed orders. Out in Reception the phone rang and clicked to the machine. It was someone from the Dudley News, looking for a comment on the Okeke death.

Helen went to pick up Trevor's wife and bring her to the hospital. I followed the ambulance to the Sandwell. There was a radio car with the Pulse FM logo driving very slowly along the road. They were looking for the surgery. Fortunately, the only bit left of The Lindens sign was NS so it looked like taking them a while to locate us.

When they wheeled Trevor into A&E his colour had

improved but he looked steamrollered.

'Poor little sod,' he kept saying. 'Poor little sod.'

Helen called me while he was waiting to be seen. She said Mrs Buxton was in no state to come to the hospital.

'She's three sheets,' she said. 'He's not dying, is he?'

'He's calling the nurses 'sweetheart' and asking to be taken outside for a smoke. Should I stay?'

'No, go home. Give them my number in case of emergency and I'll see if I can get the son's number from Mrs B. It's on the local news, by the way, about the Okeke baby. What a goddamned mess.'

CHAPTER 21

I threw a Ready Meal in the microwave, poured a glass, then tipped it down the sink after one sip. I needed to think. My notes should definitely cover Trevor's back. He'd be in the clear. But what if this finished him, health-wise? I still had eight months left at The Lindens and Trevor was what I most liked about the place. Pam Parker and Vaz were nice enough but I now had serious doubts about Mac. And with Helen I never knew where I stood. One minute a sharp word, the next a lingering hand on my back.

Just after 9.00 my phone rang. I nearly didn't answer it. What if the West Midlands newshounds had tracked me down? What if Trevor had taken a turn for the worse? But it was Chloe.

The first thing she said was, 'What the fuck, Dan?'

'What the fuck, yourself. Where are you?'

'You do know you're on the news? Your crappy Lindens practice?'

'Why have you left me?'

'I told you. I needed some space.'

'I've been going out of my mind. Why don't you come home? We can talk.'

'Don't pressure me. Mummy just called me. She'd seen about the riots on TV.'

'What riots?'

'Anti-racism. In Handsworth. It's because of your surgery's up-fuck.'

'Our surgery didn't fuck up. We did everything by the book.'

'Are you personally involved?'

'Come home. Please.'

'I don't know. Things are complicated.'

'Have you met someone else?'

'I need to think.'

Don't ask, Dan. Don't mention Jamil.

'So if you don't want to talk, why did you phone me?'

'To find out what's going on and tell you that Daddy's going to call you. He can advise you. You must listen to him.'

Laurence Swift was just about the last person I wanted to speak to. I was probably going to get a roasting for failing his princess daughter in some way. Pressuring her! I have never in my life pressured anyone. Talbots don't do pressure.

Laurence called me within minutes of Chloe ending her call. They'd obviously been conferring. Smoke signals between The Chummery and wherever Chloe was hiding. In Jamil's luxuriously appointed love nest, possibly.

He said, 'This is a bad show. Have you seen the news? Some damned rabble-rouser predicting mayhem. Rent-a-mob. Who's your brief?'

I said, 'Laurence, there really isn't a case to answer. The child's mother asked us to circumcise the baby. Our senior partner refused. I was there. I witnessed the entire consultation. He told her a circumcision had to be done in a hospital. But it seems she went off and made her own arrangements.'

'Went to some bloody jigaboo woman, apparently.'

'Bloody's right. And now the child's dead. It's a tragedy, but there's no way we're culpable. Anyway, we're talking to the GMC in the morning.'

'Who's your senior partner?'

'Trevor Buxton. But he's in hospital himself at the moment, collapsed under the strain. I imagine Helen Vincent will handle things, if there's anything to handle. She's taking over on January 1st anyway.'

'Assume nothing, my boy. Tell your man, Burton, I know

a couple of excellent silks, should the need arise. Now I'm putting Vinnie on. She wants a word.'

Vinnie said, 'Dan, you do seem to have got yourself in a pickle.'

I wasn't having that.

I said, 'What do you mean?'

'Well, mismanaging things with Chlo. And now this scandale.'

It amuses me when Vinnie drops a bit of plummy French into her speech. Tant pis, is one of her favourites. Quelle horreur! That's another.

I said, 'Vinnie, there is no scandal. And I don't manage your daughter. I love her and I thought we were happy, but she's giving me the run-around. Do you know where she's living?'

'I'm not at liberty to say.'

'Is she staying with a work colleague?'

'Possibly.'

'Male or female?'

'I won't be quizzed, Dan. But you really need to consider some of the choices you've made. It would have made Chloe so happy if you'd gone to work with Laurence. Good night.'

Exhaustion suddenly overtook me. We were in for a difficult few days at The Lindens and I had to face the fact that I might have lost Chloe. I ironed a shirt for morning, went to bed and slept deeply in spite of a very vivid dream involving Vinnie Swift, Hilda Ruck, Helen in a bubble bath and an angry crowd baying and hammering on the surgery's locked doors.

The next morning there were a few reporters sitting in cars outside the surgery. Not exactly a media frenzy but still worrying. I just turned up my coat collar and hurried past them. I was the last to arrive, apart from Pam Parker who wasn't really expected but came in anyway.

She said, 'I thought you might be glad of another pair of hands, seeing as Trevor's out of action.'

Trevor had been admitted to a Respiratory ward for a few days. Helen was taking Mrs Buxton to visit him after lunch.

Pam said, 'Kyle Bibby's outside, by the way, giving interviews.'

Moira said, 'That's the earliest he's ever been up in the morning.'

Stephanie called us to order. She said we'd open for surgery as usual at 9.00 but if there was any sign of trouble we'd close for the day. Mac had offered to speak to the GMC legal department.

Helen said, 'Cliff says…'

Stephanie cut across her. She said, 'I told you we don't need your husband's advice. I told you not to talk to anyone about this.'

I said, 'Stephanie, it was on the news last night. They'd even heard about it in Bishop's Wapshott.'

Helen continued anyway. 'Cliff says if they claim for clinical negligence, the Bolam test applies, which is, was there a failure of duty of care? Trevor advised the Okeke woman to go to hospital, Dan was a witness to that, therefore he surely met all reasonable standards. And if it should go to a tribunal, the standard of care would be judged by a panel of doctors, so there's no way we have anything to worry about.'

Stephanie said, 'You mean the Old Boy network?'

Helen said, 'Call it that if you must. It works in our favour. They're all going to be thinking 'that could easily have been me.''

Mac said, 'There's the Bolitho test as well, if they sue for damages. Even if they proved a breach of duty, which they won't, they'd also have to show that the failure actually caused the injuries or contributed to them. Never in a million years. So now can one of us step outside and tell the vultures to clear off? There's no story. Nothing to see.'

Stephanie said Helen should do it. Helen said it was Stephanie's job. Stephanie said she was only willing to read a short statement that had been okayed by a lawyer.

Pam said, 'Why don't we just leave it all to Kyle Bibby?'

There wasn't a single no-show for surgery. Word had gone round that there were TV cameras outside so all the usual offenders from Brook Glen and Cherry Tree turned up, hoping to get their faces on television. When I went out to Reception to fetch more prescription blanks Kyle was leaning against the counter. He had a dog with him, a brindle bull terrier.

'Morning, Doc,' he said. 'I'm just telling Moira here, I put them telly people straight. I told them, you couldn't ask for a better man than Dr Buxton.'

Moira said, 'And I'm telling Mr Bibby, he can't bring that dog in here.'

Kyle said it was his Social Anxiety Dog.

He said, 'Guide dogs for the blind, right? You let them in. Well Tyson's my Social Anxiety Dog. I'm not so liable to go off on one now I've got him.'

I said, 'That's good to hear, Kyle, but as far as I know that's not a recognised category of assistance dogs. You'd have to talk to the practice manager. And frankly, today's probably not a good day.'

'Got you,' he said. 'I'll come back later in the week. I can put it in writing if you like.'

'That's a pedigree dog you've got there. How much did he set you back?'

'No, I'm fostering him. I got him off Rocky Dearlove. They just sent Rocky down for two years, so I'll be looking after Tyson till he gets out. You tell Dr Buxton, he don't have nothing to worry about. Everybody in my tower, we're all behind him. We won't hear a word said against him. Mind how you go, Doc.'

He left.

Moira said, 'All the Bibbys and the Dearloves behind him! That'll be a comfort. They haven't got a case, have they, these people with the little baby that died?'

'I don't think so.'

'Poor Trevor. Will you be visiting him?'

'I thought I'd go at lunchtime.'

She fetched her purse and gave me a pound coin.

'Get him a Mars Bar from me,' she said. 'He'll be missing his smokes.'

Trevor seemed to have shrunk overnight.

He said, 'Well this is a mess. What did the legal bods say?'

'I don't know. Have you ever had anything like this happen to you before?'

'No, not a thing. I've gone 37 years without a smudge. I mean, I had a couple of patients falling in love with me, years ago, when I was still full of vim and vigour. But there were never any accusations, unfounded though they'd have been. Just little notes and unsolicited gifts.'

'What did you do?'

'Passed them along to Mac or Helen. The women, I mean, not the notes. There was never anything I couldn't handle. This little lad though. I keep picturing him, lying on the desk, chortling at me, piddling on the files. I've lost a few sick kids, Dan. It happens. But not like this. Not a perfectly healthy one.'

'What's the care like in here?'

'They do the best they can, lad. At least I can walk to the bog unaided. You might wait a long time for a bedpan. Do something for me. When you get back, call the Liver Unit about Glenys Allsop. I meant to do it yesterday.'

'Anything else?'

'Yes. Tell me something to cheer me up.'

'Kyle Bibby has vouched for you, on local television and on radio. He told them you were a top doctor. A bit stingy with the temazepam but a caring and sympathetic physician and straight as a die.'

'Phew,' he said. 'I was afraid he might not step up. At times like this you find out who your friends are.'

'There's something else.'

'Go on.'

'He's acquired a bull terrier. It belonged to one of the Dearloves, who is now doing time, so Kyle has adopted it.'

'Kyle Bibby. Cherry Tree's very own Good Samaritan.'

'He claims it's his Social Anxiety Dog and he wants to be allowed to bring it into the surgery, like a guide-dog.'

'A Social Anxiety Dog?'

'Yes. He says it helps him to stay calm. I told him to apply to Stephanie for a permit to bring the dog into the surgery. Moira chucked him out, pending his application.'

Trevor laughed so much a nurse came running.

'Mr Buxton,' she said. 'This is quiet time. Patients supposed to be resting.'

'Haven't you heard?' he said. 'Laughter's the best medicine.

'Helen's bringing Mrs Buxton in later.'

'That's good of her. Do you think Kyle'll be asking for tins of Chum on prescription?'

'It's quite a big beast to feed. I suppose he might qualify for supplementary benefits.'

'Name of dog?'

'Tyson.'

'Anything else?'

'It wears a scarf. A neckerchief. Union Jack.'

'Thank you, Dan,' he said. 'And thank you Kyle. You've dispersed the black cloud that's been pissing on me since yesterday evening.'

By the end of the afternoon the mood at The Lindens had lifted a little too. The cameras and reporters had moved on to Handsworth where a Mrs Agu had been charged with involuntary manslaughter and bailed, the window of a Pound Land shop had been bricked by boys with scarves over their faces and their trousers at half-mast, and some community blowhard was ranting about institutional racism in the health service. I had also established that Glenys Allsop was being assessed for a liver transplant.

Pam Parker and Nurse Linda were in the kitchen. They asked after Trevor.

'He's disturbing the peace of Mary Seacole ward and raring to go home.'

'Helen's happy. The lawyer says there's no case to answer.'

I said, 'I have a question. Trevor's wife? Does she have a name?'

'Mrs Buxton,' they said in perfect unison.

'Does she usually come to the Christmas party?'

'Yes.'

'So when I meet her, what do I call her?'

'Mrs Buxton,' again in unison.

CHAPTER 22.

Kelly Tomlinson had her baby with her. Levi. Her other two children were at nursery. Kelly herself had a rash. Levi didn't.

She said, 'It don't itch, Doctor, but it don't half hurt.'

She took off her shirt. There were blisters, running from her armpit across the top of her left breast and behind her left shoulder.

I said, 'You've got shingles.'

'I've heard of that,' she said. 'That's terrible. You can go blind.'

'Not where you've got it. Yours is along the axillary nerve, see? Nowhere near your eyes.'

'Can you cure it?'

'No. We just have to let it run its course. You need to rest and take paracetamol if the pain gets too bad.'

'Rest!' she said. 'On me own with three babs?'

I looked at her file. She'd been one of the first patients I'd seen at The Lindens. Two children with pink-eye. I remembered her exact words when Trevor asked her about her partner. 'He's fucked off with some minger.'

I said, 'So your partner's still not around?'

'Yeah, no,' she said. 'He did come back, but he's inside now. He got time for robbing.'

I was at a loss. She looked exhausted and shingles can be very debilitating.

'No family you could ask to give you a hand?'

She said she'd ask her Mum if she'd pick Coco and Sienna up from creche but she might not be willing.

She said, 'She's got a new bloke and they're in bed all day, shagging.'

And there was me thinking grannies wore cardigans and

made fairy cakes.

I said, 'I can see things are difficult for you, but shingles are a sign that your immune system is at a low ebb so you do need to look after yourself. Get as much rest as you can. Eat some decent food. Fresh fruit, vegetables, and drink plenty of water.'

'And there's nothing you can give me?'

'Not really.'

'Will the bab get it?'

'If he gets anything it'll be chickenpox. It's caused by the same virus. Is it going around at the creche?'

'Don't know,' she said. 'Chickenpox. That's all I fucking need.'

Helen looked in.

She said, 'I've got Keith Sideaway coming in, if you're interested. The chap with a Pancoast lung tumour? He's had his first round of treatment. Might be an interesting one for you to follow.'

I expected to see a change in him, but I was still shocked when he walked in. He'd lost weight and his eyelid droop was much worse.

'Thought I'd come in to thank you,' he said. 'They told me at the hospital you'd done well to spot what was wrong.'

Helen said, 'It was only a lucky hunch. So what have they planned for your treatment?'

'Three lots of this chemo. I've got three weeks off now, then I go for the next dose. Horrible stuff. I've been as sick as a dog. And you're there all day. It's a full-time job this cancer.'

They were giving him intravenous cisplatin and paclitaxel, plus lorazepam to reduce the nausea.

'After that I have to have radiation for three weeks. Twice a day, Monday to Friday. Only they said sometimes they have to stop it, after the second week. Some people can't take it. It all depends how I hold up.'

She said, 'It's a balancing act. They want to shrink the tumour as much as possible, but they don't want the radiation to damage your bone marrow.'

'That's what they told me. Shrink it, so they can take it all out when they operate. I tell you, it's marvellous what they can do these days.'

His left arm was weaker and it was swollen above the elbow. Pressure from the tumour that was still growing. I asked him if his employer was being okay about sick leave.

'Brilliant. The boss said, "you take your time, Keith. Your job'll be here for you when you're ready to come back." The wife worries of course. It's putting a lot on her shoulders. I shall take her and the kids on a nice holiday once I've beat this cancer.'

'How old are your children?'

'Thirteen and eleven. Hardly kids any more. I've promised them we'll go to Euro Disney next year, as soon as I'm right. You're never too old for Disney, are you? Any road, that's the latest. I won't keep you. I just wanted to say thank you.'

He went off, very cheery. Helen was pensive.

'What are his chances?'

'I don't know what the figures are. I mean, it's not a hopeless case but he's got rough times ahead. Chemo, then they add in the radiation. And that's before they operate. If they operate. We're talking major surgery, Dan. It's a bastard of a place for them to access, and if they're not confident of doing a clean resection they might not even try. They might decide on palliative care only.'

'He was so upbeat today. That first time he came in, with his drooping eyelid, he hardly said a word. Just now he was like a different man.'

'You're right.'

'Do you think it's possible they haven't spelled it out to him, at the hospital?'

'The treatment he's having, you'd have to have your head very deep in the sand not to know it was serious. And he'll have talked to other patients, while they're waiting around. I don't know him well enough to gauge his mood. Did you think he seemed a bit disinhibited?'

'You mean because of the meds?'

'Not really. Lorazepam doesn't make you chipper and chatty. I don't want to be the voice of doom but I'm just wondering if he might have a distant metastasis starting to announce itself.'

'You mean a secondary in his brain?'

'Personality change. It can happen. He's already got bone secondaries.'

'What did the hospital say about his lymph nodes?'

'They didn't. Well, we'll know soon enough.'

'Daunting though, what he has to go through to have a fighting chance.'

'It is. He'll be thinking of his kids. That's what'll keep him going. If he was 20 years older, he'd probably fold his hand after a week of radiation treatment. I would.'

'Really?'

'I probably wouldn't even start the chemo. Spend the last year of my life waiting around in hospitals and heaving my guts into a bedside bucket? No thank you. But if I had an eleven year old, it'd be a different story. They still need you at eleven.'

'How old is Miles?'

'Twenty. Right, I'm off. I've got a meeting in Wolverhampton. I'll be back later. Anything you're not sure about, Pam's here and Mac should be in around four.'

'And are we over the Okeke crisis?'

'I think so. If there's an inquiry you and Trevor might be

asked to attend but I don't think there will be. I hope Trevor thanks you for covering his ass. He can be shockingly bad about notes.'

'When do you think he'll be well enough to work again?'

She said, 'No idea. Not for a week or two. I'm not sure he should be working at all. He's losing his touch.'

I didn't think Trevor was losing his touch. I just thought his kind of touch had fallen out of fashion. But I didn't say that to Helen.

Kyle Bibby likes to get a late appointment. He thinks we'll give him what he wants so we can be rid of him and go home.

He came in with his cheeky chappie grin.

'Terrible about them riots,' he said. 'And your main man finishing up in hospital. That'll have been the upset caused it. Stress can kill you. People don't realise.'

I said, 'Kyle, what can I help you with today?'

'Just my usual.'

I said, 'Your usual? This isn't a pub, Kyle.'

He sniggered.

'Just me mazzies. For me social anxiety.'

'What happened to the dog?'

'Rocky's fucking sister took him, didn't she? Said he belonged with family. I mean, Rocky percifically asked me, but he won't stand up to her. Well he can't. He's inside. Fucking cow. She'd bottle you as soon as look at you.'

He seemed very twitchy, very hyper for somebody on temazepam. I asked him what else he was taking.

'Nothing much,' he said. 'Couple of dexxies. I loved that dog.'

'You've been taking Dexedrine? But you do realise that has completely the opposite effect to the temazepam?'

'I only take a dexxie if I'm having a bad one. If I don't see

241

no purpose in life.'

'And did that happen today?'

'Yeah. Things kicked off a bit.'

'And where do you get Dexedrine?'

'I can't tell you that. More than my life's worth.'

'That'd be the same life that seemed so without purpose that you took a strong amphetamine.'

'I think you're having a little dig at me there, Doc.'

'So you buy Dexedrine on the street. Anything else?'

'Only the usual. Bit of Benzo, bit of Vanilla.'

'And Vanilla is what?'

'All legal, doc. It's just to get you in the party mood, know what I mean?'

I said, 'Kyle, one of these days you're going to take something that kills you.'

He said, 'Maybe it will, maybe it won't. I could walk out of here and fall under a bus. Main thing is to enjoy life, right?'

I wrote him up for temazepam 20mg.

'Only twenties again?' he said. 'You're a hard man, Dan. Dan the Man. Only you're not. Sometimes you're Dan the killjoy. You have a good one, Doc. Get yourself a screw of Benzo. And tell Dr Buxton, Kyle says get well soon.'

Vaz was waiting for me at the end of surgery. He had questions about the Christmas party. First, could I tell him about the song?

'What song?'

'Tradition of Lindens medical practice. I have to sing 'twelve chronic backaches' but I don't understand why.'

'Neither do I. Who told you this?'

'Moira.'

We went to Reception. Mary was on duty. Did she know anything about a Christmas song?

'Of course I do,' she said. 'Hasn't Dr Mac given you your line? I think you're fungal toenails.'

It was a special Lindens rendition of The Twelve Days of Christmas. She brought out a list.

'Yes. Dan Talbot, 'eight fungal toe nails'. You happy with that?'

'Oh yes. Thrilled. Are there enough of us?'

'Not quite. Some of us double up. If Trevor doesn't come you might have to do an extra line.'

I borrowed the list and Vaz and I went to his office. I took him through the song as best I could. He still looked baffled.

I said, 'Don't worry. On the night, just stand next to me and when I nudge you, sing "on the twelfth day of Christmas my patients brought to me, twelve chronic backaches."'

He said, 'This is a very strange custom. Now I would like to ask you about Secret Santa.'

I'd clean forgotten about Secret Santa. I needed to buy something for Helen.

'Who did you draw?'

'I'm not supposed to say. What should I buy?'

'Male or female?'

'Female.'

'Chocolates or smellies.'

'What are smellies?'

'Bath bubbles, cologne, that kind of thing.'

'If you had to buy something for, say, hypothetical example, Miss Moira, what would you choose?'

'In the purely hypothetical case of Moira, I'd buy milk chocolates.'

'Thank you. You're a very helpful fellow. Will Chloe come to the party?'

'I don't think so. Chloe left me.'

He was devastated.

'I didn't know,' he said. 'Of course not. This is a private matter. But now I've caused you distress.'

'No, you haven't. I should have told you. I suppose I was

243

waiting to see if she came back.'

'Perhaps she will?'

'Perhaps.'

I only said that to make him feel better. With every day that passed it seemed less and less likely. True, she hadn't left her engagement ring with her note. True, half her clothes were still at the flat but that could be for any number of reasons. Stuff she didn't like any more, stuff she only wore in specific circumstances that I'd never quite got the hang of. But this wasn't a five minute Chloe flounce. This was a serious walk-out and though the evening of the Vaz dinner had triggered it, it surely couldn't be the cause. She must have been having second thoughts about me and now - I couldn't deny it - I was starting to have second thoughts about her.

I went Christmas shopping on my way home and I didn't buy anything for Chloe, not even a pair of cashmere socks that I knew she'd love. I picked them up and then I put them down. I got Mam a necklace from the 'Downton-inspired' collection, a pair of Shaun the Sheep slippers for Da and two boxes of soap, Lily of the Valley flavour for my Nan and lemon-shaped ones for Helen Vincent's Secret Santa present. Done and dusted. I don't know why women make such a fuss about it.

Funny the things you only do when you're home alone. Like drink milk from the carton and eat your chip butty over the sink to save washing a plate.

CHAPTER 23

Stephanie was on my case to fill in her survey about ways we might get more from the Patient Participation Group meetings. 'Added value' was one of her phrases. 'Going forward' was another.

I ate my pasty at my desk and read through her damned questionnaire. Mary tapped and came in.

She said, 'I'm sorry to disturb your break but I've got Margaret and Rene Spooner outside.'

'Did they have an appointment?'

'No. I wouldn't have let them in only Margaret doesn't look so good and she's not a person to expect special treatment.'

They were in the waiting room. Rene was wearing a nightdress under her coat. She was gathering up magazines. She had quite an armful.

She said, 'They stole these from my house.'

Margaret was leaning back in a chair. She was very, very still. Her face was grey. Lunchtime and her mother wasn't yet dressed. She must have been feeling rotten.

'Strained a muscle,' she whispered.

'Is the pain in your back?'

No answer.

'Did you do it lifting something?'

The tiniest shake of the head.

'Can you show me where it hurts?'

She pointed to her throat and her chin. Pallor, jaw pain. Her pulse was racing. Mary was standing behind me.

I said, 'Is anyone else in?'

Only Stephanie. It was 1.30, the dead hour. Vaz was doing visits, Mac too, probably. Trevor was still off sick, Pam

Parker wasn't due till 3.00, Helen was either on her way to a meeting or on her way back and I was close to another brain freeze moment. It wasn't that I didn't recognise what I was looking at, more that I lacked the courage of my convictions.

Then Mary said, 'Would you like me to phone for an ambulance?'

And I heard myself say, 'Yes. Tell them a possible MI. Is there somewhere in here I can plug the ECG machine in?'

She pulled a chair away from the wall. There was a power socket.

I trundled the machine in from the nurses' room. My hands were trembling. It was a long time since I'd handled ECG leads and to make matters worse, Rene took exception to me undoing her daughter's blouse.

'What are you doing to her?' she kept saying. 'Leave her alone. Are you interfering with her?'

I attached the leads. I had one left over. Think, Dan, think. Right arm, left arm, right leg, left leg, 4th intercostal space to the right of the sternum, ditto to the left, one in the armpit, one on the left side level with the axillary lead, V4 goes in the 5th intercostal space in line with the centre of the clavicle. I still had a lead left over. Where was V3 supposed to go?

I heard Mary open the front door. Nurse Chris had come back from lunch. She didn't even take off her coat. She took one look, picked up the orphan lead and whispered, 'Between V2 and V4. Have you given her aspirin?'

Rene was trying to hand Margaret a magazine to read.

'She'll be all right,' she kept saying. 'She's just got a touch of neuralgia.'

Mary took Rene to the kitchen to make a cup of tea. Chris came back with chewable aspirin and a glyceryl nitrate spray. Margaret seemed to relax a little, then she sat forward and vomited on my shoes. We looked at the ECG strip. Deep breath, Dan. You know what you're doing if you just take your time.

I could see at once that it wasn't a normal trace but what exactly was abnormal about it?

Chris said, 'the ST wave.' She traced it with her finger. The S segment never returned to the base line. It just blended into the T segment. Margaret was having a heart attack.

Mary swears the ambulance arrived within ten minutes. To me it seemed more like an hour. The paramedics gave Margaret oxygen. They said they'd start thrombolysis en route to the hospital. Was there a relative who could go with her in the ambulance? Only a demented one.

Chris said, 'Don't worry about your Mum, Margaret. We'll take care of her.'

I'm not sure Margaret was even listening. She was on a trolley and out of the door. She got the blue light ride, and we were left with Rene. I suddenly felt high. Adrenaline. That must be what Rob lives on, working in Major Trauma.

Chris said, 'An almost silent heart attack. It's an easy thing to miss, particularly in women who don't like to make a fuss. That was a good catch, Dan.'

I said, 'I need to practice with those ECG leads. How come you were so fast with them?'

'I worked in A&E before I had kids. I could do it in my sleep. It's different here. You're not up against the clock. Not usually anyway. You'd better wipe the puke off your shoes before it stains. I'll call Social Services about the old lady, then we'll have a cup of coffee. You look like you need one.'

Vaz came back from house calls.

Chris said, 'You missed all the excitement. We've had a myocardial infarct in the waiting room.'

Vaz asked what had made me suspect an MI.

I said, 'I couldn't think of any other reason for jaw pain so severe she seemed afraid to move. And she was a terrible colour.'

'Was she sweating?'

'Yes, a cold sweat. Both of us, actually! You don't expect that kind of emergency in a GP's surgery.'

Chris said, 'You probably saved her life though, Dan.'

Which was an uplifting thought but turned out not to be the case. Margaret arrested on the way to hospital and they weren't able to restart her heart.

I went back into Trevor's office and closed the door. I needed to compose myself. It was all in a day's work. I needed to prepare for afternoon surgery and brush the Cornish pasty crumbs off the desk. I took a piece of paper, wrote,

The Participation Group sessions get mired in personal stories, unrealistic expectations and the requirement to respond respectfully to patients' views even when they're talking cobblers. In my opinion. D Talbot

and stapled it to Stephanie's Improved Outcomes questionnaire. Boy, did I feel better for doing it.

Sadly none of Rene's other children were in a position to come and collect her. She sat in Reception for three hours, eating Mary's toffees, until Mac conjured up an emergency bed for her at the Sorrento nursing home.

'Where's Margaret?' she kept asking.

'She's gone to the hospital for some tests,' we told her. 'So we'll be taking you to a nice hotel for the night.'

'Hotel?' she said. 'How much? I'm a pensioner, you know?'

Mary said, 'It's free. Dinner and breakfast included.'

'I'll need a nightie.'

'You're already wearing it, Rene. Under your coat.'

It was getting towards the end of surgery. I heard voices out in Reception, slightly raised, but I had Lisa Packer in with me and I wanted to give her my full attention. Lisa had returned, triumphant, to show me that the purple Serotide inhaler she had so coveted and which I had refused to prescribe, had done her no harm.

I said, 'Where did you get that?'

'Swapped with Jordan,' she said. 'Nice, isn't it?'

I said, 'You may like the colour, Lisa, but it's completely the wrong medication for you and I strongly recommend you give it back to your friend and stick to the Ventolin.'

All she said was, 'I'm not swapping back. We're not even speaking no more. She's just a div. They ought to make them in more colours, though.'

I updated her notes. Using a friend's Serotide inhaler against my advice.

'Keep good notes' was one of Yasmin Panwar's first pieces of advice when I started as a trainee with her. 'You never know when you'll need to rely on them. It can be years later.'

The commotion was still going on outside, so I followed Lisa as she left. Miles Vincent was haranguing Mary. I heard Mary say, 'She has a full list and she has a patient in with her. Now sit down and wait.'

'Fuck you,' he said.'

I said his name and he turned to face me. Watery eyes, top lip sweaty, pupils dilated. He was probably coming down from a hit of speed.

I said, 'Miles, if you can't be civil, you'll have to wait outside the building.'

He sneered. 'Like to see you make me, Mr Learner Doctor.'

He squared up to me. His knuckles were white. A woman peered out from the waiting room and shot back in again.

Mary said, 'It's all right, Dr Talbot. I'll take care of things. Miles just needs to calm down.'

'Fuck you, old bitch,' he screamed. 'I'll get you fired. Time you fucked off and died anyway.'

I grabbed him by the sleeves of his parka. We were nose to nose. Mary was saying, 'Don't rile him, don't rile him.'

I'm not sure how that would have ended. I'm not a scrapper but I'm not a pushover either. I played lock for Y Fenni Under 16s and Miles Vincent had no muscle, but a desperate man can surprise you with this strength. I was saved by the bell. Helen's door opened, her patient came out, then Helen.

'What the hell?' she said. 'What the hell do you think you're doing?'

I'm still not sure which of us she was speaking to. I opened my mouth to say Miles had been vile and aggressive with Mary but then thought better of it. Risk sounding like a whiny tattle-tale? Why bother? She knew what her son was like.

Miles said, 'You were supposed to leave me some money. Where's my fucking money?'

Helen gestured to him to go into her room. Then she shot me a furious look and muttered, 'None of your business, Dan. Get back to your patients.'

She followed Miles into her office and slammed the door shut. Mary shook her head.

She said, 'Talking to his mother like that. In my day we'd have got a pasting.'

It was only then I realised we'd had an audience. Stephanie and Vaz and Nurse Chris all standing with their backs to the wall, lost for words.

Mary said she was fine. 'I don't like to hear language but in this job you get used to it,' she said. 'And if you ask me, that boy's been trouble since the day he learned to walk.'

It was nearly midnight when I got home from Sterling. The doctor who was on the shift after me had turned up late. Sometimes an empty flat is okay but not that night. That night I would have loved to have Chloe there to tell about my day. About Miles Vincent and poor Margaret Spooner, about Lisa Packer and her Serotide fashion accessory.

My phone rang just as I'd nodded off. As soon as I saw Chloe's number, I was wide awake. The voice wasn't Chloe's though. It was Hua, and she was whispering.

'I would like Chloe to go home,' she said. 'I only have small apartment.'

'She's staying with you?'

'Yes. She sleeps on my sofa. She is very messy girl.'

'Has she been staying with you all along?'

'Yes.'

'Not with Jamil?'

'Jamil doesn't want her. He has girlfriend, in Beirut. They will have big wedding next year. You must allow Chloe to come home.'

'I haven't stopped her. She still has a key. And she was the one who walked out on me. Just be firm with her. Tell her she has to leave.'

'I did. She cries when I tell her. I think you must ask her. I think you must ask her very nicely.'

I said, 'Hua, in the morning, tell her to pack her bag. Take back your key. If she doesn't want to come home to me, she can go to her parents' place. I'm certainly not going to beg her to come home. Now I really have to get some sleep.'

I took two calls before morning surgery. The first was from Trevor.

'I'm out on parole,' he said. 'Meet me in the Black Bear at lunchtime. Just for a pineapple juice.'

'You're not drinking?'

'No, you won't be drinking. I'm slipping the leash. Both

of Mrs Buxton's sisters are visiting. Their usual pre-Christmas routine, like a pincer advance with gift-wrapped weapons. It's no place for a sick man. About 1 o'clock?'

I said I'd try. My mobile buzzed. Chloe. She said she supposed we ought to talk.

I said, 'Yes, I suppose we ought, but not now. I'm about to start surgery.'

'I need to drop off my stuff. Have you changed the locks?'

'Of course not.'

'You don't sound very pleased to hear from me.'

I told her I was neutral, which wasn't quite true, and that I wasn't even sure why she'd left, which was a whopper but I didn't want to bring up Jamil's name until I could see her face to face. I also had fourteen patients to see.

I said, 'We can talk tonight. I'll aim to get away promptly.'

Mam always says, 'Don't let the Devil know your plans.'

CHAPTER 24

Did Chloe really want to come home or was she simply out of other options? Was I the consolation prize after someone else had won Jamil? Had he led her on? Had she been a mug? Was I one? My mind kept drifting to these questions.

The patient with an ingrowing toenail got less than my full attention, likewise the woman who wanted me to do something about her thread veins. Then Connie Riley came in and I snapped out of it. I did a Trevor Buxton and pulled my chair round to sit beside her. She said she was having trouble sleeping since Jimmy passed away.

I said, 'It's not surprising. You can't have been sleeping properly while you were nursing him.'

'I do miss him,' she said. 'I keep thinking I hear him cry out, like he used to, near the end. But of course, he's not there.'

'How long were you married?'

'Fifty two years. He used to say he'd have served less time than that for murder.'

I said, 'Shall I give you something to help you sleep?'

'I don't want to turn into a junkie.'

'No,' I said, 'We won't let that happen. We could try something mild. What we really need to do is remind your body how to sleep. Do you get out at all? Do you go for a walk? A bit of fresh air every day would help.'

'To tell you the truth,' she said, 'I don't like going out because I have to walk past Harry Darkin's house. He's always waving to me from the window. He's always on at me to go to the Seniors' Club with him.'

'The Seniors' Club sounds like a good idea. A change of scene, a bit of company. Don't you like Harry?'

'It's not that. He's a good neighbour. But I know what he's after.'

I said, 'He's 92, Connie.'

'I know he is,' she said. 'But he told me he's still got lead in his pencil.'

I gave her a prescription for Ambien but I doubt she'll ever use it.

Trevor was sitting alone in the lounge bar of The Black Bear. He looked much better.

'Aha,' he said. 'What news from the coalface?'

I told him about Margaret Spooner.

'Margaret?' he said. 'You don't mean Rene?'

'No, Margaret.'

'Well that's a shocker. I tell you lad, we know not the hour. What are you having?'

'Tonic water.'

'Margaret Spooner gone. So that seals Rene's future. She'll live out her days at the Sorrento or some other departure gate, and you know what? I bet she'll love it. All those people to argue with. And poor old Margaret never did go back to choir practice. She flogged herself into an early grave. Well, that's a turn up. What else has been happening?'

'Miles Vincent was in again, raising hell.'

'Looking for the Bank of Mum?'

'Yes. We nearly came to blows.'

'All the fun of the fair when I'm not around. Who blinked first?'

'Neither of us. Helen intervened. She told me to mind my own business. It's not right though, letting him treat Mary and Moira like shit, causing scenes when we've got patients in the building. Why does Helen let him get away with it?'

'Search me. Misplaced mother love? Mind you, Clifford's just as bad. He got a couple of Miles's shoplifting charges dropped, a few years back. The lad probably thinks he can get away with anything now. Being a parent, it's easy to get things wrong. There's no exams, no aptitude test. You just buy a pram and off you go. It's amazing how few disasters there are.'

'Will you see your kids over Christmas?'

'I very much doubt it. We only see James when he's between women and he's currently enthralled with a very beautiful Slovakian girl. And Alice doesn't do Christmas. She's into solstices and all that stuff. Equinoxes. Anyway, the Alice situation is complicated.'

'Because she's gay?'

'Funny word, gay, isn't it? You wouldn't remember when it had a different meaning. I don't think there's much gaiety in Alice's life. It's her partner, Micky. She knocks Alice about.'

That was a surprise. I thought women were supposed to be the gentler sex. Trevor said that had been his belief too, but he now had good reason to see a more mixed picture.

'Why doesn't Alice leave?'

'A very good question. Why don't women leave? Because they think it won't happen again? Because they think they've somehow brought it on themselves? I don't know, but I've seen enough of it in my time. Women who get beaten up and still stay. They always think it's going to get better and it never does. Then, if they do make a run for it... we had a patient, years ago, in the Eighties, she was always 'falling over', always 'banging into things' and bruising herself. She left him eventually, went to one of those women's refuges. He coaxed her to meet him, to talk things over, see if they could make a go of it. Know what happened? He strangled her. Know who he was? Local GP, just like you and me. A respected member of the community. So I understand why Alice puts up with Micky. It's a gamble. Stay and get hit again or leave and risk something worse? I'm a betting man and I don't know what I'd choose. All we can do is keep the emergency exit clear. Our door is always open. She knows that. Doesn't matter how old they get, Dan, they're still your kids. Miles is Helen's boy and Alice is still my little girl.'

I said, 'I'd be very tempted to help this Micky meet with an accident.'

'Get thee behind me, Satan,' he said. He laughed, but he wiped away a tear as well.

'Tell me something cheery.'

'Harry Darkin told Connie Riley he still has lead in his pencil.'

Trevor choked on his beer.

'Did he, the old goat? How did that conversation come about?'

'He's been trying to persuade her to go out with him. To the Seniors' Centre.'

'Probably not the best approach. A bit too direct, and far too soon after Jimmy. Mind you, get to their age you wouldn't want a long courtship. Harry Darkin! I wonder if he's been buying Viagra online.'

'So now Connie won't even go for a walk because she has to go past his gate.'

'Bless her. Should we drop Harry a quiet word on the art of seduction?'

'That'd be betraying a confidence. I think Connie can handle him.'

'Sounds like that's exactly what Harry's hoping for. What else? No bon mots from Kyle Beeby? No gynae adventures with our Amber?'

'No.'

'Have you patched things up with that girlfriend of yours?'

'Tonight, possibly. She's coming round so we can talk.'

'That's a good sign.'

'I suppose.'

'You sound a bit lukewarm.'

'Because I'm not sure if she's opening negotiations for the right reasons. She's been sleeping on a friend's sofa. When do you think you'll be back at work?'

'After Christmas. Am I missed?'

'I miss you.'

'I'm surprised they didn't get a locum in.'

'We've all done a bit extra. Pam Parker's increased her hours. Are you going to sit here all afternoon?'

'Till about 3.00. The sisters-in-law generally make a move around that time. There are worse places. Racing on a big screen telly and this Puddler's bitter isn't bad. If they let you smoke in here it'd be perfect.'

As soon as I walked back into the surgery I knew something was up. There was an argument going on behind Helen's closed door. I asked Moira if it was Miles again. She shook her head but didn't offer any information. Vaz and Linda were in the nurses' room.

Linda said, 'Mac's getting a roasting about something. Stephanie's in there as well. There'll be nothing left of him by the time that pair have finished with him.'

But then Helen's door opened and Mac emerged. He was wearing a very nice Crombie overcoat and he didn't have a mark on him.

Linda said, 'Problems, Mac?'

'No,' he said. 'Just the Big Chief getting her skivvies in a tangle. I'm away to Waterdene. Lilian Rowe's had a stroke.'

Stephanie was the next to appear and her stony face told a different story. She went straight to her office and shut the door. Linda quizzed Moira.

'All I know,' says Moira, 'is a letter came, recorded delivery. Then the balloon went up.'

257

Freda Jarrold was on my afternoon list, the first time I'd seen her since her magnesium deficiency flap.

I said, 'How are the palpitations?'

But she didn't want to talk about palpitations. I'm not sure she even remembered having them. Freda was concerned that she had an under-active thyroid.

She said, 'My eyebrows are getting very sparse, Doctor, and I cannot lose weight no matter what I do.'

'And you think it might be your thyroid?'

'Yes. I was reading about it.'

Been on Google, as Trevor would say.

I could have explained patiently that she didn't have the classic appearance of hypothyroidism: thinning hair, dry skin, puffy face. Her hands weren't cold, she wasn't constipated, her pulse was normal. I could have reassured her that a sub-clinical deficiency, even supposing that to be the case, was nothing to worry about. Or I could just give her what she wanted. Tests.

'Well,' I said, 'let's take some blood.'

How far have you slipped from your high ideals, Dan Talbot? Whatever happened to being empathetic but firm?

Stephanie was still grim-faced when I encountered her at the end of surgery.

'Not helpful,' she said. 'Not helpful at all.'

'What?'

'Your note on Patient Participation Groups.'

'You asked for my opinion.'

'No I didn't. I asked for constructive suggestions.'

'What was all the yelling about with Mac?'

'You'll find out soon enough.'

There was one patient left in the waiting room. He said he was for Dr Vincent. As soon as I heard him leave, I shot across to her office.

I said, 'About yesterday. My little set-to with Miles?'

But she waved that away, told me to sit down.

She said, 'I'm glad you came in. I was going to have a word. We've got another situation on our hands.'

She passed me a letter. It was from a London firm of solicitors, acting for a Mrs Michelle Sanderson in the matter of alleged professional misconduct by Dr Bruce Macdonald, attending physician to Mrs Sanderson's aunt, Miss Hilda Ruck. The facts had been reported to the General Medical Council.

Helen's eyes were closed. She looked exhausted.

I said, 'What does Mac say?'

'That this patient, what's her name?'

'Hilda Ruck.'

'That she has the mental capacity to make financial decisions and anyway he's no longer her Attending. That Vaz is now her GP. Do you know her?'

'I saw her once, when Mac was away. This is about the house sale?'

'You know about that?'

'I know there was a rumour that Mac had bought her house. Trevor asked him about it and it turned out it was actually Mac's sister who'd made an offer for it. Thinking of moving down here, apparently.'

'And Trevor accepted that story?'

'I'm only saying what I heard.'

'You should have come to me. Damn it, Dan, no-one tells me anything. That Okeke woman was potential trouble, playing the cultural discrimination card but the first I knew about it there was a dead child and we had reporters on the doorstep. Now this. Why am I always the last person to hear what's going on?'

I might have said, because you're always running off to meetings. Others, braver than me, might have said, because you're a moody bitch and we never know whether we're going to get stroked or savaged. All I could say was, 'Helen, I'm just the blow-in trainee. If Trevor was satisfied with Mac's explanation, it was hardly for me to question it.'

I handed back the letter.

She said, 'There'll be a tribunal. It can't be avoided.'

'Maybe there's no merit to the claim. Mac doesn't seem concerned.'

'You've spoken to him?'

'No, but he came out of your office and started whistling Scotland the Brave.

'All bluster. Of course there's merit. How old is this Ruck woman?'

'Around 90. What will you do?'

'I don't know. He'll have to take gardening leave until this is sorted. It could take months. How am I supposed to keep the place going?'

'Isn't that Stephanie's job?'

'Stephanie! She's threatening to leave, says she's a manager not a firefighter, and anyway, I'm not inclined to stop her. Everything about her irritates me. Have you noticed how her jacket sleeves are all too long?'

'Perhaps Trevor could delay his retirement? I think he'd like to.'

'Trevor's got one foot in the grave. We'll have to get a locum. We're haemorrhaging money. I get no support, no gratitude. And I know the kitchen cabinet talk about me. Useless mother, addict son.'

There didn't seem any point in a flat denial. How could we not discuss her?

I said, 'I haven't heard anyone call you a useless mother. But they do worry about Miles's aggression. The way he spoke to Mary yesterday was shocking.'

'She's used to it. It doesn't bother her.'

'I'll bet it does. And the way he speaks to you bothers all

of us. Is he like that at home?'

'It's the drugs. He gets anxious. He can't help himself.'

'I thought he was about to hit me yesterday. Does he ever hit you?'

'Not really. He throws things, sometimes.'

'Is he like that with his father too?'

'No. They just ignore each other.'

'And you're caught in the middle.'

'Pretty much.'

I didn't know what to say. It didn't matter. Helen's floodgate had opened.

'Cliff's only interested in one thing. Getting laid. And it's not that I mind that so much, as long as he takes them to hotels, but he's started bringing them to the house in the middle of the day. Economising, I suppose. He's getting too old for the back seat of the car, and now he's too bloody cheap to get a hotel room. I caught him at it in the spare room with some idiot blonde last week. I binned the duvet cover.'

A tear dribbled down her chin.

She said, 'It isn't always blondes. As long as they're young and they wear skirts. He doesn't like girls in trousers. Ease of access, you see? I mean, am I really so unattractive?'

She needed an answer, of course, and quickly.

I said, 'Helen, you're a very attractive woman. You don't need me to tell you.'

That sounded about right. Something else they don't teach you in med school: how to comfort your weeping, quite fanciable boss without overstepping the mark. I'm a bit hazy about what followed but I think it went like this. She stood up. I tried to wipe a smudge of mascara from her cheek. The phone rang in Reception and flipped to the out-of-hours message. We were standing very close. I could smell her perfume and coffee breath. She ran her fingers through my hair.

Then she said, 'I've wanted to do that for a long time. Such sweet curls. Bad idea, though. Very bad.'

I think I agreed with her, but temptation was still close. Her mouth is slightly lopsided, not perfect like Chloe's but strangely sexier. I wondered what she'd taste of. Did I dare?

'Still,' she said, and pulled away from me. 'We're both sensible grownups. No harm done. Fancy a quick drink at the Bear?'

'Well, Dan Talbot,' I thought. 'The way you handle this is either going to ruin your time at The Lindens or oil the wheels.'

She clocked my hesitation.

'No, you're right,' she said. 'Pub, alcohol, another bad idea.'

Someone tapped on the door.

'Yes!' she yelled. 'Now what?'

Vaz peeped in. He was wearing his red anorak. He'd bought it in a charity shop and I hadn't liked to say anything but the consensus in the kitchen was that it was a woman's style.

'Helen, sorry to bother,' he said, 'but there's a gentleman.'

'Where?'

'Outside. I found him as I was leaving.'

'Is he ill?'

'I think he's lost.'

We went out. There was an elderly man on the front step. Padded coat, tweed cap. He had a Tesco bag hooked over his wrist. Helen asked if we could help.

He looked at us and said, 'I think I'll go home now.'

I asked him if he needed a lift.

'Thank you,' he said. 'Mother'll be wondering where I've

got to.'

Helen and I took him inside. Vaz had to leave. He was working the early shift at Sterling.

The man said his name was Joe Smith. He didn't know his address. First he said he lived in Willenhall, then he said he was from Gospel End. There was nothing in his pockets apart from a Murray Mint. I checked our patient lists. We had two Joseph Smiths, one deceased and one aged 52.

Helen called the police. The only missing person they'd had reported was a 15 year old girl. In the carrier bag I found a pair of pyjamas, still with the price tag on, a pack of Bic razors, a new toothbrush, a tube of Steradent tablets and five pairs of pull-up incontinence pants.

'Ah,' says Helen, down the phone, 'my colleague has just pointed out that our Joe has an overnight bag. I think we've got a case of festive season grandad-dumping.'

The police said it'd be at least an hour before they could get anybody out to us. Evenings just before Christmas they're run ragged. We took Joe to Helen's office and I made him a mug of Pam Parker's hot chocolate.

I said, 'You don't seem surprised. Does this happen a lot?'

Helen said as far as she could remember it was a first for The Lindens but she knew a GP in Stourbridge who'd had one, just before Christmas. People decide they fancy some winter sun, a week in Lanzarote, 400 quid all-in and they think, "I'll have a bit of that, thank you very much. Get shot of Grandad and off we go."'

I called the social services out-of-hours number. They said we might have quite a wait. Joe kept asking to go home to Mother. It could have been his wife. Grandad Talbot used to call my Nan 'Mother'.

But Helen shook her head. 'Probably anterograde amnesia,' she said. Joe was living in the past. He was quite sharp in some respects. He could count backwards in sevens and he knew he was born in 1936, but he couldn't tell us who had dropped him on our doorstep or what he'd had for lunch. Helen finished signing letters, then I fetched an old pack of playing cards from Trevor's Bureau of Doom and we played three-handed rummy.

It was around 8.30 when two WPCs arrived at the very same time as the emergency social worker.

I said, 'What's the procedure?'

One of the WPCs said, 'The procedure is, first you let me use your toilet because I'm busting. Second step is to make us a cuppa. Third step is we get him in somewhere for the night.'

The social worker said it'd be no easy matter finding him a bed.

Helen said, 'Well he can't stay here, and we don't want him sleeping at the nick, poor old sod.'

'No room there anyway,' says the WPC. 'It's chocker with drunk and disorderlies.'

I said, 'What about tracking down his family?'

She said they'd get Joe's picture on the breakfast news. Do you recognise this man?

'Course,' she said, 'his nearest and dearest are probably well on the way to sunny Spain by now. But once we know who they are we can arrange a nice welcome home party when they get back. A nice reception committee at the airport.'

It was getting on for ten o'clock when Woodleigh Grange agreed to take Joe.

'Dead man's shoes,' says the social worker. 'Lucky for some. They just need half an hour to clear the room and remake the bed.'

Joe got to his feet. 'Am I going home now?' he said. 'I shall get the strap from Mother for stopping out so late.'

He went off very cheerfully. Helen said I should go too. She'd close up. It didn't feel right leaving a woman alone at that time of night in a building with a drugs' cupboard, but she laughed when I said it.

'Aren't you a sweet, old-fashioned boy,' she said. 'Go on. Go home to your girlfriend.'

That was when I remembered I was about five hours late for a very important conversation with Chloe.

CHAPTER 25.

Chloe was not only at the flat, she'd also eaten, left her dishes in the sink and gone to bed. She surfaced when I fell over her boots.

'You're late.'

'Emergency at the surgery.'

'You're a GP. You don't have emergencies.'

'How little you know. So, you're back. Not back just to talk but actually back.'

'Hua needed her couch.'

'I'm going to have a drink. Do you want one?'

'I think I might have finished the wine. I'll have tea. And toast.'

She was wearing one of my rugby shirts. Was that because she knew it was a look I couldn't resist or because she couldn't be arsed to unpack her bags? Maybe Hua hadn't offered laundry service.

'We had an old bloke dumped on our doorstep this evening, with his PJs in a carrier bag. Imagine doing that to your Dad or your granddad?'

'We went to endless trouble to find the right place for Granny and Grandpa to live.'

'But most people can't afford those kind of fees.'

'They could if they were thrifty. Mummy's very careful with her money.'

That part was perfectly true. Vinnie Swift will cook bacon when it's turned green and the sheets at The Chummery have lumpy seams where they've been turned, sides to middle, when they started to wear thin.

I said, 'Now you've come back, don't you think you should tell me why you left?'

'It's complicated.'

'No, it's not. You thought Jamil was a better catch.'

She said, 'He's just a friend,' but she didn't look me in the eye.

'It turns out he's just a friend. You were hoping he'd be something more.'

'I didn't sleep with him.'

'I suppose that's something.'

'You don't seem very pleased to see me.'

'I am pleased. I've missed you. But you can't blame me for wondering whether you've come back for the right reasons. Hua wanting her couch back doesn't make me feel great. Jamil turning you down doesn't really do it for me either. I feel like I'm the second prize.'

Well then she threw herself into my arms and sobbed and snotted and swore her everlasting love and generally made me feel like such a hard-hearted bastard that I told her I loved her and I was willing to give things another try.

I thought she'd fallen asleep but then she whispered, 'Have you really, truly, never fancied anyone else since you met me?'

'Really, truly,' I said, although, hand on heart, if poor dumped Joe hadn't happened along, if dear, innocent Vaz in his Cancer Research lady's anorak hadn't knocked at Helen's door, I knew that my evening might have unfolded very differently. Furthermore, it wasn't a completely unpleasant idea.

By morning Chloe was full of bounce. I wasn't. I was tired, I was longing for a few days off and I was nervous about seeing Helen. That silly moment between us couldn't be un-had. She might revert to being distracted and testy, she might continue flirting. With Helen there was no predicting. And I'd have liked to tell Chloe the latest about Mac and Hilda Ruck, but it wasn't the time. She'd say it was no more than she expected of the kind of practice I'd insisted on joining and I was in no mood to hear about the errors of judgment she thought I was making in my life.

She said, 'You're not being very nice this morning.'

I said, 'I've told you I'm glad you're back. Nice is going to take a bit longer.'

'Let's go out for dinner tonight. Let's go to Anderson's.'

She was really making an effort to please me because Anderson's is a steak house. I felt a heel for turning her down.

'Can't do. I've got the practice party tonight.'

'That'll be cheapo wine and peanuts.'

'I suppose it will. Why don't you come? Everyone's been very keen to meet you.'

'Why?'

'Because I've told them how brilliant you are and Vaz has told them how beautiful you are.'

'Yeah, right. I bet you told them we split up, as well. I bet I've been discussed. Barrington took us to Simpsons for a pre-Christmas lunch.'

'Very nice. What, all of you?'

'Senior housemen, the regs and senior reg.'

'Not the juniors?'

'They were left holding the fort.'

'I'm glad I didn't need urgent cardiac care that afternoon.'

She said, 'Barrington's confident about my exam results. He reckons I'm twice the doctor I was a year ago. He made me sit next to him at lunch.'

'I thought that was Mun-Hee's privilege.'

'Not at all. Actually, I don't think they spoke. He kind of ignored her. She must have done something to annoy him.'

'Either that or they're having an affair.'

'What do you mean?'

'Isn't that what happens when people who work together

are secretly getting it on? Don't they go overboard with the 'not speaking' routine?'

'You seem to know an awful lot about workplace affairs. Something you want to tell me?'

'No, I'm on speaking terms with all my colleagues and they're all either too old or too male to attract me. So, you think you're well in with the Great Man?'

'Seems like it. Which is good because there are three of us and there are only two openings for registrar.'

My first patient of the day was Dawn Beamish. The surname was familiar, but I knew I hadn't seen her before. Then I made the connection. Her daughter was Tara Beamish, who'd had the hair dye rash. Dawn looked pretty rough. She had a hacking cough and she was hot to the touch. 102 degrees. She said she'd been ill for more than a week, shivering one minute and burning up the next.

'Did you have a 'flu shot this year?'

'No. Any road, I had the 'flu while I was away.'

'When was that?'

'Last month.'

'Where were you?'

'Nigeria.'

Then it really came back to me. Tara's Mum, with the African Internet boyfriend.

I said, 'Okay, where did you go for your vaccinations, before you travelled?'

'How do you mean?'

'You should have had some vaccinations, quite a few actually, against tropical diseases, and you should have taken anti-malaria pills. From your notes I can see you didn't come to us for any of it.'

'Don't know nothing about it,' she said.

Helen was in the nurses' office.

'Morning, Dan,' she said, bright and breezy, not a flicker of embarrassment or regret or lust.

I said, 'I've got a patient, Dawn Beamish. She's been back from Nigeria for three weeks, had no vaccinations before she went, took no anti-malarials, and now she's feverish. I need Linda to sit in while I check her spleen.'

'Nigeria? Without any shots? So we're dealing with a moron.'

'She's got an Internet toy-boy over there. Can we fast-track her bloods?'

'Yes. You think it's malaria? Ask for thick and thin smears, PCR and serum antigens.'

'PCR?'

'Polymer Chain Reaction. It's very sensitive. If you mark the samples PRIORITY you should get the results this evening, or tomorrow morning at the latest. Mind you, it is the start of the silly season. What are you going to prescribe?'

'I thought artemisinin?'

'A combi treatment might be better. Or you could start her on the artemisinin and wait on the blood results. And she definitely didn't take anything prophylactically?'

'Nothing. I'm not convinced she even knew where Nigeria was.'

'Okay. Have a prod at her spleen, see what that tells you. And Dan, if it is malaria, don't forget it's notifiable.'

Linda chatted to Dawn about her boyfriend while I palpated for the tip of her spleen.

'Good-looking, is he?'

'Yeah. He's dead tall. Dead well-built.'

'A long way to go though, Africa. What was the food like?'

'Horrible.'

When you're searching for the spleen you start in the lower right quadrant of the abdomen and work diagonally upwards. I knew the moment I'd found it because she flinched.

'There it is. As I thought.'

'Is it cancer?'

'No, your spleen's enlarged. There's a very good chance you've got malaria. Did you get bitten by mosquitoes when you were in Nigeria?'

'I got bitten by everything,' she said. 'And I had the runs. I didn't like it there. God's going to come over here, as soon as I can get him his papers.'

'God?'

'It's short for Godwin.'

I said, 'Dawn, malaria is a very serious infection. We can treat it, but I can't overstate how important it is, if you plan on going back to Nigeria you must get up to date advice before you set off.'

'Don't worry,' she said. 'I won't be going back. I thought it was a right dump.'

I made sure Dawn's bloods were sent off and then I raced into Wolverhampton at lunchtime, to House of Fraser. I grabbed a pair of satin pyjamas, some Jo Malone and a roll of wrapping paper. I was set for a romantic Christmas reconciliation, as long as I could persuade Mam to put Adam on the airbed and let me and Chloe bunk down together.

Two cases of wine had appeared behind Reception and the fridge was packed with plastic boxes of party food. When I called my last patient in Moira and Mary were standing at the ready to rearrange the furniture in the waiting room. Usually it's one or the other behind the front desk. It was strange to see them together.

Alma Geddis suffers from acid reflux. Trevor had tried her on diet changes, and he'd tried her on antacids and a proton pump inhibitor. Nothing seemed to help.

I said, 'I'm inclined to send you for a barium meal.'

She said, 'That don't sound very tasty.'

I did the referral letter while she was with me. By the time she left, a bar had been set up in the nurses' room, the food was laid out in the kitchen and Jingle Bell Rock was playing on an old CD player. Nurse Linda was hanging a feeble little sprig of mistletoe over the waiting room door.

Alma said, 'You'd better watch out, Dr Talbot. Looks like somebody's puckering up for a Christmas kiss.'

But I knew it wasn't me Linda had in mind. I had wondered whether Mac would show his face at the party, under the circumstances, but I gathered from Linda's glamorous red dress that she expected him to come. Vaz appeared wearing a very tight jumper decorated with robins. Helen emerged from the toilets in jeans and a big sparkly, fluffy sweater and even Mary and Moira had put on flashing Christmas pudding earrings they'd bought at a Pound Shop. Only Stephanie hadn't changed out of her business suit.

She cornered me, asked me if I'd heard.

'Heard what?'

'About Mac. Swindled an old lady out of her property.'

'Is that definite? I thought it was under investigation.'

'There's no smoke without fire. This practice, it's one thing after another.'

'Things will probably change once Helen's in charge.'

'Think so?' she said. 'She's as bad as Trevor only not as nice. She can't even control her own kid. I'll let you in on a little secret. I'm leaving. I've got a second interview after Christmas. A nice practice in Solihull. I can do better than this place.'

I wished she hadn't told me. I hate secrets.

Pam Parker arrived wearing reindeer antlers. She was followed by her husband, Bob, her father-in-law, Bob Senior, and a teenage daughter, Melissa. A pale, doughy complexioned girl with a metal brace on her teeth. Mac came in behind the Parkers. He was in full Highland dress and carrying an accordion. He did not look like a man living under the shadow of a GMC tribunal. Helen barely greeted him.

'Oh Mac,' says Linda, 'Is it true what they say about men in kilts?'

And Mac said, 'Every year you ask me that and every year I give you the same answer. Whatever rumours you've heard I can tell you this Macdonald goes nowhere without his boxers.'

Stephanie announced that there was plenty of zero alcohol wine for those who had to drive and Mac growled, 'You're welcome to it, you peevish cow. This fellow has a bottle of Glenmorangie and a taxi booked for 8 o'clock.'

Nurse Chris had her coat on. She said she couldn't stay long because her boys were home alone. The oldest is fifteen.

She said, 'They're good lads but if there's any trouble they can get into, ordering a pizza and watching Snowmageddon, they'll find it.'

Her husband's a plumber and he was on call-out.

I tried chatting to Melissa Parker. What school did she go to? Oldbridge Girls. What was her favourite subject? She didn't have one. What was she hoping to get for Christmas? Anything, really.

Pam said, 'Give it up, Dan. Recognise a conversational desert when you see one.'

Melissa asked if she could sit in Pam's office and play Candy Crush.

'Yes, but keep the door open,' says Pam, 'and don't meddle with my computer.'

The other daughter had declined to come.

'Hannah's sixteen,' says Bob Junior. 'Far too sophisticated

for this kind of gathering. She'll be at home trying to uninstall the porn filter.'

Bob Senior introduced himself to me several times. Everyone said Trevor was coming but there was no sign of him. It was like waiting for royalty to arrive.

Chris said, 'They've probably stopped at a pub on the way. Mrs Buxton sometimes needs to prime the pump before she meets her public.'

Mariah Carey was playing on the CD. Bob and Pam Parker were throwing some gentle shapes. Linda was slow-dancing, alone and trying to catch Mac's eye.

Vaz said, 'It would be polite for someone to dance with Nurse Linda.'

I said, 'It would. And I think you're the man to do it.'

I'm told I'm not a great dancer myself but even I have a better sense of rhythm than Vaz. Still, it was gallant of him to try and stop Linda from looking quite so desperate. I felt a hand on my waist. Helen said, 'I think I'm owed a dance. It's in the small print of your contract.'

The next track was Queen. One of Mam's favourites: Thank God it's Christmas. Mary and Moira got up and started some kind of ballroom dancing. Helen's hand was still on my waist. I wasn't sure where to put mine.

I said, 'Those malaria blood results didn't come back.'

I actually said that. She smiled, leaned in closer. She said, 'Like I said, it's the start of silly season. Relax, Dan. It's just a little dance with the boss. Christmas party? You know what I mean?'

I knew exactly what she meant.

CHAPTER 26

There was a welcome blast of cold air. The front door had opened. I heard Trevor's cough and the sound of him locking the door from the inside and then, there they were, Dr and Mrs Buxton. A cheer went up.

He said, 'I see you impatient buggers have started without us. No respect for your elders and betters. I hope I'm not too late for a sausage roll.'

Trevor was wearing a red and green bow tie. He looked well. He steered his wife straight towards me. I disengaged myself from Helen. 'To be continued,' she said.

Mrs Buxton was blonde, with old-fashioned curls, like a film star from bygone days. Pale pink nail polish, heels, a touch of midriff bulge, but a great figure for her age. Miss Cannock Chase 1967, or was it 1968?

'This is Dan Talbot', says Trevor. 'Dan, this is Mrs Buxton.'

She smiled and took my hand, but she seemed unsure of herself, as if she couldn't quite focus. She said she'd heard all about me.

Trevor said, 'Good grief, what is Vaz wearing? Did someone dare him to buy that sweater? No wonder he can't get a woman.'

I found Mrs Buxton a seat and brought her a glass of white. She grabbed my hand again.

'Don,' she said. 'Trevor's not been well, you know?'

I sat beside her.

I said, 'I do know. He's looking on good form tonight though. And he'll be retiring soon. Are you looking forward to that?'

'Oh yes,' she said. 'It'll be very nice. But he's not been at all well.'

Bob Senior introduced himself again.

I said, 'I hear you were a dentist over in Walsall.'

'Was I?' he said. 'If you say so.'

Chris asked if we could please get on with Secret Santa and the song because she needed to leave, so Moira distributed the parcels. I got a game called Toilet Football. A little green mat, a ball, a goal post and tiny boot on a stick.

'What a ridiculous present,' says Trevor. 'Everyone here knows Dan never gets the chance to squat on the bog, let alone sit down long enough to play footie. We keep him far too busy.'

His present was a desk sign. It said PLEASE WAIT. SENIOR MOMENT IN PROGRESS. We all laughed, but I thought it was quite sad. He wouldn't have a desk for much longer.

We were about to start the song when there was a sound of hammering at the front door.

Trevor yelled, 'We're closed!'

More hammering.

'Try Sandwell A&E!' he roared, but he went out anyway, to see who it was. The door was unlocked, there were voices, laughter, and then in walked a man whose face was vaguely familiar, followed by a face I was getting to know well. Miles Vincent, minus his usual woolly beanie and yes, then I remembered where I'd seen the older man before. At Twycross Lodge, after the death of Albert Gosling. It was Helen's husband, Clifford.

'Bunch of drunkards,' he said. 'Are you all deaf? And we found this gorgeous young lady wandering around outside, trying to get in, half dead from the cold.'

It was Chloe, who did indeed look gorgeous. She was wearing that duck egg blue dress with the sticky-out skirt. Her cheek was icy cold.

I said, 'Why didn't you let me know you were coming?'

'Your phone was turned off, doofus. Is it a nice surprise?'

Nice, and more welcome than you'll ever know, I thought. You and Clifford Vincent have probably saved me from another slow dance with Helen.

I told her she looked fabulous.

'Say it in Welsh.'

She likes to hear me say 'fabluss'. She doesn't always get the difference between actual Welsh and English with a Welsh accent.

'You look fabluss.'

'Anyway, I thought I'd better come and inspect your working environment. Check for hazards. See what temptations you might be exposed to.'

'Temptations?'

'You know what I mean. There doesn't seem to be anything to worry about, though. Who's the one in the cheap cocktail dress?'

'That's Linda, one of the nurses.'

'So the one in jeans must be the famous Helen Vincent.'

'And that was her husband. Your knight in shining armour.'

'Yes, he told me. He's very handsy. As if I couldn't walk through an open door without his guidance. I wouldn't like to share a cab with him.'

'He has that reputation.'

'The guy in the kilt? Is he the one you thought might be scamming old ladies?'

'Keep your voice down.'

'He's quite cute. Shall I go and chat to him about patient-doctor ethics?'

'It's not funny, Chlo. He's in trouble. Come and meet the Buxtons.'

But Mac had picked up his accordion. It was time for the

song.

'Wet your whistles,' says Trevor. 'Everybody got their lines?'

Chloe went and sat between Bob Parker and Clifford Vincent. I beckoned Vaz to come and stand by me.

'On the first day of Christmas,' sang Pam, 'my patient brought to me, a Nokia in a place it shouldn't be.'

'On the second day of Christmas,' bellowed Mac, 'my patients brought to me, two bum crack rashes and a Nokia in a place....'

And so it went. Three jippy tummies, four gummy eyelids...'

'Five hacking coughs!' That was Mary. She had a good strong voice.

'Six knee-joint twinges.' That was Helen.

'Seven nasty sniffles.' Moira, followed by me, 'Eight fungal toe nails.'

Then Mac again, 'Nine fallen arches.'

'Ten swollen ankles,' wheezed Trevor.

'Eleven septic piercings.' That was Chris.

I nudged Vaz. 'Twelve chronic backaches.'

All together, 'and a Nokia in a place it shouldn't be.'

I suppose it was more fun to do than to watch. Clifford Vincent spent the whole time murmuring in Chloe's ear.

Vaz said, 'Thank you, Dan. I don't think I made any mistake. But I still don't understand this custom.'

Chris was leaving. She gave me a peck on the cheek.

She said, 'Your girlfriend's lovely.'

I noticed she had the box of lemon soaps in her hand.

'Helen got them from Secret Santa,' she said. 'Only she doesn't use soap and I don't like dark chocolate, so we swapped. Did you buy them? Don't worry. I'll give them a good home.'

One thing about Chloe, she's great at circulating. I think

she learned it from her mother. Laurence tends to surround himself with listeners and hold forth, but Vinnie keeps on the move, darting from group to group. It's not that she's interested in people. She doesn't really listen to anything you say. I think it's more a habit. Circulate, circulate.

Chloe introduced herself to everyone, loaded her plate with quiche and coleslaw, put her arm around me in a very flattering, proprietorial way.

Vaz was sitting with Mrs Buxton but he looked like he was struggling. He's not great at small talk and Mrs B was very likely baffled by his accent, though she was smiling very amiably. I went over and joined them. I told her I was going home for Christmas, to Wales.

'That's nice,' she said. 'It's Don, isn't it?'

'Dan. Dan Talbot. I believe your daughter lives in Wales?'

'Yes,' she said. 'Somewhere in Wales. Trevor could tell you where.'

She's got a slight touch of the shakes I noticed, in one hand, and her head wobbles a bit. Could be Parkinson's but more likely just essential tremor.

Chloe gave me her 'when can we leave?' face. I signalled ten.

A figure loomed over me. Miles, scrubbed and shaved but definitely wired. He hadn't come to exchange the season's greetings.

'Hey,' he said, 'Mr Learner Doctor, you'd better watch yourself come January.'

I said, 'And why is that?'

'Because come January my old lady's in charge here. Mess with me and you'll be out.'

I stood up. At that very moment Bob Senior tapped Miles on the shoulder and said, 'Bob Parker. Thought I'd introduce myself. How do you do.'

'Fuck off, grandad,' says Miles.

I said, 'Do you want to try that again? How about "pleased to meet you, Bob? Can I get you a drink?"'

He sniggered. 'Don't think I'll bother,' he said. 'Bunch of losers.'

Bing Crosby was singing White Christmas, but the room had gone quiet. I heard Melissa Parker say, 'Hi Miles. Want to come to Mum's office and play Blockheads?'

He said, 'You're the fucking blockhead, fatgirl.'

Helen said his name. Pam, who can move with surprising speed considering her size, crossed the room and embraced him from behind. She said, 'Dan, are you close enough to palpate Miles's cauda epididymidis for me?'

I grabbed him by the balls, not too hard but enough to concentrate his mind. Credit to him, he didn't cry out.

Pam murmured, 'Listen, baby boy. Dr Talbot here is a rugby player as well as a skilled physician. One twist and your nuts'll be in a bowl along with the dates and the satsumas. Now get out of Dodge until you can mind your manners.'

His face was white. He was shaking. I let go of him.

Bob Parker said, 'You all right there, Pammy?'

'Yes darling,' she said. 'I was just asking Miles to play nicely.'

Helen said, 'Cliff, why don't you take Miles home.'

And Clifford said, 'Why? Is he bored?'

The Vincent males left but not, I noticed, before Clifford had made a little detour to whisper something to Chloe.

Mac's taxi came. Linda stationed herself under the mistletoe. He kissed her hand. It was a clever move. Maybe he's been there before with Linda. He didn't exactly snub her, but he made it clear he wasn't interested.

'See you when I see you,' he said. Mac was starting his midwinter gardening leave.

The party began to break up. Pam and Helen went into

the kitchen to have words, mother to mother.

'Pam said, 'He was threatening Dan. He was nasty to Bob's Dad. All I did was tell him to stop behaving like a pillock.'

She was shovelling the leftovers of the food into a Tupperware box. Melissa chimed in. 'And he called me fatgirl.'

Helen said, 'Why is everyone so touchy? He's just a kid. He doesn't mean any harm. And I think you did more than speak to him, Pam. I think you hurt him.'

'No,' said Pam. 'I wrapped him in a warm and loving embrace. And it worked. He was as meek as a lamb after that. You know me, pet. See a job that needs doing, I'm in there. But actually, he's not just a kid, not anymore. He's a grown man and he's volatile. I worry for you, Helen. One of these days he's going to hurt someone, and it could be you. Do you want to take this guacamole? It won't keep.'

The Buxtons were leaving.

Trevor said, 'Dan, is it true you had young Vincent by the gonads just now?'

'Slightly. He seemed to be squaring up for a fight.'

'So you nipped things in the bud, so to speak.'

'It was Pam's idea.'

'Why do I miss all the excitement? Merry Christmas, lad.'

Bob Senior introduced himself again. Stephanie locked the booze away. I asked Chloe if she'd like to see my office.

'What, you mean your time-share ashtray? I don't think so, thanks. Let's see if we can get a table at Anderson's. I'm craving a steak. All Hua keeps in her fridge is water and pak choi.'

She and Helen met in the doorway to the loo.

Helen said, 'Sorry we didn't get to talk. Great dress, by the way.'

Chloe said, 'Thanks. Lovely party.'

And then, after Helen had gone, she whispered, 'bitch.'

Chloe was good to drive so we left my car at the surgery.

I said, 'What was all that about?'

'What?'

'Calling Helen a bitch. She complimented you on your dress.'

'It was a fake compliment, Dan. She had a bitch face on.'

'I don't understand.'

'You wouldn't. It's a woman thing. She's probably like that with any female who's younger and more attractive than she is. Does she have a little cougar thing for you?'

'Are you kidding?'

'Yes, I am, totally. What's with that awful song?'

'It's a Lindens' tradition.'

'And what about the crappy, vandalised illegible sign outside? Is that a tradition too?'

'This is Tipton, Chlo. The sign may be vandalised, but we still practice good medicine.'

'And what was going on with the boy? Was he drunk?'

'Drugs. He was either on his way up or on his way down. I'm not sure.'

'He looked like he was about to throw up. I mean, he was ashen. And that Parker blimp had her arms wrapped round him.'

'Yes, Miles wasn't feeling great. So overall impressions?'

'The Mac guy seemed okay. Quite a doll, in a mature kind of way. He has the legs for a kilt. What were you going to tell me about him?'

'He's facing a Medical Practitioners' Tribunal.'

'About that old lady?'

'Her family aren't happy about Mac's sister buying her house.'

'His sister? Not really anything to do with him, then.'

'That's a generous way of looking at it. One degree of

282

separation. Other impressions?'

'Helen Vincent's an ice maiden. I don't know why you said she was attractive.'

'I didn't.'

'I'm sure you did. You also described Pam Parker as jolly, but I think you meant to say obese. She looks like a Weeble.'

'A what?'

'A Weeble. They were these little characters we had when we were kids except Flo was very possessive about them. I was hardly allowed to look at them let alone play with them. Little ball-shaped creatures. I mean, what kind of example is she setting her patients?'

'Many of our patients don't look to us for example. They look to us for drugs. Pam's a good doctor. Patients feel they can talk to her, but she doesn't stand for any shit. What about Trevor? Don't tell me you didn't like him.'

'No, Trevor's sweet. All those years working there, though. A lifetime. You'd have thought he'd have had more ambition.'

'But that was his ambition. What did you make of his wife?'

'A lush, obviously.'

'Where I come from 'lush' is a term of approval.'

'Where I come from it means a dipso. What is he doing with a woman like that?'

'She was a beauty queen, a long time ago. They've been together for, what, 40 years? Two kids. I imagine they love each other.'

'And what's her name? Why does everyone call her 'Mrs Buxton'?'

'I don't know. Perhaps she doesn't like her name.'

'You mean like 'Beryl' or something? Anyway, the fact that Trevor's a sweetie is irrelevant to your future. You can't think of staying on there after you're registered. He's retiring and then you'd be left with Bitch Face.'

'I noticed Clifford Vincent bending your ear. What was his story?'

'He seems to think he's a big shot solicitor. I mean, really? Personal injuries claims. Some mickey mouse outfit in somewhere or other.'

'Willenhall.'

'Never heard of it. I just kept nodding.'

'Mac calls him an ambulance chaser.'

'He asked me out to lunch.'

'Who, Mac?'

'No. The big shot. He gave me his card. He said if I enjoyed fine dining, he knew a very nice place in Sutton Coldfield and to give him a bell.'

'Sutton Coldfield?'

'A safe distance from his home patch, I suppose.'

'The slimeball. I hope you told him to fuck off.'

'I didn't even bother. Let him dream. Little does he know that a) I hate the expression 'fine dining' and b) I also hate the expression 'give me a bell'.'

'And c)?'

'And c) I'm going home with Dan Talbot, who is the pick of the crop.'

CHAPTER 27

Mam was in a pother about Chloe's ever-changing plans for Christmas. First she'd said she might go with me to Wales, then she wanted to go home to the Chummery, then she'd left me. Now we were back together and she was trying to make amends, so Aber was on again.

Mam said, 'What it is, Dan, I'll put you together in your old room, only don't tell your Nan.'

'I don't think Nan needs to know the sleeping arrangements. But she must know we live together?'

'Knowing it's going on in Birmingham is one thing, having it right under your nose is another.'

'So Adam gets the airbed?'

'Yes. I'll buy a new one. To be honest, your Aunty June's Li-Lo is getting a bit manky. I wouldn't want Chloe to go away with a bad impression of us.'

'She won't.'

'What does she like for breakfast?'

'Just do the usual. When I go to her folks, they don't make a fuss. It's take it or leave it at The Chummery.'

'I've seen how they do it in those big houses, though. All the dishes kept hot on a sideboard. Bacon, kidneys, tomatoes. The egg yolks must get hard, mind, anyone coming down late.'

Mam's definitely been watching too much Downton.

'When's Adam arriving?'

'He'll drive over on Christmas morning.'

'And if I know him, he won't stay the night, either. He'll be gone by 5 o'clock. I tell you, he's got a secret life in Cardiff.'

'Secret life! He doesn't have the time for one. People think teachers have it cushy. They don't allow for all the marking they have to do, and then there's this Ofsted business, and the paperwork.'

'We all have paperwork, Mam. No, Adam's definitely got someone he rushes home to. I suppose we'll find out, eventually.'

'But not on Christmas Day, please, and not in front of your Nan and your girlfriend. I want things to be nice.'

'Me too. We'll see you mid-afternoon.'

'Champion. And drive steady. Christmas Eve there'll be people behind the wheel who've had a few.'

So we were all set. Chloe worked till late on Saturday. We slept in and the plan was to go to Gas Street for pancakes and the Sunday papers. Her phone rang. All I could hear were various permutations of, 'Oh my God. The fool. What does Daddy say?' Then she said, 'I'll come. My bag's packed anyway. They'll understand.'

She got off the phone.

'Who'll understand what?'

'Your Mum and Dad. I can't come with you. I have to go home. Something awful has happened to Slow.'

A car crash was the obvious. Charlie drives with his foot to the floor. I pictured him in traction. I pictured him on life support. Wrong, wrong. He'd been arrested.

'Drink-driving?'

'Cocaine, actually. Driving under the influence.'

'That's not good. Where is he now?'

'On his way to The Chummery. Daddy's picking him up from the Shag Pile.'

The Shag Pile. My future brother-in-law's Docklands penthouse.

'First offence. Right?'

'Of course. The thing is, he was also in possession. I have to go.'

'Why? You're a doctor. He needs a lawyer. Cocaine is Class A, Chlo. That's jail.'

'Fortunately, Daddy knows someone.

'What does that mean?'

'Hopefully Slow might get off with a caution, or a fine.'

'That doesn't sound right.'

'Don't go all holier than thou on me. If it was your brother, you wouldn't want him to go to prison.'

'Did you know Charlie was a cocaine user?'

'Not exactly. I mean, I'm not surprised. His crowd, they all like to party. And everyone uses something. The point is to make sure you stay on the right side of the law.'

'What do you mean, everyone uses something? I don't.'

'Because you're an adorable square.'

'Do you use anything?'

'Not really.'

'Let's stick to yes or no.'

'The occasional spliff if I'm round at Dee's.'

'You smoke marijuana?'

'Have been known to. Shock horror.'

'Anything else?'

'Fuck, Dan, lighten up, would you?'

'Sure, I'll lighten up. It's not my brother who's in deep doodoo. What else have you used?'

She sighed.

'I've tried Bounce.'

'What's Bounce?'

'A legal high. It gets you in a party mood. Dan, I have to go.'

'So you're walking out on our Christmas, letting my parents down, because of your fool of a brother.'

'Mummy needs me. She's hysterical.'

'If she's hysterical now, wait till she has to visit him in Wormwood Scrubs.'

She said I was being beastly. I suppose I was. It wasn't her fault her brother had more money than brains or that Vinnie was freaking out in case people got wind of it at the golf club. I just didn't see what help Chloe could be.

I said, 'What about Flo? She lives closer. Can't she administer the smelling salts?'

'No. In fact she's threatening not to go to The Chummery on Christmas Day, in case the she-brats find out what's happened. They're sure to ask questions.'

'That's a joke. Poppy already knows the F word. She probably knows as much about drugs as her Uncle Charlie. And, it now turns out, as much as her Aunt Chloe.'

She called me a prig. I said she was childish. But we made up before she drove away. The Swifts are a very different tribe to the Talbots and if we were going to spend the rest of our lives together, I had to get used to that. Also, I didn't want her to drive angry. What if there was another coke-head, Charlie Swift type on the roads?

Abandoned again, and I couldn't even set off early for Abergavenny because I had a surgery on Christmas Eve morning. How did I spend my weekends before I met Chloe? Hanging out with Rob and Matt mainly. Drinking too much possibly. Now Rob's the other side of the world and Matt's become a bit of a tit. I went for a mooch around Gas Street, had a flat white, listened to the Sally Army band playing carols, came home, thought I'd wrap some presents, went out again to buy Sellotape, felt sad, ate my body weight in Pringles and fell asleep on the sofa. It was around ten o'clock when Chloe phoned me.

She said, 'I left in such a hurry I didn't give you your presents. They're in my side of the wardrobe. Your Mum's is in the green paper. Your Dad's is a voucher, in the envelope.'

'Not flying lessons, I hope.'

'No. The Italian Stallion Driving Experience.'

'The what?'

'He gets to drive a Ferrari for three miles. The other two boxes are yours. Why are you laughing?'

'I'm not. It's just the idea of putting the words Italian Stallion and my father in the same sentence.'

Chloe had never witnessed my Da's driving. I've seen him use hand signals.

'So you're definitely not coming with me? There's still time.'

'I'm really, really sorry.'

I heard men's voices in the background.

'Who's that?'

'Daddy and Daddy's friend. He's a silk. We're just getting some legal advice. And Pig and Giles are here too.'

'Who?'

'Pig and Giles. They're Slow's mates.'

'He has a friend called Pig?'

'They were at school together. I think his real name's Peregrine.'

'And your hysterical mother?'

'She's got one of her horrific migraines.'

'Does she have Migraleve?'

'Paramax. This could knock her out for days. I'll probably have to cook Christmas lunch.'

'You mean turkey and the works? Do you know how?'

'Damned cheek. I can read a cookbook. Anyway, we have pheasant.'

'I'm told it can take years to master gravy. You'd better give Flo's caterer friend a call. What was her name?'

'Bloody Annabel. I love you, Dan.'

I said, 'That's good to hear because I love you too.'

'Say it the Welsh way.'

'Dw i'n dy garu di.'

'Aww,' she said. 'Who's Gary?'

We were operating a reduced service on Christmas Eve. Just me, Vaz and Linda. Stephanie was on Reception to give Mary and Moira time off. Vaz was waiting for me in Trevor's office when I arrived. Could he have a quick word in private?

He said, 'Dan, I think I have done a terrible thing.'

I sat down.

'A prescription error?'

'No, it is a personal thing. After the party, I drove Nurse Linda home. Her taxi didn't come so I offered her a lift.'

'Right. And?'

He was looking at his shoes.

I said, 'Crikey, Vaz. Did you stay the night?'

'No, no, no. This is my problem. She invited me, but of course I said no thank you. Linda is a single lady. She lives alone. How could I be her guest?'

'I don't think she wanted you to be a guest. I think she wanted sex.'

'Dan, this is what I feared. English ladies are not like Indian ladies. Now perhaps she will be offended? I didn't mean to offend. This is very, very bad situation.'

'Okay, well perhaps not as bad as you think. The first thing to bear in mind is that she'd had a lot to drink at the party. She's probably forgotten all about it by now.'

'You think so?'

'More than likely. The other thing is, Linda's very, how can I put this? She's very open about her needs. I'm sure she was hoping to get Mac into bed. And I've seen her flirting with one of the delivery drivers. I think she just puts it out there to see if there are any takers.'

'Takers?'

'Don't worry about it. Have you seen her this morning?'

'No. I hid from her.'

'I'll bet when you see her it'll be as if nothing happened. Which it didn't.'

He said, 'Dan, this is very shocking to me. Where I come from ladies do not offer sexual intercourse in this way.'

I looked in on Linda before I started surgery.

I said, 'Nice party on Friday.'

'Was it?' she said. 'It's usually dead boring. Now Saturday, I went to a real party. Oh. My. Lord. I don't remember a thing except we were drinking tequila shots. I feel like I've had three weekends, not one.'

When I'd finished surgery I took my sandwich in to Vaz's office.

I said, 'No need to hide. Linda has had a hectic weekend and from Friday afternoon onwards her memory is a complete blank.'

He smiled.

'Thank you,' he said. 'Thank you very much. But Dan, for future information, if a lady offers herself to me will she be offended if I say no?'

'Surprised, possibly. And yes, some might be offended. Or they might think there was something wrong with you.'

'There is nothing wrong with me.'

'I'd say, Vaz, that any woman worthy of you would appreciate your gentlemanly behaviour. Heaven knows, they scream blue murder if you make a move on them and they're not interested. And for the record, I think you made a wise decision regarding Linda. Mixing sex and work could get very messy.'

Said he, who wasn't entirely clear how he felt about Helen Vincent's murmured 'to be continued.'

'What are you doing for Christmas?'

'I have Out of Hours shift tonight and tomorrow I will help at soup kitchen, at Holy Redeemer church.'

'That's very admirable.'

'What about you?'

'I'm going to see my parents. Setting off as soon as I've drunk this tea.'

'And lovely Chloe?'

'She's with her parents.'

'I have another question. My gift from Secret Santa. What is its purpose?'

He took it out of his briefcase. The box said Novelty Ball Scratcher. It had been personalised, but they'd spelled his name ATNOTHY.

'I don't understand. What ball?'

'Testicles.'

'Perhaps it is a kind of joke?'

'Yes,' I said, 'perhaps it is.'

I got to Abergavenny in the daylight. Mam came running out in her slippers, peering into the car for Chloe?

'You've not fallen out again?'

'Family crisis. She had to go home. I'll tell you about it later. She's really sorry.'

Chloe hadn't actually expressed any regrets although I was sure she'd meant to.

Mam said, 'If I'd known I wouldn't have bought new towels.'

Old Mrs Price from next door happened to be coming along.

She called, 'Is that your Adam, Eirwen?'

'No,' says Mam, 'It's our Daniel. He's a doctor now, you know.'

We went in.

I said, 'I've been a doctor for seven years now. I don't think you need to put it out on the news anymore.'

'Mrs Price won't remember that. And she's as blind as a mole. Edward, our son's here!'

My Da's Ed to everybody. Mam only calls him Edward for dramatic effect.

'And guess what? No girlfriend.'

'Chloe, Mam. Her name's Chloe and she's your future daughter-in-law.'

'If you say so.'

Da said, 'You can put the best china away then, Eirwen.'

It was months since I'd seen them. Mam looked the same as ever, but I saw a difference in Da. Less hair, more waistline. I suppose he's what I'll look like in thirty years or so.

He said, 'Come on the M50, did you?'

'M5 and the M50 to Ross.'

'The A40 was backed up by the Newport turn-off last week. There was nothing moving.'

Mam said, 'What your father means is, how nice to see you son, come in, have a cup of tea, Merry Christmas.'

'Is Adam still coming in the morning?'

'Should be. What it is, he couldn't come today because he's waiting in for a new telly to be delivered. By 8 o'clock, they told him.'

I said, 'Do they deliver that late on Christmas Eve?'

'I suppose they do in Cardiff. Anyway, it doesn't matter. You're here safe and sound and we can have a nice cosy evening. There's that carol service on at 6 o'clock.'

One of Mam's Christmas Eve treats is to watch Carols from King's and have a little cry when the boy chorister sings the first verse of Once in Royal.

'What about Nan? Shall I go and fetch her?'

'Not till tomorrow. She said she's sooner stay at home tonight, with her memories.'

I took my bag up to my old room. Our old room. Adam and I always shared because Grandad Merrick was living with us in those days. Then Adam went off to uni and I had the room to myself for a couple of years. It's been redecorated since we left home, but Mam still put our bits and pieces back. Adam's Manic Street Preachers poster, my Coldplay tapes and my Wade Whimsies. Nan Talbot used to buy us the little animals. Hedgehogs, squirrels, foxes. Adam kept his in their boxes, so they wouldn't get broken or chipped. He could be very pernickety. He still is.

I called Chloe. Vinnie was still lying in a darkened room wearing an eyeshade, but Charlie and Laurence had been out for a day's rough shooting with Charlie's friend, Pig.'

'So this cocaine crisis isn't affecting anyone except me and your mother?'

'It's affecting me. The bloody Aga's playing up and I'm going to spend Christmas chained to the kitchen sink. Were your parents hugely disappointed I didn't come?'

'Devastated. The fatted calf had already been killed.'

The truth was, aside from the new towels and the best teacups, I think Mam was quietly relieved. She could relax and enjoy having her boys home without trying to run things to Downton Abbey standards.

'What's your evening looking like?'

'Granny and Grandpa are bickering. They've both been on the sherry since lunchtime. Granny says she wants a divorce.'

'At her age? Hardly seems worth the bother.'

'That's what I said. She's accused Grandpa of looking at another woman's privates.'

'From a wheelchair? Does he get around that much?'

'She says when they go to the day room he always asks to be parked opposite a woman called Ada who sits with her legs wide apart. I don't imagine there's much for him to see. They all wear big knickers.'

'How does the accused plead?'

'He says Granny has bats in her belfry, which is perfectly true. I miss you.'

'I miss you too. I'm standing in my old bedroom looking out of the window. You can see across the rooftops to the Black Mountains. There's a sprinkling of snow on the Sugar Loaf. Has Flo put in an appearance yet?'

'They'll be over in time for champagne and stockings. Say that Welsh thing again.'

'You mean, "Nadolig llawen?"'

'No, the Gary thing that means "I love you."'

What Chloe doesn't realise is, that's about the extent of my Welsh. I learned a bit in school and a bit from my grandparents but it's not a big thing in Monmouthshire.

Mam called me downstairs for tea and scones.

'Just to keep you going,' she said.

'I'd forgotten what a great view it is from the bedroom.'

Mam said, 'Perhaps you'll have a view like that again someday. It'd be nice if you came back.'

I didn't like to tell her that a little Welsh market town wasn't likely to fit in with Chloe's career plans.

I'd brought two bottles of pink fizz but there was no room for them in the fridge.

I said, 'I see we're on war rations again. That's a very big joint of meat. Are you feeding the whole street tomorrow?'

'Best Welsh beef. And I've got burgers and mince for you to take home with you. Your Da always buys too much. Put the bubbly on the back step. It's as cold out there as Jenkins' feet when they buried him.'

'Won't it get nicked?'

'No. This is Abergavenny, not ruddy Birmingham. Don't tell your Da but I've got one of those mini nut roasts for Adam. I never know what to give him since he turned vegetarian.'

There's a Christmas Eve routine at our house. Tea and

scones, in case you can't last till dinner, put the presents under the tree, listen to the carols so Mam can reminisce about the year I sang the first verse of Ar Hyd Y Nos solo in the school concert, watch Da ruin a perfectly good fire by putting too much slack on it, eat fish pie even though you're still stuffed from the scones, argue over the evening's viewing then let Mam have the last word, open a box of After Eights.

We watched the Christmas Special of Call the Midwife. Mam was hawk-eyed for any errors.

She said, 'It's the mother who needs to puff and pant, not the midwife. If that nurse carries on hyper-ventilating, she'll faint in a heap on the floor and be no use to anybody. They ought to get me in, when they're making these programmes, to advise them. You done any home deliveries, Dan?'

'We don't offer them. I don't think there's any demand. Our patients quite enjoy a couple of days in hospital. Three meals and no whining kids to look after. Anyway, Helen Vincent won't take the risk.'

'Very few GPs will. And I mean, hospitals aren't like they used to be, not like when I had you two. Take Nevill Hall. We've got everything they could ask for. Bean bag chairs, those big balls you sit on, birthing pools. They're a ruddy nuisance. You're down on the floor, craning your neck, trying to see what's going on, watching for the head to crown. Very popular though, with the mothers, and with the dads. Some of them put their trunks on and get in the pool. It's quite home from home. And if anything goes wrong, we can have them in theatre in a trice.'

'Funny though. Babies always used to be born at home.'

'Yes, well, that's as maybe. You have to careful these days. If things don't go according to plan you can end up getting sued.'

Mam said she'd had a number of stillbirths over the years,

but she'd only ever lost one mother. A retained placenta and a massive post-partum haemorrhage.

She said, 'The baby was fine. A little boy. He'd be a teenager now. I'll never forget the look on the husband's face though. The doctor went out to break the news to him. I could see him through the glass in the door. His whole world turned upside down, just like that. Are you getting used to giving people bad news?'

'No.'

'I suppose you will.'

'I was with a patient when he died recently. Old chap, stomach cancer. He died at home and we happened to be there, me and Trevor Buxton. It was very moving. His wife lay beside him on the bed.'

I though Da was asleep but he suddenly said, 'Well this is cheery talk for Christmas Eve. Have you got a padlock on those After Eights, Eirwen?'

There seemed to be a culinary theme to Chloe's Christmas gift shopping. I got a pizza stone and a fermentation crock. You use the crock to make your own sauerkraut, apparently. I'm not sure if I like sauerkraut but Chloe had been telling me we should eat it because it's good for you, so it seemed I'd been given a new project. Mam's gift was a vegetable spiraliser.

'Very interesting,' she said, 'I'll have to study it, see what it's all about.'

I had to explain the Ferrari drive voucher to Da. The nearest place he could redeem it was Bridgend but as Mam said, it was a very nice thought.

I peeled the spuds before I went to church. Mam trimmed the sprouts.

She said, 'Are you going to tell me what's been going on with Chloe or should I mind my own business?'

'We had a bit of a wobble. We just needed some time apart.'

That sounded about right. No need to mention the Jamil factor.

'Time apart. Of course, in our day you didn't live together before you got hitched. We had to settle for a kiss and a cwtch on the doorstep. We didn't need time apart.'

'I know you don't approve.'

'Look, your Nan didn't approve of me making your Da help with the washing up. Your Grandad Talbot never held a tea towel in his life. Times change, I realise that. So, you two are back together but not for Christmas.'

'We were all set to come here but then her brother got himself into some trouble and Chloe felt she was needed at home. They'll be having a big family pow-wow, deciding how to handle the Charlie situation.'

'What's he done? Murdered someone?'

'He got pulled over for drug-driving and they found cocaine in his car.'

'He'll be going to prison, then.'

'That's what I think. Chloe's hoping he'll get a suspended sentence. Her mother's gone to pieces.'

'Well she needs to pull herself together. Mothers can't go to pieces. And where's the father in all this? If either of you boys did anything like that, I'd expect your Da to give you a walloping. And if he didn't, I would.'

'Not allowed nowadays. Walloping. You'd end up in prison too. And anyway, I'm bigger than you.'

'I'm serious, Dan. Don't you go nipping at drugs. A lot of doctors do it, writing themselves prescriptions. Next thing they know, they're addicted. You'd better get your skates on if you're going to church. You going to Chapel Street?'

'No, I thought I'd go to St Mary's.'

'Gone up in the world, have we? Where will you be getting married, Westminster Abbey?'

'It'll be the Swifts' nearest church, I imagine. Not that Chloe's religious.'

'Oh dear,' says Mam. 'Well say one for me while you're down on your knees. And when you get back you can go with your Da to pick up Nan. I'll be interested to hear how you think she is.'

My Da's a very careful driver, irascible and unforgiving. On Christmas morning you don't get a lot of people on the road but Da managed to find somebody with a dirty, unreadable number plate and another culprit who didn't position himself correctly to make a right turn. I'm not at all sure he's the right man for a spin in a Ferrari.

Nan was sitting with her coat on. She has that lovely soft

old lady skin that smells of talcum powder. She called me 'Ed.'

Da said, 'It's our Dan. He's home for Christmas.'

'Well I know that,' she said.

We put Nan up front and I sat in the back. She kept asking if they were dropping me somewhere and Da kept saying, 'It's our Dan. He's coming for Christmas dinner.'

There was an immaculate Ford hatchback parked outside the house.

'Wonders will never cease,' says Da. 'Your brother's here.'

It was a couple of years since I'd seen Adam. He's never met Chloe. He shaves his head now.

I said, 'What's this? Are you going bald?'

Mam said, 'No he is not. He's got a lovely head of hair, if he'd only let it grow. All my men have good hair.'

Adam said he went swimming most mornings before work so shaving it was easier. His head was shiny, like a skull.

I noticed Nan called him 'Ed' too. Her husband was an Edward, her son's an Edward. Now we've all become Eds. I tried to get her to sit and talk to me, but she preferred to be in the kitchen teaching Mam how to roast potatoes so we Talbot men were left to ourselves, trying to make conversation. At least, I tried.

'How's work then, Adam?'

'Not bad.'

'Kids not beating you up?'

'No.'

'You seeing anybody?'

'Not particularly.'

'Chloe and I are hoping to get married next year.'

'Oh yes?'

Da said there was talk of closing the Abergavenny livestock market and building a new one, all mod cons, out near Raglan.

'How do you feel about that?'

'I'll be sorry to see it go, but you've got to move with the times. Monmouth's gone. Newport's gone. It's an Asda now.'

I said, 'Nan's getting forgetful.'

'Bound to,' says Da. 'She's getting up in years. I forget things myself.'

Adam poured a lot of gravy on his nut roast, which annoyed me. He always did hog the gravy. And the custard.

I said, 'So you're not really a vegetarian?'

He looked at me.

I said, 'Because that gravy was made with beef dripping.'

'That's all right,' he said. 'I just don't eat meat.'

Mam gave me one of her 'don't upset your brother' looks and Da said, 'That was a tidy roast, Eirwen. Most enjoyable.'

Adam clenches his jaw a lot. You can see his masseter muscle working away. I wonder what that's about. Gritting his teeth to get through a festive get-together? As family's go, we're not that bad.

Nan was very chatty, telling us about people from chapel and the seniors' centre. Mam whispered to me when I was helping her to clear. 'Half of them are dead. Ask her about her new neighbour.'

She'd bought a guaranteed suet-free Christmas pudding in honour of Adam. She needn't have bothered. All he took was a teaspoonful of pudding and a greedy helping of custard.

I said, 'Nan, who have you got living next door to you now?'

'Baines,' she said. 'Her name's Mrs Baines. She's from Pontypool so I don't know how she's wangled a flat here. And I'll tell you something else about her. She stole my floor cloth.'

'That's a strange thing for a person to steal. Was it pegged out on your walkway? Perhaps she took it by mistake.'

'Oh no,' says Nan. 'She came in my house and took it. A brand new floor cloth.'

We watched the Queen's Speech. Mam observed that she was wearing well.

'She damned well ought to be,' says Da. 'Kept in the lap of luxury.'

Mam said, 'I don't think she is, Ed. I read she's a very frugal person.'

Nan said she wanted to get home before dark. Mam put the kettle on and asked Adam if he'd run her and make sure she was settled in, after we'd had a cup of tea, but he said he couldn't wait, he had to be getting back himself. He went to fetch his anorak. Mam looked crestfallen.

She said, 'I thought you might stay over?'

'I didn't say I would.'

I said, 'What's the rush to get back? Have you got somebody waiting for you at home?'

'No,' he said. I think he had, though. I walked with him to his car, asked him how he thought everyone seemed.'

'Not bad,' he said. 'Why?'

I said something about people getting older, about needing to keep an eye on things and wishing I lived nearer. He shrugged.

He said, 'Nan's going a bit senile, that's all. Nothing we can do about that.'

I'm not sure how you're supposed to feel about a brother. I only have the one and he's a closed book.

I went with Da to deliver Nan back to her maisonette. As we turned onto Nan's estate there was a man coming towards us, pushing a stroller.

Da says, 'There's Gareth Driscoll.'

302

He pulled over and lowered his window.

'Alright or what, boy?' he said. 'Out with the family?'

There was child bundled up in the stroller and a little girl on a new bike with stabilisers. I was at school with Gareth. His grandparents farmed over by Clydach.

'Merry Christmas, Ed,' he said. He nodded at me. I don't think he recognised me. 'I heard things were slow at Ruthin last week.'

'Yes, not much doing. Cast ewes were going for £30 a head.'

'Might be worth a punt. Put them to the tup, get one more lamb out of them and then sell them on at weaning.'

'That's what I said. Feed them well enough, you might even get twins out of them. Phil Challenger bought a few broken-mouth ewes last year, gave them a lick tank with liquid feed. He did pretty well out of it.'

'It's a thought, Ed. Well I'd best be getting the nippers home. Merry Christmas, Mrs Talbot.'

Gareth Driscoll, the last boy in Middle Infants to learn to read, now running a very successful mobile sheep-dipping service and married, with two kids. He'd also had more conversation with my Da in two minutes than I'd managed in 24 hours.

Every time I see my Nan I wonder if it'll be the last time.

I said, 'You look after yourself now. I want you fit and well for my wedding.'

As Da took her in I heard her say, 'I didn't know Ed was getting married.'

Boxing Day morning Mam was wearing her Downton-inspired necklace and the apron Da had bought her. He is an utterly useless present buyer. Even I know you don't give a woman an apron. She cooked me one of her monster breakfasts, to keep me going, like I was driving to the other end of the country.

I said, 'Before I go, there are a couple of things I'd like to talk about.'

'The wedding?' says Mam, brightening up.

'No, we can't do anything about that till Chloe gets her exam results. About Nan. She's definitely not right.'

'See, Ed? Dan agrees with me.'

Da said, 'What am I supposed to do about it? It comes to us all.'

'Could you bring her to live here?'

'She's happy where she is.'

'Until she drops a tea towel on the gas hob and cremates herself.'

Da said, 'If she was living here, she'd still be on her own all day. I'm out. Your Mam works. It'd just be our house burning to the ground instead of her flat.'

Mam said it'd be easier to arrange something when she retires. She's got eighteen months to go.

She said, 'Don't worry, Dan. We do keep an eye on her.'

'I know you do, and I'm sorry I'm not around to help, but I see a big difference in her. She had no idea who I was, nor Adam. And he's the other thing.'

'Don't start, Dan. Not at Christmas.'

'He's just so weird, Mam. It was two years since we'd seen each other. He didn't ask me a single thing about my life and he didn't tell me a single thing about his. He's like a human black hole. And he didn't bring you a present.'

'I don't need presents. And he's never been the chatty type.'

'Chatty? He's practically mute. Why does everyone pretend he's normal?'

Mam said, 'We've never pretended that. He's a genius, practically.'

I said, 'He's not a genius. He teaches maths in a

comprehensive.'

'Well,' she said, 'whatever. He's very, very bright, I know that much. He's not like the rest of us.'

Her eyes teared up. She was packing up a freezer box of meat for me.

'Grass-fed Welsh Black,' she said. 'And properly hung. I'll bet you can't get beef like that in Birmingham.'

We had a long hug.

'Dr Talbot,' she said. 'Have you got your name on your door?'

'Not yet. I'm still the trainee. I share with Trevor Buxton. Anyway, most of them call me Dr Dan.'

'Dr Dan. That's nice.'

'I didn't mean to upset you about Adam.'

'You didn't. What it is, Dan, I'm used to his funny ways. He always was an oddity.'

'Are you sure you brought the right baby home?'

She clipped my ear. Da shook my hand. They came out to see me off. I watched them in my mirror as I pulled away. Da patted Mam on the backside as they went back into the house. He's a dark horse, my father.

I went straight to Sterling and did a four hour shift. We took several indigestion calls. Too much food or the start of a heart attack? I was on with Neil, a nurse practitioner. He's an experienced pair of hands. He said one of his criteria was fear. If he sensed fear, in the patient or the person making the call, he'd advise them to call an ambulance. We had a couple of weepers too. The Boxing Day blaahs, he called them. They just needed someone to talk so we referred them to Samaritans.

CHAPTER 29

When I pulled in at home there was no sign of Chloe's car. Just as well because there was a red Vauxhall parked in her space. I went in, thinking she must still be at The Chummery, but the lights were on and there she was, trying to get the blender working. It won't start if the lid's not snapped on firmly.

I said, 'What's with the Astra in your space?'

'My Christmas present,' she said. 'Mummy got it in November but then she saw a something she liked better, so they've given the Vauxhall to me.'

'That's a very generous gift. What's happening to your old car?'

'It's not a gift. It's part-exchange. Slow's going to sell it and give the money to Mummy. How was home?'

'This is home. Wales was nice. Comforting. Nothing changes very much. We all just get older.'

'Henry said Abergavenny's quite a nice town.'

'It is. How does he know?'

'No idea. Probably something to do with pigs. What did you get for Christmas?'

'A rugby quiz book, a pair of thermal gloves and half a beef carcase. Also a parcel for you which I believe is a book of photographs of scenic Monmouthshire, not to completely ruin the surprise. What are you trying to make there?'

'A super-greens smoothie.'

'Why?'

'It's good for you.'

'It looks like bile. How's your mother? And what's happening about Charlie?'

'Mummy's feeling better. Daddy's barrister friend thinks we might try a medical defence.'

'Less of the 'we' if you don't mind. What kind of medical defence?'

'Get a doctor to say Slow was under severe stress and acting quite out of character.'

'Get a doctor to perjure himself, in other words.'

'You've come back in a nice mood. Anyway, nothing will happen for yonks so Slow's gone to Dubai for some sun, the lucky so and so.'

'Hasn't he had to surrender his passport? Isn't he a flight risk?'

'Of course not. Why would he run away? He owns a very successful business.'

I realised that Charlie Swift put my brother in a better light. Adam might be deficient in social skills but at least he wasn't a reckless, coke-sniffing bell-end.

Surgery reopened on the 28th. When I arrived, there were two vans in the car park. SmartSigns were erecting a new sign. I remarked to the guy that what we really needed was something scrubbable but he said peel-off vinyl was what had been ordered. Cheaper, I suppose. The other van belonged to an office cleaning service.

Mary was on Reception. She nodded towards Trevor's room.

'Out of commission. You're getting steam-cleaned. A waste of good money, if you ask me. They'll never get rid of the smell. There's years and years of cigarette smoke in there.'

'So where do you want me to work?'

'Use Dr Parker's office. She's not in today and Dr Mac, well, heaven knows when we'll see him again.'

She handed me a printout. Dawn Beamish's blood results: a Plasmodium falciparum infection. Not good. Dawn had a serious case of malaria.

Helen appeared. She had her busy face on and didn't even say 'Good morning.'

I said, 'The steam-cleaning? Does this mean Trevor's not coming back?'

'No,' she said. 'But he's taking on the nursing homes, until we know what's happening with Mac, so he hardly needs a room. Consider it yours, for the time being but do not, under any circumstances, allow him to smoke in there.'

'That might be tricky. His office, his practice.'

'Your office now, Dr Talbot. And by this time next week, my practice.

I was back to being Dr Talbot. No more hair ruffling, no more threats of slow dancing. The silly season was over.

Pam Parker may have shared her office with Mac, but it had the stamp of a woman. Pastel-coloured tissues, photos of her daughters and her cats, Norwegian Formula hand cream beside the sink. Vaz looked in on me. He had a big smile on his face.

'I have good news, Dan,' he said. 'I have met a very nice lady.'

It was worth keeping my first patient waiting while I heard about that. He'd met her volunteering at the church soup kitchen on Christmas Day. Her name was Teresa and she was a primary school teacher. They were going on a date the coming Friday.

'Where are you taking her?'

'On this I would like your advice.'

'I'll think about it. Talk to you after surgery.'

'Thank you,' he said. 'I am very happy.'

All I could think was, don't let this be another disappointment. Vaz is possibly the nicest man I've ever met but he's a bit like a puppy. He's happy to meet everybody so he assumes everyone will be kind and decent and friendly.

Mary said, 'Dr Talbot, I've got a Mr Humphries on the

phone. He's not one of ours and he won't say what it's about, but he insists on speaking to you.'

The name Humphries rang a bell. I couldn't think why.

'My poor wife,' he started straight in, 'is very, very upset with you and anyone who upsets my wife can expect to get a piece of my mind.'

I was still in the dark. I asked him who his wife was and what I'd done to upset her.

'So you don't even know the names of your patients. Typical!'

I said, 'Mr Humphries, this practice has nearly 8000 patients. It would help if you told me your wife's name and how exactly I can help you.'

'My wife is Barbara Humphries and thanks to you they've taken her foot off.'

Of course. Barbara Humphries. The diabetic who'd wanted her bunions done before her daughter's wedding. I'd uncovered the deep ulcer on the ball of her foot, but it was Trevor who'd noticed the patches of gangrene.

I said, 'I'm very sorry to hear that. I knew she was scheduled for debridement. When did they decide to amputate?'

'Last week. It ruined our Christmas. All she wanted from you was a letter about getting her bunions fixed and now look at her. She's a cripple.'

'Cripple' isn't a word we like to use these days, but Mr Humphries was of a different generation.

'I can certainly understand her shock but she's actually very lucky. It was Dr Buxton who examined her...'

'That's right, pass the buck.'

'It was Dr Buxton who examined her foot after me and if he hadn't noticed the gangrene things might have turned out much worse.'

'How so?'

'If the gangrene had gone unnoticed for much longer, she might have lost all of her lower leg.'

And what I didn't add was that she still might.

'You don't know that. Her foot might have healed.'

'Clearly the hospital didn't think so, and as a matter of fact, neither do I. The blood supply to her foot wasn't great. That's what gangrene is. Tissue that's died because of lack of oxygen. There's no easy fix for that.'

'Well why weren't we told, that's what I want to know.'

He'd gone from angry to whiny. He was running out of steam. It wasn't the moment to remind him that Barbara knew perfectly well the risks with diabetic feet.

I said, 'She'll be offered a prosthesis, of course. An artificial foot.'

'So they say. But when? All she's got right now is a stump.'

'You'd have to ask the surgeon. Sometimes they fit a temporary foot as soon as any swelling has gone down. A permanent prosthesis takes longer. Five or six months, I'd say.'

'That's no use to Barbara. Our Joanne's getting married in July. How can she be the mother of the bride with a plastic foot?'

I told him I was sure she'd look so elegant no-one would notice her foot.

'We're having it at the Country Club,' he said. He sounded defeated.

I said, 'I think the best way to look at this is to be thankful the gangrene was noticed before it progressed any further. You've still got your wife, Mr Humphries. Your daughter's still got her Mum.'

He said, 'Barbara's always worn lovely shoes.'

And then he rang off. No 'thank you', no 'see you in court'. Just click and gone.

310

Vaz was doing house calls. I said I'd go with him so we could talk about his hot date along the way. His idea was to take Teresa to a fancy restaurant, if I could suggest one.

I said, 'It's your first date. If I were you, I'd keep it lower key than that.'

'What does this mean?'

'A fancy restaurant could be a bit intimidating. Maybe she's a confident person, maybe she isn't. You want to be able to relax, get to know one another.'

I suggested a couple of places.

'What should I wear?'

'What were you wearing at the soup kitchen?'

'Robin jumper and Christmas paper hat.'

'In that case whatever you wear will be an improvement. I'd say, no tie, casual trousers. The key word, Vaz, is relaaaax.'

'Relaaaax. This is very helpful. Where did you take Chloe on your first date?'

I told him our story. The thing is, I was always a bit of a ditherer when it came to girls. Chloe was a year below me in Medical School, so I'd seen her around, but I didn't know her. At first I thought she was snooty. After a while, I started to really fancy her, but I'd heard her being voted Best Rack of the year by some of the other blokes, so I didn't think I stood a chance. Then one day, in A&E, a few of us had been summoned to see a thoracic aortic aneurism, and after the consult she cornered me and said, 'Okay, Dan Talbot, seeing as you're never going to ask me out, I'll do the asking. Want to help me take a llama for a walk one of the weekends?'

I was so stunned the only thing I could think to say was, 'Any particular llama?'

'Not the Dalai. My sister gave me a voucher for my birthday. It's pretty dog-eared so I think she must have won

311

it in a raffle. I think it's had several previous owners. You go to this llama farm and they put a halter on one of the animals and you take it for a walk. They're quite tame, apparently, but they can spit.'

It was a brilliant first date. We laughed so much it was very easy to segue into our first snog, especially when the llama tried to join in. That was Vaz's next question.

'At the end of the evening, should I give her a little kiss?'

'If she seems as though she'd like you to.'

'How will I know?'

How indeed.

I said, 'I think it's more that you'll know if she doesn't want you to. If in doubt, you can always ask. I think women quite like that. It lets them make the next move.'

'Thank you, Dan,' he said. 'You are very wise.'

Like I'm some big expert when it comes to women. Nobody ever gave me any guidance. The only thing Mam ever said to me was, 'don't do anything to a girl you wouldn't want a lad to do to your sister.' But I didn't have a sister so that wasn't much help. And Da tends to see the world as it applies to sheep. If a ewe isn't in the mood for the ram she'll make it abundantly clear and the ram won't take offence. He'll just trot across the field and try another one. Llamas are probably the same.

Vaz was going to see a Mrs Hands, on the Brook Glen estate. She was in an old folks' bungalow, not warden-controlled, and one of her neighbours, a Mrs Chaplin, was concerned because she hadn't seen her since the day before Christmas Eve. Mrs Chaplin had been watching for Vaz's arrival. She came out to the car.

She said, 'I've knocked and I've knocked, but there's no answer. And her curtains are still drawn. It's not like Doreen.

I'm wondering if she's had a fall.'

She came across with us to Mrs Hands's bungalow. I called through the letterbox. No reply.

I said, 'Is it possible she went away for Christmas?'

'Never,' she said. 'Where would she go? There's a daughter in New Zealand, but that's all.'

Vaz called the police and the three of us sat in his car to wait. Mrs Chaplin kept saying, 'I don't like the look of this.' She said Mrs Hands was in good health and in her early eighties, as far as she knew.

She said, 'We don't stick our noses into other people's business around here. We're friendly enough but we don't live in each other's pockets.'

It was half an hour before the police arrived. They broke a glass pane in the back door and let us in. Mrs Hands was dead, of course. She was in an armchair, fully clothed, no sign of injury, no sign of a struggle. The bungalow was freezing cold.

The WPC said, 'Looks like another case of hypothermia. We had two yesterday.'

Mrs Chaplin was very upset.

'The poor woman,' she said. 'I should have raised the alarm sooner. This'll prey on my mind now.'

I said, 'Was Mrs Hands sparing with the heating?'

'Oh yes,' she said. 'She was very careful. We all are. You have to be when you're on a pension.'

There was mail on the mat inside the front door. A few Christmas cards, a menu from a Thai takeaway and two fliers from local churches. The Christian Fellowship Centre, where everybody is somebody to our Lord. And one from All Saints. Let's Keep the Christ in Christmas. Midnight service on December 24th will be at 6pm for reasons of safety and security. A warm welcome to all.

We left the police searching for Mrs Hands's daughter's

phone number. Vaz called Mrs Chaplin's daughter to tell her that her mother had had a bit of a shock and might be glad of some company.

'What did she say?'

'She will come after work.'

'They say hypothermia's not a bad way to go.'

'Yes.'

'But how do they know?'

'The lady looked peaceful.'

'Yes. But dead people do, generally. Growing old can be pretty shit.'

'What does this mean?'

'Even when you've got family you can still end up dying alone in a freezing cold house. Are your parents still alive?'

'Oh yes. But we are eleven children. One brother is in Toronto, one sister is in Vancouver. The others are in India.'

'Are they near your parents?'

'All in one same building. And Dan, hypothermia is not a problem in Kerala.'

I felt really depressed. Dawn Beamish trolling off to Nigeria to see a man she'd never met and wrecking her health. Midnight Mass being said at 6 o'clock because of hooligans on the street. And Doreen Hands, spending Christmas alone and too worried about money to light her gas fire in December. What a bloody world. As we pulled into the surgery car park Helen and Trevor were standing by the new signboard and Helen did not look happy.

'Have you seen this?' she said. 'The fuckers. And in broad daylight.'

Yet again The Lindens' name had been violated. The smart new sign had lasted barely five hours. It now said SHIT END and the spare letters were nowhere to be seen.

Trevor was laughing so much he had to brace himself against Vaz's car, to get his breath.

'Priceless,' he said. 'Dan, can you take photos with your mobile phone?'

I took a couple of pictures.

'It's a strange thing,' he said, 'but stuff like this gives me hope. Most of the time we think we're dealing with dead-eyed swamp-dwellers, but this took a measure of intelligence and initiative, don't you think?'

'No,' says Helen. 'I do not.'

I said, 'Have you thought of having a printed sign? It'd be harder to vandalise.'

She gave me a withering look. 'Really, Dan?' she said. 'Haven't you heard of aerosol paint?' And off she strode.

'Well,' says Trevor, 'that told you.'

CHAPTER 30.

Vaz was away on a one-day course - de-escalation training for health professionals, how to deal with potentially dangerous situations - so I did the house calls. There were only a couple, both hospital discharges who needed checking on. I looked in on Marion Flitwell although she wasn't on my list. She was looking even slimmer, and not as tearful. Someone was giving her lifts to visit her husband and it seemed he'd soon be coming home anyway.

I said, 'Only mind you don't slip back into your old habits. No snacks in the middle of the night. If you keep this up, you won't need an operation. You'll just need a lot of new clothes.'

'I do already,' she said. 'Terry says I'm starting to look gaunt.'

Marion did not look gaunt. There were no prizes for predicting how that story was going to end.

I was on my way back to the surgery. Things tend to be pretty quiet around the estates until early evening. The residents aren't early risers. Even on giro day, a lot of them get up, fetch their money and then go back to bed. But as I drove through Cherry Tree something seemed to be occurring outside Karim's Kabin. There was a body on the ground and two women were stooped over it. One of them ran into the road and waved her arms. I slowed down and opened my window a crack. I asked if anyone was hurt.

She screamed, 'It's my boy. Phone for an ambulance would you? I haven't got no credit.'

I said, 'You don't need credit to call 999. What's wrong with him?'

'I think he's dead.'

As I got out of the car the shop owner, Karim, appeared. He'd already called for an ambulance.

He said, 'I don't want this body outside my shop.'

The 'body' was Kyle Bibby, except he was suddenly very much alive. He sat up, wide-eyed, pupils very dilated, and started flailing his arms, as if he was fighting someone. His pulse, when I finally managed to feel it, was racing.

One of the women was his mother, the other was his sister. It was hard to tell them apart.

I said, 'I know Kyle. I'm from The Lindens Medical Centre. What has he taken, do you know?'

Just his usual, they said. Temazepam. But I knew he must have taken something else. He was hallucinating, boxing the air. I asked Mr Karim if he'd noticed Kyle hanging around with anyone, maybe buying something. He said all he knew was he'd sold him a can of cider and a Zippo lighter.

I said, 'So he might have smoked something?'

Mr Karim shrugged.

'Or sniffed,' he said. 'They go round the back. Kids, most of them. They send a big one in to buy a lighter. They're damned nuisances. They leave the plastic bags behind my shop.'

I said, 'Why do you sell them lighters if you know what they're going to do with them?'

'I'm a shop-keeper,' he said. 'It's not my business to tell people what they can buy.'

I went through Kyle's pockets. He had three butane lighters and two of them were empty. Karim said he'd only paid for one and he had a good mind to ban him from the Kabin. One of the Bibby women made a suggestion as to what Karim should do to himself.

He said, 'Your brother is a shoplifter. He is a thief. And now he is littering my shop front.'

Kyle's sister said, 'And you're an overcharging Paki.

Talking about a dying man like that.'

The dying man himself was trying to get to his feet.

Mrs Bibby said, 'You're a doctor. Can't you do something?'

I said, 'He seems to be over the worst of it. The best thing is to keep him calm till the ambulance gets here.'

She said, 'What about artificial inspiration?'

I said, 'That's for when people aren't breathing.'

Kyle wasn't making any sense, but he was definitely breathing. Then he went quiet, his eyes rolled back and he crumpled. Mrs Bibby started wailing, 'I've already buried one boy.'

I remembered Trevor telling me about that. Kyle's brother had died in prison.

The ambulance arrived. I told the paramedics what I knew, which wasn't a lot. They seemed to know all about butane sniffing. It was kids usually, they said. A low cost, quick hit. But Kyle could well have taken something else as well. Cider, mazzies, butane and who could say what else.

I said, 'I need to get a handle on all this.'

'Good luck with that,' says one of them. 'There's something new every week. Computer screen cleaner, that was one we had a few weeks ago. Kid sprayed it into his mouth. Gave himself frostbite of the pharynx. What else have we had recently, Chelle?'

Chelle was checking Kyle's heart. She said he was still quite tachycardic.

'Whipped cream,' she said. 'That's getting to be quite popular.'

Apparently if you puncture a Whiperoo can into a plastic bag you can inhale the nitrous oxide and get high, although not always with a happy outcome.

'They get hypoxic in no time.'

'Brain damage?'

'Brain, heart, you name it. But try telling them. Tennis balls, that's another one I've heard about. New ones, fresh out of a canister. I don't know if it's true.'

Chelle said, 'That'd be more for the country club set, Vic. Not a lot of new balls around here. Do you sell tennis balls, Karim?'

Karim said, 'Please remove this body. I'm trying to run a business here.'

'We're just making sure he's stable,' says Chelle, then we'll be on our way.'

As they were loading Kyle into the ambulance, he started shadow-boxing again. I mentioned his brother's sudden death.

I said, 'There might be a heart defect in the family. The brother was in prison when he died so he can't have been sniffing.'

Vic, the paramedic, gave me a pitying look.

'Nothing to get high on inside? You are joking? It's like World of Candy in Winson Green. It's like the Pick'n'Mix. I'm sure there is a defect in the family, Doctor, but I don't think it's in the heart.'

Kyle's Mum went with him in the ambulance. The sister said, 'What about me? I haven't got no taxi money.'

Karim said his son was going to the Cash & Carry so he'd drive her to the hospital in their van.

'Wait there,' he said. 'I'll tell him.'

I thought that was pretty decent of him considering the names she'd called him.

I said, 'I think you owe Mr Karim an apology.'

'How'd yer mean?' she said, and she gave me that bleary Cherry Tree look I'm getting to know so well.

I called Sandwell A&E at the end of afternoon surgery. They said Kyle had arrested on arrival at the hospital, but they'd shocked him twice and he'd survived. He was stable and being kept under observation.

I spent a while on MIMs finding out about malaria treatment options. Then I looked up recent trends in street drugs, but I couldn't see anything about tennis balls. Helen was in the kitchen.

I said, 'You're a tennis player.'

'No,' she said. 'What gave you that idea? I run or do treadmill.'

Then I realised my fantasy of her in a tennis skirt had morphed into an actual belief. I'm sure I blushed. Not that Helen could have had the faintest idea why.

'My mistake,' I said. 'I must be thinking of someone else. A paramedic told me kids are sniffing new tennis balls.'

'It wouldn't surprise me,' she said. 'Shoe polish, that's another thing. Have you heard about that? Probably not that easy to find though. I mean, who polishes their shoes these days? Apart from my husband on court days. Energy strips, they're another new problem.'

She had some in her desk. They're gel strips impregnated with caffeine. She said she'd used them when she ran a 10k.

'So anyone can buy them?'

'Sure. The thing is, you're just supposed to use one. But kids get hold of them and cram half a dozen into their mouth. Next thing you know you've got a 12 year old having a heart attack. Overdosed on caffeine.'

Moira said, 'Dr Vincent, your lad is outside and would like a word.'

Helen said, 'Then tell him to come in. It's freezing out there.'

'I did,' says Moira, 'but he said he'd sooner wait out there.'

Helen went out to Miles.

Moira said, 'I don't know what you and Dr Parker said to him at the Christmas party, but you've properly put the wind up him. He wouldn't come in because you're here.'

'We just gave him some friendly advice.'

She laughed.

'Good for you,' she said. 'About blooming time somebody did.'

Trevor had been doing Mac's nursing home rounds.

He said, 'Ever felt you were nothing but a supporting act? Just the warm-up before the big star appears? I hadn't realised how popular Mac was. He's got a lot of old ladies pining for him. If this tribunal thing drags on, I reckon we'll have a few deaths due to broken hearts.'

'I know. I've seen him in action.'

'But word is getting around, about the Ruck business. A couple of the nursing managers asked about it. I hope there's nothing else lurking in the woodpile.'

I told him about Kyle Bibby.

He said, 'I was about to say men like that would do the gene pool a favour by dying young with their head in a butane bag, but in Kyle's case it's too late. He's already spread his DNA far and wide.'

'His sister was a charmer. Lynn, I think she's called.'

'Oh yes. There's a whole dynasty of them. I'm not sure who the Founding Father was. Some old lag, long gone. The Bibby women are particularly terrifying. Missing teeth and Tipton facelifts. We used to have the whole family on our books but most of them transferred to a practice across in Wednesbury. They'd heard there was a new doctor there who was a soft touch. Only Kyle stayed with us. Should we be flattered? Actually, when I think about it, Kyle's about the best of the Bibby crop. Certainly the least frightening.'

'I felt really relieved when I heard he'd survived.'

'That's because he's seduced you, with his naughty but nice routine. I don't blame you. I've always enjoyed his consultations. He's quite a card. But get it in perspective, Dan. Here we are, working, burning the candle at both ends, paying income tax, and Kyle Bibby spent the morning behind Karim's Kabin getting out of his head on nicked lighter fuel. And now he's in Sandwell getting a delicious hospital dinner that we've paid for.'

The lights were on. Chloe was already home. She was curled up on the bed with her stuffed Eeyore and she'd been crying. When Chloe resorts to Eeyore you know it's something serious. Then I noticed the crumpled envelope. Her exam results.

'Did you fail?'

She shook her head.

'You passed?'

A nod.

'So why are you crying?'

I thought she said 'bunny.' Then she blew her nose. 'Mun-Hee.'

'Did she fail?'

She sat up.

'Why the hell would I be crying if Mun-fucking-Hee failed?'

'Sorry. I'm confused.'

'Barrington gave her my job. I'm out.'

'Ah.'

'What do you mean, 'ah'?'

'I did wonder about Mun-Hee. The way she chucked us to have dinner with Barrington. And then you said they ignored each other at your Christmas lunch. I thought it sounded a bit sus.'

'That's what Hua said. All very well for her. She's been offered a job too. How come everyone is so smart all of a sudden? How come everyone sort of wondered about Mun-

Hee and Barrington but didn't bother telling me?'

'I think I did try.'

'I'll never speak to her again. And she's still got my Prada skirt.'

'I didn't know you had a Prada skirt.'

'Well that's my career down the toilet.'

'Chloe, you've just passed your MRCP. Barrington's not the only consultant in the sea. What about another firm? What about Kirkpatrick?'

'He doesn't know me. He's got his own housemen he's been bringing on.'

'You don't have to work at the Queen Elizabeth. You can get a job anywhere.'

'I don't want a job anywhere.'

'You could get a job at Sandwell. They'd snap you up. We could drive in together every day. Maybe I could stay on at The Lindens after I'm registered.'

'Why would you stay there a moment longer than you need to? The place is run like a goat gymkhana.'

'No it isn't. It's real medicine and it's something different every day. I've got a malaria case.'

'In Tipton?'

'A woman just back from Nigeria. She went there without any vaccinations or any anti-malarials.'

'Is she an idiot? What's her erythrocyte index?'

'Five percent.'

'Fuckadoodle.'

'What's for dinner?'

'Gastropub salmon en croute but I'm not hungry. I bought them before I knew Mun-Hee had ruined my life.'

'Such a tragedy. A highly talented and well-qualified cardiologist on the scrap heap at 29. What about the Wolverhampton Heart and Lung place?'

'That's mainly surgical. I need to talk to Daddy. He knows

people.'

'I'm sure he does. Wouldn't his contacts be in London, though? Can we focus on finding you something in this area, at least until I've finished my training?'

'I can't believe Barrington's done this to me.'

'Like you've always told me, you're in a cut-throat specialism. You could change. I did.'

'I am not going into general practice.'

'I didn't mean general practice. I know it wouldn't suit you. I meant ENT. Go and work with your father. Get him to open a clinic in Birmingham. Swift & Swifter. You have so many possibilities. So fuck Barrington, fuck Mun-Hee and the horse she rode in on. Let's eat and then you can talk to Big Daddy.'

'Let's have sex first.'

'Okay. But not with Eeyore watching.'

Afterwards she said, 'Have you ever had sex with an MRCP before?'

'I don't believe I have.'

'You mean you're not sure?'

'It was just a figure of speech.'

'So how was it?'

'Fabluss.'

'Are you serious about staying on at The Lindens?'

'Maybe. I'm there till September anyway.'

'That limits me a bit.'

'Yes, but we always knew there'd be times like this. Two doctors, two careers. We can work it out. Who's going to cook the en croute thingummies?'

'I think it falls to you.'

'Why, because you out-rank me now?'

'Yes.'

'Okay. Just one question. You've got your Part II, we've had sex and I've given you some career advice. Now can we get married?'

She smiled and did that funny thing where she makes Eeyore shake his head or nod. According to Eeyore, the answer was yes.

ALSO BY LAURIE GRAHAM

THE TEN O'CLOCK HORSES
DOG DAYS, GLENN MILLER NIGHTS
THE DRESS CIRCLE
PERFECT MERINGUES
THE UNFORTUNATES
MR STARLIGHT
AT SEA
THE FUTURE HOMEMAKERS OF AMERICA
THE IMPORTANCE OF BEING KENNEDY
GONE WITH THE WINDSORS
LIFE ACCORDING TO LUBKA
A HUMBLE COMPANION
THE LIAR'S DAUGHTER
THE GRAND DUCHESS OF NOWHERE
THE NIGHT IN QUESTION
THE EARLY BIRDS
ANYONE FOR SECONDS?

Dr Dan will be back in early 2020
If you've enjoyed meeting him and would like advance notice of his
return, go to Laurie's website, http://LaurieGraham.com and join
her mailing list.

Printed in Great Britain
by Amazon